Accepting

She was taking a [...] statues ... or what sh[...]

They appeared in her headlight beams so suddenly she almost didn't have time to stop.

They weren't statues at all, she saw, but costume headpieces worn by a large group of revelers as they crossed the road. Some turned to wave in apology, others in recognition, and a few, oddly, in invitation.

Then one of the giant-headed figures blinked its eyes, parting its lips in a smile. Sarah realized that they weren't costume headpieces at all; these beings were real, corporeal, flesh and blood ... and utterly fantastic.

An antlered turtle—who, from all appearances, was a child—came over to the car, its right hand making a small but insistent circular motion: *Roll down your window.*

"Hello," it said in the voice of a little girl.

"What are you?"

"The first moment your aunt ever dreamed about falling in love," replied the turtle-child. "She wants you to know that it's time, if you've got the courage."

From "Rights of Memory" by Gary A. Braunbeck

NEW AMAZONS

edited by Margaret Weis

DAW BOOKS, INC.

DONALD A. WOLLHEIM, FOUNDER

375 Hudson Street, New York, NY 10014

ELIZABETH R. WOLLHEIM
SHEILA E. GILBERT
PUBLISHERS

First Printing, February 2000
1 2 3 4 5 6 7 8 9

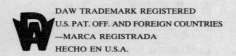 DAW TRADEMARK REGISTERED
U.S. PAT. OFF. AND FOREIGN COUNTRIES
—MARCA REGISTRADA
HECHO EN U.S.A.

PRINTED IN THE U.S.A.

ACKNOWLEDGMENTS

Introduction © 2000 by Margaret Weis
Scarifices © 2000 by R. Davis
Emrys © 2000 by Nancy Springer
Prices © 2000 by Jo Clayton
Sleep With One Eye Open © 2000 by Linda Baker
Messenger's Plight © 2000 by Robyn McGrew
Gifts of Wonder and Darkness © 2000 by
    Kathleen M. Massie-Ferch
On the Brink © 2000 by Lawrence C. Connolly
Society of the Knife © 2000 by Janet Pack
Brass in Pocket © 2000 by Cynthia Ward
Move . . . Tomorrow © 2000 by John Tigges
Demon Drink © 2000 by Kate Novak-Grubb
Look You On Beauty and Death © 2000 by
    Livia and James Reasoner
Hannegan's Health © 2000 by Nick O'Donohoe
Seven Grains © 2000 by Kevin T. Stein
Love, Trouble, and Time © 2000 by Linda Mannheim
Rights of Memory © 2000 by Gary A. Braunbeck
Shadow © 2000 by Felicia Dale
Three Choices: The Story of Lozen © 2000 by
    Jane Lindskold

CONTENTS

To Jo Clayton
who fought cancer and lost,
but was not defeated

INTRODUCTION
by Margaret Weis

Legend tells that an Amazon warrior woman would sacrifice a breast in order to improve her aim in archery. I thought about this legend a lot when I was going through my battle with breast cancer. For me, the idea of sacrificing a breast to achieve victory came to be very symbolic. That is why this book is called "New Amazons," a book that tells the stories of women who make sacrifices in order to gain victory over a foe.

This book came to be very special in a number of ways. Usually when editors send out invitations to authors to be part of an anthology, the author sends back a postcard with nothing more than an impersonal checked reply, either yes or no. In this instance, we had more than checked replies. We had many personal notes from the authors. Roger Zelazny wrote back a very kind letter sending his regrets, but hoping that the book was successful in its goals. Within months, he was dead of cancer. Jo Clayton is a contributor to this book, sending us one of her last stories before she, too, succumbed to this dread disease. Many other authors wrote stories which they personally dedicated to a loved one who had suffered from cancer. One author wrote that her mother had died of breast cancer and that she felt too close to the subject to be able to contribute.

This book was originally intended to help raise awareness about breast cancer. Because we have lost so many of the science fiction/fantasy community to cancer, and because we have others in the community battling the disease, we want to raise awareness about all types of cancer. We want to urge all of you, men and women, to go out beyond the walls and fight the enemy before it lays siege. Most battles against cancer can be won if the cancer can be caught in the early stages.

1

Know the early warning signs of cancer. Take them seriously. Act on them if you find you have any of them.

Perform breast self-examinations. This is so very important. Mammograms cannot take the place of self-examinations. I know. I found the lump in my breast. Two mammograms in two years missed it. Even when the doctors knew where it was, the mammogram could not locate it.

Don't think that you are too young to start self-examinations. It is important that you become aware of the physical aspects of your breasts so that you will recognize a change. Make this a part of your monthly routine. Start a buddy system with a sister or girlfriend. Call each other up and remind each other. You may save a life!

If you know your family history, pay attention to what it's telling you. My mother died of bone cancer. My grandfather died of stomach cancer. My grandmother was a breast cancer survivor. Two of her sisters had the disease, as did three of their daughters. I was a likely candidate!

Don't smoke. If you're smoking, stop. I spent a year in chemotherapy. Whenever I see someone with a cigarette, I want to take them and lead them to the "infusion room" where they stick a needle into the back of your hand, because the veins in your arm have all collapsed. The room where they give you the medicine that, if you're fortunate, will keep you from vomiting. The room where you sit for hours and watch as the various poisons flow out of the plastic bag and into your veins. This is what can happen. Is that next puff worth it?

Don't let fear defeat you. I have met women who tell me that they don't want to have mammograms for fear that the doctors will find something. They don't think they can face the pain and the trauma, the nausea and the hair loss. I know just how they felt, because I felt the same. When I first knew the lump was there, but the cancer hadn't yet been diagnosed, I was panic-stricken.

"I can't go through this," I thought. "I can't face it."

Surprisingly, those were my worst moments. Once the cancer was diagnosed, I knew my foe and I knew what it would take to try to defeat it. I discovered that life continued to bring me the same joyful moments it had brought me before the cancer. I laughed, had fun, went to Disney World, continued to write. I exercised. I lifted weights. I walked the dogs. I fell in love with the man who would be my husband. I bought a lot of great hats!

Of course, I could never have gone through the ordeal without the love and support of my friends and family and the doctors and nurses who took care of me. This is another great gift the cancer brought to me. It showed me how caring people can be. This includes: my gentle, wise, and occasionally, beautifully weird oncologist. The nurses at the "infusion" center, who made certain that I laughed through my tears. My friends, who literally filled my house with flowers (the florist delivery man came to know me by name!). My family, who were incredibly supportive. And finally, the man I would later marry, who loved me when I had no hair, who held me when my fever spiked and I was so chilled my teeth chattered, who played computer games with me during chemo treatments (and beat me, much to the nurses' dismay!).

A year that I had first viewed with fear and terror came to be a year that brought me some of my greatest blessings. I sacrificed my breast, fought my battle, and I won. But— only because I found the cancer early enough to treat it.

I hope you enjoy these stories about some very courageous women. I hope, also, that you will join in the fight against cancer of all types and that you will do your part to save yourself and those you love by becoming aware of the warning signs of cancer and, if you have any of them, acting *immediately* to deal with them.

SACRIFICES
by R. Davis

There can be no preparation—
to sit, stand, or pace will not
make this moment of cancer-cell
knowledge more bearable. Staring
at light-motes on windows, or
shadow stars on the bedroom ceiling
will not make healing wishes true.
Prayer might help.
Family might help.
Love, or simple joy in breath—
no matter the terror crawling
with needle precision under the
delicate skin of your forearm—
these might help. There are
no guarantees, no warranty cards.
Fear might help: it will remind
you that your blood still flows,
there are still children's lunches
to be brown-bagged, matching
socks to be found,
chemotherapy to attend.
It is possible, as all things are,
that you will lose a breast,
you may lose both.
It is possible that you will want
to run into an empty field,
scream at the sky, demand answers,
dig your nails deep into your palms
so that you bleed like a heart
on a machine-shop squeeze box.
   It is possible that you will die.
 It is possible that you will die.

*It is possible that you will live for
another sixty years not on borrowed time.
You can choose to fight, love, hate,
be angry, give of yourself or those
who see you with clear eyes.
You can be an amazon, willing to
sacrifice now, for a chance to fight
better battles later.
You can live, a breast, a sickness,
these are not you.
This is not about dying, its
about living, choosing to live,
for sixty seconds or sixty years,
in a jungle overgrown with questions,
in a grassland plagued by storms,
in a village where the soil is rocky,
in a city, this city, where sacrifices
make real the possibles, and life is
a single, breast-beat away.*

EMRYS
by Nancy Springer

There was no safe way for Emmy to walk around the city. If she went as herself, she had to endure the whistles and yowls and shouted propositions from the predatory males lounging along the construction site barriers. If she went as a dowdy middle-aged woman, she didn't have to put up with sexual advances, but she was a target for muggers. She could have gone as a man, but the transgender change, so opposed to her innate selfhood, was difficult to maintain and left her exhausted. Or she could have gone as one of her sister animals—that would not have been difficult at all, indeed it would have been a joy to go as a cat or a sparrowhawk—but her job required her to carry a briefcase full of papers. Besides, every time she shifted shape, there was the danger that she would be observed, discovered. This was the nineties, but still, shape-shifting was not considered a normal business strategy for a paralegal secretary in the armpit of New Jersey.

Monday morning. Paul, her husband, enjoying one of his rare days off, lay in bed and watched her getting ready for work. Her approach for now was to go as herself but lessened, diluted; by a shape-shifter's thought she diminished the bloom of her body until it no longer softened her austere gray suit. She straightened the dancing of her hips, dimmed the Welsh-gold luster of her hair, deadened the wild-rose glow of her skin. From the bed, Paul said softly, "You shouldn't have to do that."

She looked into his gunmetal-blue eyes, even darker than usual right now, shadowed by bitterness for her sake.

He said, "You should be able to walk wherever you want and nobody should bother you."

Paul was a cop, one of the good ones. He practiced old-fashioned chivalry—protect women and children—but he

6

had thought about it enough to wonder why women and children should need an armed man's protection, and when they would ever have freedom.

He said, "You should be able to be yourself."

Emmy laughed, allowing herself a fey thought, what a shock it would be to most of the people who knew her if she were to "be herself." Paul got the joke and smiled.

"Okay," he said, "within reason." He knew everything about her. Knew it all and loved it all. "You should at least be able to be as gorgeous as you really are."

"Gorgeous yourself," she told him, because he was. She kissed him, gazing into his eyes. Gunmetal blue. She loved that color—but only in his eyes. Guns themselves made her skin pucker, nasty steely things. Paul wore his holstered police-issue handgun easily, kept a .38 revolver in the drawer of the bedside table and he had shown her how to use it—but the idea made her cold. No thank you. She was a woman and a shape-changer and rather than shoot somebody she would appease or hide or flee.

Emmy kissed Paul once more and went to work.

The subway ride was uneventful. The walk from the subway station to her office was no worse than usual. Her boss, Charlene, a carrot-haired older woman in a Chinese-red suit, was there before her and glanced up placidly as she walked in. "Morning, Emmy."

"Am I late?"

"No, I'm early. Lenny brought me in."

At the mention of Lenny, Emmy turned away and discreetly added a roll of fat to her waist and several zits to her face. Lenny was all too aware of being the boss's son and Lenny was a leering dickhead. As bosses go, Charlene was a nice enough woman, but Lenny was the light of her life, so bright she called him sonny and blinked blindly as she basked in the glory of his presence. This partly explained why Lenny had never learned that he was not irresistible to women.

Right on cue, enter Lenny from the back office. "Yo, Emmaline! You want some company around town this morning?"

"My name's not Emmaline."

"So tell me what it is. Emma Lou?" He grinned like a snake. He resembled a snake altogether—lean, rippling and reptilian. Emmy would have eaten rattlesnake stew sooner than tell him her real name. She ignored the question, busy at her desk, getting her morning delivery to the courthouse in order.

"I asked Lenny to help you run that over, Emmy," Charlene said. "The streets are so unsafe these days."

"I'll be your guard dog," Lenny said. "Your Rottweiler."

A guard dog would have been a better deal. If it tried to hump her leg, she could have kicked it where it hurt. But Lenny was the boss's son. When he propositioned her (today he waited until they reached the first corner), all she could do was say, "No."

"Emma Louise, I'm hurt. I'm devastated. I'm sure I can change your mind. Meet me for lunch?"

"No. I'm not interested, Lenny." She kept her voice polite and refrained from saying she had met slime molds that attracted her more, because she had to try to get along with him. She wanted to keep her job.

"Of course you're interested. You're a woman, aren't you? A drink after work, then?"

"No! Lenny, let me alone."

It was no use pointing out to him that she was married; she had tried. The concept of marriage, love, fidelity meant nothing to him. All he understood was his own testosterone.

"Aw, Emma Lou—" He slung an arm over her shoulder. When she tried to slip out from under it, he crooked his elbow around her neck and grabbed at her breast.

The total dickhead! Hot with fury, Emmy forgot about being polite. She brought a heel down hard on his instep—it was heartening that the stupid high-heeled pumps she had to wear to work were good for something. She did her best to punch a hole right through his foot, and at the same time she attacked his ribs with her elbow.

"Ow!" He let go of her. "Bitch! You hurt me!"

"Oh, poor wittle *thing*." She strode off, wishing she could take a couple of minutes off from being a paralegal secretary and show him what a real bitch was like, a Rottweiler bitch with two-inch fangs to sink into some soft, cherished part of his anatomy and hang on.

"You just don't get it, do you, psycho bitch?" he yelled

after her. "I'm going to ream your ass! I'm not going to take no for an answer!"

Who just didn't get it?

She managed to say the right and normal things as she ran her errands at the courthouse. Lenny was gone when she got back to his office. Blessedly, it appeared that he hadn't gone crying to his mommy; Charlene looked as placid as ever.

It occurred to Emmy, not for the first time, that Charlene was a shape-changer too. Charlene in Wonderbra and control-top pantyhose and four-inch heels and silicone implants. All women were expected to be shape-changers.

The world was a bizarre place. Just in case Charlene transmogrified into a maddened mommy before her eyes, Emmy spent her lunch hour looking at the help-wanted ads in the newspaper.

Paul phoned in the middle of the afternoon. "I'm called in, babe."

Emmy sighed; another lonely night. It wasn't easy being a cop's wife. But she'd known what she was in for when she married him. "Be careful, honey."

"Always."

Springtime. There was an hour of daylight left when she got home, and tiny iridescent-blue butterflies were swirling like azure mist in the creek bottom. It was for this that Emmy worked her scutty job, for this that she and Paul needed the double income, to live in this place where her heart felt at home, in this farmhouse in the country. She ran inside and upstairs to their bedroom and yanked off the pumps, the irksome pantyhose, and drab gray suit. She flung open the bedroom window and let in the fresh tawny sunset. A moment later she flew from the windowsill, her russet feathers shining in the westering light, a sparrow-hawk.

She soared over the woodlot rosy with new buds, her strong wings carrying her like a swimmer on the currents of the sun-stirred air. She skimmed, she swooped, she dove. As a hawk her vision was so acute that she could see tadpoles hatching in the creek water a quarter mile below her. She saw a black-velvet dragonfly with mauve wings; she saw a red salamander scampering. Sunset turned to after-glow, then twilight; in the shadowed fundament of the woods white starflowers closed as stars opened like spirit eyes in the darkening firmament above. Songbirds chittered Emmy away from their nests as she swept low, lower. In her hollow-boned chest her great heart beat like her wings, and only hunger filled her. A deer mouse rustled last year's oak leaf and Emmy plummeted, scarcely noticing how her wings beat the red twigs aside as she drove her talons deep, deeper into loamy darkness to capture her soft gray supper.

Later, back in her house and her innate human form, with the window closed and locked and curtained and the security system turned on, Emmy slipped on one of Paul's T-shirts and lay in bed and read the poetry of Anne Sexton. Later yet she turned out the bedside light and slept.

It was around two in the morning when the security system went off.

Emmy awoke, her heart thudding. She had thought Paul was being a wee tad obsessive when he insisted on the expensive alarm system, when he said that a house in the country, isolated, needed good security worse than an apartment in the city, when he said he didn't like leaving her alone there when he had to work nights. She had thought he was being a bit paranoid when he put the .38 in the bedstand drawer. Now she thought differently.

There was an intruder in the house.

Even above the thudding of her heart she heard his footsteps downstairs. He wasn't even trying to be quiet.

Emmy slipped over the edge of the bed and by the time her hands touched the floor they were padded feline paws. A slim gray cat, she squirmed out of the T-shirt and darted silently through the bedroom doorway.

Crouching by the doorpost, she watched as her uninvited visitor started up the stairs. "Whoo-ee, the alarm's going off," he said, laughing. "So arrest me."

His face was only a shadow to her, but she knew that rattlesnake voice. Lenny.

Lenny, and he acted like he'd been spending his mother's money on the street. Lenny, high on acid and drunk on his own arrogance. So the cops would show up in fifteen or twenty minutes, so what? This woman wouldn't press charges against *him*.

"Where are you, proud piece of ass?" Something fishy-silver flashed in his hand. A knife.

Emmy could see him more clearly now, his face grinning, level with hers as she climbed the stairs. Her front paws twitched under her furred chest; she wanted to jump him and sink her claws into his eyes. But she shrank back. Her mother—a shape-changer too; it was a trait that ran in the females of her family—her mother had taught her to fly as a bird, run as a fox, and hide and be secret as a cat. What was the sense of confronting a knife large enough to cut her in half? To fly, run, be secret and hide; those lessons were all she needed to survive.

At the top of the stairs he flicked a light switch. The glare pounced, catching her crouching and trembling in a corner. He saw her.

"Relax, cat." He spoke with contempt. "I don't want you. I want the big pussy." He laughed at what he perceived as his own coruscating wit. "Where is she?"

He strode into her bedroom, the bathroom, the spare room, knife at the ready in one hand, whacking on lights with the other. He ripped back curtains, threw open closets and dumped clothing, tilted up beds and let them crash to the floor again. Emmy stayed out of his way and watched him violate her home. He ran up to the attic; she heard him flinging things around up there. He came down, and he wasn't laughing anymore. He was white with fury and calling her vicious names just because she was not spreading her legs for him, because she was not gibbering in terror under the blade of his ego. He rampaged downstairs—she heard the thud as he flung the sofa over. He savaged the first floor, tore his way to the penetralia of the basement, then gave up.

"Goddamn cunt, she must have gotten past me somehow. Out the door."

Poised at the top of the stairs, Emmy hoped he would leave now. But he did not.

"The slut. She ain't going to get away with this." He pounded up the stairs again.

From the doorway she watched as he raged into her bedroom—the bedroom she and Paul shared—lifted his arm high and thrust his blade deep into the warm indentation her sleeping body had left in the bed. He slashed the pillows, hers and Paul's, ripping and flailing with the knife.

Enough.

As Emmy leaped, she was aware that no amount of shape-changing could ever make her safe from men like him, that all women were expected to spend their lives watching and placating and bending themselves out of shape and it wasn't right it wasn't fair it wasn't freedom—

She leaped noiselessly to the bedside table, nudging the drawer open with her paw, and even as she bloomed into a woman again she was grabbing the revolver and slamming six cartridges into it with the quick-load and cocking the hammer and taking steady two-handed aim at him.

"Back off," she said.

Maybe it was the sight of the gun that made him stagger away from her with his mouth not functioning even to curse. Maybe it was the fact that she was suddenly there when he had not been able to find her anywhere.

Or maybe it was the sight of her.

Naked and proud she stood in all her Welsh glamour, breasts like wild roses, dewy dawn skin, her belly a tawny sunrise above her wide free hips and thighs—staring him down, her glare as hard as the gun in her hands, she stood like a goddess of one of those ancient tribes that used to go naked into war. He wobbled away from her, gawking.

"Drop the knife," she ordered.

But he didn't do it. He didn't have enough soul. At first he comprehended her, but then his smelly crotch of a brain started functioning again and he understood her nakedness only as his limited vocabulary allowed. "Bitch," he said. "Cunt, where you been hiding? Prick tease. You know you ain't going to shoot me." He raised the knife and started toward her.

Even then she couldn't kill him. She shifted her aim downward before she pulled the trigger.

He howled and fell writhing to the floor. His knife skittered under the bed. Hurt and unbelieving, he gazed up at her from the carpet, both hands clutching the wound.

"Look at me," she said, and she was the blood-red Welsh dragon aiming the pistol at him with its clawed hands. "Look at me." She was the ancient, skull-headed crone of the dark of the moon. "Look at me." She was an angel-winged willow-thin girl-child laughing and taking aim at him, she was a harpy whose gray pinions spread wide enough to shadow the room, she was a hag with the head

of a lioness, she was herself again. "I am Emrys," she told
him. "I am the seventh daughter of a seventh daughter.
Don't mess with me."

When the police arrived a few minutes later, Paul with
them, they found Emmy wrapped demurely in a sheet and
sitting on the edge of the bed, holding at gunpoint a moaning man who looked white enough to die.

"I aimed at his knee," she told Paul after the ambulance
had taken Lenny away. "Really."

"Well, you missed, babe." Shaking as she was not, Paul
could not let go of her; he held her and held her and trembled. He was trying to match her tone but his voice quivered as he said, "You got him in the thigh."

"The thigh? Is that all? Damn."

He could not joke about it yet. He laid his head on her
shoulder, his face pressed into the warm winglike curve of
her collarbone. He whispered, "Why didn't you just fly
away? Or be a mouse or something and hide?"

She didn't answer at first. Then she said something that
didn't seem to connect. "I was looking at the want ads
today."

"Huh?"

"Job openings. There's a position at Women's Advocacy.
They need somebody with some legal knowledge. I'd take
a cut in pay, but I think I might go for it."

Beginning to understand, he let her go. With only his
hands resting lightly on her shoulders he looked at her. She
looked steadily back at him.

"I'm never going to hide again," she said.

PRICES
by Jo Clayton

In the Year of the Snake when the snow was barely off the ground and there were green buds everywhere, the apothecary and bonesetter Hanoz Morel was called to the riverfront of Zedar Hirubai to deal with the broken leg of a sailor. When he left the ship, it was late enough that most were sleeping and those who were awake and not on watch had taken themselves to places of entertainment, so Wharf Street was empty, wetted by the rain from the storm earlier in the evening and filled with the unobtrusive noises from riverboats breathing and stretching, rubbing against the fenders strung from piling to piling. Through these noises Hanoz Morel heard a soft whimper coming from the darkness in the walkway between two warehouses. Being a curious man, he turned to look.

Hair shining silver in the moonlight, a child crouched next to what he first thought was a bundle of rags. Small and delicate, little more than a baby, she was crying quietly, like a wild thing too frightened to make a noise.

When he bent over the bundle, he saw it was a woman's body. Her head was horribly broken and her face beaten until it was impossible to say what she looked like, but the tattoos on what remained of her cheeks and chin told him she was a witchwoman from one of the nomad clans that roamed the wide grasslands to the east of this river valley. Why she was here, why she'd been killed, he would probably never know.

She was still wearing the bracelets and beads that marked her rank and role in her clan. They were carved wood and had no value to anyone other than her, but they might someday provide clues for the child if she wanted to discover just who her mother had been, so he hardened himself, took the beads from around her neck and slid the bracelets from her wrists.

He put the ornaments into his satchel, then sat on his heels, frowning at the little girl. It was very late, his neighbors would be long abed and the Foundling Hostel closed for the night. His wife had just come through a difficult pregnancy and had lost the baby in a premature birth despite all that he and the midwife could do. She tried not to impose her grief on him, but he suffered with her and he couldn't bear the idea of causing her more pain by bringing into his house a baby not hers.

He stiffened as he heard the scrape of a foot. The little girl's eyes went wide with terror. She crawled to him and tried to hide inside the skirts of his long coat. He got to his feet, lifted her and held her cuddled against him. *In the morning,* he told himself, *I'll know what to do with you.* In the morning.

Indardura was waiting up for him, her face pinched with weariness and her eyelids pinked with the tears she'd washed away before she opened the door. Her breath caught in her throat as she saw what he carried, a small sound that twisted his heart.

"Someone killed her mother," he said, apology in his voice. "I think the baby saw it, poor thing. I'll take her to the Foundling Hostel in the morning, but I couldn't leave her in that alley."

Indardura held out her arms, her face lighting with the first true smile he'd seen in weeks. "What a little love she is. So quiet. So sad. Of course you had to bring her here. Give her to me. Are you hungry, baby? We'll go wash that dirty little face and then I have some milk for you."

Later, as Hanoz Morel lay in his bed, listening to his wife's slow, deep breathing, feeling her relaxed and warm against him, he thought, Whoever you were, I bless you, witchwoman, for the gift of peace you've given my Darry.

Indardura named the child Lirayn because she was a grace given by God, and Hanoz told the neighbors she was the daughter of a cousin who'd died. As time passed, Lirayn forgot entirely her first two years and the violence that ended them; she was bright and loving, filled with imagination and energy, and she brought great joy into their lives.

In the Year of the Wolf, when Lirayn was fourteen, she began to dream—frightening dreams of burning and blood, death and mutilation. She grew thin and anxious. Her throat locked on her sometimes and she couldn't eat; what she did get down more often than not came up again. Hanoz Morel's simples and possets and tinctures gave her no ease and he ran out of things to try until one day he came upon the gruesomely stained bracelets and beads he'd taken from her blood mother's body and he remembered her heritage.

He rented a mule, set her behind him and rode into the hills west of Zedar Hirubai, taking her to see the Guren who would surely know what caused her torment. As the mule jogged along the path to the holy hermit's dwelling, he told her for the first time that though by all the ties of the heart she was his daughter and Indardura's, by blood there was no link between them, and he related the story of how he'd found her.

She was quiet when he finished, and he could feel her withdrawing from him. "I should have told you before, my Lyr, but you were my heart's delight and Darry had truly forgotten that you weren't born of her body. I didn't want to hurt her by reminding her of that." He felt her tremble and heard a catch in her breathing that was not quite a sob. "Lyr . . ." But he couldn't find the words he needed, so he retreated to unhappy silence for the rest of the journey.

The hermitage was a low, shaggy hut built 'round the trunk of an oak tree whose heavy branches arched above a pool in the creek that curved 'round the glade. A man sat on a flat stone in the dappled sunlight, watching the flow of the water and the shift of clouds and leaves reflected in it, an old old man with long white hair and a shaggy gray beard. He was called the Guren and it was whispered that he was very wise. Though many hermits had that reputation simply because they were hermits, it was said that the Guren was greater than all the others and learned besides, that even the Baroi respected him and sent to ask his thoughts on this and that.

Hanoz Morel dismounted, helped his daughter down, and tied the mule to a tree. He took Lirayn to a place where last winter's leaves were thick on the ground and left her kneeling there while he spread a clean white cloth before the Guren and laid his gifts on it, a fresh-baked loaf wrapped in a square of linen, butter, cheese, and a box of tea. Then he, too, knelt and waited.

Lirayn watched all this without truly seeing it as she tried to sort out some meaning from an existence that had just had its props knocked away. Dada wasn't her father. Mama wasn't her mother. She wasn't Town kat but Plains har. Her mind was full of fog, and putting two thoughts together in any kind of coherence seemed beyond her reach.

She felt heat on her face and looked up. The Guren was gazing at her.

He beckoned to her, raised his hand to stop her father . . . not her father not her father not her father . . . from speaking or moving. "Come here, girl."

When she knelt again in the place he indicated, he reached out, placed his thumb on her brow, and closed his eyes.

The storm calmed inside her. She leaned into his arm, her own eyes closed, tears of relief dripping from beneath the lids and sliding down her face.

He took his thumb away, and she gasped as the wretchedness filled her again, pressing her hand tight across her mouth as her stomach rebelled and threatened to eject everything in it. Through the roar in her ears, she heard the Guren speak. "Go into the house, girl. On a table just inside the door you will find a copper basin. Take it and fill it from the pool there, spit into the water, and bring the basin to me."

The hut was dark and had an old person smell to it. It seemed to hunker around her and stare at her. She snatched the basin and went out.

The Guren sat hunched over the basin for what felt like an hour but probably was not. Finally, he spilled the water out and lifted his head. When he spoke, his words were rusty whispers so faint she had to strain to hear them, and he went on and on, until her head was tired with listening.

"Look at the stream that runs beside us. See how the water bends and slides and even the small turbulences are subsumed in the whole. This is how it should be. When the snow melt overfills the bed, though, this modest flow turns dangerous and can destroy its own banks. You are like the streambed, but instead of water, the pneuma of your gift gushes through you. You are in a time of snow melt and must be taught how to build your banks higher and stronger, how to channel that raw and unshaped power which tears at you." He blinked, stroked his beard. "Now go home, reconcile yourself with your heart-parents, and learn that nothing has changed and you are still who you were. When you have done that, come to me and I will teach you."

The Year of the Wolf ended and the year of the Vulture passed by. Lirayn cooked and cleaned as her mama had taught her, aired the bedding, hung potted ferns to sweeten the rooms and let sunlight into the hermitage. When her self-imposed chores were done, she sat at the Guren's knee and learned what he had to teach her. In the autumn before the first snows she went down the mountain to spend the Harvest Festival with Hanoz and Indardura, a happy time for all of them, though she was glad to return to the hermitage when the visit was done.

When the cycle of Years turned and it was the Year of the Snake again, Zopal Eranz came stumbling into the apothecary shop. "It's Barta, Hanoz," he gasped out. He let his crutch fall and leaned on the counter, struggling to catch his breath. He was a friend and neighbor to Hanoz Morel, lived with his wife in one of the outwall villages, two houses down the lane from Hanoz and Indardura. His sons had grown old enough to get work on the river and his daughter was married to a clerk employed by the Registrar's office.

"Easy, Zop. Yanni!"

"She was in the back yard, Hanoz, doing some weeding, and she just sort of fell over. She's not dead, she's breathing, but I can't wake her up."

As Hanoz Morel pulled off his apron and reached for his satchel, his apprentice, a young man with a pleasantly ugly face and large, soft brown eyes, came from the back of the shop, wiping his hands on a towel. "Yes, Master?"

"Keep an eye on things for me. I expect I'll be gone for the better part of an hour. If Madame Bruhil comes in, give her the powders I've mixed for her. The packet has her name on it."

"Yes, Master."

Barta lay among the yam hills, her thin sharp face dusted with dirt and flies. Her eyes were open, but empty of life, though her bosom lifted and fell at long intervals and Hanoz could feel a slow strong beat in the touch spot under her jaw.

"We'd best get her inside, Zop. I'll carry her, and you go find a boy who'll run word to your daughter. Barta will need to be bathed and dressed in night clothing and I'll want your Callina to look everywhere for insect bites while she is tending her mother. I must tell you I've never seen anything like this. It most certainly isn't stroke or brain fever."

Face drawn with worry, Zopal Eranz, hobbled back into the lane to call one of the boys playing there.

Barta Eranz continued to breathe, her heart continued to beat, but she did not wake from that curious state, nor did she respond to any of Hanoz Morel's tissanes or tinctures.

Three days later Bernari Gargador, a tavern keeper's daughter, fell into the open-eyed sleep and could not be roused. Then it was the turn of Madame Tijario who cared for the abandoned children in the Foundling Hostel. After these, one or two women a day went down, some of them women who didn't know each other, had never even passed in the street. As panic spread, Hanoz Morel and the two other apothecaries in Zedar Hirubai put aside their differences and struggled to discover a pattern in who was taken and who passed over, but there was none that they could find.

On the sixteenth day after Barta Eranz fell, Hanoz discovered Indardura stretched out on the kitchen floor.

"Darry . . ." He went to his knees beside her, thrust his fingers up under her jaw. After a terrible moment he felt a throb, a long pause, another throb. She was alive. At least she was alive. When he could thrust himself to move, he carried her to the second floor, got her into a clean nightgown, and put her to bed.

For a moment he knelt beside the bed, helplessness washing over him. He'd tried everything he knew for those other women and there was no hope in him for Darry—nothing left for him to do but to take care of her until she failed as Barta was beginning to fail.

He dropped his head onto his hands. There was no one he could get to come in and help tend her; people were too afraid, and because they were afraid, they were growing angry and desperate. It wouldn't be long before they started burning houses . . . he straightened his back, brushed at his face as if he brushed away that thought. "Lirayn," he said aloud. "I shouldn't bring her here . . . I have to . . . I can't do this alone."

That afternoon Hanoz rented a mule for Yanni the Apprentice and sent him up the mountain to fetch his daughter home.

Lirayn was distressed when she saw how bad her father looked; from what Yanni had told her on the ride down, she'd expected weariness but not this hollow despair.

She slipped off the backpack, hugged him hard, then went to the bedside and was shocked again as she looked down at her mama. For as long as she could remember, Indardura had been a plump, comfortable woman with skin soft as velvet and smoother than cream. Lirayn had loved the feel of it when her mama hugged her or touched cheeks as they danced a Pozkor Round. The woman on the bed looked deflated, her skin dry and leathery.

Lirayn leaned over, set her palm on her mother's brow—and gasped as she read the absence inside.

"What is it, Lyr?"

She straightened. "This isn't a sickness, Dada. Not of the body. Someone has stolen Mama's soul."

"I don't know if you want these." Her father hesitated, then held out a leather pouch. "They belonged to your blood mother. Maybe they can help you in the Deadlands."

Lirayn took the pouch, pulled the drawstrings loose, and

upended it over the bed. Four carved wooden bracelets and a string of carved wooden beads tumbled onto the coverlet, dark stains mottling the polished wood. When she touched a stain, it burned her and she snatched her hand away. At the same time, the last thing the Guren told her before she left came leaping into her mind. Follow the blood, he said. And it will lead you to the heart.

She slipped the bracelets over her hands, took up the string of beads, and dropped it over her head so the beads lay against her neck and fell down past her breasts. She unrolled the prayer rug she'd spent last winter weaving, set the trance drum at its front edge, then turned to her father.

"I've never done this alone." She brushed at the fine blonde hairs that escaped from her braids and tickled her face. "I've walked the Deadlands a few times, but the Guren was holding my hand. It's easy to get lost there, he said, if you don't have a guide and someone to call you back. Dada, I'm depending on you to do that for me. I left a small linen bag on the table beside my bed. If I haven't returned to myself by midnight three days from now, bring a brazier in here and burn that bag. Don't open it. Please. If you do, you will destroy its virtue."

"Lyr . . ."

"Hush, Dada. You know I have to do this."

Hanoz Morel closed his hands into fists and looked helplessly at her. "It's just . . . I don't want to lose you, too."

"I don't want to lose me either." She forced a giggle and was rewarded when she saw a smile struggle out from behind his worry. "See that I drink some water every few hours, but don't try to feed me. That could be dangerous."

Alone in the bedroom, Lirayn went to stand looking down at her mama. "I wish. . . ." She shook her head, laid her hand once more on Indardura's brow, closed her eyes, and tried to remember the whole woman, not this fragment that lay on the bed. "Follow the blood and you'll find the heart," she murmured. "That's what he said. One could wish he'd been a trifle more forthcoming."

She settled herself on the rug, arranged her legs, rested the small round drum on her crossed shins and tapped tentatively at the head—but found no rest within, no focus to which she could turn, using it to separate soul from body.

There were too many memories here. All here, present to her now, turning her away from what she needed to do. She'd swept this room and mopped it and made the bed and washed the windows and watched her mama sitting in that worn old armchair sewing things, had herself sewn many a seam and darned many a sock as she perched on the hassock beside the chair.

The distractions of familiarity. The Guren had warned her of those. It was why he was a hermit, he said. Why he knew he was not Wise. Walking the road to wisdom meant accepting the All in its complexity and shadings, he said, accepting the good and the evil and the ordinary merging of the two. It meant living in the All and apart from it at the same time. The abrasions of daily life wore away my focus, he said. The blows of daily life fractured my being. When I at last understood my limits, I came here where life is pared to the bone and changes are subtle enough that I can contemplate them with pleasure and trace the lines that connect them to the All.

A fly came buzzing in the window and landed on her mother's face where it walked across cheeks and eyes and nose and mouth in erratic, ill-formed curves.

At first Lirayn felt revulsion. Her muscles tensed as she started to rise and brush the fly away, then she forced herself to acknowledge this distraction and use it, to watch the fly walk, to think of nothing but those angular legs translating up-and-down into horizontal arcs.

The fly expanded until it was huge enough to fill the room, then exploded into shards of jet and mica and she plunged into that black-and-crystalline glitter, swooping down along a thin silvery thread undulating beside her, the tie that linked Indardura's soul to her body.

She found herself standing in a gray land where grass and leaves were black and the sky a silver bowl.

And she'd lost the thread.

A wolf howled and the wooden bracelets clattered, the stains on them burning white hot. She lifted her head.

On a rocky outcrop a short distance away, that wolf stood looking at her—a silver beast with a creamy white ruff and belly fur and luminous blue eyes, startling in this land without color.

Follow the blood, Lirayn thought. If the bracelets tell truth, that is my blood mother. How do I speak to my Mother about my Mama without provoking anger or hurt? What do I say?

The wolf yipped, a sharp impatience in the sound.

Lirayn sighed. Just ask, she told herself, the more bends you go round the likelier you are to fall on your face. "Mother I never knew, lead me to my Mama's soul."

The wolf curled black lips in a snarl that bared her tearing teeth, then she turned and began picking her way down the outcrop to the short furlike black grass on the flat below.

Stung by that hostility, Lirayn wanted to snarl back, but she contained herself and hurried after her Guide.

As she walked through the grass, she began to feel weak. The beads about her neck jumped lightly against her skin. Was that a warning? She looked around, but she couldn't see any threat. When she looked down, though, she saw that her feet had hundreds of tiny cuts. They were leaking black blood and the grass was lapping at it.

She ran.

The grass hissed, tried to trip her, but she reached bare stone still on her feet. As soon as she'd gotten clear, the cuts healed over and her strength came trickling back.

Far ahead of her the wolf looked 'round and yipped, then trotted on.

She came to a river filled with black boulders and wild white water that slapped into them and leaped into fans of spray. The wolf waited until Lirayn had almost reached her, then she jumped onto one of the boulders and leaped from that to another and another, zigzagging across to the far bank.

Lirayn drew back a few paces, ran at the stream and leaped, landed, leaped again almost as soon as her feet touched the cold stone, trying to remember exactly where the Guide had stepped. She had almost reached the other side when she made a mistake, came down on the wrong boulder.

It turned under her.

The water seized her, sucked her under and rolled her along the gravel bottom, cast her up again and slammed her into a jagged stone slab. She caught hold of it and levered herself out of the race into the shallows, crawled up the bank and lay there, trembling and panting until she felt eyes on her and turned her head.

The silver wolf stood a short way off. After a long moment she seemed to smile with satisfaction, then she turned and trotted off.

Scraped and bruised, bloody and cold, Lirayn struggled to her feet and followed.

A black fragment whipped by her, flat and ragged like burned paper blowing in the wind. She thought she heard a faint scream, but the thing was past so quickly she couldn't be sure. She walked on, weary and sore, following the silver wolf who seemed to ride the horizon as if each of her paces pulled it to her.

Another fragment appeared as if spat out of the air itself. It flew by her on a wind she couldn't feel, trailing that almost-not scream. A moment later more of the fragments burst at her, drowning her in mewls and wails, stinging like gnats when they brushed against her. They came at her until the air was black with their fragile tumbling forms and her head ached from the constant high whine.

Then she was through them. Her skin was covered with red blotches, much as it had been after she got into a thicket of thistles when she was six.

The wolf waited at the horizon.

Lirayn sighed and walked toward her Guide, anxiety growing inside her. She knew that time ran differently in this place, sometimes faster than in the mortal world, sometimes more slowly. It was impossible to tell whether an hour or a day had passed where her body was—or perhaps only the space of a breath and a beat of the heart, so she had no notion of how much of her allotted three days had already passed. If she were called back before she found her mama's soul, if she went home without an answer, Dada wouldn't blame her, but the look in his eyes. . . . She shook her head and forced herself to move faster and faster, until she was almost running.

The air went chill, and tendrils of fog swirled around her.

This fog was one misery too many. Suspicion became certainty. The wolf was deliberately leading her into these hazards and would not take her where she had to go until forced to it. Lirayn shouted "NO!" then dropped to the ground and sat with her legs crossed, her hands on her knees.

The fog thickened. The bloodstains on the bracelets and the beads burned her ghost flesh, ice burn, so cold, so very cold . . . it came to her suddenly what this was. Cold anger made tangible.

Anger? Why?

She stripped off one of the bracelets and held it with her hands curved round the outside. Before she could use it as a focus for meditation, the chill lessened and the sense of looming threat backed off slightly.

What?

She stripped off the other bracelets and set them on the ground, lifted the string of beads over her head and let it fall in a heap beside them.

The fog rolled aside.

The wolf stood in front of her, blue eyes burning into hers, demanding . . . something . . . she didn't understand what.

With a yip of impatience that was absurdly like the sound her mama made when Lirayn had done something thoughtless or silly, the wolf brushed her paw over the pile of ornaments and then stood waiting.

"Is that it? Is that what this is about?" Yes, she thought, it must be. Her blood mother was furious because she was wearing those beads and bracelets. She'd assumed rank without earning it. And in doing so, she had trampled on her mother's accomplishments and pride.

"My father . . ."

The wolf's eyes narrowed, and she growled a warning.

Lirayn swallowed nervously and began again. "The man who found me and raised me as his daughter gave these to me because he thought they would help me. He didn't know, nor did I, that wearing them would be a presumption. I apologize and return them to you, Mother who bore me." She lifted the string of beads, leaned forward, and managed to drop it over the wolf's head. The bracelets were more of a problem. "I don't know how I . . ."

The wolf pawed at the bracelets, separating them, then she lowered her head, nosed at one of them, pushing it toward Lirayn.

Lirayn picked it up and looked at it. The carvings were long lean running wolves. A gift or something else? She slid it over her wrist. "The others, too?"

A growl.

"We leave the others where they are?"

The wolf trotted a few steps away, then stopped, turned her head to look back and whined.

"All right. I'm following."

They went 'round a rock outcropping that Lirayn recognized with a flare of anger that she quickly suppressed, then down a long slope to a wide hummocky plain with a river flowing dark and powerful between groves of black-leaved oaks with pewter trunks. The ground moved oddly beneath her feet as if each step were somehow a thousand paces long instead of one, so she was soon following the wolf through those trees and into a wide swale where the grass was a creamy white, soft as fine velvet.

The bodies of women were laid out on that grass in neat rows, head to foot to head to foot, their eyes closed, their hands crossed over their ribs, faint silver threads curving up from between their breasts to vanish in the silver sky.

Lirayn walked cautiously down the last slope and began moving between the rows of souls. The first was an older woman, very beautiful despite the petulant lines in her face and an ugly growth affixed to her head. The second was Barta Eranz. Seeing her neighbor's ghost body lying there naked and vulnerable like that startled and disturbed Lirayn. She didn't want to look, but she felt she must. There was a swollen black egg where Barta's heart should be.

All of the women she walked past had such stigmata, a mottling of the face and head, a black tree growing through the body, a withered and blackened breast, a swollen leg, a nose eaten away, wormy growths from the ears, black puffballs where the eyes should be. When she found Indardura, her mama had something rather like a huge prune attached to the side of her body, a prune grown two spans tall, black, wrinkled, ugly and frightening.

She knelt and set her hand on her mama's brow—and felt nothing except a coolness against her palm, nothing it to tell her why this had happened or give her a thread she could pull to undo it. Nothing.

"Mama, wake up. Know me. It's Lyr. Please?"

There was no answer. As she knelt there wondering what she should do now, a new soul came drifting down and settled on the white velvet grass, a woman with black marbling through her body like the mold in blue cheese.

"Mama. Please."

A cold nose touched her shoulder.

"What?"

The wolf moved off a few paces, looked back, and whined. When Lirayn got to her feet and came toward her, she leaped over a ghost body and trotted to the beginning of the first row of laid-out souls. She waited until Lirayn was beside her, then she sank her teeth in the shoulder of the ghost body, shook her head vigorously, sending that soul flopping about like a dishclout whipped by the wind as it was hung out to dry.

With a mewling cry, the soul opened its eyes and tried to sit up.

The wolf shook her teeth loose and backed off a few paces. Looking expectantly up at Lirayn, she sat on her haunches with her tail brushing back and forth over a body in the second row.

Now that animation and arrogance were returning to that superlatively beautiful face, Lirayn recognized the woman. She was the Barronin-lehn, mother of the current Baroi of Horren. Though he was nearly thirty, wed and with two sons of his own, gossip said that he was apron tied and as much in thrall to her as if he were an infant suckling at her breast.

The Barronin-lehn's ghost got to her feet. Her head lifted, and her dark eyes glittered. "Li Tay," she said. Her voice was beautiful, a warm, rich contralto, but shockingly loud in the stillness of the swale. "Where is my maid? Bring Li Tay to me."

A low growl woke Lirayn from the subservience that custom had pulled her into, the residue of all those times when she was in the shop and her father took her outside with him to bow to the Baroi and the Barronin when they rode past. Lirayn ran her thumb over the carvings on the bracelet she wore. Name, she thought, What is her name . . . I know I heard it somewhere . . . name . . . ah! Haygra. Barronin Haygra . . . no, just Haygra, I'm the one with power here, not her.

The wolf rubbed her head against Lirayn's thigh, showing approval of the change in her stance. A muted joy at this recognition warmed through Lirayn and gave her yet more confidence. "Haygra," she said. "Be still."

The Barronin-lehn opened her mouth to blast this impudence.

Lirayn licked the palm of her right hand, clapped it across her own mouth and fixed the Barronin Haygra with as commanding a look as she could achieve.

Haygra's cheeks bulged as her mouth sealed and her attempts to speak produced nothing but a distortion of her face. She lifted a hand, took a step forward.

Lirayn whipped her hand from her mouth, held it out with the fingers pointing at the sky and the palm facing the angry ghost.

Haygra slammed into an invisible wall, took a hesitant step back.

"You may speak," Lirayn said. "But only of what brought you here."

Her voice petulant but much softer, the Barronin-lehn said, "Where is this place? Who are these people?"

"Forget that. Tell me what you remember."

Haygra's shoulders slumped and she looked away. "This year . . . just this year . . . I had terrible pains in my head . . . and falling fits. I would forget things. I could look in the mirror at my own face and not know who it was I saw. And there were . . . other problems. I don't want to talk about those." She looked from the corners of her eyes at Lirayn to see how that was received. When there was no rebuke, she went on with more assurance.

"My son did not trust the apothecaries of Zedar, so he sent men all the way to Grand Har to bring back the healer most in favor at the court of the Regge. The man could not be tempted away by gold, so they took him by force and brought him to me. My son showed him three bags of gold. Those he would receive if he cured me. Then he showed him a rope. By which my sweet Jaun meant he would hang from the barbican gate if he failed.

"It soon became apparent to me if no one else that this self-called healer was a fraud, a half-taught Spell-man with a handsome front and a few flashy tricks. He bled me and dosed me, made me do disgusting things. Despite everything he tried, I got worse until I could not even speak. When the words I saw so clearly in my head came through my lips, they were an idiot's babble.

"He tried to run, but my Jaun dragged him back and

gave him one last chance. What he did next . . . there was a stench . . . something burning . . . words . . . ugly . . . evil . . . the sound of them felt like slime oozing on me . . . don't ask me what they were, I don't know . . . I don't think I could bring myself to say them even if I did . . . I don't remember anything more . . . until I woke here. What is this place?" The Barronin-lehn looked frantically about, her hands plucking at her hair, her face, her mouth working, spittle escaping from the corners.

"Barronin-lehn Haygra, return to your sleep. Sleep. Sleep." The wolf's whine mixing with her voice, Lirayn chanted the word over and over until the animation left Haygra's face and her legs folded under her. In moments she was stretched out again on the white velvet grass.

Lirayn frowned down at her, then turned to the wolf. "Mother, it sounds like the Spell-man tried a Black cantrip and the pneuma leaked. And it's still spreading, taking any woman with something wrong in her body, something hidden that even the woman might not know about . . . Mama!" She wheeled and ran.

She knelt beside her mama's ghost and forced herself to touch the ugly wrinkled growth that stretched from Indardura's hipbone to her lowest rib. The soft, spongy feel of it nauseated her, but she stroked it as the Guren had taught her, flattening her left hand, her healing hand, and drawing it across the growth, slowly slowly, repeating the act over and over again.

As she worked, she felt a growing fatigue and knew that her own substance was flowing into Indardura's body to replace what she wiped away. This did not frighten her; on the contrary, it rather pleased her. It seemed a way to repay the tenderness and care Mama and Dada had given her from the moment she entered their lives and the pain she'd given them with her anger when she thought everything she knew was a lie.

The blackness shrank and shrank again. Her arms grew heavy, so heavy she could hardly lift them, her hands trembled.

Distantly she heard a soft whine, then a warmth spread through her. It was the wolf, it was her blood mother, feed-

ing her, spending her soul stuff to heal the woman who'd
reared her daughter.

The blackness dwindled to the size of a pea, but that last
bit was stubborn. Lirayn kept brushing and brushing at it,
yet it simply sat there black and hard, defying her. She
reached again. The wolf knocked her hand away and bit
the black seed loose from Indardura's ghost body, spat it
out and collapsed beside Lirayn.

Because she'd given so freely of herself, she was skeletal,
translucent, a ghost of a ghost, this mother in wolf shape
whose name Lirayn didn't know. For a moment her eyes
were still shockingly bright in this color-drained land, blue
as Lirayn's eyes were blue. Then lids fragile as the thinnest
parchment closed over them. The wolf sighed and lay still,
her muzzle resting on Indardura's breast.

Summoning the last dregs of her strength, Lirayn gathered her blood mother into her arms and sat on her heels,
holding the wolf form tight against her body, fumbling for
a way to keep the soul from the not-being into which it
was fading, searching through the lore that the Guren had
taught her until she found the one way open to her.

"Once you carried me for nine months, Mother, let me
now carry you. Come into me," she crooned, then spoke
the ritual words, the compact she offered. "This is a gift of
my heart, given freely and without reservation."

She felt a faint stirring against her skin, a warmth, then
her arms were empty.

With a sigh she raised herself onto her knees, meaning it
to shake Indardura awake as the wolf had done to Haygra.

Smoke blew into her face, her eyes watered, her nose
twitched, and she sneezed.

And found herself looking into her father's worried eyes.

The herb packet was burning on the brazier beside a
steaming pot of something else she didn't know what, and
she was weary beyond any tiredness she'd ever known.

"Lyr, did you . . . ?"

"I know what happened and I know why." A hiccup
caught her by surprise; eyes wide she pressed her hand
against her mouth, startled again by the kicking, scratching,
and poking inside her that had caused that eruption. Her
blood mother was making herself at home. "And I think I

know what to do," she finished. She hiccupped again, clicked her tongue in annoyance.

"You can tell me later, Lyrrie." Hanoz Morel brought her a mug, closed her hands about it. "Drink this," he said. "It's broth. You've been three days without food and you need to build your strength again. Get as much down you as you can manage." He rose from his knees and went to sit on the stool beside the bed, holding Indardura's hand as he watched Lirayn sip cautiously at the warm soup.

When the cup was half empty, she looked up. "It wasn't deliberate, what happened to Mama. It began with Haygra, the Barronin-lehn. . . ."

The Great Hold of the Barois of Horren was a vast gray complex of stone that nested atop a high rocky hill a few leagues north of Zedar Hirubai. Rumor said there were three springs inside those walls, springs that never went dry even in midsummer heat. It was certain that in the memory passed from grandfather to grandfather, the Hold had never fallen to any siege.

Lirayn sat high in a huge old oak tree, contemplating the Hold and trying to discover a way she could get past the guards and inside the walls.

Her blood mother Maymoy was visible as a projection outside her mind, standing on a clump of leaves and scowling at the Hold as if she were willing the Spell-man to come forth and surrender to them. Maymoy had a very *firm* mind.

Lirayn didn't exactly regret her exalted generosity in the Deadlands, but she was starting to understand the consequences of impulsive acts. It was all very well to preserve her dead mother's existence by housing the soul in her body, but when Maymoy started being her mother in earnest, wanting to run Lirayn's life from inside where she couldn't get away from her . . .

Her eyes narrowed as she inspected Maymoy's image. Whatever means her mother used to create that projection, she had done it with an effortless ease. Jealousy nipped at Lirayn, but she quelled the feeling and went back to contemplating the Hold. Maymoy had confirmed what she'd suspected. There were only two ways it to negate the cantrip, stop the leak of its pneuma, and thereby free the souls of the trapped women from the Deadlands—the Spell-man could cancel his spell or they could cancel him—which meant they either had to go into the Hold, find him, and confront him or they had to compel him to come out and face them.

The Hold's main gate was open. In the Gatehouse built across the arch, the Gatekeeper drowsed in the window that overlooked the drawbridge, coming alert only when he didn't recognize a man seeking entrance. There was a trickle of people moving across that drawbridge, mostly farmers driving wagons filled with the Baroi's hirur, the portion of crops he collected in addition to the rent.

"I suppose I could hide in one of those wagons." She felt rather than heard Maymoy's snort. "Well, if you don't like that, what do you suggest?"

The figure turned and Maymoy's eyes snapped blue sparks at her. *Walls!*

Lirayn put her hand over her mouth, hiding a grin. Walls said like that sounded like the worst of curse words.

Fool's game, going into a trap without fixing a way out of it.

"Well, how do we get to the Spell-man?"

The sun is almost on the peaks. When the moon is up and the dark is on us, I can find him, break him loose from the Baroi, and chase him here to you. If you are willing to pay the price.

"Price?"

You'll not come nearer death while you walk in that body, daughter. I will take what I must and that might be every-thing you have.

I have already paid a price, Lirayn thought. *And the pay-ing is not yet done.* She closed her eyes. Mama was fading and Dada was grieving, and she could stop both. She had begun this with a confidence and vigor born of ignorance, convinced she had the strength and skill to bring it off. No more of that comfortable folly. She sighed. And even less choice. "I will pay," she said.

Good. If you want something, you must always be pre-pared to pay its cost. Hm. It's time I taught you your heri-tage, daughter. You'll need it when you face the Spell-man. He's a fool and a fraud. Such men never believe, deep down, that there's a trap they cannot talk themselves out of. The bracelet I gave you, look at it. Leave it on your wrist, but see what is carved there.

Lirayn turned the wooden round over and over; she'd laid the beads and the other bracelets away, but this was her blood mother's gift and she only took it off to sleep. The long, lean wolves ran nose to tail in their eternal circle.

This is your heritage, daughter, the gift of running on four legs and reading scents that ride the wind. My mother taught me and her mother taught her and so it was in an unbroken line back to the first who wore fur. KNOW YOURSELF.

As those last words clanged in her head, Lirayn felt a brief agony, then she was a point of awareness encysted within a fierce, hot mind, drowning in a sea of scents, looking through eyes that saw in black and white. She cried out for help, the sound a wolf's whine. From somewhere the words came again. *Know yourself.*

And she was once more in the skin she'd known all her life.

The Spell-man fell off the rope he'd used to climb from the Gatehouse window, ran frantically across the drawbridge and along the road that crawled in sharp switchbacks down the rocky slope. Broken chains rattled from his arms and legs and his eyes glittered with the terror that drove him, a terror engendered by the huge silver wolf which loped along behind him, a blue-eyed wolf taller than a warhorse, whose soft growl spurred him on whenever he thought to slow and catch his breath.

Down and around he went, then out across a flat with piles of rock and clumps of withered grass and into the oak grove growing beside a curve of the River Baizin, one of the three that met above Zedar Hirubai.

A growl froze him in place when he burst into a glade where a young woman lay on a prayer rug. A fire crackled beside her in a ring of stones. On a grate over the fire a pot was boiling, the steam rising from it sharp with the scent of the herbs in the water. The wolf brushed past him, leaped onto the girl's body and melted into her.

Careful to conceal her trembles, Lirayn sat up. The drain hadn't been quite as bad as Maymoy had warned it might become, and the return of the wolf-soul to the body

brought a replenishment of its strength. Nonetheless, Lirayn was glad that she didn't have to stand up right now.
"You're not very good at Black work," she said. She kept
her voice casual and smiled at him, relishing the mix of
anger and confusion in his face.

He was an impressive man, tall and lean, handsome in
his way with jutting cheekbones and a fierce black mous-
tache. She could feel his slyness oozing back as the terror
of the wolf faded and he saw that it was a girl he faced.
He struggled a moment, trying to wrest himself from the
spirit chains Maymoy had thrown 'round him. When he
discovered he couldn't shift them, he tried another ploy.
"What do you want, sweet child?" he asked and smiled at
her, a tender caressing smile meant to melt her bones. She
saw what the Barronin-lehn had meant. Charlatan and good
at his trade.

Lirayn reached for the staff she'd cut on Maymoy's instructions, used it to help her onto her feet. Leaning on it,
she stood facing the Spell-man. "You have a choice," she
said. "Three roads. You can remove the cantrip you wove
around the Barronin-lehn. You can tell me the exact spell
you used, so I can remove it. You can refuse to do either.
Choose one of the first two and I'll let you go your way.
Choose the third and I'll cancel the cantrip the only way
left to me. I will kill you."

"Kill me? I don't believe you, not a pretty, young thing
like you." His voice was rich and mellow, like the cream-
heavy coffee that Indardura fixed on deep-winter mornings
when the wind blew icy cold 'round the corners of the
house.

"To save my Mama and bring her soul back to her, I'd
boil you in a stew pot and suck the marrow from your
bones."

He smiled at her, sighed, and shook his head, his deep-
set dark eyes glowing with warmth and compassion. It was
false, she knew that, something he'd practiced till he was
very very good at it, but she found that look disconcerting
because it reminded her he was a man not a devil, that the
evil he'd done came from weakness and incompetence, not
from malice.

"Your mother? I thought that Barronin-lehn had only one
child, a son. No matter." He leaned forward, having loosened

the spirit chains enough to allow the movement. "In any case,
I saved her life. She'd be dead now without me."

Lirayn scowled. "Will you tell me what I ask?"

"No." He lifted a hand to show her how soon he'd be
free and ready to do what she would not like. "Go home,
child. You're dealing with matters beyond your understanding."

"So be it." Lirayn swallowed and swallowed again. She
could see this going on and on, because he'd never believe
she meant what she said. And after all the words, the end
would be the same. "Maymoy, help me."

The Change was agony, but she knew what to expect
this time.

The wolf leaped, she felt the rush of triumph and rage,
the solid thud against the man's body, the pleasure as the
teeth closed in flesh and tore, the taste of the hot salty
blood.

Then she was in her familiar body, standing some steps
away from the dead man and trying to control the faintness
that flooded over her and the nausea that threatened to
rob her of the rags of her strength.

When she could move again, she used a fold of her skirt
to take the pot from the grill; she emptied it over the fire
in the ring of stones, then rolled it up in her prayer rug.
The grill and the stones could stay where they were; they'd
tell no tales to the curious.

The rug under her arm, she stood a moment looking
somberly down at the Spell-man. "I'll pay a price for you
also."

She turned away and started walking home. One mother
lay dormant within her and the other would be waking and
waiting for her. She had done what she came to do, but
right now all she felt was weariness and all she wanted was
a bath that could wash away not only dirt and sweat, but
the taint of death that clung to her.

SLEEP WITH ONE EYE OPEN
by Linda P. Baker

The man was a Killer and he had come for her.

Laura knew it the moment he stepped through the scarred inner doors of the inn.

She froze only steps from the stranger, stilled like an animal caught in a hunter's sights, a sudden sickness in the pit of her belly, heavy and sodden and writhing, gluing her feet to the floor. For a moment, a face from her childhood was superimposed on the Killer's. Laura blinked, and the memory wavered, then disappeared.

He was a big man, so tall his head blocked the twinkle of the glass lamp high on the barroom wall. A normal man, with tanned skin and hair sunbleached the pale blond of ripened wheat. Except for the aura—a halo of blood-red writhing around his body, the glint of copper/gold in his eyes—the traits of a Killer. Traits Laura recognized from childhood rhymes. Traits no normal person could See. Traits so strong she couldn't blink away the Seeing.

He paused just inside the entrance, and his gaze zeroed in as if she stood alone instead of in the crowded bar. He showed no surprise at finding her there.

Behind the Killer, the wooden inner doors hesitated, giving a little screech before they reversed direction and began to close. Both inner and outer safety doors stood open in unison. The night sky, black and menacing and filled with burning stars, silhouetted the man's head.

Three years before, in the town before Drale, she'd had to leave in the night. Through wasteland where the ground sucked at her boots. Through forest where ruined trees loomed, branches black and gnarled like greedy, grasping fingers. Twisted trunks hiding things unimaginable. All under a black sky filled with fiery pinpricks of light. The journey still haunted her.

But even knowing she might have to face the night didn't frighten her as much as knowing what the man was. Seeing it so plainly before her eyes and not being able to push the recognition away, tamp it down, ignore it . . .

He was a Killer and he had come for her.

Mesmerized by the recognition in his Killer's eyes, the swirl of his Killer's aura, she backed away slowly, around a table. The mugs of beer on her tray rattled against each other like teeth chattering.

"Hey—" A fist loomed into Laura's vision. "Hey!" The owner of the fist opened his hand and jiggled a handful of coins, eager to exchange them for a mug of foamy beer.

Only one of the coins was real.

It glinted dully, tarnished copper, mundane amongst the handful offered up in the man's grubby palm. The others, the ones which had been Dreamed into being, glowed brighter than shiniest gold, shimmered like a trick of the sunlight on desert sand.

Laura gasped and stepped back. No! Not now, with a Killer in the room! Her gaze darted across the faces of those about her, automatically searching for evidence that anyone else Saw what she did. Or, more important, that anyone else could tell that she Saw.

"Hey! Gimme a beer."

The Dreamed coins flickered between solid and insubstantial, vibrated with a high-pitched whine that Laura saw as much as heard. The coins, and the man, set her teeth on edge, set the skin on the back of her head to crawling and tingling.

A litany, the result of twenty years' hiding, played softly in her thoughts. *Be calm. Be calm. Act normal.* Her body responded, slipping into the usual, slump-shouldered, subservient, blend-into-the-background posture.

Brushing her long brown hair back from her face, Laura thrust her tray under the man's hand rather than touch the money. If he noticed, he didn't comment on it. He thumped the coins onto the tray and greedily grabbed a beer.

The Killer seemed to have lost interest in her. He was scanning the crowded room.

The Xillenwood Inn was an old building, built long before the Dreaming Wars, long before Laura was born. It still had single sleeping rooms on the second floor above the huge bar. Its walls and floors were wood plank. In the tall windows across the front, there was still real glass, although it only showed from the inside. The windows of all inhabited buildings had been covered with heavy iron safety shutters during the Wars. They had never been removed.

The mutter and quiet of the room slowly penetrated through the haze of Laura's shock, and she realized that conversation and the clink of bottles had dulled as the crowd slowly noticed the man. Their faces were painted with suspicion and distrust for a stranger arriving in the middle of the night. And with a glint of interest for the distraction from the slow pace of their nights.

Laura knew they wouldn't be so interested if they could See what he was, as she did. A warning coiled in her throat, pressed against the back of her tongue. These people, still strangers though she had worked in their town for almost a year, didn't know what she did, couldn't See the blood aura writhing about the man. And she wouldn't—couldn't—tell them.

To the people sitting at the bar, the families crowded around the tables, the noisy men and women playing hiland, slapping worn cards on top of each other with shouts of glee, all things looked the same. Even if their own sleeping minds created a thing out of their Dreams, they would not discern it from the real world.

Only a Killer had the Sight to distinguish all things Dreamed. Only a Killer could look at someone and know if he or she possessed the power of a Dreamer, someone whose sleeping thoughts could create a rose, money . . . or a monster.

Killer. The word reverberated in her skull.

He moved slowly toward her, surveying the room, graceful, assured, agile for such a big man. "Hello, Little Sister." His voice was low and sinister and pleasant. He caught her arm as she turned away.

Laura shivered at the words of welcome, of recognition and condemnation, and pressed her chin firmly down, gaze glued to the dust-filled cracks in the floor. His scent was warm and masculine, but corrupted somehow, like something forbidden, something that grew only in darkness. Mixed with the smells of whiskey and dust and the press of too many bodies, the scent left a cloying, cinnamon taste in the back of her throat.

Firm but gentle, the Killer's callused thumb slid across her cheek, along the line of her jaw, and tilted her head up. His eyes were blue, bluer than anything she had ever seen, as blue as the pictures in the old books of the sky before the Dreaming Wars. Even in the dim light, she could see the bright, hot understanding in them, the glimmer of red gold.

She could feel the blood aura pulsing with life and malevolence on his fingertips. It enveloped her, crawling on her skin like tiny, buzzing bees, bearing a repulsive arousal that coiled at the base of her spine. Her nipples hardened against the coarse cloth of her work dress.

He tucked a finger under her chin, leaned close so that his breath slithered around her neck. "You have the Seeing, Little Sister."

As smooth as water on flesh, the words, the caress of his voice washed through Laura's mind.

She remembered suddenly a dress a classmate had worn. She remembered the way the cloth had shimmered and gleamed, had seemed almost to vibrate. Six-year-old Laura had known the dress wasn't true. Had known it was from a Dream. But even then, she had known the hard lesson of silence.

"No." Laura shook her head and twisted around him, a quick, elusive movement borne of many hours working amongst the mine and farm workers who kept nightwatch in the bar.

The stranger caught her arm once more as she tried to slip past and forced her up against his body. His coat smelled of trail sand and wool and night air. His hand was hotter than the summer sun on her bare arm. And his gaze, his blue clouded over with red-gold gaze, wandered down her face, the front of her dress. It settled, like a spider in the center of its web, on the scattered coins. They sparkled with a red-gold fire that matched his aura.

"Once you have Seen the world as it is, there is no turning back." He whispered the words, breath warm and caressing across her ear, her neck.

"I don't know what you're talking about." Laura pulled away, and her arm, where his fingers had dug in, throbbed and pulsed as if the flesh had been poisoned. Head down, straight brown hair hanging in a mask across her face, Laura wheeled and escaped through the crowded tables. She ignored orders for ale, sidestepped the sly fingers that would have pinched and patted, pretended not to see familiar faces peering up at her with suspicion and curiosity.

Old Soli, drunk and grinning, stood up and staggered along in front of her. She glanced back fearfully as she tried to get past the old man, expecting to see the stranger pursuing, but he was no longer even looking at her. He was looking past her at Soli. He glanced at her, then back at Soli, eyes narrowed.

She slipped past the old man and edged behind the bar. Smoothly, the bartender took her tray, greedily ferreting out the scattered money from amongst the dirty glasses.

She shivered as his fingers counted the coins into the drawer, imagining the awful screech that would have traveled along her nerves had it been her fingers touching the vibrating Dreamed money. In her twenty years, she'd become accustomed to many things—the need for secrecy and solitude, for maintaining an exterior show of normalcy, the need to constantly move on just when she found a place she liked. . . . She had never become accustomed to watching others handle the Dream things as if they were nothing.

The bartender thrust an empty tray and a damp towel toward her. "Clean up the booths."

She took the tray and towel and went in the direction he pointed, grateful he had indicated the back corner, away from the stranger. As she slipped into an empty booth and plopped the wet towel onto the table, there was a gasp from someone in the crowd, a soft oath from a woman sitting nearby.

Safely hidden in the shadows, Laura looked up. Everyone was turned toward the stranger.

He had removed his heavy, knee-length coat and hung it on a hook beside the door. Visible now to everyone was evidence of what he was. Holstered tight against his ribs, beneath his left arm, was a Wakener, the weapon of a Killer.

Laura shrank farther back into the shadows, biting her lip to stifle a whimper. The shining, tubular surface of the Wakener picked up the candlelight and flung it back in spangles of blue-green. Bright, hot spangles, like the light a Killer's power would make it fire.

She gripped the table until the old wood creaked and the pain in her fingers pushed back the faintness. *Calm. Calm,* she litanized the word in her mind. *Be calm.* If she was calm, an opportunity to escape would present itself. All she had to do was bide her time. The years of running had taught her that. Wait for the right moment.

In the silence, the man returned the frightened, hostile stares of the crowd, his right hand laid casually across his chest, fingers near the Wakener. The mocking pleasure which lit his eyes tugged at the corners of his mouth.

His gaze slid carefully over the room, and each person cast his or her eyes up, then down, then up again, unable to bear the man's inspection, unable to look away. Almost teasingly, he hesitated over some faces, checking twice, thrice, before he passed on to the next. An unspoken ripple of relief went through the crowd when he turned his back and moved to the bar.

A Killer in their midst, figure of song and rumor! They settled back into their games and conversations, but the timbre of voices in the room had changed. Had she not been able to hear the words of those nearby, Laura would have still known the essence. It was always the same, whispered in tones of reverence . . . resentment . . . dread.

"What's a Killer doing in Drale!?"

"They never visit the small towns!"

"We keep nightwatch faithfully. We don't need them!"

"The Killers saved us when the wizards gave Nightmares form. During the Dream Wars—" This from an elder, an old woman with careworn skin and white hair, in a reproving voice.

A younger voice interrupted, "But there are no more horrors such as those from the old days! Perhaps somewhere where the people aren't so conscientious about the laws . . ."

Another joined in, voice conspiratorial, gossiping, "I hear there are wizards still practicing Dream spells in the cities. Trying to cure what was loosed . . ."

The old one said softly, "They're gone, long ago. And even if they were not, they would never heal the wound. Some things, once unleashed, cannot be undone."

"But there are no more horrors . . ." the young voice repeated, softly, plaintively.

Laura shuddered. There were no more Sleep horrors in Drale, just coins and dolls and flowers. Except . . . only a few days before, the remains of a body had been found, at the edge of town. The bones of a woman, picked clean of flesh, bone-ends gnawed and splintered as though from teeth.

The crowd's rumble changed once more, as the true significance of the Killer's presence sank in. The protests lowered to hostile, speculative whispering. Suspicion, turned at first only on the figure of the Killer, now shifted equally to the those who sat across the table, to parents down the street at nightcare, to friends at work in the farming sheds. Which friend, relative, daughter, father, brother, would not live to see another nightwatch? Which was a Dreamer?

The Killer watched the reflections in the mirror behind the bar, outwardly nonchalant, a sardonic smile creasing his face as if he knew the turn of their thoughts. Accepting the whispers and stares, the fear and hate and reverence as his due.

Laura could see, now that he had shed the heavy coat, that the man's belly pressed against his belt, as if the heavy muscles which rippled beneath his shirt were segueing into fat. She could see the tiny sun wrinkles lining his face, the beard shot through with gray. Not quite so imposing as he had first seemed. But still she saw the seething blood red limning his body. The awful pulsing aura that she couldn't shut out of her Sight.

Shoulders hunched, Laura stared at the table without seeing the sticky surface, swabbing with the towel in the same small circle. She squared her shoulders and stretched to widen the path of her towel. He wouldn't do anything here, or in the sleep dorm, in front of everyone. That would be the opportunity. At daybreak, once everyone else was asleep, she would be gone. Into the wastelands. On to another town, one where she could pretend to be no more than a lone drifter. Where she could pretend to herself that she saw no shimmering coins or blood auras.

Black worn-down boots coated with dust intruded into the edge of her vision. Their owner blocked her exit from the booth. The man held out his hand. "I've taken a room. Will you lie with me today?"

Laura stared at his open palm, her mind refusing to respond to the words of ritual she'd learned in adolescence. Everyone slept in dorms, in the presence of others. Even married couples and families who could afford their own rooms did not sleep in them. Only a Killer was safe sleeping alone. Only a Killer was immune to the Dream spells.

His offer was an honor, but unexpected. Totally unexpected. The thought of his weight pressing her into a mattress was arousing the way turning over a rock and watching the things squiggling underneath was repulsive. She was unable to turn away even though she wanted to.

She glanced past him, at the people beyond. The significance of his recognition, of his singling her out, was not lost. They stared back at her with the same antipathy she felt for the man standing before her. Their expressions of suspicion and loathing threatened to overwhelm her.

Swallowing to rid her mouth of the hot taste of fear and anticipation, she laid her small fingers in a hand powerful enough to crush it and allowed him to lead her up the stairs.

When they reached the second floor, the first thing the Killer did was inspect the shabby room with the same thoroughness as the room below. He looked under the bed and in the closet, he tested the heavy nightshield which was double locked over the window. Then, satisfied they were alone, he removed the holster which held the Wakener.

It seemed more intimate than the disrobing Laura expected would follow. Fascinated, she stared at the shining wand in a leather holster worn smooth and supple from years of wear. With its buttons of glittering crystal, the weapon looked innocuous, more like a child's toy than something that would end the life of a Dreamer.

He held it out, cupped in both hands like the precious thing it was, and she touched the barrel, imagining the clean, precise beam slicing into her body. How would it feel, the spilling of nightblood? How would he feel, watching the redness soak into the dust of a quiet street or pool and clot on white bed linen?

He put the wand on the rickety nightstand and sat on the edge of the bed, slowly unbuttoning his shirt. His chest was strong, browned as if he'd ridden many weeks without his shirt.

A half smile crinkling the sun-etched lines at the corners of his eyes, he waited patiently for her to come to him.

His touch was as gentle as it had been on her face. Warm on the pulse beating at her throat, callused and scratchy on the tender flesh between her breasts. He drew her down onto his lap and kissed her, his tongue tasting her eyelids, her bottom lip before slipping between her teeth.

His touch was light and tender, deceiving. Laura sighed and pressed against the hardness burning into her thigh. Such hands should have been rough, should have made her afraid. Instead they made her imagine she could slip inside his thoughts, feel the sibilant hiss of blood rushing through his veins. His hands made her think she could turn him from his purpose, if only she could reach into his mind and make him feel her fear as surely as he pressed his face to her breasts and felt the rhythm of her pounding heart.

He twisted, lifting her back onto the bed, covering her with his body. A heavy garnet pendant, warm from lying against his chest, fell out of his shirt onto her breast.

A Killer's amulet! Laura stiffened, tried to twist away from the stone. Trapped in a delicate web of copper and silver wire, the garnet hung from a chain woven of the same metals. The stone was as blood-red as his aura, as molten as the heat he awakened between her legs.

He laid his face against the amulet, holding it against her heart, and it felt strangely warm, electrifying, almost alive. "Tell me what you See." His voice was strange, husky and strained, muffled against her skin.

Her languor, the opening, swelling sensation of arousal stuttered. "I do not See."

He thrust his fingers into the strands of her long hair and shoved her head backward. His voice rumbled against her exposed throat. "Do not deny what is!" His teeth scraped the pulsing jugular.

"I don't—!" she choked.

His fingers tightened on her head, deliberately hurtful, until she thought he would crush her skull. "Do not lie to me!"

Laura clutched the edges of her blouse together and tried to turn her body away from his.

His fingers closed on her throat, then he stopped himself and relaxed back onto the bed. His eyes, which had glinted red-gold with anger, settled back to blue. The squinting lines across his forehead eased, giving him back ten years on his sunburned face.

"You See me." He reached out and caught her hand, and the tickle of the aura crawled up her arm, down her belly. "You feel me. Do you think I cannot See you?"

Laura froze, rigid against the tug of his hand, resisting the siren's call of his body. She still felt the strange ambiguity of his touch, like fire crawling on her skin, like worms crawling in her mind.

He sighed and released her hand. "Say if you do not want to share my bed. I'll not force you."

Laura rolled away from him and stood up. Her fingers shook as she fastened the carved wood buttons of her dress. "I don't want to." But she did. Her fear couldn't wash away her desire for roughened hands on secret flesh, could not ease the ache of emptiness in a mind which had felt rushing blood and heat. To tell someone the truth. After all the hiding . . .

He remained on his back on the bed, staring up at her. "Tell me your name," he said softly.

"Laura."

"Your blood-name."

She wheeled away, suddenly afraid of what she could See. If she looked at him, she would See the aura of a Killer in a sparkling halo around his face. She would See the secret Dream name of his soul, painted in blood in the air. The same way she would know her own, if she but looked inside herself. "I have no blood-name."

His voice stopped her just as she reached the door. "Walk with both eyes open, Laura . . ."

When she hesitated, fingers touching the doorknob but not curled around it, he continued, ". . . sleep with one eye open."

The way he said her name was the gentlest caress, as if he had drawn his thumb down her bare spine. Laura waited, expecting he would explain the strange words. When he didn't, she dared to peek over her shoulder.

He appeared just as an ordinary man. Solitary, tired, lying on his back, staring at the ceiling.

"What does that mean?" she asked when he didn't even look at her.

"Walk with both eyes open. It's the first lesson a Killer learns." The bed creaked as he sat up. "It's unusual, you know, to find one as old as you who hasn't been trained."

"I'm not—" she started angrily, then choked off the words. The words, the truth, threatened to choke her. Bile, bitter and metallic, hesitated at the back of her throat. The room was suddenly as cold as a cloudy afternoon in the depths of winter.

The trembling started down deep and radiated outward. The room was warm, but suddenly it felt as icy as the wind blowing across the wastelands. Laura moaned. "I don't want to See."

The Killer nodded with understanding, as if he could taste the nausea rising into her throat, feel the chill that had nothing to do with temperature. "Wanting does not change a thing."

Laura pressed her back against the wall and slowly sank to the floor, aware only on a surface level of the roughness of the wood tugging at her dress.

"What are you afraid of, Laura?"

She wrapped her arms around her drawn-up knees, closed her eyes. Tears burned her eyelids. "Nothing," she whispered.

After a long time, when she said no more, the bed creaked again as the man lay back down.

Laura sat, arms clutching her knees. Willing him to ask no more questions. To forget she was there. As if in answer to her prayer, he shifted, sighed deeply. After a long time, his breathing took on the even rhythm of sleep.

For almost an hour, she remained where she was, rigid, barely breathing. Finally, when she could wait no longer, she rolled forward, crouched on her knees, waiting again to be absolutely sure that he was asleep.

Calm, calm, calm. Be calm.

Again, when she had waited as long as she could, she rose slowly, cursing the rustling cloth of her dress, the squeak of the ancient floorboards. As patiently as she had waited before, she waited again, standing tense on the balls of her feet, to make sure he remained asleep.

Satisfied that his breathing had not changed, she tiptoed

to the door, waiting again with her hand on the doorknob. As she turned, ready to open to door, she saw the Wakener, laying on the bedside table. The cold brightness of it was like a knife in her brain. In her heart. She wanted to rend the cold metal, tear it with her bare hands. Beat the tube over something hard until it broke into jagged pieces. Until it glittered no more. Fired no more.

She turned back to the door, back to the wand, back to the door, then gave up trying to resist. She walked to the bed, careful to keep her feet on the same wide pine board, to avoid the noisy joints.

Heart pounding, as much in pride at her control as in fear, she stood beside the bed and watched the man. His tanned face was ageless in sleep, serene. The aura, so dazzling before, was muted now, was almost the soft, warm glow of a winter fire.

She picked up the Wakener. The worn leather holster was soft and pliable in her fingers. The metal buckle jingled faintly, like the chime of a tiny bell, and she froze, not even daring to breathe.

The man shifted, murmured her name softly in his sleep. For a moment, his forehead creased in a frown, then his breathing continued, slow and regular, threatening every few breaths to become a snore.

Enclosing the offending buckle in her fingers, Laura fled, planning her flight as she hid the wand inside her dress and slipped down the stairs.

She would head north, across the wastelands. She would find a new home. One where she would blend into the crowd, where she could be anonymous, as she had been in this one.

As she descended the stairs, the noisy conversation below died, replaced with speculative, sidelong glances. Only a fraction of the original crowd remained, the usual group of singles who straggled behind every morning. In their faces, she saw the hostility, fear, loathing. And reverence.

Laura exchanged her apron for her jacket. It hung on a hook beside the door, beside the stranger's heavy coat. She glanced back, expecting to feel the weight of his hand on her shoulder at any moment. The only thing she saw was lurid curiosity and fear where, just yesterday, there had been smiles.

*   *   *

The sky was beginning to lose the muddy gold shimmer of morning when Laura looked back at the bar. She was alone on the main street of town, surrounded by buildings shuttered tight against the creeping sand of the desert. And the creeping things of nightfall.

Soon, offshift nightwatchers would crowd the walkways, stopping for a meal, heading for the sleep dorms. The usual routine would slow as word of the Killer spread. They would gather, wasting a few moments of daylight, to whisper among themselves of the Killer, to count their friends and neighbors and see if any were yet missing.

Laura knew she would be among those counted. She would be one of those whose name, if spoken at all, would bring downcast eyes and a shaking of heads.

Once you have Seen the world as it is . . . She shivered despite the growing warmth of the morning and walked faster, looking back several times to see if anyone was following. As she had in the saloon, she expected at any moment for the Killer's hand to descend heavily onto her shoulder.

In her sleep dorm, the bedroll and pack she kept always ready was there, pushed far back against the wall under her bed. She paused only long enough to collect it, to exchange her work dress for sturdy pants, shirt, and jacket, to grab a waterskin from an equipment shed.

She took the east road out of town until it dipped and she was no longer visible to anyone watching. Then she dropped down into an arroyo that would take her past Drale and, in a narrow, jagged fashion, north.

She walked for most of the morning before climbing out of the arroyo, scrambling and clawing her way up its steep, soft wall.

Drale was visible on the horizon, a brown grouping of buildings, gray lines of farm sheds, protected swathes of precious green, growing things between. She scanned in all directions, squinting against the reddish autumn glow of the rising sun.

She turned twice, slowly, carefully surveying the land all round, the town left behind, the desert to its east, the wastelands into which she was heading. The flat, featureless land was empty save for low dunes of the desert and the scraggly skeletons of the wasteland trees, clutching without hope at the sky.

It was said the wizards who had begun the horror were not evil men, just unwise to meddle with spells and magic they didn't understand. Unwise to turn their power away from healing and making fire, finding water and casting glimmers. It was only after the power of Sleep, the power of Dreams had become known that the evil ones had come forward, the greedy ones, the ones who craved power. They had left pitifully little to rule over.

Despite the empty land, she was unable to rid herself of the feeling that the Killer was right behind her. She sipped sparingly of her water, slipped, and slid back down into the gulch and continued on.

As the sun rose higher, her uneasiness grew. The wand was cold, jabbing against her ribs. She shifted it and tried matching her footsteps to her litany of calming. She paused often to listen.

Every hour or so, she climbed up out of the gulch and scanned the horizon all around. Each time the land was as empty as the time before. The only sound was of the soft breeze disturbing the desert floor. It cooled her skin and filled her lungs with the scent of warm sand.

For the fourth time in as many hours, Laura sighed and slid back down into the arroyo. All about her was quiet and empty.

Just as her feet thumped into the hard-packed floor of the arroyo, Old Soli lurched around a bend in the arroyo! Laura was so surprised she yelped. She would have lost her balance had her bottom not been braced against the wall of the gulch.

Her heart did a hard, hammering turn in her chest, then settled down to quick, alert tripping. "Soli! What are you doing here?"

The old man stumbled toward her, slurring, "I know you," as he advanced. His breath, sour and reeking, touched her as his gnarled fingers grasped at her shoulders.

She shoved him back, not roughly, and wrinkled her nose at the smell of cheap wine and unbathed, sweaty man. "What are you doing here?" she asked again.

As his mouth twisted, struggled around an answer, the familiar face of the old man shimmered. First he was Old

Soli, with sun-wrinkled skin and faded brown eyes, then a second image shifted and shimmered across his features, blurry until it settled into place.

A horrible thing, with inhuman eyes and hide like gravel!

Laura screamed and scrambled back, into the center of the gulch, kicking up puffs of sand.

Soli mumbled in his whiskey-ruined voice and yawned a smile full of needle-sharp teeth.

Laura didn't pause to scream again. She just turned and ran. And fell over nothing, over sand, over her own fear. Dust puffed into her open mouth, choking off her cry of dismay.

The thing she could now See shambled after her on huge, misshapen feet, flexing its claws, grinning its needle smile. For a moment, terror held her, then she was up on hands and knees, clawing for purchase in the dry dirt.

The thing caught her ankle and yanked her back.

She spat dirt and opened her mouth to scream.

And the litany grabbed her. *Calm. Calm. Calm.*

It didn't work, but it helped.

Back. Away. Anywhere. Away from the thing's claws. Scrabbling for the wand. Tearing at her own ribs. At the thick cloth of her jacket. The Killer's wand. Her wand. Cloth ripped. The holster snap clicked and the Wakener was free in her palm, cold and smooth and metallic.

Soli was almost upon her again, and she retreated farther down the arroyo, careful of her footing this time. Her breath was loud and harsh in her own ears; her heart thudding like drumbeats. She aimed the smooth metal wand, but she didn't know how to use the Wakener!

She backed away, holding the useless tube up with shaking hands.

Grinning, slathering, Soli reached her. Reached *for* her!

Screaming, Laura fell away from him. And something clicked. For the second time in her life, the power of a Killer blossomed in her mind, erupted into life around her. For a moment, her eyes felt as if a thin, opaque layer had been placed upon them. Then her vision cleared.

Soli glowed with a noxious, venomous, glittering, green blackness.

The shining crystals of the Wakener cut into her fingers, burned her palm. There was a soft hiss, only a little louder

than air escaping a sealed bottle. The thing that had been—
that was—Old Soli froze as it leaned toward her, its claws
touching her wrists. Light, guided by unthinking instinct,
coming from her, coming from the Wakener, skewered its
chest, enveloped it. Cut through its insubstantial facade and
exposed the blackness that was its center.

Her Killer's light and the light of the sun ate at the
shadow core. The monster's grip went lax. Liquid, as red
as the sky at midday, blossomed out from the spout of its
mouth. Its brittle gray eyes darkened to dirty black.

The monster teetered, gushing blood on Laura, and she
scrambled back to keep it from falling on her. It crashed to
the ground with a crackling sound like waxed paper being
crumpled, like rocks breaking. Dust puffed up around its
broken body. Lines, fine as the age marks in porcelain,
splintered across the thing's pebbled skin.

Laura was kneeling beside the body, the Wakener cradled in her lap, when the Killer rode around the same bend
as Soli had, hours before. The sun was almost out of sight
of the edge of the arroyo. The temperature had just begun
to cool.

Laura looked up into the blue eyes of the stranger. Her
neck ached as she moved, reminding her of how long she
had been sitting there.

The man reined in and sat astride his horse, staring down
at her. "You remembered the first lesson, girl. Do you still
say you do not See?"

"I Killed it," Laura said and looked up. The coldness
inside her was gone, replaced by something hard and stiff
and fierce. With something she hadn't yet named. The sight
of the man no longer made her feel like fleeing.

He smiled at her with approbation, as if he knew. Nodded as if bestowing a blessing.

His expression was nice, but the warmth in her was already so strong, the smile did little to add to it. It was too
much to take in. She looked away, gestured at the crumpled
corpse. "What— What was it?"

"A thing which should not have been. A very old one,
I think."

"But . . . *What?* I knew him. I—"

The man shrugged. "A statue. A painting. An imagination. A stone thing, brought to life by some Dreamer's errant thought."

"But how could he have survived all this time? I know he's been here longer than I have! Why didn't you See him last night?"

"Who says I did not?" He paused while she digested this, then continued, "The very old ones are always knowledgeable in the ways of hiding. The longer they have life, the better they become at evading death."

"But I didn't See him before now!"

"The Seeing comes on when it comes on. Some are born to it. Some come to it late. Some hide from it until it overtakes them." He smiled again to soften his words. "The first Killing is always the worst. Especially when it comes so late in life. I myself did not See until I was nineteen. It will not be so bad next time."

Laura shivered and drew her coat closed over her breasts as if the sun had suddenly gone away. The coldness hovered behind her ribs, eager to blossom again.

"What are you so afraid of, Laura?"

She opened her mouth. For a moment, nothing came out. But the coldness that had always threatened to freeze her when she thought of telling was easy to push back. She swallowed, cleared her throat. Tried again. "The way they look at you. At me."

"They?"

"All of them. Everyone. Strangers, teachers, friends . . . Parents. Everyone who had ever known or guessed what I am."

"The way they look at you . . ." Her voice cracked again, and she paused to swallow. Then spoke another word. And another, then another, slow, halting, as if her throat was rusty. "It's like— Like you're the bad thing. You're the inhuman thing!"

The stranger's saddle creaked as he shifted. "What happened to you?"

She paused, remembering. Shivering with a chill that had nothing to do with the coolness of the air. Words jammed in her throat, then started to spill out, to flow, a torrent of memories. And horror. "None of the others saw the Dream things. Not my brother. Or my friends. Not my parents. Not my friends' parents. I was the only one, and I knew. I knew, that made me a bad girl. Because of the way they looked at me.

"I learned not to mention the toys, the books, the things that weren't quite solid. The knife my aunt used to whittle toys . . . it was sharp. So sharp. The chalk my teacher used in math class. The rose my boyfriend gave me on my sixteenth birthday."

Laura clapped a hand to her mouth. The memories were there. All there, springing up from the shrouded places in her mind, the places into which she had shut them. Some of the memories were cloudy, some as clear as if from yesterday. "There was a monster. They knew because they found what was left of its Kills. Pets . . . A man . . . A child . . . The town was in a panic. No one went out. No one left the sleep dorms unless they had to, to tend the crops." The torrent of words slowed as Laura drew a shaky breath. She stared at the patterns the creature's blood had made in the sand, lost in the past.

"And you Saw the Dreamer?" the man guessed.

Laura nodded, mute with remembered pain. The pale green aura of a Dreamer, crackling around a soft, boyish face. An angelic face, full of life and laughter. A face very much like her own. "He was— It was— My brother."

Her mouth opened, stretched wide with a pain so strong it couldn't escape. She stared up at the man whose shadow seemed to reach across to her. She couldn't tell him. Couldn't tell him the rest. Couldn't put into words the expressions on the faces of her father, her mother. The horror that said they were more afraid of her than they were of a Dreamer. A strangled gasp emerged from her throat.

The man allowed the reins to fall to the ground as he dismounted. The great spotted horse stepped daintily aside, then stood as if tied when its master walked away.

The Killer knelt between Laura and the body of the monster and dipped a finger in the congealed gore on her blouse. With the solemnity of ritual, he touched the bloody fingertip to his tongue, then to Laura's lips. His finger slipped between her teeth, lingered on her tongue.

She gasped and would have fallen had he not caught her shoulder. The blood cut through her senses, like sand in her bones, like glass between her teeth. It tasted of iron and stonedust, of things which never should have been, of nightmares come to life. Of kinship and acceptance and sympathy.

And it told her the blood-name of the man. "Denn," she breathed, staring up into his bluer than blue eyes.

He nodded, pleased. "You don't have to be afraid anymore, Laura. You are what you are, as your brother was what he was. There is no choosing. The Sleepers don't understand. They don't See. They don't *feel*. But none of your own kind will look at you like that."

His aura glowed in the evening light, clean and bright, as did the pendant resting on his chest. So pure it made him difficult to gaze upon.

Laura picked up the Wakener. It was warm where it had been lying across her thighs and spotted with the blood of her first kill. The stains wiped away easily, leaving shining metal and faceted crystals looking like new. She held it out to its owner, holding it in both palms like an offering, but he waved it away.

"It's yours now."

She held the wand suspended in midair, not moving closer to him, but still not taking it back. The weight of it, the smooth warmth, was so very right in her hands, and yet so malevolent, so . . . powerful. The thing tugged at her, as it had in his room. She wanted to destroy it. And she wanted to tuck it back into the holster strapped across her shoulder and feel the warmth of the Wakener against her ribs.

Finally, she closed her fingers around it, cradled it against her stomach. The crystals were rough and bumpy under her fingertips. "You weren't asleep. You let me take it," she accused. "You knew Sol—that thing would come after me."

He shrugged. "You needed to learn for yourself."

"To Kill," she said, her tone quizzical, fearful, very bitter.

He shook his head firmly. No. "To *cleanse*."

He swept his arm up to indicate the land beyond the arroyo. "It's not much now, but each generation reclaims a little more of the land that was lost in the wars. If our children reclaim a little more. And our grandchildren a little more . . .

"If not for us, the Dreamers and the things they birth would come out of the night and cover the earth, Killing and destroying the little we've rebuilt. Last season, another city was lost to the night things, ravaged and burned to the ground to keep them from escaping. Because we are too few, and the Dreamers are too many."

When she met Denn's gaze with solemn eyes, he removed the pendant from around his neck and held it out toward her. "Someday a generation will be born who will not remember this."

Laura stared at the amulet, half expecting it to leap across to her hand on its own. It radiated the same repulsion and attraction that she felt for its owner.

Denn said softly, persuasively, "Someday a generation will be born without sons and daughters who have to destroy each other."

Still she hesitated.

He held the amulet closer to her. "The time for hiding is over."

She looked up into the red/gold/blue eyes that burned with determination. And acceptance. She took the heavy pendant and slipped it over her head. The stone dropped into the collar of her blouse and came to rest over her heart, cold for only a moment. In its heated depths, she felt the name she would take, now that Laura was no more. "Tell me the first lesson again."

Grinning, Denn pulled a silver flask from his coat pocket and took a deep drink from it, then handed it to her.

"Walk with both eyes open. Now you See the creatures of Sleep, and in turn, they recognize you." He leaned in close, almost nose to nose with her. His finger against her breastbone punctuated each word. "Always! In the dark or in the light, walk with both eyes open. See what is before you. See what is behind you. Use the Sight you have been given."

She sipped from the flask. Smooth, warm whiskey burned its way down her throat.

"And the second lesson?"

"Sleep with one eye open."

MESSENGER'S PLIGHT
by Robyn McGrew

A gust of wind hurled heavy flakes of snow into Hsing Li's face. Behind her, Sonpa, her brother's horse, whinnied nervously and limped forward. Li would have to leave the stallion behind and secure a new mount in Chun Bai. "Come on, Sonpa, it's not much farther to the inn."

The storm had blown in from the north just after dawn. Like a northern marauder it transfigured everything in its path. Midway through the morning, Sonpa had slipped on a treacherous decline and twisted his right foreleg. The snowstorm, combined with the horse's injury, had slowed Li's progress intolerably. She had to get to Shaun Yi by the full moon or her family would lose their honor. Yet she still had to trudge across another ridge to reach the High Lord's city.

An hour before noon, sodden and deeply chilled, Li led Sonpa into the shelter of a small wooden structure attached to a timeworn stone inn. The building had one weathered door and above it, a sign bearing faded illegible strokes of calligraphy. Pale yellow light leaked from the edges of the door to the inn. Li resisted the temptation of the warm inn and turned instead into the stable. She removed Sonpa's saddle and strapped a blanket over him. "I'll get you some grain," she promised the horse as she led him into the first of three empty stalls. Satisfied Sonpa would be all right, Li left the shelter of the stable and crossed to the inn.

The wind resisted her efforts to enter the building. She managed to get one leg and shoulder through the door, when the innkeeper saw her struggles and came over to help. "Welcome to the White Dragon. On such a stormy day, I did not expect guests. I am Chow Yuen, the owner." Yuen pushed the door closed. He bowed formally from the waist. Waving a hand toward the middle of the room, he gestured to a small fire burning in the center of a round stone hearth. "Please, sit and warm yourself. I will bring you hot wine and a blanket."

Li fought the cold wrought stiffness in her face and smiled at him. "Your offer is kind, but I cannot stay. I need to cross Yu Soong Ridge today if I am to reach Shaun Yi by tomorrow night. Can you recommend a stable where I can trade horses? Mine twisted a foreleg crossing Mei Ridge."

The innkeeper placed his long-fingered hand on the small of Li's back and firmly guided her to the cushions near the hearth. "Chun Bai is a simple town. We do not have a blacksmith or a stable. Besides, the High Lord's city has rested at the foot of Yang Mountain, in the shadow of Bai Lung Temple for more than six hundred years. I am sure it will remain in place for a few days, if you wait out the storm here."

Li chuckled. "I'm sure, but my business requires I reach the city by the full moon."

Yuen plucked two ceramic cups from a teakwood shelf positioned about the hearth and focused his pale eyes on her. "What business is so urgent that it cannot wait a few hours or a day?"

"I bear an Imperial message."

The innkeeper's white eyebrows disappeared into his hairline. "Many Imperial Messengers have stayed here over the years, but not one of them has been a woman."

"My brother Hsing Tsu is the messenger. He stopped at our mother's home on the way here. My mother mentioned a loose tile on the roof and Tsu insisted on repairing it before traveling farther. He fell. The healer said he broke his leg in three places and would not be able to ride for weeks. I promised to deliver the message for him." She did not dare tell the innkeeper the rest of what Tsu had imparted to her. If General Kuan's message did not reach the emperor in time, they would dispatch the reserves to the wrong location. If she failed, many would die.

Yuen returned the cups to the shelf next to a grouping of wooden bowls and spoons. "Let me see what I can do for your animal. Hang up your wet clothing on the pegs by the fire and let them dry." He pointed to a series of wooden pegs on the hearth. "You will not make good progress if you are weak from hunger and cold. The large copper kettle contains stew, the small pot—brandy wine." The old man crossed to the door and pulled it open. Snow blew in past the threshold and pushed back his long white hair and mustaches like so many silk ribbons. He did not seem to notice the cold as he walked calmly into the storm.

Left alone, Li decided to follow the man's advice—to a point. She removed and hung her now dripping cloak and mittens on the peg nearest the fire. Next, she poured herself a cup of the brandy and opened her pack. Her reflection in the kettle mimicked her movements. The copper revealed a young woman with a round face and a sinewy build. Cold had softened her normally gold complexion to a pale yellow and her thick black braid glistened with droplets of snow turned to water. She looked like a doll a noblewoman's child might own, except for the dark blue male attire of a long tunic and pants. In the kettle, her eyes reflected the firelight, making them look like inverted stars.

First, she removed the scroll bearing the General's message from the leather satchel. On the missive, Kuan's huge thumbprint provided security. Flint, candles, a direction finder, cook pot, eating sticks, and a small bag of kindling followed. Court garb, food, and the note of passage from her brother remained in the large shoulder bag. Her blankets, shelter, and other large items she had left with Sonpa.

The brandy wine warmed her throat and stomach as she sipped it. Within a few minutes the sweet feeling had spread to the rest of her body. She stood to reach for a bowl when the door opened and a gust of wind announced Yuen's return. Casually, he brushed the heavy, wet snow from his tunic sleeves and crossed the stone floor to join her. "Your horse's ankle is sprained. He will need several days of rest before he can travel."

Li bit her bottom lip and considered the possibilities. Only thirty-six hours remained before the High Lord marched with his army. On Sonpa, she could have reached Shaun Yi by late tonight. The storm had slowed her too much. Now, even riding, she could not reach her destination before tomorrow morning. "Is there a farmer or a merchant in Chun Bai with a horse I could borrow?"

"The only animals you will find here are chickens, dogs, and pigs. I am sorry." Yuen reached beyond her to recover a bowl and spoon. "You must surrender to providence. Eat, and I will prepare a room for you."

"No. Thank you for the offer, but I cannot remain here. The message must reach the High Lord. If I must walk, I have no time to lose."

The lines deepened the innkeeper's forehead. "You are a determined young woman. It grieves me to see you take such a risk. Perhaps . . ."

"Yes?"

"I have never seen him, but they say that a hermit lives in a cave a three-hour walk north of the town. It is also said, he sometimes rides a horse. If you can reach his grotto, he may lend you aid."

"Thank you, Master Chow."

She'd left the town of Chun Bai three hours ago and still, she'd found no evidence of a grotto. The road cut an icy path through a pine forest. Tree boughs heavy with snow and icicles angled sharply toward the ground. Some of the larger branches lay broken from the strain. Among the treetops, the wind played an unearthly song. The only other sounds were the crunching of Li's feet and the rasping of her labored breathing as she fought her way through the high drifts. She must find the hermit by the time she reached the promised split in the road or turn west for the pass.

Two hours later, Li arrived at the split or so she thought. The wind had grown steadily worse, and she could not see more than a few feet in front of her. With the visibility so poor, she might have passed the hermit's grotto without knowing it. Little matter now, she would have to keep moving or freeze to death.

It took several fumbling tries and the removal of her right mitten to get the direction finder out of the pack. Her path had veered slightly to the west already, which meant she must follow the left split.

"Fool!" The word cut through the wind as easily as if the speaker stood next to her. He, or at least Li assumed the stranger to be a man, stood an arm's reach away on the road bearing north. His long white hair looked like a mantle of snow and ice. He was dressed simply in a ragged tunic and half-pants. With one swift look he assessed her, then turned away. "Follow me."

Li hesitated. This strange old man wore no boots, not even sandals, yet if she wanted to borrow his horse, she had no choice.

He guided her through a maze of trees and snow shrouded bushes until they came to a large cave with a small opening. The entrance looked like a giant eagle's talon had scraped it from the mountain. Li stopped at the entrance. The hermit's grotto contained no fire, torches, or lamps. Light came from glowing green moss that beetled from the upper reaches of the cave. To her right, water flowed out of the wall and into an ice edged pool. Against the back wall, a small patch of white-and-brown winter mushrooms flourished. In contrast, the left side of the cave contained only a small pallet of woven rattan. She did not see a horse or any evidence of one ever being there.

"Satisfied your curiosity, or will you stand at my threshold all night?" The hermit regarded her with pale, ice-blue eyes that made her think of Yuen. The inflection in his voice sounded at once irritated and amused. His furrowed brow and half smile, expressed the same sentiments.

Not reassured in the least, Li forced herself to smile politely and enter the musty hollow. "Your home is lovely."

"My home is a hole in the mountain. You didn't come here to lie about the splendor of my abode. What do you want?"

"To borrow your horse."

The hermit crossed to the mat and sat with the bonelessness of a cat. "What makes you think I have a horse?"

"The innkeeper at the White Dragon told me that you might have one. If you do not, I will leave now. I have far to go, and the storm is impeding my progress."

Her taciturn host arched an eyebrow at her. "You do not approve of the storm?"

"How could I approve or not? For me, it would have been better if the White Dragon King would have chosen another time to bestow his blessing on the land."

"I see. Have you ever thought that if this inconvenience did not occur now, the farmers in the valleys bellow Yang Mountain would not have enough water for spring and summer?"

"It needs to snow, but I wish it would stop long enough for me to get off the mountain." Li started to edge back toward the entrance. She did not want to affront her host, but she must continue her journey—and soon.

"You think your needs are more important than the exigencies of others the spirits guard?"

"No, not really," Li edged another step toward freedom.

A blast of icy air encompassed Li and pushed her away from the entrance. "No, you may not leave yet, my little mortal. You have yet to tell me why I should make the snow stop."

Li turned and ran into a sheet of ice where the entrance once stood. She bounced off the stone-hard wall and fell to the cave floor in a heap. The hermit made a rasping sound like ice being shaved, which Li took for laughter. Angry and afraid, she stood and turned to face her captor.

The hermit had changed. Instead of a thin, crotchety old man, she faced a wondrous beast. His head looked like an albino camel, except that the large rabbit eyes were the same icy blue of the hermit's. His ears would have been at home on a cow, but the icicle horns made her think of a deer. A sinewy neck twisted and raised like a white snake revealing the only scale-free area on the beast, much like the soft belly of a frog. Legs longer than a tall man, although short for a dragon's body ended in pawed feet with huge white talons. Short fins like junk sails fanned out along the length of huge body and long tail. Despite her best efforts not to, Li gasped.

The White Dragon King lowered his sinewy head until he could look directly into her eyes. "So tell me, little mortal, what message is so important that it cannot wait three days until your horse heals?"

"Great Sir, I bear a message to Lord Ao. If I do not deliver my message in time, the reinforcements will go to the wrong place. Many will die."

"Many will die if I do not provide enough snow to melt in the spring. Their deaths will take longer and have no meaning."

"Forgive me Lord Dragon, but how can the delay of a storm make any difference in the spring melt?" Li held her breath hoping He would not take offense to the question.

The white dragon sighed, and his breath covered Li with

a thin layer of ice. "Things are not as simple as you think, little one. To cause a great storm like this, I must work with my cousins, the air dragons and the water dragons. The latter must provide the needed moisture, while the former must guide the clouds to the correct place. It is only then that I can breathe upon them and cause the clouds to weep snow. My cousins and I planned for many weeks. I grieve for your sake we cannot reschedule, but next week my cousins and I must provide for others. You will find everything you need to live for a week or two here in the cavern. For your own safety I must seal you in, for I must make the storm stronger tonight and your roads will become impassable."

"Please, you must not."

"Have I not said it is for your safety, little mortal?"

"Lord Dragon, I do not worry about my safety. Please let me do something to prove my need to you. It's not just for me. It's not just for the Lord Ao or General Kuan or the men in the army. I gave my word to my brother, and he gave his to the General. My family will lose face if I fail. I'll do anything. I'll go to your temple after I deliver the message to serve you for the rest of my life if that's what you want."

Icy blue eyes locked with her dark ones and Li felt herself weighed and judged. Like an acupuncture treatment, she felt him probing into her soul. After a moment he withdrew. "Very well, I will test you. Find a way to open the door to the cave by morning, and I will help you reach your destination. Fail . . . and you will remain here as a hermit for the rest of your life."

A test! The Dragon King would decide her family had no honor to preserve if she refused. To say yes meant she would have to get out of the ice-sealed cave. If she failed— She could not think of that. She nodded firmly and said, "I accept."

The dragon reared and nodded in return, before vanishing from sight. His parting words echoed hollow against the walls of the cave. "You may use anything you have or anything you can find in the cave."

Li emptied her pack onto the floor, seeking something she could use as a pick on the ice. Failing to find anything useful, she extended her search to the cave. She found a

stalagmite cluster growing near the mushroom garden.
Wrapping both hands around a hand-sized stone, Li pulled
back and applied all her strength to it. After several minutes of trying with no success, she moved to a smaller stone.
Then to a smaller stalagmite, until finally she found a stone
piece twice the size of her thumb. This, she snapped off for
use. Warmed by the exertion, she shed her cloak and mittens and left them by the mushrooms.

She chipped at the ice barrier slowly and methodically
for several hours. After making only a small indentation
near the middle, she had to stop. Partially because she had
fatigued herself, but also because she felt weak and needed
to eat. Lord Dragon said she would find everything she
needed to live for a week. He should have left food, water
and hopefully wood. The pine logs when she found them,
looked like they came from a full-grown tree ripped to
pieces by the dragon's talons.

Deciding she would want the fire pit by her mat if she
needed to sleep, Li set up a boxlike cooking pattern with
the logs. From the pile of her belongings, she retrieved her
kindling chips and flint. The small, dry wood caught
quickly, and Li encouraged the flames to transfer to the
ripped edges of the logs. In only a short time, she had a
strong fire with which to cook her travel stew. She filled
her pot with water from the wall and set it on the logs to
boil. This done, she returned her attention to the ice wall.
Her progress looked unimpressive. The fire had warmed
the small cave considerably and Li removed her outer tunic
to compensate. Fire—how foolish of her not to think of
it before. She should build a fire near the door and melt
the ice.

It took only a few minutes to move the fire and replace
her cooking pot. The ice took on a glassy cast and tiny
rivulets of water traced their way down its surface to the
floor. "It's working!" Excited, Li added more logs to the
fire. The heat increased. Water sluiced down the door, and
the ice looked clearer. Relieved she would not have to chip
her way out, Li replaced her items in the pack, except a
food packet and the pot. She would eat and then leave.

A hissing sound was the first warning of trouble. Gray
smoke filling the room confirmed the problem. The ice
turned water had traveled the short distance to the fire and

was extinguishing it. She tried to pull the logs away from the wall, but more of them fell into the water and the fire died on contact with the water. Worse yet, her stew water looked ready to tip over and she would burn her hand if she tried to stop it. The Dragon King might find her trapped and hungry in the morning, but at least she wouldn't have to explain away an injury.

The cooking pot turned over, dousing what little remained of her fire. Water splashed onto the ice door and collected at the bottom of the ice block. Weary, and disgusted at herself for not thinking far enough ahead to anticipate the problem. Li sat on her haunches and waited for her pot to cool. She admonished herself to make the best of it and pressed the pot against the ice wall. Except the ice wall had a significant dent at the bottom where the water had spilled.

Fight water with water—not fire. Li retrieved her kindling and flint from her bag and started a new cooking fire over by the pallet. She used her mittens to retrieve the pot and filled it with water. When the water boiled, she carried it to the wall and splashed it against the bottom. While more water heated, she kicked at the wall where the ice had thinned. An hour of alternating force with hot water resulted in a head-sized opening in the door. Hours later, fatigued and aching, Li crawled out of the opening.

The Dragon King's voice called from inside the cave. "Congratulations, little mortal. You impress me. I did not think you could do it. Since you have, you might as well rest until midmorning and I will take you to your Lord Ao."

Li stuck her head through the opening. The cave appeared unoccupied. "Lord Dragon, are you in here?"

The scraping ice laughter sounded as the white dragon appeared. "Yes, I have been here the whole time, Even when you made it miserably hot, I stayed. You could not see me and assumed I had left. Come back inside, where you won't freeze."

Li crawled through the opening, then faced the white dragon. "My lord, the message."

"It must wait. The storm has almost reached its climax."

Pressing her lips together, Li looked out the opening she had created and considered trying to walk. Snow swirled in chaotic circles, obscuring the landscape. If she tried to hike, she would lose her way in only a few feet. Only a snow dragon could navigate a blizzard. Perhaps she could convince him to take her immediately. "The snow is your element. Can you fly to Shaun Yi in such a storm?"

The dragon tilted his head and twisted his spike-toothed mouth into the semblance of a human grin. "I could, but why should I? You're the one with a message to deliver."

Li bit her lip, drawing hot, salty blood. "You promised to take me to Lord Ao."

"Yes, but I did not say when."

"Please, I must go now."

A sad tone entered the dragon's voice. "If I take you now, you will most likely die."

When Li answered, her voice was barely a whisper. "If I do not go, many will die. Did not Lao Tzu teach that we should embrace all things? I know my brother would offer his life to see the message delivered. I cannot do less than he."

"Very well, little mortal. Gather your belongings and we will leave."

When Li joined the snow dragon outside, the massive beast laid his head on the ground in front of her. "Get in."

Li looked at the gaping mouth and lurched back a step. "I thought I would ride on your spine or that you would carry me."

"The razor edges of my spine would separate your legs from your torso. If I carried you in my talons, the cold would kill you in minutes. Your only hope for survival is in my mouth."

Forcing herself to move forward, Li climbed into the icy cavern of the dragon's mouth. Teeth which could have passed for massive ice-shrouded stalagmites and stalactites closed. The dragon's tongue was like hard snow and his breath a frosty breeze. Li huddled into her cloak and prayed to the spirits of her ancestors that the lord dragon did not forget her and swallow.

Even in the dragon's mouth, Li could feel the buffeting of the wind and the difficulty of the flight. She had not thought it would take so long, and she felt so very cold. She knew she dared not close her eyes. Sleep in such a cold place would certainly bring death and failure.

Li gasped as she jerked awake. She had to fight, had to stay alert. It could not take much more. . . .

Bright white light bathed her face, penetrating her closed eyelids. A babble of voices filled her ears. Her whole body burned as if touched by a million sticks of incense. Painfully, Li regained consciousness.

"Lord, she wakes now." The obeisant tone in the voice told Li the man spoke to someone of high rank.

"Wha'?" Li opened her eyes. She sat in the middle of a meditation garden. Tiny trees and winter flowers were covered in light, powdery snow. A small group of nervous-looking courtiers and soldiers watched her. Uncomfortable under their intense scrutiny, she struggled to rise.

A smooth-faced soldier in the red and gold of imperial service helped her to sit. "You should remain still," he warned her. The cold has sapped your strength."

Li worked the stiff muscles of her mouth to loosen them. "Please, where am I?"

"In Lord Ao's garden, at Shaun Yi."

"How?"

"A snowstorm descended on the palace with a fury, but stayed only a moment. When the wind calmed, we found you lying on the ground."

"Then, I am not too late?"

"Too late for what?"

"I must see Lord Ao. I bear a message for him." Li looked around the snow-shrouded garden in search of the great lord. A warrior with a crimson face veil edged in gold and armor painted with the five-fingered imperial dragon, sat observing her from a rattan chair. Li focused her attention on him. "My Lord, I bring a message from General Kuan. Please I beg you to allow me to deliver it."

The veil moved with the breeze of the High Lord's breath. "Give the message to Lord Shih."

Li fished the scroll from her pack and passed it to the crimson-liveried courtier. He examined the seal. "It is from General Kuan."

"Bring it to me," the High Lord ordered. The courtier crossed the garden and presented the scroll with a deep bow. Lord Ao broke the seal and skimmed the scroll's contents. "This changes much." He passed the scroll back to Lord Shih. "See that my officers learn of the new route."

Shih bowed and scurried out of the garden. Lord Ao turned his veiled face toward Li. "You have done well and at great personal risk. You have my thanks."

Li bowed her head in response. The emperor rose and left the garden. His entourage followed. The only ones remaining in the garden were the smooth-faced soldier and a white-haired man with pale eyes, who looked similar to, but not exactly like the innkeeper and the hermit.

Li smiled at him. "You have been most kind, my lord. When the weather allows, I will go to your temple."

"Nonsense. I do not want you to serve me because you have to—you would only make yourself and everybody around you miserable. Rest a few days and go home. Travel by way of Shaini, we will not make a storm there for another three weeks. In the spring, come visit and collect your horse. Farewell, little mortal."

GIFTS OF WONDER AND DARKNESS
by *Kathleen M. Massie-Ferch*

Winds stir the tall pines as moonlight slips between the branches and bathes the high cliffs in ghostly light. Two youths stand boldly at the cliff's very edge, staring down into the deep shadows. One boy's dark hair glistens a midnight blue in the cool light of the full moon. Rushing water calls to him from the impenetrable shadows, and the murmuring wind fills his young mind with a new, potent song. His hand moves in the pale light toward his older brother standing so near, too near. . . .

The dream dissolved.

What was it?

Only dark, quickly forgotten impressions teased the edges of my thoughts. I shook off the hypnotic effect of the fire's crackling yellow-and-orange tongues. The more I tried to resolve the vague dream, the farther it slipped from my grasp. The wind howled in the chimney, sending a sudden chill along my spine. The wind—it was something about the wind. But what? It slipped farther away. I turned from the dancing flames to glance at my husband even as I caressed my slightly swollen abdomen.

Chuck's thoughts felt far away, unreadable, unconcerned. He concentrated on sharpening his pocketknife in the fire's warm glow. The scrape of steel on stone blended with the hiss of burning pine. His auburn locks, still damp from his recent shower, just brushed well-muscled shoulders. I studied his straight nose and square chin, pleased with my healing gift. No trace remained of the broken nose and jaw he had suffered that spring in a logging accident.

He glanced up, but in that moment the *now* blurred: before me sat my husband still, but—

Auburn hair strewn with white, gray eyes framed by laugh lines. For a brief moment his mouth tightens as tension rules

*his features, but then the darkness passes, and an easy smile
deepens his wrinkles.*

I blinked. Time shifted, and the present returned. A thrill
moved through me, replacing my earlier unease. This vision
was so like the time I had seen Chuck on the fairgrounds,
during a school picnic, and *saw* we would marry. If only
my gifts weren't so infrequent. Should I tell him of them
and our happy future? But no, Chuck can never keep secrets from the other Elders. I relaxed my mental barriers
and found his barriers already gone.

A good life, perhaps with many children? The thought
slipped from me to him. The life of our unborn son stirred
under my gentle caress.

Chuck's smile broadened. *With many children. As many
as you want.* Chuck reached out and lightly clasped my
hand in his callused grip. "I'm not as concerned with the
Charter's vision on this subject as your wants." The tele-
phone rang. He tightened his grip momentarily.

"It's Betty," he stated softly with certainty. "For you."

"I wish I had your talent for *hearing* across phone lines,
especially when Mrs. Johnson is calling." I moved the three
steps to the nightstand and hesitated only another ring.
"Hello, Betty."

"Ann, did I wake you?"

"No."

"I just finished the last test. The baby's perfect! Not a
strand of DNA out of place."

I strengthened my mental barriers as a shiver coursed
through me again.

"Ann?" Betty asked.

"That's great. But I told you he'd be fine. You didn't
have to rush the results. Tomorrow would have been
soon enough."

"No problem. I had time. I'm here with Mrs. Glime."

"Oh, then there wasn't a mistake with her test. They
came back bad again?"

"No mistake and she wanted to abort right away."

"She okay?"

"She's fine, but tell Chuck I want the Council to re-
evaluate this match. Three bad tries is more than a coincidence. There's a mismatch in their genetic code."

"Tell her," Chuck added loudly as he put aside his knife

and crawled into bed, "We've already got it to the agenda for next week."

"You hear that?" I asked Betty.

"Yes. I'll tell Mrs. Glime."

I returned the handset to the cradle as the wind howled in the chimney again. The scent of pine forest lingered in my memory as I climbed into bed and Chuck's warm embrace, and still the dark thought eluded me.

Late the next day I stood in the patio doorway delighting in the bright fall flowers and lush grass surrounding my secluded home. Lisse happily sang to her dolls on the grass between rose beds. I enjoyed watching her play and couldn't love her more, even if she had been born to me. It was difficult remembering what it had been like before she came to live with us.

The sunshine felt good in the shelter from the wind. Autumn was still young. We had cleared just enough trees to carve our earth-shelter home from the hillside and allow a northwest view of the lake. Across the lake I could make out the break in the tree line where the Brule River snaked through the forest that spread out in every direction. Beyond the break lay the Upper Peninsula of Michigan. The summer had been dry; the sugar maples were in a hurry and already painted the hills with brilliant oranges and reds. Soon the poplar trees would follow with a splash of yellow. The distant clouds gathered, sculpting the western sky with dark, boiling shapes—rain clouds that in a few short weeks would carry snow. In a way, I looked forward to the isolation of winter—the quiet days, the smell of fresh baking as the insulating snow blanketed the land and my home. But it was still early September, and the strengthening breeze carried the fragrance of roses and something else.

A faint tremor in the psychic currents drifted through the woods, tickling a corner of my mind. I sent out a questioning thought. The Johnson's baby was colicky again. I toyed with the idea of retreating inside the house and the protection of its thick layer of covering earth. The dirt, combined with the surrounding trees, would shield me from most intruding thoughts, both of the Charter and not. I could escape the thoughts, but not the phone.

The perfumed wind surrounded me, caressed my shoulders. Perhaps a soothing thought, sent drifting upwind, would reach the non-Charter child and ease his pain, otherwise it would only be a matter of time before Mrs. Johnson phoned to ask for advice. But a mere phone conversation never satisfied Mrs. Johnson. I didn't want to go out tonight—not with the storm coming—over simple colic. The currents soon quieted.

Where is that son of mine?

Only Lisse's soft voice and the birds singing filled the breeze.

"Lisse, have you seen Rickie?"

"He was over there." The little girl pointed around to the other side of the house.

As I rounded a group of tall shrubs, I saw my five-year-old son throwing rocks at a gathering of feeding birds. I froze as pain coursed through my thoughts. In an instant I was a young girl again.

The wind caressed the feathers of wing, neck and tail—spring winds, fresh winds. There! I could see me sitting below. How silly I looked with my eyes closed, yet not asleep. I nudged my friend to return. The mourning dove landed on my lap. With each contact I honed my skills. At the end of the flight I'd coaxed the small bird back to my hand and the offered bread crumbs as I had every day for a week.

Today I was barely back in my own mind with the bird perched on my wrist when suddenly a shadow loomed over us. Still deep in mental rapport with the trusting dove, I looked up absently to see my father's stony blue eyes.

No! part of my mind screamed at the sight of him. But I could not move fast enough.

He grabbed the bird, wrung its neck with deft and practiced hands, and returned the body. I sat stunned, almost as limp as the warm, lifeless bird in my hands. The pain, the brief, sharp pain—the emptiness—in place of my friend.

"Birds are food, not toys," he had said mockingly. Pleasure radiated from him, bombarded me, freezing my thoughts in horror. "If you can trick birds from the sky, perhaps there are other skills the Elders can test you for. You'll be worth more. Tomorrow I'll show you how to trick other creatures with your gift—or better yet, how to trick Townies."

Emptiness. So empty. Was there no place for my friend to linger? The wind. I remembered the wind. Pleasure, Father's pleasure. I threw my thoughts against his, pushing his away. A clang rang through my head. I felt his thoughts beat against mine. No!

Their sound retreated until only my thoughts remained. Nothing else existed. I could hear him screaming at me, but I could no longer feel his thoughts or my mother's, who had come running to my side.

I leaned against the sun-warmed bark of a birch tree, pushing the past away. Yet I remembered how for days I felt nearly blind and deaf. It had been painful, at first, to keep all others out. Now I welcomed the barrier to my wondrous gifts, hiding most of them from Father and the Elders. The wrenching nausea I had felt that day so long ago threatened to overcome me again. The northern winds blew, cooling my face. I let them take away the old pain, the hurt. Father was dead; so was the past. I wouldn't let either haunt my now-contented life.

I pulled my sweater up about my shoulders. "Rickie."

The child looked around. The sunlight glinted red in his dark auburn curls so like Chuck's.

"That's cruel! Those birds have never hurt you."

"I like to see them fly," he responded innocently.

The pain was still there, new this time. I looked around until I saw a stunned dove lying at the base of a nearby poplar. I knelt on the grass and gently picked it up.

"Oh, but I didn't mean to hurt any," Rickie cried.

The secret chamber within my mind opened, and my greatest gift flowed forth. My inner eye saw this dove's ruptured blood vessels and swelling tissues. The pressure was building in the tiny brain. I directed the energy currents with my thoughts. Cells knitted together again, fluids drained, blood flowed evenly within the vessels, and after a few minutes the tissues returned to normal. The bird awakened, ruffled its brown-and-gray feathers, and flew into the poplar tree.

"Ahh!" Young Rickie cried, his gray eyes wide as they followed the bird's flight. "I'm sorry I hurt it, Mother. I didn't mean to. I won't again."

"Do you promise?"

The boy nodded solemnly. "I promise, Mama."

"Then watch this."

Rickie sat down beside me on the grass as I sent a thought out to the bird. It flew back and landed on my outstretched palm. The boy stared, open-mouthed.

"I've told him you want to be friends. Would you like to touch him?"

Rickie stretched out a cautious finger and stroked the creamy-brown breast feathers that shone with an iridescent pink and blue as they reflected the last rays of sunlight. The dove hopped onto the boy's finger. I *watched* my son intently. He was too young to hide any thoughts. I felt his wonder and *knew* he'd never be like my father.

"Teach me to call him when I want! Please?"

"When you're older and your gift is better developed, yes. Both Papa and I have a talent for working with animals. Perhaps you will, too. But until then, you'll just have to trust him to come to your voice. Adding a treat each time will also entice him back. But tomorrow. Now, he needs to find a cozy place, out of the coming storm, and we need to begin dinner before Papa gets home. It's your turn to set the table."

"No, Lisse's turn."

I smiled. "I don't think so. But let's go find her anyway."

Night descended quickly on the woods as the autumn storm approached. A fire burned brightly in the bedroom's hearth, warding off the deepening chill, leaving the child's room friendly and fire-bright. I pulled back the covers as Rickie hopped into bed and snuggled down into the pillow. As I tucked the blanket up around his shoulders, the *now* again darkened and blurred:

A ten-year-old Rickie lies beside a younger boy whose hair is as black as the deepest night. Both boys are asleep. Rickie's arms intertwine with the other boy's.

Another vision so soon after last night? Wonderful!

I leaned over Rickie and brushed his hair from his eyes. My single, long, dark braid fell forward. It was the same blue-black as the hair of the younger boy in my vision. I tickled Rickie's nose with the braid's end. Rickie had Chuck's auburn hair and looked so much like hm; I was glad this baby would look like my side of the family.

"Would you like to have a little brother, Rickie?"

"I'd even let him play with my dove."

"I'm sure he'd like that." I kissed the boy's forehead and watched him drift into sleep. A flash of lightning brightened the quiet room. I went to the deep-set window to shut the thick drapes. Lightning danced across the night sky, illuminating the steep slope below the window on this side of the house, and the lake beyond. Continuous flashes lit the night as brightly as if a full moon shone overhead.

The night is clear. Only a breath of wind slips through the pines. Silver moonlight shines on two brothers—the older with auburn hair—the younger with hair as dark as the clear night sky. The youths stand side by side on the edge of the cliff, high above the Brule River. Rushing water from the deep shadows and the wind fills the younger mind with a new, potent song. He is one with the forest around him. He feels its essence more intensely than ever before. His gift is strong; his desires burn bright. He becomes the marten as it lunges from a low tree branch, and enjoys the sweet taste of warm blood as it feasts on a mouse. Edward's mind flows farther, riding the wind through the woods. He becomes a lone yearling doe as she is hunted by a wolf pack. He lives her heart-thumping race through the brush, and relishes her pain as flesh is torn away by gaping jaws each time she stumbles, until she no longer rises for another sprint.

Again he hears the endless rushing waters calling, the wind whispering above his head, all demanding more blood. Edward reaches out. A quick, hard shove sends his trusting brother over the edge. Time slows. Edward's mind seizes Rickie's. Thoughts twist. Fear mingles with betrayal in the seemingly endless fall. Unanswered cries pierce the night and echo off rock walls. Terror becomes consuming pain as Rickie hits the jagged rocks at water's edge. For those who can hear, the echoes of his thoughts fade more slowly into the still night than his youthful voice.

Calmly, Edward pulls all the cascading emotions, the fear and terror mixed with anger, inward. His eyes are half closed; his mouth holds a faint smile. The adrenaline sets his blood boiling.

A nearby lightning strike, closely accompanied by rolling thunder, brought me back to the *now*. My chest constricted; the hair on my neck and arms raised. I yanked the drapes together, trying to shut out the horrifying vision burned into my memory. My hand weakly reached down to cover my abdomen even as I sought out a sleeping Rickie in reassurance.

"Now, yes, but how do I keep him safe?" I whispered to the night, as a deep cold seeped through my bones and into my mind.

I sat at my dressing table brushing my hair, not wanting to sleep, or rather dream, just yet. The dancing flames of the evening's fire kept me occupied and nearly free of thought, until gentle hands rested on my shoulders.

"You've been distracted for days," Chuck murmured softly. "And you haven't been sleeping well. I phoned your nurse. She told me this isn't unusual, that maybe you're just worried about Edward—or is there something else wrong?"

I could sense his avoiding mention of my two previous miscarriages, as if discussing the subject was bad luck. I searched his gray eyes. Rickie's eyes—and so, too, the eyes of the son I now carried. As far as I knew, I was the only Charter member to develop the gift of visions. What could I say to make Chuck believe my fear without revealing all my gifts?

I took a deep breath. "I've had some bad dreams about Edward. I dreamed he grew up like my father." I waited; Chuck didn't say anything for a very long moment. His eyes didn't betray his thoughts and, afraid to betray my own, I kept my mind closely guarded.

"Well," Chuck finally said, "I suppose that's possible. But if we give our son enough care and love, I'm confident he'll grow into a good man. How could he not?" He half smiled, trying to lighten the tone of the conversation.

I chewed my lower lip before answering. "What if some behavior is hereditary, as our gifts are?"

"Behavior isn't like our gifts. Behavior is learned. Our gifts are selectively bred—"

"Father would have been as he was, no matter who raised him. He'd still have raped those women and beat others. You helped erase their memories of the horror, even as I healed their bodies. I can't forget them, their pain, both mental and physical. Can you? Parents can only do so much to make the child, the man."

"We'd never allow our child to—"

"My grandparents never taught Father to be a rapist or bully," I interrupted.

Chuck answered slowly. "I don't know why your father was as he was. We never did learn how to control him. The Elders took a chance in permitting him to father children by a Charter woman. Or perhaps it wasn't their choice. Your father usually got what he wanted despite the Elders' wishes. But that was then. He taught us all a lesson. No one else will ever get away with even half of what he could. Besides, things worked out well. All five of his children are assets to our Charter. I should know."

"Right!"

"Your brothers aren't cruel. You're not like your father. Nor is your sister. Rickie certainly isn't. Our children *will be* as we are." His smooth brow puckered. "Why worry about something that may never be? We can't know for sure until little Eddie's older, or at least born."

Suddenly I couldn't meet his eyes and looked at the fire. Chuck went on. "You need more rest. Between your canning and running over to the Johnsons every other day to look after their sick child, of course you're tired. It's no wonder you have bad dreams."

"Even though you're an Elder, you don't really understand genetics, do you? Breeding our special abilities is only a small part of our Charter. Even reading minds is only—"

"So science is beyond me," he interrupted. "You're right. There is more to the Charter. Our financial investments make all of this possible. Without my hard work poring over stock tables and returns, none of this would exist. We'd all live in tiny homes in town. That's as important as genetics."

"Sometimes you're so practical, Chuck."

"If I were that practical, I wouldn't be in love with you or be having this discussion about nonsense. I'm not the telepath you are, but I can feel his presence almost as easily as I can Rickie sleeping down the hall. This baby is a part of our lives already. How can you even suggest he'll turn into your father?"

"What if he's worse?"

"Nonsense! You're just anxious and worried. You're making up excuses before you even miscarry."

Should I tell him of my visions? Could I make him see

how small a gift it had been before now? I could picture, even feel, his disappointment, his hurt over my *secrets*. I couldn't face that pain, not now.

"Ann? Your thoughts are buried so deep, even I can't feel them. Why? What else is bothering you? Let me in. Let me help."

"I like canning," I said stubbornly, guarding my secrets. "And you seem to like eating my canned foods, be it peaches or my jellies."

He frowned as if uncertain. "Of course I do, but we can do without if it makes you tired. I'd even settle for TV dinners three times a day. We can certainly afford to buy anything you want."

"Anything?" I teased, but he didn't sense the sharp bite of my jest.

"As long as the mailman or UPS man can deliver it, order away from your catalogues." He reached out again and brushed my cheek with a feather-light touch of his callused hand, then flopped into bed. His words floated across the fire lit room. "The nurse wants to see you soon if you still can't sleep. And she said no vacuuming. That I should do it. Just tell me what you want done and when, and I'll do it."

I remained at my dressing table, staring into the semi-blackness, trying to penetrate the darkness of my own thoughts, looking for any spark of hope to soothe my fears about this baby. Soon Chuck's soft snoring added to the rustle from the slow-burning fire. Hours later I reluctantly climbed into bed, still without an answer, and lay close to Chuck without touching him, my thoughts buried deeply.

I sat in my bedroom, resting after having healed the broken back of a Charter neighbor. Resting wasn't necessary. Everyone coddled me, just because I was pregnant. I felt strong and so did my unborn son though I wished otherwise. Could it be otherwise?

All I could think about was the child within me, about my visions. I pushed aside my lunch. So many visions. This morning after I had healed the man's back, his wife came in the room, carrying their toddler. For a brief moment I had seen the child as a young man in a coffin and knew

Edward had somehow been involved in the car accident, if not responsible.

In the month of restless nights since my first awful vision, I had foolishly decided I could prevent my sons from being on the rock ledge that night, or send Rickie away. But that would only delay the inevitable. Again I *saw* Rickie murdered for no other reason than to have his death experienced through Edward's strong, gift-enhanced senses! I told myself again it was only a dream, but I knew it was not.

Would Rickie's death be the first? How many others would there be after Rickie? I was afraid to guess. Edward would be as he would be. I could see the man Edward of my visions. I knew him. Part of me, and Chuck, were in him, but so was my father. Changing the people around him would change neither him nor his needs. As he grew, so would his needs grow and change.

I remembered my father's pleasure when inflicting pain on others; his delight over tricking everyone with his gifts. He had been selfish and mean. Even the Townies avoided him whenever possible. Edward would be different, and worse. He would have Chuck's charm. It would take Edward time to learn about the darker emotions, and their strengths, but he'd be clever, and eventually would learn. His enjoyment and craving of darker emotions would destroy my family. I knew that and knew time would be in Edward's favor. My choices?

A chill settled on me. Edward would have to die to save Rickie and all the others I didn't yet know about. What else could I do?

I hugged myself as if to ward off the fear and pain that tore through my chest.

It was a perfect time. No one with the gift was close enough to detect my actions. Chuck was out logging; Rickie and Lisse were napping. The house, even though on a hill, was shielded from our gifted neighbors by the dirt covering and the surrounding trees. It wasn't likely anyone would sense my actions, though in truth I doubted anyone had the ability.

Tears welled up. My intellect told me I was right. And I had a convenient alibi. Healing the broken back had been too much strain. The stress caused a miscarriage, again. Just like the stress of Lisse's mother's death had caused my first miscarriage. No one would ask questions of a grieving woman. For I already grieved over what had to be. I would lock the truth away in the corner of my mind like my other secrets. No one would ever see them. Chuck could never know. He'd never understand. He wanted this son. So had I. But there would be other sons, other children. I *knew* it.

Tears slid down my cheeks. It would be easy. I had done it before when I helped Jenny Pierceson, one of the women my father had raped. Jenny had been so sure of what she wanted, if only I could be so sure.

I turned my thoughts inward and found the brightness of my son's life. My gift wrapped around the spark. The glow from his life was warm, much like a fire on a winter's night—and so innocent. I remembered my joy when I first felt this life. Chuck's happiness. He'd given me an expensive diamond pendant. The present in and of itself meant little. I had smiled and accepted it because it made him happy, and cherished it because he'd braved the crowded, psychic jungles of Iron Mountain's shops to buy it. For days I had basked in the glow of his love. The warmth from him was so different from my childhood.

Why did that have to change?

The room seemed darker, as if the sky abruptly clouded over, though the sun still shone brightly. It was suddenly hard to remember my purpose, to remember the vision of Rickie's broken body. I loved this baby! I forced myself to see Rickie's twisted image and continue. Edward must die! But as I closed my grasp and began to squeeze the life from my son, he moved.

Did I hurt him? Was he crying? I saw another vision as if through a smoky veil:

A twelve-year-old Edward ducks into the shadows near a darkened window. An angry Lisse is fast on his heels, but instead of finding Edward she meets up with an equally angry Rickie, also in search of Edward. The two teens stare at each other, their anger melting away. Their breathing slows, filling the silence. Edward steps from the shadows and chuckles, a light, child's laugh.

"You two should never fight or even try. The only way either of you can stay angry is to pick fights with anyone else who loves you. Which is usually me." His voice is filled with mock indignation as he points to himself. *"You both*

know you can't stay angry at each other, especially if you're in the same room. So why try?"

The young lovers slowly embrace as Edward comes forward, and puts his arms around them both. The boy feels Lisse's gentle emotions. He feels Rickie's soothing love for her.

But it's the changing of emotions, from anger to calm and the reverse, that is more exciting than the intense emotions— like the changing weather, or a strong storm brewing. They call to Edward.

"Though it is more fun teasing you both when you're testy."

"Edward, you're impossible," Lisse says softly, but with deep fondness.

"I must be, and that's often hard work. Sometimes I think that without me, you two would spend your whole lives living near each other and never talk about important things."

"What important things, Edward?" Rickie asked.

"Why love, of course!"

I couldn't close my psychic grasp. The love and kinship Edward felt for the young couple was strong. Perhaps it was a reflection of their love, and not genuine. At the moment, I found it hard to believe Edward would be capable of either love or hate. But I wasn't sure. A fluttering passed through my middle as Edward stirred again.

Vision fragments swirled through my head and haunted me. Over and over I watched Rickie fall, felt his terror, saw his broken body on moon-washed rocks as Edward stood above calmly and drank in the sensations. Edward helping Rickie and Lisse find their love.

"Yet you will be capable of kindness, even if for selfish reasons. How do I destroy the monster in you without touching the good?"

I knew I must act. Edward's charming side would be deceptive and led, no, I reminded myself, would lead Rickie and others to death. Unlike Father, Edward would have his charming nature to hide behind. A charm which would hide him for years. Edward's gift would be so much stronger and better focused than Father's. If Edward ever gained control of the Charter? Perhaps he'd cause the collapse of the ninety-year-old secret society.

There was no choice. I reached for the focus of my gifts, but instead a wave of fatigue passed through me, quickly followed by deep hunger pains. My child needed food. I needed food, now. Absently, almost unconsciously, I reached for a cookie from the ignored lunch tray as Rickie and Lisse came running into my room, excited over the find of a butterfly in Lisse's room. The mother in me forced me to concentrate on the children and their needs, forgetting my failure. We sat munching tidbits while watching the butterfly eating the sticky honey from its own piece of confectionary. Lisse reached out with a pale finger to brush a thin brown wing.

The back of Lisse's hand is cut. Her blonde hair is matted with blood, her face swollen and blackened. Tears well in her blue-green eyes. Edward strikes her again, thriving on the pain and anger. He needs these emotions. It proves he lives. The striking hand is covered by a black glove lest its perfection be marred. . . .

A light touch startled me.

"Auntie, are you all right?" Lisse's voice sounded suddenly too young. She would always be too young, too innocent to deal with Edward's bizarre gift, and so, too, would Rickie.

I reached out, gathered both children in my arms and hugged them tightly. "Yes, but I'm still tired. Why don't you and Rickie go outside and play until dinner?"

The children hesitated. Lisse's slim hands rested against her pale blue dress. Hands that I knew I would again see in my dreams as broken and crippled. Dreams that must never become reality.

I found a reserve of inner strength and spoke calmly. "I'm fine. Go, play, both of you, so I can nap for a while. But stay in the yard."

Once alone, my resolve was in place. My father was many things: cruel, sadistic, lusting, but what emotions he felt came from within him. They were his own. It would not be so with Edward. My father taught me how the darker emotions were always the more intense, sharper, and more forceful—those emotions would beckon to Edward.

I looked out the window at the peaceful lake. Sunlight glistened off water littered with the fall's colorful offering. I sighed. My son would be both kind and evil, loving and monstrous. "He'll soak up emotions as a towel does spilled wine."

Again my thoughts surrounded my son's life. He stirred as my powers touched him. He tried to pull away. I felt the blood pulse through his developing heart. My gift revealed his still-large head and eyes. He was as yet a strangely formed being, but Edward would grow into a perfect baby and someday he would be a handsome man, even as Chuck now was.

Edward pushed my touch away.

"Already so much power!"

Could I destroy only the gift? Edward's ability to feel other's emotions? I sought his budding mind, and my brief hope despaired: the gifts were interwoven too tightly throughout his other brain functions. Even if my own healing gift was strong enough, I lacked the training, and doubted if anyone else possessed such skills. The Charter's purpose was to enhance all forms of natural skills, not destroy them.

There had to be a way. If I could control my future sight, that might compensate for my lack of skill.

Energy currents coursing through the child's brain resembled glowing blue rivers: some caused his heart to beat, others controlled his arms and legs. He stirred again under my mental gasp.

I felt tired. Maybe if I napped first.

"No! Edward wants that!"

I concentrated on my task, on the thought of Edward not being able to hurt others. Everything blurred for a moment before clearing. One blue pathway seemed to glow a bit brighter and stronger than it had a moment before. I let instinct guide me. My power severed the energy river. The child remained strong and alive. What had I done to him? Was this enough?

I shifted concentration and truly willed another vision to come to me—forced my own gift to heed my need.

Teen-age Rickie and Lisse are racing across the woodland meadows on their horses. Summer flowers are in bloom. Laughter fills the cool air as the young couple chase each other in a game of tag. Edward watches from a tall white pine at the clearing's edge. He sends an illusion to the horses' minds until they see and smell fire. The animals burst across the pasture in panicked flight. Lisse's horse stumbles, falls and breaks its neck. Rickie throws himself from his panic-

stricken mount and limps to where Lisse grieves beside her unmoving mare. Edward's face warps into a mask of sickened delight as his mind drinks in the fear from humans and beasts until . . .

I broke off the vision. Again I reached into my son's mind, to the glowing pathways contained therein, this time with less hesitation, less concern for the crying that only my imagination heard. Always I concentrated on his inability to hurt others. A second river was severed. I felt his mental anguish and steeled myself to my task. There was no other choice. More and more blue rivers brightened with my inquiry and I severed them, yet the boy's life-force remained strong and viable. It must. I truly wanted Edward to live, but only if my family, my world, would be safe. In time, when I had learned more about my gifts, I might be able to reverse my present actions and heal Edward. But that seemed a fool's dream.

Finally, I was too tired to do discern which pathways were brighter and thus should be severed. I withdrew from my son's mind. My baby slept peacefully.

The room explodes with the sound of a dozen young feet running across the hall's wooden floor. One child is burdened. Fifteen-year-old Rickie carries a younger boy with blue-black hair on his back. Edward's thin, trusting arms hug his older brother's neck. Rickie sets the boy on the ever-present pillows that must support his slight frame.

The boy's face indicates it harbors a near-vacant mind that will never think as others do. His staring eyes see the world, but cannot comprehend its complexity with his simple thoughts.

A young woman lovingly helps to arrange her foster brother. Lisse's and Rickie's hands frequently touch and linger over each other's as they settle Edward on the pillows. The boy feels their thoughts, thriving on them, radiating them back to those around him. In response, everyone in the room feels happier, safer. Their spirits are always lighter, glad in Edward's presence. Edward is never far away from his siblings, and never alone.

Lisse's pale golden hair brushes the boy's face. He forgets the young lovers' emotions and smiles at her tender caresses and the feel of her silky hair, though he stares at a place in the room only he sees.

Other children settle themselves closely about the pillows. A young boy takes Edward's hand and holds it, waiting to help Edward when his turn at the game comes. None of the children notices the mud and water that covers their pant legs or sneakers.

Two identical girls of six gently set their own precious cargo on the floor. Not a drop of water spills from the bucket. The twins each dip in a hand and squeal with delight as tadpoles tickle their fingers. Edward's smile broadens. His eyes follow the motions around the room in a bizarre manner. He doesn't see the movements, but he lives them as the people do. One elusive emotion replaces another from moment to moment. There is never a lack of stimulation for his thirsty mind in the large Charter household.

ON THE BRINK
by Lawrence C. Connolly

The bitterness lingered. Kate swallowed again, forcing down the taste that clung to her tongue, and it was then that she felt her grief stirring in the shadows behind her. "It's not really there," she told herself as she felt the atavistic tingles along the back of her neck—the icy prickling of skin that she always felt when things stirred behind her back.

"Ignore it," she whispered to herself. "There's nothing there." She closed her eyes and tried filling her mind with things that she knew to be true. She was alone in the kitchen, alone in the house, and more alone in her life than she had been for a very long time. The tingles on her neck were from the tea. The stuff had evidently been full of caffeine.

She opened her eyes and looked at the empty cup on the table in front of her. The cup's sides bore the faded imprint of Canada's Niagara Falls—the place where she and Terry had spent what she remembered as being a perfect honeymoon. Inside the cup, black leaves lay like sludge. She had swallowed the tea in a single gulp—just as the tea lady had told her to do. She had thought that the stuff would calm her, but here it was giving her nerves that were even worse than the ones she had been getting from her usual seven to ten cups of coffee.

Again, the grief shifted behind her. Kate dared not turn to look at it. Her imagination could do crazy things if she gave in to it. So she sat quietly with her racing heart. "I should never have done it," she told herself. "I should never have let that crazy woman talk me into drinking the tea."

"Tea," said the woman on the front step after Kate opened the door to find her standing in a veil of afternoon flurries. "I have your tea," she said, raising the sample case that she carried in a gray-gloved hand. "May I come in?"

Kate hesitated. "*My* tea?"

The woman reached into her pocket and produced a card. She flipped the card over, letting Kate read the name and address that had been scrawled across the back. The name, address, and handwriting were all Kate's.

"But I just mailed that card this morning," Kate said, although she realized that she might be getting her days confused again. Lately the days had been swirling together like churning mist.

"I wouldn't know about *when* you mailed it," said the woman. "All I know is that I have it *now,* and now I have your tea."

Kate decided that she could use the company. She let the woman in.

At the woman's request, Kate filled the kettle and set it on the stove to boil.

"And we'll need a cup," said the woman.

Kate rinsed the coffee dregs from her Niagara Falls cup while the woman set her sample case on the kitchen table. Clasps rattled as she raised the lid. Inside the case, tea tins stood on satin-lined shelves. The decorated containers bore strange, hand-painted names: *Generosi, Respectabili, Hones, Digni, Tenaci. . . .*

"Looks like Italian," said Kate as she scanned the words. "Are these Italian teas?"

"No," said the woman. "Not Italian."

The kettle rattled as the water started to churn.

The woman removed a large, slender package from the bottom of the case.

"What's that?" Kate asked.

"A gift," said the woman. "Something you'll put to good use." The package clunked heavily as the woman set it on the table.

"What kind of gift?" Kate asked. "What is it?"

"You'll see," said the woman. "But first we'll brew your tea." She opened one of the tins. Kate caught a whiff of sweetness and musk. The woman picked up the cup and looked at the picture on its side. "Niagara Falls," she said as she ran a crooked thumb across the faded image. "Honeymoon?"

"Yes."

"How long ago?"

"Eighteen years."

The kettle screamed.

"Tea," Sara said.

"Tea?" Kate asked. It wasn't that she hadn't heard; it was just that she wasn't sure of much of anything these days.

Kate raised her Niagara Falls cup, sipping her coffee while Sara slid a postcard across the kitchen table. "I got this for you."

Kate studied the card. The address on the front was for a company called T Leaves. A scripted slogan in the lower left corner read: *Tea Lends Enchantment and Vitality Every Season.*

"You want me to send away for tea?" Kate said. "What do I want with tea?"

"You're drinking too much coffee. You have enough things agitating you right now. You don't need to add to it with caffeine."

"I'm not agitated. I'm grieving. There's a difference."

Sara sat back. Winter sun streamed through the window, filling her hair with tangled light. At fifty-one, Sara projected a natural, effortless confidence. Looking at Sara now, it was hard to believe that five years ago her life had been in ruin.

"It's funny," said Sara. "After Bryan left, I hated you for still having the things that I'd lost. Now here I am, on the other side, trying to convince you that life doesn't end when a husband leaves."

"Terry didn't leave me."

"Dying is leaving," Sara said. "It's not voluntary, but it's still leaving."

Kate picked up the tea card. Anything to change the subject. She looked once again at the printed slogan. *Tea Lends Enchantment and Vitality Every Season.* Her gaze lingered on the line. She had always been a painfully slow reader, but sometimes that slowness caused her to notice things that more facile readers missed. "T Leaves," she said.

"Excuse me?"

"The initials in the slogan spell out the company name—T Leaves."

"Oh," Sara said. She glanced at the card. "I didn't see that. Cute!"

"So what do you know about this company?" asked Kate.

"Nothing. I saw the card in a health food store. It was part of a display for caffeine alternatives. I thought of you."

"Thanks, but no thanks."

"Throw it in the trash if you're not interested," said Sara. "But try cutting back on the caffeine. You've got enough to deal with without having to battle coffee nerves." She squeezed Kate's hand, and Kate felt the weight of things unsaid.

The concern in Sara's eyes whispered the things that her lips had the kindness to keep silent. And the eyes said, "I'm worried. You're letting your grief carry you away. It's destroying your home. Destroying your life. You need to get rid of it before it washes you over the brink."

Kate held Sara's gaze, and with her own eyes she tried to say, "You think you know me, but you don't. There are secrets in me that only Terry knew, and if you knew them—if you knew even half of them—they would drive you mad with concern. If you knew one fourth of them, you would be amazed that I have even made it through two weeks without him. If you knew a fifth of them, you wouldn't waste your time talking to me about tea . . . and you would never dare leave me alone in this house."

"What're you staring at?" Terry asked after he found her in the back of the gift shop.

She realized that he had already asked the question once before, but his words had gotten lost in the roar of the distant falls.

"What do you have there?" he asked.

She turned toward him. "A cup," she said. She turned it over in her hand, letting him see the imprinted image of the falls.

"Cute," said Terry.

"Can we buy it, T.?" She always called him T. whenever they were alone. In a group he was always Terry. Alone he was T. T. for two, and *Terry* for three.

He slipped behind her, looking over her shoulder as she went back to studying the cup.

"Can you make it move?" he asked.

"Yes," she said.

She had told him about the thing that she could do with her eyes—how she could look at pictures and patterns and make them come alive. It was a secret that she had shared with no one but him.

He tucked his chin against her shoulder. "So what does it do?" he asked.

She touched the picture. "The water churns, the mist swirls, and this little boat—" she pointed to what for him must have been nothing more than a brass-colored speck among a tangle of painterly strokes, "—this little boat sails out of the mist."

"Then we have to get it," he said. Just like that. No argument. No debate. He understood the pieces of her that no one else even knew existed, and for the eighteen years that followed he became the anchor that rooted her to the world in ways that no one could have understood. And sometimes, whenever she awoke at night and the darkness swirled into frightening shapes, she would listen to his breathing and feel his warmth, and the darkness would go back to being darkness. Terry made her whole. With him, her life developed a continuity that had never existed in the days before T.

The woman lifted the whistling kettle from the stove. Water spilled into the Niagara Falls cup. The musky smell grew stronger, filling the kitchen. "Let it steep for at least five minutes," said the woman as she set the kettle back on the stove. Then she closed her case, secured the latches, and turned toward the arch that led into the living room.

"That's it?" said Kate.

The woman walked out of the kitchen. Kate heard the front door swinging inward. "Wait a minute!" She hurried out of the kitchen to find the woman standing in the doorway. Outside, the snow had stopped falling. The sun tossed low, winter beams against the front of the house. Days were so capricious this time of year; it was hard to know what to expect. The tea lady's slender body threw a twiglike shadow across the carpet as she turned to look back at

Kate. "Wait at least five minutes," said the woman. "Open your gift while you're waiting. When the five minutes are up, drink the tea. It's most effective when you drink it fast. One gulp is best. It might burn a bit, but it'll be a good burn. Trust me. You'll see. Tea has a way of making everything right."

The woman stepped outside; the door closed behind her as if it had been drawn shut by a gust of winter wind.

"Wait!" said Kate. "There's something I need to know!" She dashed across the room. She pulled the door open and stepped out onto the porch.

The wind whipped along the blanket of unbroken snow.

Kate returned to the kitchen. The water in the Niagara Falls cup had turned an opaque black—more like coffee than tea. She looked down into the cup and saw her reflection looking up through the drifting wisps of surface clouds. A chill shot through her; she sat back and glanced at the clock. How much time had passed since the woman had added the water to the leaves? Thirty seconds? A minute? Kate had never been good with clocks. There was something about the shifting progression from left to right and then right to left that always confused her. And digital clocks with their segmented digits were even worse.

She took a pencil from the drawer beneath the sink and drew a line on the clock face beyond the tip of the minute hand. Then she counted ahead five lines and drew another line. God, what would people think if they ever knew about these things? She shoved the pencil back into the drawer. She sat down and started to wait.

She reached for the slender gift that sat beyond the cup. The package was wrapped in silver paper. Kate picked it up. It felt heavy. She set it on her lap. Again, her own face looked back at her, this time reflected from the silver wrapping that covered the long, narrow box. Her fingers found a taped fold along the top of the package; she peeled back the fold and tore the paper down the center, cleaving her reflection and exposing a foot-long cardboard box on which had been embossed the name T LEAVES. She opened the lid. Inside she found a sheath of neatly folded tissue paper. She peeled back the paper, and saw—

"What is it?" she said, whispering aloud to the silent room.

It looked like a wrought-iron *t*—a bold, lower-case letter with serifed arms and a barbed stem. She took hold of it, gripping it by the stem—"Shit!" She jerked her hand away. Blood flicked from her fingers, staining the white paper with a spattering of red stars. She rotated her hand and moved it into the light. Blood snaked down along her wrist. Her palm, thumb, and index finger had been sliced nearly to the bone.

She moved the box back to the table and ran to the counter where she grabbed a handful of paper towels. As she wrapped her bleeding hand, she turned, looked back at the iron *t* in its bed of bloody paper, and whispered, "What are you?"

The *t* didn't answer. It only lay there, cold and silent.

The kitchen had filled with shadows. Kate flicked on the light and returned to the table to take another look at the iron *t*. Now, in the ceiling's incandescent glow, Kate realized that what she had at first taken to be the curved stem of a *t* was actually the hooked blade of a dagger. "What kind of gift is this?" she asked the room.

The room, as it had for most of the past two weeks, responded with brutal silence.

She glanced at the clock. The minute hand had moved beyond the second pencil mark. She picked up the Niagara Falls cup and downed the tea. It had a pleasant taste— bitter but silky—not unlike coffee. But after she had swallowed it all, a cruel aftertaste gripped her throat. She clamped her lips as she set the cup on the table. She swallowed again, forcing down the taste that clung to her tongue, and it was then that she felt her grief stirring in the shadows behind her.

She sat still, trying to deny the atavistic tingle on the back of her neck. But then something happened that made the intruding presence impossible to deny.

Her grief screamed.

Kate turned and looked behind her.

A few feet behind her chair, the patterns in the kitchen carpet had begin to churn. Something was rising from the piles. Yes, she could make it out now—the thing looked like a piece of twitching liver, but it was changing, growing, sprouting tendrils that hardened into jointed arms. The arms sprouted claws. The claws dug into the carpet, and the nylon piles groaned as the thing pulled its cankered haunches from the churning fabric.

And then, with a spastic jerk, it stood up. A head festered from its twitching shoulders. Eyes formed. A mouth gaped. The thing coughed and gasped for air in the darkening room. Its rancid breath filled the kitchen. It looked at her, licking its lips with a blistered tongue. "Hurry!" it said. "Let's finish it!"

It ran from the room.

She followed it through the long hall, passing the rooms that made up the first floor of the large house—the bathroom, the game room, the guest room, the solarium, and the room for the child that she and T. had never had. When she entered the master bedroom, she found the beast standing on the king-size bed. It was driving its claws into the plaster wall above the brass headboard.

"What're you doing?" she screamed.

Its hooks snagged a beam within the wall. The wall buckled and split as the creature tugged.

"Stop it!" she yelled.

But it kept rending the wall. Wood snapped and groaned while the room filled with squalls of flying plaster and splintered wood.

She had to stop it. She ran back into the kitchen to get a broom. The thing was strong, but it was no larger than a terrier. Perhaps she could shove it into the hall and out the door. But she had second thoughts as she pulled the broom's aluminum handle from the closet. She might as well try swatting a fly with a straw. She tossed the broom aside. It gave a hollow clank as it toppled and fell against the stove. She needed something lethal. . . .

She looked at the table. The hooked dagger was still there, sleeping in its bed of bloody paper. It looked lethal enough, but to use it she would have to get close. She reached for it with her blood-crusted hand. This time, she gripped the dagger by the hilt. The ribbed iron chilled her skin, and its heaviness fought her as she pulled it from its papery bed. But the iron warmed as she entered the hall, and its mass found balance in her hand until the weight was no more apparent than the weight of her arm.

The carpet churned beneath her as she raced back to the bedroom. She felt the swirling patterns as they rose and flowed like river water about her ankles. By the time she had splashed into the bedroom, the thing had torn a jagged opening in the wall behind the bed.

Beyond the opening a gas lamp flickered above the porch, a streetlight blazed beyond the walk, and an evening star twinkled on the darkening edge of night . . . and flowing beneath those points of light, the currents of a churning river spilled over the brink of a thundering precipice.

The view frightened her, not because she believed any of it was real, but because seeing such things marked a major regression in her life. Not since adolescence had she seen things so out of control. Now that she was seeing them, however, there was nothing to do but ride them out and play along.

She splashed into the room, raising the dagger and bringing it down so that its hook sank deep into the beast's pulpy hide.

The thing shrieked and looked up at her. Their faces nearly touched as she tried retracting the blade, but the barbed hook held fast to the creature's flesh, and pulling the blade only drew the beast closer.

"What did you expect?" it asked as its barbed hands swung forward to take hold of her neck. "That dagger's made for gaffing, not for rending!" Its claws dug in, breaking her skin. "Work with me!" said the grief. "Help me ruin what's left of your life."

She twisted the hook. The thing shrieked as Kate climbed onto the bed. She set her foot on the beast's belly and yanked the hook. The barb came free in a shower of pasty blood.

"I was only helping," the grief shrieked as she brought the barb down once again. This time she cleaved the thing from chest to groin. Its organs spilled out, running across the bed and into the rising currents that swirled toward the precipice beyond the shattered wall.

The beast stopped screaming. It lay motionless, drained. She drove the barbed dagger into its head and tossed it—

dagger and all—toward the thundering cataract beyond the bed.

She had killed the beast, but the fantasy wasn't done with her. The currents were rising; the bed rocked from the floor and sailed forward until it wedged in the jagged break in the wall. Plaster crumbled. Beams shattered. The bed broke through into the foaming night.

Kate gripped the brass headboard as the bed careered toward the thundering falls.

The bitterness lingered. Kate swallowed again, forcing down the taste that clung to her tongue, and it was then that she felt the weight of Sara's concerned gaze. She realized that the two of them had been sitting in silence a long time. Sara was good that way. She gave a person time to think, time to wander the inner landscapes—no questions asked. Perhaps Sara understood a lot more than she let on.

"What're you staring at?" asked Sara.

"Nothing," said Kate. She put down her cup, setting it atop the T LEAVES card on the table. "Just thinking."

"What're you thinking about?"

"About getting on with my life," said Kate.

She studied her cup. The little brass boat had faded, but it was still there, still afloat and sailing beneath the veil of churning mist.

THE SOCIETY OF THE KNIFE
by Janet Pack

"Jereth, it's so good to have you home again. I've missed you."

"I missed you also." The older woman kissed Meryn's high cheekbone and tried not to wince while trading hugs with her niece. The scar from her recent surgery needed aging, stretching, and a good deal of massage with warm fedalis unguent to become an integral part of her body again.

"Mother of my Heart, I'm sorry." Meryn's pale brown face darkened with embarrassment as the older woman disengaged from their embrace, clearly uncomfortable. "I forgot. This time it's you, the Goodhale of NorthMarch, who needs time and the appropriate atmosphere for healing."

"True," Jereth nodded. "But that seems to be going well, even by Goodhale Surgeon Seldar's exacting standards and my own impatient ones."

The wound from the invasion of the surgical knife appeared clean, the incision a bright, healthy pink. Knitting tissues sang their paen of health to her. For this favor Jereth was very glad.

But was she purged of the insidious growth? Would she ever be? The doubt wriggled in her mind like a maggot, surfacing several times each day and visiting her with nightmares when she slept. The most disturbing thing about her situation was that she did not know the answer. Burying her unease yet again, the Goodhale looked around the comfortable main room of the house that had once served as sanctuary for her father.

The Marshal of the Northern March had died from a hideous stomach disease which had sapped his vibrant energy and had turned him from a burly man into a scarecrow. Helping him from the earliest stages of his illness, almost nine years past now, Jereth had discovered her talents as a Good-

hale. She had not been able to save her father, but her inno-
vative treatments had prolonged his good days and made
him more comfortable during his bad ones.

When the Marshal could no longer cope with the excruci-
ating pain in his middle and wasted muscles that no longer
obeyed him, he had asked for release from life through
his daughter's rare skill. She had provided the overdose of
sleeping potion and herbs with love, and had attended the
revered fighter's bedside as he slipped from life with
dignity.

But a Goodhale seemed all she could be. She had not
yet been able to pass beyond an extreme mental turmoil
that had consistently prevented her from becoming a Goodhale Surgeon, one on the same plane as Seldar. The older
woman damped that thought, too, hiding it beneath the
trivia of arriving home, confining it far from her niece's
discerning gaze.

Smiling now, Jereth turned slowly, soaking in the atmosphere and the memories of the manor. "It's so good to be
home. I love it here."

"Sit down, Aunt. I'll bring tea."

The older Goodhale sank down at the refectory table in
the main room. The place was still filled with Steene Catoyan's things—his crested riding gloves lay on a table, his
heavy cloud-colored wool cape cascaded to the floorboards
from the staghorn stand next to the front door. Each time
she laid a fire in the great hearth, Jereth thought she heard
an echo of the big man's thundering laugh amid the ghostly
talk of the Marshal's compatriots who had gathered wherever
he was. Despite their boisterous brawls, the large house had
always seemed a happy place, and somehow peaceful. The
Marshal had always claimed that NorthMarch House was
a place of healing for body and soul, a place of rest.

Meryn had come to learn goodhaling from her aunt
shortly after the Marshal died and Jereth's petition to
Queen Girande to stay at NorthMarch House had been
approved. The women had added their own touches to the
place. Drying healherbs now festooned rafters and walls,
adding a subtle, almost spicy, perfume that permeated the
space beneath the thick thatched roof. Their stones, quartz
and pearl, amethyst and garnet, all used to enhance concentration and to induce healing trances, caught glimmers of

firelight and hoarded them in the corners of shelves where they lived. Jereth's diaries and a few precious laboriously-copied volumes of proven techniques for setting bones and conquering infections were stacked on a large chest against one wall. Mortars, pestles, and jars of all descriptions sat ready for the unguents, salves, and tinctures that helped keep the aches and symptoms of the residents of North-March town at bay. Black iron pots of medicinals always steamed on the hearth, sending tangy, sometimes exotic, vapors into the rafters. The atmosphere of the house was now more quiet than during the Marshal's occupation, and still peaceful.

The short older woman drew in a deep breath and released it in a contented sigh, even though the action stretched the scar under her right breast. Her clear gray eyes, deep as the cold mere at the foot of the hill, turned to the inner doorway as her apprentice carried in a tray with steaming mugs and placed it between them.

"And I truly missed you, Meryn," Jereth sighed. "There were few willing or able to take time to hold my hand or read to me while I was convalescing at Skrael's Goodhale House. It's so busy there." Her brow wrinkled. "I think that's wrong. No patient can make a full recovery left alone."

Narrow, strong fingers gripped Jereth's bony ones as the younger woman sat down. "I should have been there," Meryn said, her soprano soft with remorse and her dark blue eyes anguished. "I could have helped."

"Doubtless, Daughter of my Soul," the older woman comforted. "Those at Skrael would have welcomed your talents, especially your quick eye for diagnosis. But you couldn't have come. I don't know what the town here would have done with both of us far away in Skrael for an unspecified time. I had no idea how long I needed to stay. You know there are no other proven goodhales between here and there. And I'm better equipped than most to deal alone with the tortures of recovery after a pass from Seld-ar's magic knife."

"Seldar said you are well now?" The young healer's hope opened like a flower on a sere plain.

The older woman nodded. "He claims to have excised a growing body of disease, and believes he did so before it released its poisons throughout my system. It was small, about the size of a pea. I'm to drink a dreadful-tasting, stomach-twisting tea several times a day. That's what's making my hair fall out. See?" She ran a hand over her dark auburn hair. Meryn gasped when Jereth's palm came away covered. The Goodhale dusted the strands onto the table and left the hair abandoned, gleaming dully under the light from the lamp on the tray.

"Seldar says I must concentrate positive thoughts into my personal quartz to assist the healing process. But yes, both he and I think I am cured. I feel no ill inside me."

Jereth spoke with more confidence than she felt. What if Seldar, the best Goodhale in all Rannerlan and one of only two surgeons, hadn't found all the bits of the venomous growth? What if the hideous disease was again increasing? What if she herself couldn't ascertain its development? She controlled a shudder before her niece could see it. There was so much she didn't know, so much she needed to learn!

"Thank the Wise One for that," Meryn breathed, dragging the older woman's attention back to their conversation. Her eyes brightened. "Did you ask him?"

"Seldar doesn't give away his secrets to just anyone."

A hard line of disappointment appeared at the corners of the young healer's mouth. "You're not just anyone. You're the Goodhale of NorthMarch."

Jereth's full lips quirked upward. "It took a few days for me to marshal my courage to ask Seldar, especially after the surgery. At first I wasn't going to do it. I felt too weak, too violated by the disease. How could I hope to cure anyone else when I'd had such a horror inside my own body? Then I remembered all the people that could benefit from Skrael's Goodhale sharing his techniques, and all the extra hours I spent studying so I'd be ready to become part of the Society of the Knife." She sipped from her mug while Meryn waited impatiently. Jereth tried to ignore the voice in her mind that repeated over and over, *"You can't do it. The noise, the horrible noise!"*

"I finally made the request. At first Seldar refused, saying I was not well. I wasn't. But after the third day I told him I was not so ill I couldn't learn, and that a challenge would speed my recovery. That sang to some beliefs he holds very close about a positive attitude assisting recovery. The morning of the sixth day we began private sessions."

Meryn's oval face shone with eagerness and joy. "So he *did* teach you surgery. And as I progress, I can learn the techniques from you and become part of the Society of the Knife, too."

Jereth put down her mug, her hand seeking that of her niece. She turned the young palm up to the glow of the tallow lamp, studied the steadiness of the tapered fingers. "You have the aptitude to wield the knife, Child of my Soul. I'll teach you what I know, which is very little. I must go back." She damped the pang of fear before it had a chance to ice her own hands. "He promised to show me more. Seldar's knowledge of bodies and diseases is too vast to impart in only a two sevendays. I kept detailed notes on what he said and did. The books are in my carrybag. You can study them when you find time." Her fingers moved away from Meryn's to lift her mug again. She sipped the steaming honey-sweetened bark tea, relishing a taste different than the bitter stuff she had to drink every day.

"But when will I find the time to go back to Skrael?" The corners of the older healer's eyes and her mouth turned downward. "NorthMarch is a large area. There's so much to do here, how am I to get back there to learn more goodhaling? And Seldar is busy also."

"You'll find time, and so will Seldar. I doubt he has the heart to refuse such a talented student," the young woman said earnestly. "He'd be stupid if he didn't realize that another surgeon in this area of the country would benefit both the ill and himself."

Jereth smiled and shook her head. "Heart-daughter, your compliments are prejudiced but appreciated. Seldar can find students better than I." Her fear silently nudged her mind, saying much the same thing.

"Perhaps. But none more dedicated." Meryn's pale brows, so unlike Jereth's own dark auburn ones, pulled together as she changed the subject. "I considered an idea while you were away," the young woman began, then hesitated and took a new breath. "We might continue as we are, as Goodhales for NorthMarch, until you can persuade Seldar to teach you more. Then we could turn the rooms we don't use in this house into a surgical school. People from NorthMarch to the far border of Ranerlann know they can trust our skills. Everyone says this house is peaceful, a good place to rest. It's a logical step." Her dark blue eyes pleaded. "We could do so much more to relieve suffering than we're doing now."

Dread chilled the older woman's abdomen, laid its frosty shawl across her shoulders. Jereth controlled a shiver. "I've considered that, too, Daughter of my Soul. But with only two of us?" The Goodhale shook her head. "We're both still fairly young, but that would tax us past our strengths. We would need assistants. Surgical patients take so much care—"

A thump on the big plank door startled them. Jereth jumped from her chair at the same time Meryn did. Tea slopped from their mugs onto the table. The younger woman pushed back her chair and hurried across the room. Shoving her weight down against the swooping cast iron door handle, Meryn stepped back as the thick portal swung inward.

The body of a man fell across the threshold.

"Help," he gasped in a delirium-tainted voice, fingers outstretched in supplication. "Heal."

Another figure appeared behind the fallen one. "He's my nephew," the tall man said in a baritone thick and soft as velvet, but rusted with stress and worry. "Please help him."

"We will. Put the patient in the Marshal's room." Jereth ran to open the internal door and fetched more tallow lamps while Meryn looked at the young man's eyes and felt his forehead, establishing the patient-healer bond that would last for as long as he remained in their care.

"He has fever and is in pain." Her nose lifted like that of a hound on a scent. "And something smells diseased." She reached for her cloak from the rack and tossed it doubled on the floor, intending to drag the young man across the planking.

"Here, let me." Shucking his pack and stooping, the tall stranger gathered his nephew's inert body in his arms, and stood. "Where do you want him?"

"In here." Meryn, followed by the burdened man, bustled to the Marshal's room where Jereth flipped down the covers on the featherbed. Gently the uncle laid the young man down and stood back to give the Goodhales room to work.

The young woman undressed their patient. She stopped, surprised, when she pulled off his shirt and saw the ugly suppurating knot the size of a fist just above his waist on the right side.

"Jereth."

The older woman bent to look, abruptly filled by the nausea that twisted her insides, a combination of Seldar's medicinal tea and her own deep fear. Breathing deeply through the acid stink of infection, she fought for control. "That's bad." She hoped neither the stranger watching intently from the door nor Meryn noticed the strain in her voice. "We'll start treatment with two pieces of twil bark in a cup of hot water, spoonfed to him. With honey to help his strength. Roll him away from you while I get this shirt out from beneath his body. There, good. Put two pinches of podflower powder in with the twil bark. That should help ease his pain."

Meryn draped the shirt over one arm and hesitated when she reached the door, her expression leaden with concern. "He needs healwound in the tea, too." She hesitated, looking at her aunt, assessing the older woman's strength. "Jereth, are you recovered enough to try Seldar's technique? It's the only thing that will save this man."

The senior healer probed the growth with gentle fingers, appreciating her niece's quick diagnosis and hating it at the same time. The patient groaned and twisted away from her touch. She laid one hand on his head and one on his chest, thinking peaceful thoughts and murmuring words of quiet and calm. Under the double effect of her trained voice and hands, the man became quiescent.

Beneath her outward composure, the older Goodhale trembled. This patient was certainly not a case Meryn could treat. Nor could they leave him the way he was, merely touching the surface of his disease with unguents and hoping his own body could recover with just that much help. The tumor required surgery, and soon.

This time she could not hide the tremor in her voice. "I must be ready. This growth endangers his life. I don't believe it's wrapped around his bones or reaches into his lungs, thank the Wise One. Infection is the root of this problem. Because this growth wasn't treated early, it's become toxic, taking over healthy tissues and poisoning his system." Jereth sucked in a deep breath. "I'd like to try excising it this afternoon, but that's probably impossible considering his condition. We need to give him a little time to become stronger, if he can." She looked at her niece, whose wide eyes told the Goodhale she finally knew something was wrong. "Tomorrow afternoon at the latest."

"Are you certain? Is that all the time he has?" The young healer's questions carried double meanings.

Jereth nodded, answering the second question and not the first. "He's lucky he got this far. It wasn't an easy trip for him, particularly the last few days. Am I right?" She turned to the stranger.

He nodded, fatigue evident in the long sagging lines of his face and body. "Correct, Lady Goodhale. I had doubts all yesterday whether he'd conquer the distance to your house even mounted on his pacer, but his determination asserted itself. He is Khaldurr, Second Son of the Marshal of SouthMarch, and I am his uncle Dharic Shanerisse." He bowed low in respect for the women and their profession.

Meryn's wonder showed in her expressive eyes. "You came all the way from SouthMarch?"

"We did, Honored One."

"I would have thought you'd go to Surgeon Goodhale Seldar at Skrael," Jereth said, still probing the wound. Pus oozed. To the older Goodhale's trained ears, the infection gurgled with delight at its ascendancy over healthy tissue. She shuddered at the sound, and nearly succumbed to its telltale stink. Meryn caught the stuff in a towel and disposed of it while her aunt collected herself. "It's almost the same distance, perhaps a bit closer."

"Khaldurr originally set out for Skrael, Revered Lady," Dharic said. "But when the innkeeper at Waldronn extolled your virtues, his mind locked on NorthMarch and could not be moved."

Jereth nodded, working again. "That's Rell who owns the Inn of the Moth. He was here last year, Meryn. We treated him for a badly infected cut and for joint aches."

The younger woman hesitated on her way out the door. "How about adding some gavreal to the twil bark and heal-wound? It will help push the infection out."

Her aunt concentrated again on listening to the pustulent growth, hiding her fear beneath a well-practiced placid exterior. "Excellent suggestion. Now off with you. The longer we can soak this and the more medicine we can get inside him, the fewer problems we'll have during the procedure."

The Goodhales worked through the night, alternating mixing more of the drawing salve with spooning bark tea laced with podflower powder, twil bark, and gavreal into the sufferer. Jereth found surprising areas of soreness in her own body as she labored. Concentrating on her patient, she tried to ignore her own hurts. Tiredness, however, set in much faster than she cared to admit.

Alert to subtle hints of discomfort and fatigue that flitted across her beloved aunt's face, Meryn insisted on taking over some of the older woman's tasks. Dharic refused a bed and rest in one of the extra rooms and hovered in the background, fetching tea and assisting when asked by holding dressings or bowls for waste.

As the sun rose, weary Jereth checked their patient. "I believe he'll be ready by this afternoon," she sighed to the young woman. "I'll do the procedure when the sun reaches through the western window. Seldar calls it 'operating.'"

"Will *you* be ready, Aunt?"

There was more than one level to that question. Jereth squeezed her niece's hand, also very aware of Dharic's worried dark eyes on her. "I hope so," she said.

"Then get some rest, Heart-Mother," her apprentice urged. "He's quiet, I'll watch him. If I need sleep, Sur Dharic can take a turn. Should he wake and seem uncomfortable, I promise I'll call you."

Jereth laughed. "The irrepressible voice of youth and energy conquers that of age and experience this time. Very well. Although I doubt I'll be able to sleep." She rose stiffly from the chair she'd pulled beside the bed, shared a brief hug with Meryn, nodded to Dharic, picked up a lamp, and headed for her own room.

Doubts assailed her as she took off her flared knee-length suede tunic-vest and dropped it on the foot of her bed. Still dressed in her travel clothes, a full-sleeved shirt and wide-legged pants tucked into tall journey boots, Jereth lay down. She pulled a blanket over her torso and stared at the smoke-darkened rafters crossing the ceiling.

Twenty-nine years. Was she too old to accept the rigors of surgical training? What if her exhaustion and the stomach upset she often felt stayed for the rest of her life? Her hair was falling out, a side-effect of the medicinal tea, and she felt exhausted by tending the stranger for a single night. Could she recover at least part of the near-boundless energy she'd once possessed? If so, when?

It was true that she felt no illness within herself. A Goodhale could usually tell. But Seldar had said that even though her growth had been excised, even though she could feel none of the oddness inside that augured disease, she should always consider herself as having the spreading sickness. Jereth was grateful that she had discovered and diagnosed her own problem in its infancy, and that the great Surgeon Goodhale Seldar had agreed to take out the growth with his very special knife. But she felt set apart from the others of her profession by the corrupt touch of the affliction that had laired within her body. The stitched scar under her breast was a constant reminder.

Could she be missing something? Even now, could the growth's hideous invisible fingers be curling through her heart, her stomach, her bowels? Would she live to realize her dream of being a Surgeon Goodhale like Seldar, or would she, like her father the Marshal, be forced to request that Meryn release her from debilitating illness?

Another mental ache surfaced. She'd turned down several offers of marriage from local gentry, well-respected merchant's sons, and even one of Queen Girande's warrior women. Jereth could have had the normal life of a wife and mother. She'd always wanted a life-partner and a child, but that had become impossible when her talents asserted themselves. Goodhales must dedicate their energies to making their patients whole again. Even before her illness, Jereth had often fretted about gleaning enough time from patients and other necessities such as gathering herbs to teach Meryn. Attending the needs and demands of life-partner, child, and home as well as the sick would have been impossible.

And what of her horror of digging into a body with a thin blade in her fingers? Of hearing the disease sing its hideous song? Could she retain enough control to conquer her fear, build enough dominion over herself to save Khaldurr's life?

She must. She was a Goodhale, one of the best in Rannerlann. She'd studied for years so that she would be able to attain skill at surgery, her heart's desire, only to be held back by a hurdle fixed deep within her own mind.

One hot tear slipped from the corner of her right eye, sliding above the gentle brown curve of Jereth's cheek. She brushed it away and crossed her hands on her stomach. Her scar itched, a good sign. Firmly she reminded herself of Seldar's belief in positive attitude. Without it, her mending would take much longer or might never happen. He claimed that if she focused on the disease's bad side, those negative thoughts would only give it encouragement, perhaps even open the door for it to come back. The Goodhale did not want its return with so much of her life yet to live, with so much yet to learn.

With effort, Jereth turned her thoughts around. It had only been about six weeks since Seldar had used his knife on her. Her energy would surely come back: if not all, then certainly the majority of it. She'd try to be patient and let herself mend. After all, she had a niece of exceptional talent to teach. Jereth smiled. Dear, sweet, swift-to-diagnose Meryn. In a short time her niece would be a better healer than she. That young woman's careful training would be Jereth's legacy to the people of NorthMarch, as well as her tribute to the memory of her father.

The positive thinking relaxed Jereth. With a sigh more contented than worried, she allowed sleep to pull its curtain over her mind.

"Jereth."

The voice seemed familiar. The Goodhale swam toward it through tatters of nightmare. She'd been back in Skrael, operating, watching her own hands in fascinated horror as they readied to plunge Seldar's sharp, narrow-bladed knife into her own chest.

"Jereth, you have a little time before the sun touches the west window in the Marshal's room."

Her gray eyes flew open. Meryn's voice. She was back home at NorthMarch House where a patient needed her help. Jereth tossed back the blanket, pushed her body to a sitting position, and swung her legs over the edge of the featherbed. Her mouth tasted dusty, one of the effects of Seldar's terrible tea. "I should change clothes."

"You need food for strength, too. I brought fruit, warm

cheese and bread, and tea." Meryn put the fragrant dish down on a small bedside table as her aunt controlled the coiling shudders in her gut. "Need some help?"

"Thank you, no." Jereth eased out of her shirt, careful to give her scar plenty of room. "How's our patient?"

"Sleeping quietly when I left. Sur Dharic's watching him. Sur Khaldurr has been in and out of delirium all afternoon." The young woman smiled proudly, fatigue showing in bruised rings beneath her eyes. "But the swelling's down, and there's very little sign of liquid infection seeping out. The smell of the wound is better also."

"Good." The older woman pulled a clean shirt from her clothes press and slowly dropped it over her head. She rolled the sleeves above her elbows, then covered most of the shirt and her pants with a waxed leather apron. Grabbing what was left of her long auburn hair, she began braiding it closely against her head. "Have you got the purifying plant warming?"

"It's sitting on the hearth, and there's another kettle ready to take its place as soon as you finish the first." Meryn pushed herself away from the door where she'd been leaning. "I'd better go change."

"Wait, Daughter of my Soul. Are you too tired to assist me?" Jereth stopped braiding and, holding her patchy hair in place, looked searchingly at her niece.

"No, Mother of my Heart," the younger woman said softly. Her smile of excitement sparkled like sunlight on snow, bringing a heart-stopping beauty to her face like nothing else could. "I wouldn't miss this for anything." She disappeared into the darkening interior hall.

"Jereth Liana Catoyan, you are a very lucky woman," the Goodhale sighed. "First, you have an excellent partner and a Heart-Daughter in Meryn. Second, you have had the spreading disease, had surgery, and survived. Third, you can save that man in the other room if you just remember what Seldar told you. And conquer your fear." Finishing her hair, she found her hands shaking. She wrapped a thong around the braid and tied it, then took the plate of food with her to the Marshal's room and studied the young man in the bed as she ate.

His uncle nodded sleepily in a chair beside the bed. The patient looked comfortable, worn but at ease. Meryn had already brought in almost everything they'd need: clean rags, bowls, and the special curved needle and thread they'd developed for stitching wounds. The little brazier for heating, cauterizing, and cleansing their few medical instruments already glowed with coals. Dharic must have helped Meryn slide Khaldurr onto the special polished board made necessary by more delicate procedures.

Everything was ready. Was she? Denying that thought accommodation in her mind, Jereth returned to her room to leave her nearly-empty plate and unpack the precious thin steel blade Seldar had surprised her with on her last day in Skrael. It proved she was one of the Society of the Knife.

A member as yet untested, she corrected herself, feeling the implement adjust to her fingers. That testing would occur very soon. A shudder ran across her shoulders and down her back. With no one to see, she didn't bother trying to control it. Why had she been harnessed with such talent and stymied by such difficulty? Was this some oblique gift of the Wise One, meant to curb the richness of her creative gifts? Or was it a lesson set upon her, and therefore her duty to teach others as soon as she'd learned to subjugate her aversion?

The Goodhale had no answer. With an effort she stopped her ague and forced her fingernails away from the ties of her leather apron. They were patterned with nervous indentations. With a silent prayer to the Wise One for succor, Jereth steeled herself and stepped into the hall.

Meryn met her there. Silently she clasped her aunt's cold fingers in her warm ones, offering unstinting support. The older woman kissed her niece's cheek and hugged her briefly in thanks. The two Goodhales then processed back to the Marshal's room and their patient, picking up the small kettle of purifying plant from the main room's hearth on the way.

Awakened by the movements of the women, Dharic unfolded from the bedside chair and moved to stand just inside the door. The healers made final preparations by coating the stranger's wound and the skin around it several times with warm purifying unguent. Meryn positioned herself on her knees on the plank at Khaldurr's head and became still as cooled glass, gaze fixed on the patient, beginning the mental groundwork that would allow her to take him far away from pain. Finally ready, she looked at Jereth.

The older woman trembled visibly. She stared at the growth with a tense, fixed expression, as if already hearing moaning from the tissues buried within. The narrow little knife gleamed from one whitened fist, its tip shaking in time to her elevated pulse. Jereth sat for long moments while the sun brightened the western window of the room, held captive by her fear.

Something inside her stirred, gathering thews enough to finally stomp down on the maggots in her mind. *What price will you pay for this man's life?* it asked. *You have the training and the knowledge to help him. If you don't, it means death for both.*

Death? That Khaldurr would die without intercession from her knife she knew. The poisons in his system were well advanced. But herself?

Suddenly she understood. If she did not conquer her fear now, she would be consigned by it to only teach Meryn and others like her, never achieving what Jereth had always wanted. Hers would be a partial spiritual death that would cloud the rest of her life.

Slowly, slowly, the hand wielding the blade raised. Slowly, slowly, Jereth lifted her head and traded a glance with her niece. Meryn immediately plunged into the low humming and repetitive finger-stroking from Khaldurr's temples to his jaw-line that would take their patient into deep sleep.

Her singing filled the room, awakening old ghosts to Jereth's sight. Takarthiel of Marissferne stood against the wall, one of the Marshal's fighters she'd cured of a deep leg wound. Jamarth of Ravensfell, her first suitor, joined Takarthiel, as well as Halanne Lefthand, onetime female captain of Queen Girande's army whom she'd cured of blood poisons and who'd offered to marry her. The Goodhale watched the spirits of people she'd assisted in the past file silently into the sickroom.

The Marshal of NorthMarch himself followed last. Positioning himself in front of the others, he stared at his daughter with ghostly eyes that reflected her dilemma. The beloved face creased with concern, but the shade did not move.

She must act now. Catching her bottom lip between her

teeth, Jereth purified the eager knife in flame, took in a huge breath, bent forward, and cut into the head of the tumor.

The putrescent cells screamed at the touch of the thin alembic blade. Their cry was horrible, a keening that sliced through the Goodhale's mind much as her steel parted the diseased tissue. She gasped, wanting to drop the knife and catch her ears in her hands. But that would not stop the sound. Its delving was internal, personal, a demonic vibration supported by fear that shuddered through her organs and made the center of her thoughts jellid. She could no longer think, no longer act. Jereth sat frozen, her knife fixed in the shallow wound.

A hand on her shoulder startled her, consigning the cry of the tumor into the middle realm of her mind. It wasn't Meryn. The older Goodhale could still hear her niece humming to their patient. And Dharic had manners enough not to presume friendship on a relationship founded on a need for healing. The touch had no substance, light as a gentle vesper rippling the mere. Yet there was strength behind it, and something else the woman couldn't place for long moments.

Abruptly her thoughts straightened from a swirling morass into apprehensible lines again, and she understood the vigor behind it. The hand belonged to the Marshal, and the strength she felt was love and confidence strong enough to transcend death.

We cannot act for you, spoke the ghost of his voice in her mind. *But we will act with you. Forever and always, my treasure. Forever and always. Do what you must—save this man.*

Jereth's fear was still there, but somehow it threatened less than before. She gathered it mentally into a package and stashed it in a corner of her mind, knowing it would never again debilitate her. Once more her sight focused on the ugly tumor in Khaldurr's side. Once more her fingers tightened around the steel of her knife, which snuggled against her fingers and strained forward. Taking in a deep breath scented with infection, she cut downward.

The scream from the violated poisonous cells sliced into her mind, but it did not pierce Jereth's soul as it had before. A barrier had been erected there, one that put the sound in perspective. She gloried in the rightness of it, and cut again.

"Dharic," the healer whispered. "Bring the bowl." The patient's uncle leaped to her side with the vessel meant for waste. Carefully the Goodhale Surgeon laid the first narrow piece of putrescent matter in the bottom, listening as its cry faded to an incoherent gurgle and died.

Jereth became so focused on the tumor she saw nothing else. Her hearing fastened on the wound, listening to match the initial howl of protest with subsequent voicings. She sliced and listened, sliced and listened, taking small fillets away until only the outer rim of the growth rose in its original position, and she had achieved a dish-shaped cavity. With a sigh, she leaned back.

"Meryn, will you dose that with purifying plant?"

"Right away." The younger Goodhale eased herself off the patient's board, shook out the kinks in her knees, and scooted past Dharic for the main room and the next pot of warm unguent. Her soft indoor boots whispered against the floorboards, sounding to Jereth's reattuned hearing like thunder spaced against the storm winds of Khaldurr's uncle's breathing.

When the younger woman began gently painting the wound with a clean rag wrapped around one end of a straight stick, Khaldurr moaned and jerked. Meryn dropped the stick onto a nearby tray, reached for the patient's head, and began singing and stroking again. She looked at the older Goodhale for guidance.

"I can take care of that, Lady Healers. That is, if you don't mind." Dharic's long legs carried him forward, one hand already reaching for the swab. "I had experience treating patients during the last war."

Meryn caught the slight flicker of agreement in her aunt's eyes. She nodded, both permission and thanks in the gesture. The uncle dipped the stick into the kettle for more medicine, and gently applied it to his nephew's side.

Jereth cocked her head closer to the wound she'd made, this time hearing something different behind the ugliness of the tumor. There, again. A lighter sound, a different pitch. The older woman reached out with her knife, determined to free healthy tissues awakening after release from the burden of corruption.

She cut again through the center of the growth, sending purifying plant deep into its heart. Willing those lighter sounds to sing again and more consistently, Jereth began to slice off smaller and smaller sections, putting them in Dharic's ready bowl. The tumor had stopped shrieking and only moaned now as its control over the affected area lessened, as if knowing its demise under the surgical blade was inevitable.

Delicately, the Goodhale began removing the discolored corona of the growth, taking it out in small slivers in a circular pattern that never allowed the sides to collapse inward. "Disease feeds on disease." Seldar's favorite teaching phrases swam into her mind. "One weakness allows a door for other illnesses." Her healer's intuition was certain that if she allowed the tumor's edges to fold into the bowl of the wound, the remaining infection would conjoin for a final assault against her newfound strength. Jereth would not allow that.

The song of relieved tissue beneath the tumor became stronger, adding a counterpoint to Meryn's humming. The sharp scent of healthy blood and warm, healthy flesh overcame the previous bad odor. The older Goodhale took another spiral off the edge of the growth, bringing its perimeter almost even with the rest before she attacked the crater again. Carefully now she cut, smelled, and listened while Dharic hovered beside her, alternately swabbing his nephew with purifying plant, holding out the waste bowl, and sopping away bright blood and watery pus.

Jereth cut, discarded the flesh, and listened intently. All she heard now was good pain: body tissues that had been buried by infection and the weight of the tumor cried out with the bright hurt of returning life. Her fatigue-burning eyes searched for those of her niece.

Meryn stopped humming. The room filled with silence as the Goodhales listened for the last vestiges of infection. Even Dharic held his breath. Only the tallow lamps hissed with subdued tones in the room which the sun had long since abandoned.

The younger woman nodded to her aunt. "You've done it," she announced softly with a tired smile. "I hear nothing but good."

"We've done it," corrected her aunt, voice faint with fatigue. "I couldn't have achieved this without you. Will you stitch this closed?"

The apprentice healer traded places with the Surgeon Goodhale and began the delicate stitchery that would start the knitting process in Khaldurr. Trembling and weary to the depths of her soul, Jereth stood up, turned to thank Dharic, and pitched forward into his arms in a dead faint.

In the following weeks Khaldurr mended quickly and well. He and his uncle took leave of NorthMarch House a half moon pass after the surgery, promising to continue the gentle stretching exercises the Goodhales insisted upon.

From the doorway, Khaldurr had traded long meaningful looks with Meryn they thought Jereth did not see. The older woman hid her knowledge of their budding romance and the hurt she suffered for both. It seemed as though her niece was about to discover one of the agonies of a Goodhale's profession. The lingering looks Dharic turned her direction she shrugged off. She'd experienced too many bored men who only meant to pass time with harmless amorous play.

By the year's chill turn an epidemic of coughing sickness invaded NorthMarch town and the surrounding area. Jereth and Meryn took turns making calls to farms and houses, helping those who could not leave their lands even for the few hours it took to walk or ride to the Marshal's House for treatment. The Goodhales began sheltering the worst patients under their own thatch, and their extra rooms soon filled with the infirm. With just the two women working among dozens of the sick, each day soon stretched into long aching hours punctuated with wheezing breaths and wracking coughs.

By the second week of the epidemic, Jereth's sight and hearing were both slightly off-center. She tried to work through the problem, telling herself the causes were exhaustion and the terrible tea she drank daily. Her hair had continued to fall out until she was forced to wear a scarf. At least now it had begun growing in again, a fine amber fuzz.

To herself she could deny her own illness, but she could not hide it from the sharp eyes of her niece. Meryn finally confronted her with the same medicine they used to dose those with coughing sickness.

"Drink this," the young Goodhale ordered, stopping the older woman in the main hall beside the refectory table and pushing a steam-wreathed mug into her hands. "Wise One help us if we both come down with this contagion." Jereth raised one bare eyebrow—those and her lashes had fallen out, too—and Meryn nodded. "I just drank my own measure in the kitchen."

"Well-laced with honey for energy, I hope. We need all we can get." The older healer tipped the ceramic to her lips as her niece smiled. Jereth reflected that the once-normal expression had become foreign to Meryn's pretty face, and that her high rounded cheekbones had hollowed with unceasing work.

The smile disappeared much too quickly. "We're running low on wood and supplies."

"I put another big kettle of tea on to brew just a while ago, and there's podflower to powder and gavreal to shred when we get a chance," sighed Jereth, looking at the outside door with distaste. "You start that. I'll fetch wood."

"You'll do nothing of the sort," stated her niece. "I'll go—"

The portal boomed and rattled on its hinges, sounding as though it was hit with a battering ram. Two more strikes in rapid succession made it shudder. Closest to it, Meryn stepped forward. Reaching out, glancing at Jereth for support, she tripped the latch and swung the door inward.

Snow and cold wind pushed two heavily-laden figures inside. One carried an armful of wood, the other was burdened with three bulging leather carryalls. Jereth looked from one to the other of the iced fur-wrapped faces buried so deep in their hoods she recognized neither. The words "help" or "healing" were not spoken.

"What is the meaning of your visit?" she demanded as snow avalanched from their shoulders to the wooden floor. "State your business. We have work to do with the sick."

"Well I know," said a familiar voice. "I have returned to repay my debt, dear Lady Goodhales." Khaldurr, Second Son of SouthMarch, stripped off his hood and set his bundle of logs on the floor.

Meryn's hands flew to her mouth, trying too late to catch a squeak of surprise.

"We've been laboring through this storm for two days," the young man continued, "with a sledge loaded with wood and the choicest dried herbs to restock your stores. They must be near spent with all the sickness in this area." He pulled his eyes away from Meryn's, glancing quickly at his taller companion. Dharic shoved back his own hood and gave Khaldurr a nod of support. "I would also ask a favor. No, two favors."

"And what are those, Son of SouthMarch?" Jereth set her mug on the table before she lost control of it. Neither her grip nor her vision were working well.

Khaldurr dropped to his knees and captured the healer's hands in his mittened ones, holding them firmly as she tried to pull away. "I have been looking since I came of age for a life-task that would enthuse my spirit as well as challenge my mind," he said earnestly. "I found it here, after you touched me with your knife." He bowed his head. "I learn quickly. My hands are steady. I would like to become your student in goodhaling, and my uncle Dharic, also."

"But—I—"

Jereth swayed, the room momentarily going dark. Strong, gentle hands closed about her shoulders. Her eyes flew open to meet a pair as deep and dark as her father's had been, set in the strong comely face she'd come to know two months past. Dharic's grip felt warm, comforting. The man's short beard and eyebrows were still crystaled with melting ice. He seemed for a moment like a hero sent out of the legends grandnannies told around the hearth on cold winter nights like this one.

The Goodhale felt her cheeks blaze with amazement, like those of a young girl at her first meeting with a suitor. Dharic's eyes clearly told of his attraction. This time she could not dismiss his feelings as boredom or play.

But she could not give in—her energies must be focused toward her patients.

A foreign thought made her breathing stumble. What of a relationship between two Goodhales? Or between four? Could they sustain each other in love as well as assist one another in the healing arts?

"Lady Goodhale, is something amiss?" Dharic asked softly, brows contracting. Jereth didn't answer, lost in his rich voice and the sense of radiant energy flowing from his hands. She let her body and mind absorb the force freely offered. The illness establishing purchase in her system quailed and fled.

It would take very little training for this man to become

one who would calm, soothe, and lead patients to recovery by vocal talents alone. If his hands were as good, he would prove an excellent pupil, perhaps as talented as Meryn. Despite her attempt at control, Jereth let out a trembling breath and pulled in more.

"I have had disease within myself that I must treat for the rest of my life," she said distinctly, meeting Dharic's eyes. "I have been under Surgeon Goodhale Seldar's knife."

The older man's face warmed and wrinkled with concern, fascination, and something Jereth couldn't put a name to.

"I know. It only makes you more intriguing to this old soldier, Surgeon Lady Goodhale." He smiled. "You bear the scars of your own war, part of which I observed at Khaldurr's bedside."

Meryn spoke up, her voice brittle with fatigue. "She's presently ill. We both are. I believe it's the beginning of coughing disease."

"Then we've arrived at an opportune time." Khaldurr kept to his knees, shaking Jereth's hands a little to recapture her attention. "Think, Lady. In time, your student following could be as great as Seldar's. You're certainly as good as he. I suffered no complications from your treatment. NorthMarch could become famous. I've told everybody between here and SouthMarch of your talents." He smiled hopefully.

"But I have so much more to learn myself," she protested, finally getting giddy feet beneath her.

"We all do," declared Dharic. "I almost think I'm starting this far too late in my life." His head swiveled as a fusillade of coughs sounded from the Marshal's room. "Your patients need your answer. And I don't think my nephew will let loose your hands until he has your decision." His fingers tightened on her shoulders as if he, too, would not let go.

Jereth looked at Meryn. The young healer's face showed enough joy to raise the temperature in the room. The older woman turned to Dharic.

"Why are you here?"

"I fought in the last war with SouthMarch and the Battle Queen, Lady Goodhale." His tone ached with old hurts. "I could soothe the wounded with my voice, but there was so much I could not do. When Khaldurr sickened, I faced the same difficulty. When he disappeared, I was distraught. I chased him through several towns before catching up. It's a good thing I did, for he never would have darkened your doorway otherwise.

"After his surgery, when we'd been home a while, we discussed our feelings. I found my heart, like his, was set." He bent to join his nephew on the snow-wet floor, taking one of Jereth's hands from Khaldurr. They were steady and warm, his sense of energy focused and strong. "I wish, more than anything in the world, to become a Goodhale, perhaps a Surgeon. I petition your instruction." He looked up at her, waiting.

Jereth's dreams suddenly locked together. In her mind she could see NorthMarch House a hub of activity, filled with the talented wishing to become part of the Society of the Knife. Those who excelled journeyed into every corner of Rannerlan and beyond, assisting the infirm and teaching their own students.

Coughing wracked the air again. "Very well," the Goodhale replied. Her body and mind felt buoyant with energy, renewed. "Meryn, you take custody of Khaldurr, and I will take Dharic for instruction." Being students now, she dropped the honorific *Sur.* "Bring the herbs and the wood. The School of Healing at NorthMarch is begun."

Feeling more whole than she had since discovering the lump in her breast, Jereth headed for the Marshal's room with her retinue. She would find time to return to Skrael and learn whatever Seldar could teach her. She would be the best Goodhale she could be for as long as the Wise One allowed, perhaps better able to help her followers overcome difficulties after dealing with the fears that once immobilized her.

"Students," she announced, pausing at the door and smiling. "There's healing to do. Come inside."

BRASS IN POCKET
by Cynthia Ward

The sunlight slanted through the arched western windows and faded in the bright interior light, which glared on the varnished floor and hid the deep scratches. Though the day was warm, the furnace poured out heat, strengthening the smells of dust and the Lemon Pledge that Janey Middleton had sprayed on the tables.

The Williamsboro Public Library was deserted except for Janey and Mrs. Wright. Mrs. Wright presided over the circulation desk, gray-haired and dressed in gray, impassive, a granite statue. Janey dusted the shelves. Her shoulders were sore, her hands greasy.

Janey had worked at the library since '76, six years, and expected to match or exceed Mrs. Wright's forty-year career. Janey was lucky to have this job; her classmates who'd stayed in Williamsboro worked at the Shop'n'Save, Seven-11, the Eastern Maine Pulp and Paper mill. Librarian was a good career. Janey didn't have to touch anyone.

In an alley of tall bookcases, Janey heard the front doors open. Who would come willingly to the library on a 70-degree Saturday in November?

"I want the Cat in the Hat, Daddy!" An unknown child's voice.

"Don't worry, Carrie, we'll find him."

Janey stiffened. She knew the second voice, though she hadn't heard it in years. She turned her back to the center aisle.

"I want Clifford the Big Red Dog!"

"Shh, Carrie," said Lewis McDaniels. "You mustn't talk loud in the library."

Janey overheard a lot of gossip at the library; she knew Lew and his wife were getting divorced. She wasn't surprised. She knew exactly what Lew was like. She had seen him *inside*.

His daughter had been born after he'd dropped out of high school. Carrie must be five now; just learning to read. Lew had been quite a reader in school. He'd bring his daughter to the library all the time. Janey scrubbed the shelf with hard swipes.

The footsteps drew close. The heavier footsteps stopped. Janey did not turn around.

She remembered Lew sitting next to her on the porch, back when they were sixteen. Her parents had been out somewhere, and she'd been glad. She'd been stupid.

Carrie said, "Daddy, come *on!*"

Lew's footsteps moved away.

Lew had brought over some of his favorite albums ("You don't know what good music is," he said, putting on a Rick Wakeman LP), and they smoked harsh local weed on the back step as Lew talked about some old "Godard film" playing in Waterville, seventy miles away. The nearest cinema was in Bangor, only thirty miles away, but it showed movies people wanted to see. Not the stuff Lew liked. Weird foreign shit.

"C'mon, Janey," Lew said, "let's go tonight!" He grinned secretively. "I'll score a nickel of Columbian. . . ."

"You know I can't go," Janey said. Her parents, who were much older than her friends' folks, would never allow her to go anywhere alone with a boy. Especially a football player. Even if she'd known him since they were little kids.

Lew knew her parents. He said, "Tell 'em you're going shopping in Bangor with your girlfriends."

Janey didn't say anything. She didn't want to lie to her parents, but it wouldn't be cool to admit that. She didn't want to see a foreign movie, but if she told Lew, he would be really disappointed in her. Bad enough that he'd laughed at her ABBA and Heart albums.

Lew leaned toward her. His face was only a couple of inches from hers. She trembled, anxious at his closeness, but wanting him even closer.

"Janey," Lew murmured, "I don't want to go alone."

Janey said, "I'll go with you."

Lew kissed her. She'd never been kissed before. It felt so good! She returned the kiss eagerly, and Lew pulled her against him. The sensations of contact were so strong, it was like she could even feel what Lew felt: the pressure of her lips against his, her breasts against his chest. When he slipped his hand into her halter top and touched her breast, she gasped with pleasure—and shock: Lew's feelings and thoughts were as clear as her own. She felt an aching tension in him, stronger even than her own desire. She saw that he'd told his teammates he was laying her all the time, though he'd never had sex with anyone. But he wanted to. He imagined what the girl in his arms would look like naked, wanting him, spreading her legs for him—

Janey had thought that Lew felt something special for her, like she did for him—but it didn't matter who she was! She could be an *empty body,* as long as she had tits and a twat!

She pushed him away. "You don't care about me! You don't even know I *exist!*"

"What are you talking about?" Lew exclaimed. "I like you, Janey, I like you a lot! How could I think you don't exist?"

"Get out of here!"

Lew looked utterly astonished. Then his face turned stony, and he stood up. "You fucked-up bitch." He left.

Janey had shivered with the sudden fear that she'd gone crazy. Mind-reading was *impossible!* What had she been thinking? *Why* had she driven Lew away?

The library doors opened again.

"Daddy, what's *that?*" Carrie sounded frightened.

Janey turned toward the center aisle.

"Ssh." Lew's voice. "Don't stare, Carrie."

In the aisle a strange creature appeared. It was dressed all in black, its head bald except for a foot-high black mohawk. Janey couldn't tell if she was looking at a boy or a girl. She'd never seen one before, except in *Time* or *Newsweek,* but she knew she was looking at a punk.

She shrank back against the bookcase, her heart slamming her chest so hard she could barely breathe. That *thing* shouldn't be here! Punks were in London, Los Angeles, maybe even Boston. Not a small town in Maine.

Janey remembered a conversation she'd overheard yesterday between two half-deaf old ladies who thought they were whispering: "Did you hear Donny Hathaway's come back?" "By Godfrey, I never thought he'd leave California, his wife loved Los Angeles so!" "Evvie, she died in a car accident—" "How horrible!" "—and Donny's moved back to Williamsboro with his daughter. He doesn't like what California's done to the girl. Have you *seen* her?" "I don't think so—" "You'd know if you had. She looks like some kind of wild *Indian!*"

Janey had pictured a darkly tanned girl in a fringed buckskin hippie-vest and long black braids.

The mohawked punk must have glimpsed Janey, because she turned right toward her and said, in an accented but otherwise normal voice, "Where's the science fiction section?"

Even with the punk facing her, Janey couldn't stop staring. The punk had a safety pin stuck through her left nostril, and several rings in each ear. Her big dark eyes were made up like an ancient Egyptian's, her lips were black, and her face was so pale it was like she'd never seen the sun.

Why would anyone want to look like a *corpse?*

"Are you deaf, lady?"

Janey pointed across the center aisle. "The science fiction is in the fiction section, on the other side of the room. Science fiction is in the last bookcase to my right."

The punk strode away, big black boots clunking.

Janey wiped her forehead, smearing it with dust. She looked down. The ache of her shoulders had seeped into her neck. Lew's and Mrs. Wright's voices drifted to her from the desk, inaudible.

When she'd seen Lew in the hallway the next morning, she'd expected him to yell at her and embarrass her in front of everyone at Williamsboro High. But he turned and went the other way. She was relieved, even though everyone noticed, and her friends kept asking what was wrong. Finally Janey yelled, *"Nothing!"* Marcie said, "Guys are jerks." She patted Janey's forearm; in the brief contact, Janey saw fragments of Marcie's thoughts—an image of Lew gleaming in his Williamsboro Lions football uniform— *glad Lew broke up with her*—

Broke up? They hadn't been dating! Lew was still spreading *lies* about her. In sudden rage Janey spoke the worst accusation that could be made: "Lew's queer."

Her friends were so shocked they didn't say anything for several seconds. Then Marcie said, "Lew? No *way!*" The vehement denial made Janey painfully aware of her lie; but Lew had been lying about her for weeks! She said, "He's got pictures of naked guys in his bedroom!" Then her friends all gasped or squealed, except Gina, who squeezed her arm, searing her with pleasure in the chance to tear somebody down. Janey rejoiced that Lew would be hurt; yet Gina's wildfire glee made her pull back, jerking her arm out of Gina's grip and screaming, "Don't *touch* me!"

She bumped into another girl, and felt the thought: *What's* wrong *with her?* Janey jumped away with a yell, and her friends gave her the strangest looks, and all the people passing in the hall stared at her, and she didn't need to touch anyone to know everyone was thinking, *There's something wrong with her!*

For the next couple of hours, students came up to Janey to ask, "Is Lew really queer?" Avoiding their eyes, their touch, she always answered, "Yes!" The question quickly changed to "Did you hear Lew's queer?" as her rumor transformed from one person's assertion to something "everyone knew." By the end of the day, no one was talking to Lew, and everyone was whispering—and not only about Lew, Janey was sure.

She avoided her friends. She didn't talk to anyone unless she had to. She overheard her coworkers wondering why she'd gotten so shy. In crowded hallways, she felt other students' thoughts: *Ice queen* and *Weirdo!* and *What's her problem?* Her mother, who never touched her, put a hand on hers and started to say something; Janey ran into her bedroom and locked the door. She didn't want to hear her mother's words. She had heard her mother's thought: *What's wrong with her?* Everyone thought something was wrong with her. And everyone was right.

The library doors opened again.

"You call *that* a science fiction section?"

Janey jumped. She turned to find the punk glaring at her, fists on hips. The black leather motorcycle jacket hung open, exposing an oversized white T-shirt with a jagged black topographical design above the words UNKNOWN PLEASURES.

"One shelf!" the punk yelled. "One shelf of boring old farts! Don't you have *any* Delany or—"

"Please keep your voice down, Miss Hathaway," Mrs.

Wright called from the desk. Her voice was harsh as broken granite.

"I don't know anything about science fiction," Janey said coldly. She read bestsellers and romances. "Try the card catalog—"

"Never mind, this hick library would never have any good science fiction," the punk said.

The buttons on her jacket lapels bore cryptic symbols and words: X, Bauhaus, Dead Kennedys—the last offended Janey deeply, though she'd seen it before. It was the incredibly macabre and tasteless name of a punk-rock band. Janey wished she dared throw this disgusting little punk out of the library.

"Where's the psychology section?" the punk demanded.

Janey answered, wondering if the Hathaway girl was looking for self-help books. She needed them.

The punk stomped into the center aisle and almost collided with a tall, dark-haired guy in jeans and a J. Geils T-shirt. "Christ, Richie boy!" she cried. "Stop following me everywhere!"

Janey recognized Rich Vallier, starting running back for the Williamsboro High Lions. Rich never came to the library. And today was Saturday—shouldn't he be on the field? Janey remembered the late news; the Lions had lost a Friday night game.

Rich towered over the punk. She tilted her mohawk back and glared up into Rich's face; Janey realized she was barely five feet tall. Her legs looked like sticks in ragged black jeans.

"I ain't followin' you, Lisa," Rich said. His face was sullen, and pale except for the red streaks of pimples on brow and jaw. "You're always getting' in my way. Get *out* of it."

The punk—Lisa Hathaway—grabbed Rich's wrist. He gaped at her. "You want me, Richie boy. Why don't you just admit it? You might get somewhere!"

Mrs. Wright said, "Young lady—"

Rich yanked his arm out of Lisa's grip. "Lying bitch!"

"*Mis*ter Vallier!" Mrs. Wright thundered. "We do *not* allow such language in the Williamsboro Public *Library!* You will *watch* your language or *leave!*"

Rich glanced at Mrs. Wright, glared at Lisa, then disappeared behind a bookcase.

The punk went to the psychology section. Janey returned to her dusting. Lisa was in the next aisle; Janey heard occasional mutters, all inaudible until: "There's *nothing* here! Jesus, what did I expect? This podunk town sucks shit through a straw."

Lisa's boots retreated, loud and swift. The doors slammed. The punk was gone. *Big-city snob,* Janey thought. *Thinks every place should be like Los Angeles. She should go back to that hole. They deserve each other.*

Someone else left the library. Rich Vallier, Janey realized; she could hear Lew approaching with his little girl. The offspring of his macho reaction to the rumor Janey had started. He'd intended to go to college, but he'd dropped out to get a job at the mill and get married. Now he and his shotgun bride were getting divorced. Janey had changed his life completely with a word. It had pleased her; but now the memory roused no pleasure.

The footsteps paused. "Janey?"

Why was Lew talking to her? In his mind, she'd never even *existed!* And he had made her realize there was something wrong with her, and then everyone else had realized it. He was responsible; he'd gotten what he deserved.

Janey bent closer to the shelf, scrubbing at a sticky spot, a splash of forbidden soda. She heard Lew and his daughter walk away; heard the doors open and close. Gone at last! To return next week, Janey knew, and the next.

Janey lowered her head until her brow rested on her forearm. Her arms and shoulders ached, though dusting wasn't hard work. Her hands were filthy, her nose clogged and aching; the dry furnace heat pressed her with an almost physical weight. She hadn't cleaned half the nonfiction shelves, and according to her watch, it was already 3:45; she couldn't get them all dusted before 5:00. Mrs. Wright would be angry at her. And when she finished dusting all the bookcases, all the nonfiction and fiction and children's shelves, she would start all over again.

Nothing would ever change. Janey would dust shelves and shelve books for the rest of her life, decade after mind-numbing decade. She wanted suddenly to scream—she had never wanted to do anything so much! But she could hardly take a breath against the weight of heat and dust.

Janey walked to the desk, hoping her shaky legs wouldn't

give way. Mrs. Wright watched her with granite eyes. "Mrs. Wright," she whispered, "I—I feel sick. Can I go home?"

Mrs. Wright wouldn't believe it. She'd see the lie on Janey's face.

"Of course, Janey," Mrs. Wright said. "I hope you feel better tomorrow."

Janey left before Mrs. Wright could change her mind. The sun was low; the long black shadows of dead elms barred the street. The unseasonable heat had fled; a damp November breeze set Janey shivering in her dress and nylons. She pulled on her jacket as she walked up Maine Street to her car.

Her mother's car. She wanted her own car, but with her pay, she'd never get loan approval for a new car and, as her father said, you don't buy used unless you like to throw money away.

Janey slid into the Dodge and slumped over the steering wheel. She didn't have to dust anymore today.

But she'd just have to do it Monday.

And she'd only escaped to go home to an empty room.

She still lived with her parents. They didn't charge rent, and they didn't want their only child living away from them; the world had become a dangerous place. But living with her parents was kind of like living alone. They'd never said much to her outside of telling her what to do, and now they were getting deaf. Janey mostly stayed in her bedroom, reading, listening to the radio, watching TV. Sometimes she wished she had an apartment, roommates—friends—but that would *never* happen. She would remain alone—terribly alone—for all the decades of her life. She would never escape her mind-rotting job. Nothing would ever change.

There was something wrong with her, and everyone knew it.

She stiffened. There *was* one way to change her life. A vision filled her mind: the Dodge speeding, 70, 80, 90 mph, veering off the road and crashing into a tall thick pine. She could end it all.

(An unbidden question rose, silent, insistent: *If you destroy another's life, do you deserve to live?*)

She *would* end it all.

Something pounded on the car door. Fear surged through Janey, an adrenaline lightning-jolt, and she jerked upright.

"Are you okay, lady?" said the punk, her mouth close

to the window, yelling; Janey leaned away from the glass.
It was true: Californians had no sense of privacy. "You
looked sick," Lisa said, "all hunched over and shaking like
that. You're white as a ghost!"

Sick? No, the punk couldn't see what was wrong with
her. "I'm fine!" Janey said, reaching into her purse for
the keys.

"You're crying!" the punk said, and opened the car door.

"What are you *doing?*" Janey always locked the door.
But she'd forgotten.

"Lady, somebody hurt you real bad," the punk said.
"Can I do anything to help?"

"Yes! Close the door and go away!"

Lisa seized Janey's wrist. Janey felt Lisa's curiosity and
concern—and she felt Lisa feeling her own emotions. Lisa
saw her abnormality, her need to die— *No!* She jerked her
arm wildly, trying to break contact, but the skinny little
punk held on.

Emotion flooded Janey like white-hot light, Lisa's emotion. Anger: at the useless library; at the hick town with no
record stores, no movie theatres, no cable TV, no nothing;
at the yokels who all stared at her and never talked to her
except to harass her for being an out-of-stater, a Califor-
nian, a punk; at her father for dragging her to the middle
of nowhere; at her mother for dying.

Anger—and amazement that there was someone else
like her.

And she saw all the times Janey had seen others'
thoughts; saw what Janey had done to Lew after seeing
his thoughts.

The punk was seeing *everything* in her head! With the
strength of panic, Janey wrenched her arm free of Lisa's
grip.

"You're like *me!*" Lisa said. She was grinning like an
imbecile. "I never met anybody like me before! This is
great!"

" 'Great'?" Janey cried. "You must be crazy!"

"It's a *gift* from God or the universe or your genes or
something!" Lisa said. "It's like a superpower. A force for
good! You can read people's mind. You can help them."

Janey felt like she'd fallen into one of Lew's stupid super-
hero comics. "What good have *you* ever done, punk?" she

demanded. "You run around dressed like a weirdo even though you know it freaks people out, but that makes you so angry you hate everybody and everything, even your dead mother!"

Lisa's face twisted. "I don't hate my mother!" she screamed. "Fuck you! Fuck this whole goddam town!"

For once Janey couldn't suppress the angry words in her mind: "Go back to L.A.!"

"Don't worry," Lisa said. "I'm going to USC and getting a psych degree and never coming back. But you'll just off yourself, or stay here the rest of your life, even though this shit-pit makes you as miserable as me."

"You ignorant brat," Janey said. "You glimpse a few of my thoughts and think you know everything about me!"

"I'm just saying what I saw. I saw everybody calls you Janey, a totally kiddie name, but you don't object to it. I saw you let your parents smother you even though you resent it—you'd rather kill yourself than stand up to them, because you're terrified of *life!*"

"Get out of my car!"

Lisa got out of the car. But she leaned on the door so Janey couldn't close it. "Go on avoiding people because they have mean thoughts," Lisa said. "Like you didn't know that from the inside of your *own* head. Go on avoiding guys because you saw a horny boy thinking like a horny boy. Like you didn't do a nastier thing to him than he ever could've imagined! Go ahead and kill yourself— you got no reason to live!"

She turned away.

Janey slammed the door and locked it.

Two figures appeared around the corner of LaVerdiere's Superdrug; football players, gold jerseys ruddy in the dying light. Some team members wore their jerseys all the time, enjoying local celebrity. One of the guys was a big beefy fair-haired fellow, the other tall and thin, with dark hair— Rich Vallier?

No—Harry Talbot, a dropout; the beefy guy was his cousin George, star fullback, school bully. They blocked the sidewalk and grinned nastily at Lisa. She glared and tried to push between them. Harry grabbed Lisa's shoulder. Both cousins laughed maliciously. Lisa yelled, "Let me go, asshole!" Harry shook her violently.

Janey looked away. The other people on the sidewalk were ignoring the altercation. It wasn't any of their business. It didn't matter. Nothing mattered. Janey reached for the key.

"You football hooligans," Lisa said. She sounded so calm, Janey had to look. Lisa was smiling scornfully. "Afraid of anybody who isn't as *stupid* as you."

"Bitch!" George grabbed the safety pin stuck through Lisa's nose and pulled upward until she was standing on her toes.

Janey opened the car door. "Leave her alone!"

George ignored her; he was still screaming at Lisa. "Think you're so much better than everyone else!"

Lisa grabbed George's wrist. "Better than you, fag!"

George yelled incoherently and jerked his arm free, ripping the safety pin out of her nose. Blood sprayed. Lisa made a soft sound and sagged in Harry's grip. George punched her in the stomach.

Harry gaped at his cousin. "You hit a *girl,* George!"

"Lying whore *deserves* it!" George drew back his fist for another blow.

Janey seized his arm. Rage scalded her in a red roaring blaze. He wasn't a fag, even if stupid Harry sucked his joint sometimes, even if queers chased him in Portland. Everyone else was idiots, assholes, queers—nothing wrong with *him!*

"Let go!" he shouted, trying to shake Janey off his arm. She went slack, letting her weight drag down his arm. Her knees struck cement sidewalk with a sharp sound, sharp pain; nylons and skin tore.

"Hey!" The yell came from a distance, but Janey recognized the voice. Rich Vallier. "What the hell are you guys doing?"

George swung his arm, slamming Janey into the side of her car. Pain exploded in her back; her grip went slack. She heard George and Harry running away.

Janey ignored the pain and rose, to find herself facing the punk. Lisa stood hunched over a little, her arms around her stomach. Her face was white, her torn nostril pouring blood over her chin and onto her white T-shirt.

Janey grabbed her purse and reached inside. "Lisa—"

"Lisa!" Rich Vallier skidded to a halt beside them. "Jesus, George broke your nose!"

Lisa straightened and raised her hands to her face. "He didn't punch me in the face," she corrected, wiping away blood. Janey stuck a packet of Kleenex in her hand. "I'm okay."

"Bullshit!" Rich said. "I'll clean their damn clocks!" He started after the retreating figures.

Lisa grabbed his bare arm with a red hand. "You're not a macho dickhead, dude. Don't be acting like the Talbots."

"Those bastards hurt you wicked bad! I better drive you to the hospital—"

"I'll accept only a ride home." Lisa held the tissues, wadded, against her torn nostril. "I ought to get *some* use out of you following me around all the time—"

"I *never* followed you. You forget how small this town is?"

"I never forget that," Lisa said. "You know, I'm not the only one who got hurt."

"Oh, yeah." Rich turned to Janey, his face reddening. "I'm sorry, Miss Middleton. You okay?"

"I'm fine." Janey said. A bruised back and scraped knees were nothing. It was more painful being called Miss Middleton by someone only five years younger than she.

Lisa said, "Get your car, Rich!"

Rich ran off.

Lisa and Janey looked at each other. Janey opened her mouth and Lisa said, "Don't *you* start in about hospitals!"

Janey changed her question. " 'A force for good,' you said?"

"I wasn't too smart, yanking Georgie's chain," Lisa admitted. "God, I never go around saying what I see in other people's heads! Do you?"

"No!" Janey said. Yet she'd been so disturbed by what she'd seen in Lew's mind that she'd told the most damaging lie she could to hurt him.

"Thank God I didn't grow up here." Lisa looked levelly at Janey. "Small towns really fuck people up if they don't fit in."

Janey felt George's rage again, his self-deception, his self-hatred turned blindly outward. He was as bigoted as his classmates. As Janey. She had eagerly turned this hatred on Lew. If the rumor hadn't died, Lew would've gotten away from it in a couple of years, gone to college. But what boy has the patience for that? He knocked up a girl from another high school, someone he hardly knew, wrecking his own life and hers to disprove a lie.

Surely he had figured out who'd started the rumor. Yet he'd spoken Janey's name in the library. He'd wanted to talk to her.

A touch on the shoulder startled Janey. She jumped. "You stopped George," Lisa said. "You helped me."

"Lisa!" Rich's voice, yelling; his head jutted out the window of a mustard-brown Maverick. "Get in!"

Lisa didn't glance at him. She said, "Thanks, Jane."

After work the next day, she stopped by the apartment building at the corner of Maine and Water, but no one answered her knock. She walked to LaVerdiere's Superdrug to purchase a couple of items, and there he was, choosing construction paper with his little girl.

She had destroyed his life. Why had he spoken to her yesterday? There was no chance of reconciliation.

"I owe you an apology," she said. He looked up, a startled expression on his face. "I owe you an apology bigger than words can say, because I lied to hurt you."

"I know," he said quietly.

She flushed. "I'm sorry. God, I'm sorry! But that doesn't change anything, doesn't change what I did to you—"

"It's done," he said. "It's past. If things had happened differently, I wouldn't have Carrie." He placed a hand on his daughter's head; the little girl glanced up, then reached for a Crayola box. "I wouldn't change that for anything."

She didn't know what to say.

He said, "I wanted to tell you I'm leaving town. I get my GED next month and I'm moving to Orono in January, starting classes at the University of Maine."

"Oh," she said. "I hadn't heard."

"You're the first person I've told besides my daughter."

"Oh," she said, flushing again. She didn't deserve to hear the news before his parents, his friends, his ex-wife. "Congratulations, Lew."

"Thanks." He held out his hand.

She hesitated, then took his hand. They shook. He was not angry. He had forgiven her. His thoughts were with the future, and his little girl. He would still see his daughter every weekend, but he could no longer be part of her day-to-day life; he was worried.

"Don't worry, Lew. Your daughter will be fine."

He looked surprised. "Geez, you reading my thoughts?"

"You remember my folks. I know what parents can be like."

He grinned. "I swear I won't go overboard like them."

"Good-bye, Lew. Good luck at the University."

Her parents subscribed to the *Maine Sunday Telegram,* but she bought the Sunday *Boston Globe,* and a notebook. She went home and spread the classifieds on her bed. She turned the pages, pausing occasionally to write in the notebook.

A car door slammed. She looked out the window. She saw a black Volkswagen Beetle, a car she didn't recognize. Rich Vallier sat in the passenger seat, watching Lisa Hathaway stride up the walk to the Middeton front door. Her mohawk bristled like a porcupine. Mom and Dad would have a heart attack if they saw this spiky black-leather creature at their door. They'd peep out the living-room window and see her and wait silently for her to leave.

Jane opened the door.

MOVE . . . TOMORROW
by John Tigges

The Greyhound bus roared along Interstate 80, westward. For Essie Pfeltgen, it was heading toward Wentworth, Iowa, her birthplace, which lay four miles off the four-lane highway.

She looked around the bus at her traveling companions. They all appeared normal, but she wouldn't and didn't trust any one of them. She wrung her thin, bony hands together before making certain her purse, which contained all the money she had, was squeezed firmly between her left hip and the wall of the bus.

The man sitting across the aisle from her, leaned over the open space. "How far you goin' lady?"

She looked at him quickly, her eyes blazing. He wanted her money. His face, sub-bronzed and hands the same color up to his wrists where his skin suddenly turned milk white, bespoke of his farming background. But the sonofabitch wanted her money. How did he know she had any? She sure as hell didn't look prosperous. Turning her head, she stared through the window at the passing landscape.

Maybe she shouldn't have come. Essie felt nervous and uncomfortable, dressed the way she was. Her normal attire—all of her wardrobe—consisting of nine dresses, seven pieces of underwear, three pairs of cotton stockings and old tennis shoes, had been left at home. While she roamed the streets of Chicago every day, she still maintained the one-room apartment where her aunt, Tillie Stiffleman, had raised her. The place was a dump and stunk like a garbage pile, which it primarily was, but she had some good memories of growing up there with Aunt Tillie.

But something had happened two days before, and Essie had forced herself to get cleaned up, get her hair fixed and buy a "new" dress at Goodwill Industries. She'd gotten drunk on Monday, which she normally didn't do, and kicked a hole in the back wall of the closet while looking for something. The next morning she'd discovered the damage she'd caused, and inside the hole that had been covered with thin boards, found a dusty manilla folder. It contained a lot of money and two letters—one from her Aunt Tillie, one from her mother—and an old bank book. The letter from her mother was the stopper.

Aunt Tillie's letter simply told her that the money in the folder was hers and that she hadn't trusted banks after the crash of 1929. She'd found $11,111 from her aunt. Essie considered that a good omen—five aces. Adding that to the $21,475 she always carried in two pairs of heavy underwear with the leg openings sewn together, she had a total of $32,586. The $2,137.26 in the bank book had been her father's and probably wasn't any good. And all of it was in the purse she'd picked up at Goodwill for half a buck. Without sitting on the crinkly bills, her rear end felt bare, but it would only be while she went to her parents' home town.

She pulled out the yellower of the two envelopes and opened it. Her eyes teared up when she read it again.

Dear Esther,

When you read this, you will be a grown woman. I know my sister will raise you the way I would. I hope you are a beautiful young woman and that all happiness is yours. I've asked Tillie to give you this letter when you turn twenty-one. I'll try to explain about you father, Leo, and me. Please don't hate us.

When your father lost everything he'd worked so hard for, in the crash of 1929, it proved too much of a shock for him, I guess. He tried. Lord knows, he tried, but he just could not come back to where he'd been before all our problems started. I've sure missed him the two years he's been gone, and so did you, little as you was. Don't think of him as being a coward for hanging himself. He wasn't. A lot of people did themselves in when they lost everything. Love his memory.

As for me, I won't live too much longer. The doctor tries to encourage me, but I know better. I feel it inside. Sometime, when you're a grown woman, maybe with a

*family of your own, you can come to Wentworth here
in Iowa, and visit your parents' graves. If you do, go
see the house where you was born and lived. It's on the
street west of the Lutheran church, two doors away
from the parsonage. There's a round window in the
attic—the only one on the block with such a window.*

*I will always love you, Esther. Please think of me
once in a while and pray for me whenever you can. I
hope you've done what your aunt always said and have
been a good girl and woman. I want nothing but the
best for you.*

Your mother,
Marcella Pheltgen

Essie folded the letter and put it back in the envelope.
She wiped her tears away. Sure, she'd always done what
Aunt Tillie said, until she died when Essie was seventeen.
Then, Essie dropped out of school and started running the
streets. Even in 1947, there were street gangs, and she'd
gotten in with the wrong crowd. By the time she turned
eighteen, she was whoring for a living and had gotten pretty
good at it. She learned to live for the moment and not
worry about any consequences.

But when she realized she was getting old, she started
saving some money for herself. She quit selling her body
when she reached forty-five since nobody seemed to want
to buy her services any longer.

Then she turned to scavenging and did pretty good at that.

Her mother would have been so disappointed to know
how her only daughter turned out.

The time slipped by; Essie didn't notice the stops the bus
made until the driver called, "Wentworth," when he pulled
off the interstate and onto a side road that led to a truck stop.

Essie gripped her purse tightly and stood. Once she was
off, the driver handed her the cardboard suitcase she'd
bought for a buck when she got the purse. She clutched
the handbag close to her.

"This is as far as you go, lady. Wentworth's four miles
from here. Two miles to the north and two to the west on
County Highway X2F."

She thanked him and quick-shuffled away. She didn't like

the truck stop and hoped no would recognize her "bag-lady walk" in the boonies.

She found walking easy on the road's shoulder, but the October sun bore down on her, causing a sheet of sweat to form on her forehead. Off to her left, west she guessed, huge thunderheads with black clouds beneath them filled the sky. It looked as if it could rain. Wouldn't surprise her none of it did. She figured she'd walked almost two miles when she saw the road sign for Highway X2F.

Ten minutes later she turned onto the macadam road and headed west. The clouds seemed to race to meet her and, while she still had two miles to walk before she reached Wentworth, she knew the rain wouldn't hurt her. How many times had she picked through rubbish in the rain? She took off her coat and continued walking, thankful she hadn't worn her entire wardrobe the way she normally did. Sweat stood out on her forehead, and she knew it had to be at least a hundred—at least it felt like it.

The clouds moved overhead and seemed to hover there, waiting for her, waiting to vomit out their rain. Rumbles of thunder surrounded her, and Essie trembled.

She'd seen plenty of storms in the city, but being out in a place where there were no buildings she could duck into for protection, or people rushing by, scared the hell out of her. How could people not live in Chicago? She missed the man-made canyons.

Raindrops struck her in the face and the wind picked up, cooling her. A stand of cottonwood trees off to her right showed the backside of those leaves that hadn't yet blown down and when the rain picked up in its intensity, she clutched her cardboard suitcase to her body, for fear it would disintegrate.

The roar of thunder overhead scared the wits out of her. Lightning flashed from cloud to cloud until a sword of lightning seared toward the earth, scorching the air surrounding her.

Essie took one step to run, and the stink of burning ozone filled her nostrils. The bolt of lightning glanced off a cottonwood tree, shearing a huge branch before the spear careened across the road, enveloping her, and danced crazily to a huge rock, splitting it in two.

Essie collapsed and lay in a heap.

Minutes later, rain pelting her face, she opened her eyes and looked about.

"Am I dead?" she asked aloud. "Great God! What happened?" She moved a bit. Feeling no pain, she clambered to her feet and stood in the downpour, blinking her eyes in bewilderment. A buzzing rang in her head like a thousand doorbells and a million bees. Nothing like that had ever happened to her in the city. The damned countryside was dangerous. She looked around. It was almost dark and the rain continued falling. Maybe it would quit soon.

Where was her purse? She looked around and saw it under her suitcase. Her grip hadn't fallen apart, but it had to be soaked. Picking up her possessions, she checked her money and started walking in the same direction she had been going.

Then she noticed it. The road was no longer a blacktop surface. She looked back. The road behind her was a sea of mud, just like the stretch in front of her. What the hell was going on?

The rain eventually subsided until only a few drops fell and the late summerlike storm died. A timid moon tentatively peeked out from behind a bank of clouds and lighted the countryside.

That was another thing about the country that upset Essie. It was too dark. In Chicago, she could always count on the streetlights.

She walked as fast as she could and after she reached the top of a hill, stopped when she saw a light ahead. A small watertower stuck up above the trees that apparently indicated Wentworth was only a matter of a few hundred yards away. The closer she got, the more flickering lights she saw. Sure was nothing like State Street or any other place in the Loop.

She walked into the town, stopping when she reached an intersection. The streetlights, nothing more than exposed light bulbs, did little to show the houses huddling among the trees that hid them. To her right, she could see a small church, its fingerlike steeple pointing to heaven.

She felt like an intruder. A dog barked someplace as though warning the citizens, secure in their dry homes, that a wet bag lady had invaded their little town.

Hugging her purse between the suitcase and her body,

she turned left for no reason and walked down the street. She spotted a hotel sign in the weak light and went toward it.

Essie didn't like Wentworth. It was dark and quiet, and there weren't any big buildings around to make her feel at home. That, alone, was enough to drive a person crazy.

A movement inside caught her attention and she squinted, trying to make out what she'd seen. A man, holding a kerosene lamp, walked past the big window in front and stepped behind the desk. They must have had a power failure. But how could the street lights be burning?

Essie took a deep breath and slowly approached the front door. Gingerly reaching out, she turned the knob, hoping it wouldn't open and wouldn't have to go inside. Maybe she'd wake up and find herself back in the safety of her room. But the door swung in on well-oiled hinges and she stepped into the dry lobby.

The man looked up, a shocked expression on his face. "Go—good evening. I didn't hear you pull up."

"I—I ain't got a car," Essie said.

"You on the road?" the innkeeper asked, a suspicious look crossing his face.

"No. I got off the bus and walked into town. You got a room? How much is it?"

"I got a room. A dollar a night. In advance. Buck and a quarter if you want a bath." He stopped and studied Essie more closely. "Say, it's none of my business, but did you say you got off the bus and walked into town?"

Essie thought about the prices, decided she'd just washed up good the night before, and would save the quarter. "I'll take a room. And you're right. It's none of your business."

"Didn't mean to pry none, ma'am. It's just that there's only three buses a week and there ain't none due till day after tomorrow." He peered suspiciously at her over his horn-rimmed glasses.

Essie caught the suspicious tone in his voice. "I got off at the highway, and walked here."

The clerk pursed his lips and frowned. "Highway? What highway? Ain't no highway 'round here. What highway you talkin' 'bout?"

"Why, the four-lane interstate south of here. I guess that'd be the direction."

"You sure you're all right? You look sort of dazed, ma'am."

Essie ran a hand over her face. She felt all right. Just tired. The buzzing in her ears had lessened, and all she needed was a good night's sleep. Not the clerk's prattle.

"I'm okay," she said weakly. "Truth is, I almost got hit by lightning when I was walking along the road. Maybe I'm just a little mixed up."

The man's face softened. "Come on. I'll get you up to your room and you can register in the mornin'. You'll probably feel fine after a good night's sleep." He stepped from behind the desk, grabbed her suitcase, and holding the kerosene lamp in front of him, led Essie up the flight of stairs to the second floor.

He stopped at a door and unlocked it. Pushing it open, he stepped back and allowed Essie to enter. Following her in, he lighted the lamp on the bureau and stepped toward the door.

"How long you think the power'll be out?" Essie asked, concerned about having to reply on kerosene lamps for light.

"Power? What do you mean?"

Essie glanced around the room. No electrical outlets. Not even a single light bulb hanging from the ceiling like she had in her room in Chicago.

"Ain't you got no power in the house?"

"Lord, no. Someday, maybe. But not now. Where do you come from, anyway?"

"Chicago."

"In Illinois?"

Essie nodded.

"I guess you think we're a little backward, not havin' electricity, huh?"

Essie shrugged. "I just thought everybody had . . ."

"Not out here. Just a few street lights." He walked to the door and turned once more. "Forgot to tell you. The outhouse is in the back yard of the hotel if you need it. Men's on the left, ladies' on the right."

Essie shook her head after he closed the door. She'd always heard Iowa was a backward place—but an outhouse? Living like that was just plain stupid.

She undressed and laid her wet clothing on the floor to

dry. She found a washcloth and towels folded on the wash-stand and marveled that a hotel would have a priceless antique such as the pitcher and bowl set out in the room where anybody could steal it or break it.

The last thought ricocheting through her mind while she lay on the bed was hoping for good weather the next day.

Essie sat up in bed, feeling better, trying to sort through her sleep-fuzzed thoughts. When they focused sharply, she got up and put on her dress, thankful that it hadn't wrinkled too badly and walked out of the room clutching her rain-stiffened purse.

Dropping the key into her bag, she walked down to the lobby.

"Good morning," the same clerk said. "Did you sleep well?"

Essie nodded. "Where can I get something to eat?"

"Idy's got breakfast waiting for you in the dining room, ah, Miss—ah—Mrs.—"

"Pfeltgen. Esther Pfeltgen. Yours?"

"Graham. Ben Graham. Say, we got some Pfeltgens living in Wentworth. Kin of yours?"

Essie shrugged and followed him to the dining room. His wife carried in a pot of coffee.

"Say, would you like to make a visit to the outhouse before I dish up your food?" the woman asked.

Essie nodded and followed her to the kitchen.

After breakfast, Essie went to the lobby and laid a dollar bill on the desk.

Graham spun the registry around to let her sign her name.

She picked up the old-fashioned desk pen and slowly wrote her name, then the date, October 28, 1992. She turned the book back to the clerk.

Graham looked at her signature and smiled. "You made a mistake on the date, lady. It's 1929. Not 1992." He pointed to the calendar from the town bank on the wall behind him.

Essie stared at him, then at the calendar. It was actually printed 1929. What was going on? The guy was crazy. It was 1992 for crying out loud. She didn't want to get into an argument with him. Let him have his little joke. "Sorry 'bout that," she said and held her hand out for the pen. After fixing the date, she asked, "Where's the town cemetery?"

He looked at her in a peculiar way.

"I got folks buried there and want to pay their graves a visit."

"Oh." He gave her the directions and she left.

She walked back to the intersection and headed south, out of town, looking for a brick house on the left side of the road. That was where the caretaker lived. She could get directions to the graves there.

Walking up the steps to the front door, Essie hesitated, then lifted the doorbell. A grating bell-like sound tore through the early morning quiet.

The door opened and a thin, hawk-nosed woman confronted her. "Yes?"

"I want to find my parents' graves."

"What's the name?" she asked, unlocking the screen door.

Essie stepped into the cool hallway. "Pfeltgen. Leo and Marcella Pfeltgen."

The woman turned and walked into an office and opened a small file drawer. After several minutes passed, she said, "Lots 481 and 482."

Essie, standing in the doorway, felt her pulse quicken.

The woman turned and stared, her eyes boring into Essie. "Why you want to visit those graves? Ain't nobody buried in 'em."

Essie felt her jaw drop. "But—but there has to be. My parents are buried there."

"There's Pfeltgens livin' 'round here but Leo and Marcella are *not* buried where you said they should be. Leo and Marcella Pfeltgen live in Wentworth and—"

"My father died before my mother did and she died sometime after May 16, 1932."

"Don't you know the date of death?"

Essie shook her head. "I got a letter from her dated in 1932 and she was sick then. I was raised in Chicago. I—I never knew my folks."

The hawk-nosed woman's eyes softened a bit and she nodded. "I think you're jokin'. I know the Pfeltgens and

Marcella's pregnant right now, due sometime after the first of the year."

Essie could not believe what she heard. Her parents still alive? Her mother pregnant? That was impossible. Essie was sixty-two. It must be a coincidence. Another Pfeltgen couple with the same first names.

"You say you got a letter from your mother dated 1932?"

Essie nodded.

"What year is this?"

Essie looked at her. What was she driving at by asking that sort of . . . Of course. The clerk had said she'd written down the wrong date when she registered. It was 1992, and he thought it was 1929. Was everybody crazy in Wentworth? Rubbing her forehead, she thought of the way her head had hurt the night before. But that'd had to do with the near strike of lightning.

Her eyes widened. "I—I gotta go. Thanks." She turned and hurried out of the caretaker's house. She had to do some thinking about the whole situation. Something weird was happening.

She slowly walked back toward town. Church bells suddenly pealed across the countryside and she could see people walking through the intersection toward the little church. It wasn't Sunday. She'd left Chicago on Tuesday. That would mean it was Wednesday.

She half ran, half walked back to town and went to the hotel. She had to think. She also wanted to read her mother's letter again. Entering the deserted lobby, she quickly walked up the steps.

Once in her room, she took off her coat and sat down on the bed. After opening the envelope, she stopped. It looked whiter—much whiter for some reason. Dumping out the contents, the bank book fell to the bed. Nothing else. Where was the letter? She knew she had put the bank book and the letter inside. But the letter was gone. Turning the envelope over she found the front blank. Her name wasn't there. What in hell was happening?

She picked up the bank book and opened it. The pages were whiter than when she had first looked at it. What if the total had changed? She turned the page and found the last entry. The figure was the same.

She stared into space. What if it really were 1929—the way the clerk downstairs and the woman at the caretaker's house thought? Did that mean her folks were still alive? Did that mean the bank book might still be good? But how could any of that be? She was Essie Pfeltgen of Chicago, and she was sixty-two years old. She was born in 1930 and she— Wait. If that were the case and her mother wrote the letter to her in 1932, the letter couldn't exist yet. Could it? She smiled at her deduction. It made sense and at the same time seemed ridiculous.

And the only thing that had happened that was out of the ordinary was being almost struck by lightning. Had it anything to do with what was going on? That bolt had to be the reason for all the strange happenings.

Essie lay back on the bed and as suddenly sat up.

The next day was October 29, 1929. That was when the Depression started.

Why was she back in 1929? How had she gotten into such a mess? A cold sweat broke on her forehead. What if she could never get back to the year she came from— 1992? Why, the election was next month and she wanted to vote for that cute Clinton.

What if she were stuck in the past? Would she be born again next year in 1930? What then? When that Essie reached sixty-two, would she come back to Wentworth and go through the same things she was going through? Would it continue? How many Essie Pfeltgens could the world handle?

She had to do something before she went crazy. Maybe she could do something to change everything where she and her family were concerned. Her mother had written that they'd lost everything, and her father apparently had committed suicide. What if she could talk to her parents and convince them that they should withdraw their money from the bank? Maybe she'd wind up saving her parents' money, and her father wouldn't do away with himself if he . . .

She stopped in front of the mirror. "Good evening. I'm your daughter. I'm not born yet, but I *am* your daughter. I'd like you to take your money out of the bank here in Wentworth, because you're going to lose every goddamned cent you have. You're going to go crazy, Father, kill yourself after I'm born and make it so I have to grow up with your sister-in-law. I'll turn out to be a whore, Mother. Do you two want that for your daughter? Then, do what I tell you."

They'd believe her all right. Especially when she told them she was sixty-two and from the year 1992. Still, she felt she had to try.

She had to go to her parents that day or her life would be the same no matter what she did after that. She had to convince them to take their money out of the bank. Her father wouldn't commit suicide, and she'd be raised by her own parents in Wentworth, Iowa, and not become a whore in Chicago.

Essie looked outside. Dark. She had spent the whole afternoon in her room when she should have been with her parents. She smoothed her hair with a stroke or two of her hand and slipped her shoes on. When she reached the lobby, she asked for directions to the Lutheran church and left quickly. She hurried along the dirt street.

The unseasonably warm weather pressed in on her and sweat trickled from her armpits. She could see people sitting on front porches enjoying the summerlike evening. She turned onto the street west of the Lutheran Church. Her parents' home was only . . .

She stopped dead in her tracks. There on their front porch, two dark figures sat on a porch swing. Her parents. She stepped forward and walked up to the porch.

"Hello there," the man said. "Can I help you?"

Her father!

"Certainly is nice for this time of year, isn't it, ma'am?"

Essie nodded and coughed. She had to say something. But what? "Go—good evening. It *is* nice, isn't it?"

Leo Pfeltgen, her father, leaned forward to look more closely at the old woman who had walked up to his front porch. "You from 'round here? Don't recall ever seein' you before."

"Hush, Leo," Marcella said. "That isn't very polite. Good evening, ma'am."

Essie wanted to scream out who she was. *"I'm your daughter, Essie."* Instead, she managed to greet her mother.

"So where'd you say you was from?" Leo asked.

"I—I'm just passing through and thought I'd go for a walk. Chicago's my home—you know, in Illinois? It was too nice out to stay down at the hotel. Wentworth's a nice little town."

"We like it," Leo said. "It's a good little town. Friendly, conservative, and prosperous."

Essie wondered what sort of work her father had done. "What line of work you in, ah, Mr.—" It'd be terrible if she were talking to the wrong people.

"Names Pfeltgen. Leo Pfeltgen. And this is my wife, Marcella. What's your name?"

"Es—" She stopped. She had to use a last name other than her own. "Essie O'Brien."

"Essie?" Marcella said. "Is that a shortened form of something?"

"Esther."

Marcella turned to her husband. "Isn't that a beautiful name? And from the Bible, too." Facing Essie, she said, "I'm going to have a baby in late January. If it's a girl, I'm going to call her Esther. Would you mind?"

Essie shook her head. She as going to be named after herself. She shifted her weight from one foot to the other and fixed her attention on her father. "What do you do for a living in such a small town, Mr. Pfeltgen?"

"I run a feed mill."

"Is it a good business?"

Leo seemed to puff out his chest. "I been in it only six years and I'm the biggest miller in the county already."

Essie nodded. She wanted to ask him about his savings account, but how could she, out of the clear blue?"

" 'Course, I ain't foolish enough to tie up all my money in the business. Gotta have a reserve to make a person fluid."

Essie's heart leaped. "I—I don't know what you mean by fluid, Mr. Pfeltgen."

"I got a reserve of cash in the bank here in Wentworth. If business gets bad, or I need some new equipment, I always got some money to fall back on. See?"

Essie nodded.

"You gotta be fluid. The banker knows I got money and will lend me just about anything I need, based on that fact and the fact I got a good business."

Essie coughed and cleared her throat. "Mr. Pfeltgen, if I told you your bank might go bust—you know, go broke—

and that your bank book wouldn't be worth the paper it was written on after tomorrow, what would you do?"

Leo laughed. "Ain't likely to. No, ma'am. That little bank is as solid as my business."

"I'm just supposing," Essie said. "If you did know, would you take your money out?"

"I guess I might, if I knew for a fact, sure, 'cause Marcella and me need that nest egg to fall back on, what with a baby comin' and all. Gotta have money if you have a family. You got a family, Essie?"

Essie shook her head. "Not really."

"I'm sure Mrs. O'Brien isn't interested in our financial plans, Leo."

'Sorry, Miz O'Brien. What do you think of our boy from Iowa in the White House? You think he's doin' all right?"

Essie froze. Who the hell was president in 1929? "He's doing just fine, I guess." She wasn't getting anywhere. She might as well leave and turned away. "Well, I should be going. Think about what I said, Mr. Pfeltgen. If you decide to take your money out of the bank, don't wait. Do it first thing in the morning. Something awful is going to happen. A big depression is coming."

"A what?" Leo laughed. "Why things are probably more sound right now than they've ever been. The stock market is up and business is good. How can you say something like that? Why that's the silliest notion I've ever heard."

Essie slowly backed away from the porch. "I can't tell you how I know, but it's going to happen." She turned and walked away from the house, and a tear rolled down her cheek when her father continued laughing.

"If I take it out, I'd probably put it in the stock market," Leo called after her and laughed harder.

Essie hurried along the dark streets toward the hotel. She could have changed her entire life if she could have convinced them. But she'd failed. She felt terrible. She didn't belong in 1929. There was no place for her. But how could she get back to her own time and place?

Thoughts of her encounter with her parents pounded her mind. Disturbing thoughts, since she had no particular feelings about them one way or the other. It was just that she could have been born under different circumstances and could have grown up loving them and being loved in return.

But the people she'd met—Leo and Marcella Pfeltgen—may have, no would, become her parents, and they had been like any other people she might have met for the first time. There was nothing in her for them—no love, no hatred, no compassion. Just a feeling of nothing.

Was her own situation still to come in the future or was she stuck forever in the past? No matter. She was positive the next day would probably change the world and she'd always grow up to be a hooker. If only she could change something—anything—maybe things would change for her.

Without warning, a wave of nausea swept over her and a blackness closed in around her, smothering her senses. Clutching her throat, she fell to the road, gasping for breath.

Opening her eyes, Essie found the gray of predawn filtering in through the curtains and drawn shades. What had happened? She remembered walking and— She looked around. It seemed to be the same room but something was differ— The wallpaper. Much brighter. The furniture was different, too, and a light fixture hugged the ceiling where none had been earlier, The kerosene lamp was gone.

She closed her eyes. Did the change in furniture and the ceiling light mean . . . ?

She got off the bed and looked outside. An old Volkswagen sat in front of the hotel. She noted her legs didn't feel shaky anymore. Her purse stood wide open and she ran to it. Thank God! Her money was still there. The bank book, which she had put back in the purse, caught her attention and she pulled it out. It looked old again. She had to be back in 1992—where she belonged. She had to be in her own time. But what had happened? Had she dreamed the whole thing? The only way she'd ever know if she were in 1992 was to go back to Chicago. If her room was still there, she'd know.

After closing her suitcase, she went to the door and carefully opened it. She breathed easier. The stairway had been carpeted and she wouldn't make any noise going down. Halfway to the first floor, she saw the lobby had been turned into a living room and a blind television set occupied one corner.

Then she heard voices. She stiffened. She didn't want to

be caught when she was so close to getting away. She just wanted to get the hell out of there and back to her room in Chicago. The sound of voices drifted into the living room.

"I'll go up and check on her in a few minutes," a woman's voice said.

"I still think we should've called the sheriff," a man's voice said.

"I wonder who she is."

"Don't know."

'No. I mean what was she doing out in the street like that—laying there in a heap? Ain't never seen her around here before."

"Don't know."

"Well, I guess we'll just have to wait until she comes around 'fore we can find out. More coffee, Art?"

Essie tiptoed across the room and quietly opened the door. She opened it on quiet hinges and stepped outside. Once the door was closed, she breathed easier and hurried down the steps and quick-shuffled toward the intersection. When she reached it, she could see the blacktop road stretching toward the horizon. County X2F. She was back in 1992—she hoped.

When she passed the cemetery, the caretaker's house was nothing more than a burned shell. But she had been in there the day before. Should she take the time to find her parents' graves? Why? She'd spoken to them the previous evening. Granted they had only been shadows sitting on a front porch, but she'd spoken with them. All she wanted to do was get out of Wentworth.

She was used to walking and did her hurry-up shuffle and made her way to the road that would take her back to the truck stop. She continued her quick-shuffle and in less than two hours reached the service area.

When she saw the back end of a bus sticking out from behind the building, she broke into a run. A man walking to his car, which was parked near the bus, saw her coming toward him.

"Hold the bus!" she screamed at the top of her voice. "Hold the goddamned bus!"

The man turned and yelled something to the driver, who was not yet inside the vehicle.

Essie ran all the harder. "Where—where's this thing

going?'' she asked between puffs when she reached the driver.

"Cedar Rapids, Iowa City, Davenport, and Chicago,'' he said.

Essie handed him the stub of her return ticket and walked around him to board. She put her beaten-up cardboard suitcase in the rack over her seat and sat down, a bewildered sense of being tearing at her.

After leaving the depot, Essie caught a city bus to her neighborhood and walked the last three blocks humming aimlessly. She actually felt good. She felt none the worse for wear and tear.

All her life she had cursed her luck after her Aunt Tillie had died. Maybe she didn't have to curse her luck anymore. And she didn't have to stay in that dump she'd been raised in and had hung on to for what she had thought were sentimental reasons. After all, she had money. She didn't have to scavenge for a living. There had been something about Wentworth she had found comforting, despite her harrowing experience with the bolt of lightning.

It wasn't too late for her to enjoy life.

When she reached the broken concrete steps to her building, she stopped and looked up at the facade of the building. What a dump. She mounted the steps, careful not to slip on the rounded edges. A single forty-watt bulb hung from the ceiling, lighting the entryway.

For the first time in her life, she noticed the stench clinging to the building's interior. She squinted until her eyes adjusted and caught a movement off to one side. She shrank back at the sight of a huge rat sitting on its haunches, its nose sniffing. The animal, used to humans, stared at her but didn't move when Essie stepped toward it.

With more resolution than she had ever mustered before in her life, she brought her heel down hard and smashed the rodent's head to a pulp. She smiled.

Turning, she went to the stairs and marched up to the second floor and her room. Yessir. She'd do something about her situation.

By God, she'd move—tomorrow.

DEMON DRINK
Kate Novak-Grubb

"Our home was full of spirits," Cass stated. "There were muses everywhere."

Mother Una said, "That's not surprising. Everyone in your family was bright and talented."

"Not just muses," Cass explained. "There were demons, too."

The priestess nodded as she poured the tea into the cups. She had spoken in a sermon once of a demon in her own childhood home. Holding the demon up to the light of day had not made it vanish, but it had weakened it. Not everyone in the parish had been pleased to see the ugly thing, but Cass had viewed it with some interest. Una hadn't thought at the time that showing off a weakened demon would mean so much to this girl.

"I just didn't see them," Cass continued. "Terry always said they were there, but I didn't see them."

"Terry is your younger sister?" Mother Una asked. She handed Cass a teacup.

Cass nodded. "I used to blame her, I thought if she would just stop seeing the demons, they would go away. But she insisted they were there, that they belonged to our parents. She even brought new ones into the house. She played awful games with them, and they slept with her, teased and pinched her all night." Cass focused on her tea, blowing across the surface a few times. The teacups were so lovely, so balanced, too delicate to hold near a demon. She looked up at the priestess. "Terry couldn't keep the demons away." Cass shrugged. "Back then I thought Terry was just dumb. I didn't know how hard it could be to make them go away once you got a good look at even one of them."

"You said you didn't see these demons, but you saw your

sister playing with them?" Mother Una asked, trying to clarify the girl's story.

"I saw the way they made her act. I suspected she played with drinking demons and drug demons, but I didn't go looking for them."

"And your parents didn't see them?"

"They couldn't even see their own demons. But sometimes I had to work at not seeing them. That's why I played with so many muses." Cass's eyes brightened thinking about the muses of her childhood, how they gobbled up the crumbs about the hearth, chattered in the bookshelves, danced about the musical instruments and songsheets. "If I ever caught a glimpse of a demon, I went looking right away for a muse—one big enough to swat away the demon if it followed me. Sometimes I went to Nan's or Jesse's," she explained. Nan's house, she remembered, had been cluttered with thin, pastel muses who rolled in the bolts of fabric and sniffed at the tubes of paint, and in Jesse's backyard short, gnomish muses banged on the engines needing tunings.

"I didn't want to see the demons. They were so ugly, so boring, so . . . so vulgar. The muses were lovely, interesting, above it all. I was such a coward, such a snob."

"It's a natural reaction to deny they exist," Mother Una said. "No one wants the shame. Everyone tries to hide them."

"My father had a drinking demon. When my father drank, it was like the things you talked about before. He was silly. He laughed too loud. He was twice as arrogant. He argued with shouts and curses and pounding on the table. He fell asleep with guests still at the table or in front of the entertainers. Sometimes it was embarrassing, but not . . . frightening."

"What was frightening?" the priestess asked.

"My mother's demons," Cass whispered, "because they made her cry."

"Crying was bad?" Una asked.

Cass shook her head. "No. Not that. My mother was so strong. So smart. So perfect. If they could make her cry, they had to be terrible demons. Terry said mother had a drinking demon, but there were other demons, too. The kind that grew on anguish and regret and anger. I know they say those demons all feed on the drinking demon, but it doesn't mean they aren't real demons."

Una shook her head. "They become tangled, but they aren't all the same," she agreed.

"I only remember seeing them twice as a child, and if I saw them again, I've forgotten and I don't want to remember."

The priestess waited patiently for the girl to continue.

Cass set down the teacup and leaned back in the rocking chair. "The first time was when I was thirteen or fourteen," she explained. "I remember I was getting ready for school. I went into my parents' bedroom. I don't remember why. Maybe to ask my mother to sign an excuse or maybe to just to kiss her good-bye. She was still in bed. It was a time she slept a lot, which wasn't like her." Cass shuddered.

"And she was crying?" Una asked.

"I don't remember," Cass said. "I just remember the darkness over her, pressing her into the bed. She rolled away from me and she said that she wished she were dead."

"What did you do?"

"I left. I didn't know what to say, or what to do. So I just left. I felt horrible. Afraid that she meant it, afraid that it was my fault."

"You didn't tell anyone?"

Cass shook her head.

"Not even your father."

"I didn't talk about things like that to my father. I didn't think he'd care."

"Not care about your mother?"

"Not care about her pain. He acted as if people's sadness was weakness. Demons were something you ignored."

"Then what happened?"

Cass shrugged. "My mother got better, I guess. For a while. She'd gone back to barding. She told the most wonderful stories. She talked a lot about how stories were made. Maybe she wasn't always better. I don't know for sure since I spent less time home as I got older. I took jobs nannying and cleaning for the manor folk and lived away for a while."

"You said there was a second time as a child that you saw your mother's demons."

Cass nodded. "I was courting a boy. I guess I wasn't really a child anymore. Maybe that was the night I stopped

feeling like a child. I was out all night. All we did was talk,
this boy and I, but it was nearly dawn when I got home.
My parents never waited up for me. Still, I thought I'd be
in trouble. My mother was in the library—that's where she
slept when she and my father stopped sleeping together.
She was sitting up with a blanket wrapped around her, crying. I told her I was sorry for coming in so late. She didn't
answer—just kept crying, not loud enough to wake anyone,
but really hard, sobbing, her body shaking.''

Cass sniffed and brushed hot tears from her cheeks before she could continue. ''I could smell the wine then, a
horrible alcohol breath odor, and the empty jug at her side.
I looked away, but not fast enough not to see the demon.
The drinking demon or the anguish demon or maybe both
all intertwined. There were all these claws hooked into my
mother's bathrobe and a barbed tail wrapped around her
arm, and she held this horrible lump to her chest. It looked
like a malformed infant, blue from asphyxiation. It raised
a head from beneath an arm and hissed at me. It had sharp
white teeth. It said, *'You're not her baby anymore. She
nurses **me** now.'* It spat at me, leaving this yellow glob on
my shirt. I backed away and tiptoed to my room, tried to
sleep. Ever since, I've tried to keep the muses around me
tighter so I don't see the demons—''

''But the glob grew,'' Una noted.

Cass looked down with disgust at the jaundiced cat-sized
creature on her chest. She couldn't show it to just anyone,
but she knew the priestess could see it, could understand
it, could look at it without flinching. It hung upside down,
with its tail around her throat, its claw near her heart and
its teeth buried in her stomach.

''Terry left with her demons, took a job in another state.
My father stopped coming home every night, then he left
with all his demons. They left me with this demon. Some
days my mother is everything she's ever been. So brilliant,
so warm. Some nights she's nursing that awful blue thing,
its claws tearing at her flesh, its ugly purple tongue licking
at her tears. On those nights this thing grows,'' the girl
explained, hugging the yellow demon. ''It grows out of my
belly, and I can't ignore it. It whispers, *'What a useless
daughter you are. Just like your father. Unable to make your
mother happy. Too weak to yank that blue demon off of*

her.' All night long it whispers." Her voice trailed off as she touched the demon's head.

She looked up suddenly and announced, "Matthew wants me to come with him to another city to wed. He's seen my mother's demon. He's seen this thing on me. He thinks I can leave it behind, but I can't get it off me."

"You know you can't fight other people's demons for them," Mother Una said.

"That's what everyone says," Cass answered, but the yellow demon hummed in her belly and she hugged it closer.

"It will grow bigger and bigger," the priestess said. "Do you want to carry it around forever?"

"I want to drown it in a well," Cass whispered with a fierce hatred.

"That doesn't make you evil," Una insisted.

"It doesn't make me good," the girl argued.

"It makes you human. There are limits to what you can do. You have to accept that." She pointed to one of her own demons curled like a dust ball under the spinning wheel. It was the same color as Cass's but only mouse-sized, shrunken with age.

"Leave it up to the gods, you're saying?" Cass asked.

Una knew that was impossible for Cass to accept since the girl didn't have faith in gods. "I'm saying accept your limitations. Your mother must find her own way."

Cass' faith in people, and her faith in Una was enough for the moment. The yellow demon on her chest lost its grip and slid to the floor. It shrieked angrily, and tried to climb back up, but Cass kicked at it once, so it crouched in a corner. She talked longer with the priestess about friends and muses and books, until the sun began to sink. Una waved from the doorway as Cass strolled from the priestess' cottage. Cass' yellow demon scurried after her, but did not grab hold of her again.

Cass left with Matthew, fleeing her mother's demon, returning to visit her mother only once or twice a year. She would visit Mother Una then, too. Eight years passed before Cass reported that her mother had wrenched the blue demon away from her body. It was something that no one could do for her. The beast had nearly killed her, but for now it was subdued.

According to the lore of demons, though, demons never

go away. They hover about your face like flies, or paw at your knees like begging dogs, or sit in a corner glaring like a jealous cat. Some people learn the trick of keeping them at bay with faith and muses, but first you have to really see them, admit that they're real, share them with a friend.

LOOK YOU ON BEAUTY AND DEATH
by James and Livia Reasoner

Cheat death a few times and you get cocky.

The whisper of steel cutting through the air was all the warning I had as I sat at a table, staring into a flagon of ale. I dove sideways onto the wooden floor of the tavern, rolling and reaching for my sword, as a blade sliced through the space where my head had been an instant before.

My sword hissed out of its sheath as I came up on one knee and turned my shoulders to face the attack. Three men crowded toward me, bunched stupidly together so that they had little room to swing the heavy broadswords they carried. Still crouched amidst the sawdust and spilled ale, I leaned forward and thrust my blade at the one in the lead.

He gasped as it plunged into his belly, and his eyes widened in pain and surprise.

I pulled my sword free and let the dead man slip to the floor so that he blocked the path of his companions for a second. That was all the time I needed to regain my feet. I faced the remaining two and let a smile touch my lips as the point of my blade weaved a tiny dance in the air. They pushed the dead one aside but hesitated before rushing me again.

My sword was lighter than theirs, and I knew that a well-aimed swipe by one of the heavy weapons could leave me defenseless. But at the same time, I was faster, and the kiss of my steel was equally deadly.

"Lay down your sword," one of them growled through his beard, "and we'll make your end quick and painless, woman."

I shook my head and kept smiling at them.

So far their exertion had been slight, but still their chests heaved as they gulped in lungfuls of the smoky air. Fear was on them, and that swung the advantage to me.

I knew that I could kill them. I had faced men like this before, and all of them had gone down before my sword. They were afraid of me, and they were mine.

And that knowledge was nearly my undoing.

Feeling confident now, I let my attention stray. My gaze darted around the room and took in the scene. I was playing to an audience, especially to a pair of handsome soldiers in the corner, and I wanted to be sure that they fully appreciated what they were seeing.

The two would-be assassins saw my concentration slipping and lunged forward. I dropped my right shoulder and my head, and lost only a lock of hair to a hastily swung blade. Pivoting to make myself a smaller target, I flipped my wrist and sent the point of my sword raking across a throat. A crimson flood filled the man's beard, and droplets fell from the tips of the tangled hair. He staggered and fell.

And got in the way of my thrust at the last one. He was luckier than me, and I felt his blade rip tunic and skin on the top of my left shoulder. But then I was darting inside his reach and driving my sword against his chest.

There was a layer of heavy leather beneath his furs, and for a moment, my weapon was denied. I threw all my strength into the effort as he tried to slash my back with his sword, and then my blade sliced through and slid all the way to his heart. His deep-set eyes bulged and then glazed, and his sword fell to the floor with a clatter. He sagged against me; his last breath expelled hotly into my face. I shoved him away and pulled my sword free. He sprawled lifelessly on the floor next to his luckless companions.

Someone had lied to these men. Someone had told them that I was only a woman, that I would be easy to kill. They obviously had no idea who I really was. The other patrons of the tavern knew me, though, knew me to be the personal bodyguard to Empress Zora.

I knelt and wiped my blade clean on the furs of the nearest dead man, then sheathed the weapon and faced the crowd. *Look you on beauty and death,* I thought immodestly. Fat merchants in fine silks, nearly nude serving girls in bracelets and baubles, unwashed brigands from the hills in rank furs . . . All of them staring at the warrior-woman who was myself, resplendent in the tunic and breeches that made up the uniform of the Empress' service. Ah, no wonder they were impressed. Avenging angel, I was, wielder of the sword, bringer of the darkness, goddess of eternal death—

Long-winded fool.

The soldiers I had noticed earlier lifted their tankards of wine in mock-salute. They had not interfered with the battle, knowing that to do so might have made me turn on *them.* The wound on my shoulder was throbbing, but my face still wore the same self-assured smile that it had borne all through the brief battle.

"Someone haul these foolish dogs away," I said. I reached into the pocket of my tunic and withdrew a coin which I flipped in the general direction of the tavern keeper. "Already their stench makes it impossible to enjoy a flagon of ale. Pleasant evening, all."

I then turned and strode out the door, into the frost-tinged night.

I paused outside and rolled my shoulder in an attempt to ease the pain of the wound. It was not serious, but I hoped that I wouldn't have to defend myself again any time soon. I knew that the personal physician of the Empress would be glad to bind it up when I returned to my quarters in the palace, and then some rest would be all that was required further.

I was not looking forward to the reaction of Captain Galvor, the head of the Empress' guards, when he discovered that I had gotten into a fight while I was off-duty. One of the brief and infrequent times when I was off-duty, I might add. Being bodyguard to the Empress is a time-consuming task, indeed.

I drew in a long breath of the chilly air and blinked in revulsion. Never would I return to the hills that had been my childhood home, at least not willingly and not to stay, but there were disadvantages to living in the city, too. The stench of too many people living too close together reached everywhere. To someone who remembered what clean air was like, the smell of the city was a constant, nagging irritant.

Whether it stunk or not, the city was home to me now. Better that than a short, hard life spent as the woman of some oafish farmer or hunter.

"Ralna . . . Ralna . . ."

The choked, shuddery whisper came from somewhere behind me. I spun around, and my hand went to my sword as I sought the source of that hoarse plea. Lights in the city were few at night, and shadows cloaked the street. I peered into the darkness.

"Who calls my name?" I demanded harshly. "Here I am. Show yourself."

Still the whisper floated to me. "Ralna . . ."

Then there was a bubbling cough, and I knew by the sound that whoever called my name was not long for this world.

I stepped away from the glow of illumination coming from the door to the tavern. My sword was clutched tightly in my hand, and I was ready for anything.

Or so I thought.

"Ral—"

The voice came from the cobblestone street at my feet, and it broke off in the middle of my name as the toe of my boot met something soft and yielding. I knelt and thrust out my free hand. My fingers found a fur-clad form, then touched sticky wetness.

"Who. . . ?" I breathed. The wound on my shoulder was forgotten now.

"Ralna?" The voice was so low that I barely heard my name spoken again. Something about the tone was familiar. Quickly, I ran my hand over the sprawled form and discovered that it was a man, a man with a grievous wound in his chest.

There seemed to be no danger here. I turned my head and shouted, "Ho! Someone in the tavern. Bring a torch out here!"

Everyone who knew who I was knew that it was wise to obey my commands. The tavern keeper scuttled out of his establishment a moment later, bearing a torch in his hand. Several curious onlookers followed him.

As the glow of the torch fell over me and spread into a circle on the grimy street, I got my first look at the wounded man. I couldn't suppress a sharp intake of breath as recognition hit me.

"Vorn!" I exclaimed. "What . . . what are you doing here?"

The man lying at my feet, bright red life welling from

the wound in his chest, was old and white-haired. Even
injured, the air of sturdiness that had always been about
him prevailed. On the edge of death, he was, but grim
purpose filled his eyes and etched more lines on his aged
face.

I had last seen him three years before, on the day that I
left the hills for all time.

His hand caught my arm, and I felt his rapidly ebbing
strength. "Ralna," he gasped. "Praise be to the gods! I was
afraid . . . afraid that I would die . . . before I found you."

"You'll not die," I told him, and knew I was lying. He
knew it, too. There was no point in sending for assistance;
he had only moments left. The important thing was finding
out why he was here. "You have a message for me?" I
guessed.

"Your father . . . sent me here," Vorn said. "Sent me
to . . . bring you back."

I had to strain to make out his words. None of the crowd
from the tavern spoke, and I was glad that their usual rau-
cousness was under control.

"To take me back? Back to the hills?" My father was
the elder of our village, and Vorn his friend and assistant.
It was common for my father to send Vorn on errands. But
to send him to the city, this was not common at all. And
my father knew how I felt about the hills. He knew I would
not return unless it was on the command of the Empress,
as part of my duties.

Vorn summoned up his strength and nodded. "Your father wanted you to come back . . . But before I could find
you, three men . . . three men attacked me. Treacherous
dogs . . . !"

I thought I knew the three he meant. "Big men, bearded,
in furs?"

Once more he nodded. His breath alternately rasped and
bubbled in his throat. "Don't know why . . ." he managed
to say. "No reason to kill me . . ."

"Why were you sent for me?" I insisted. "Why does my
father want me to come back?"

Vorn forced his lips into a smile. "For the wedding," he
said, his voice suddenly clear. "Your sister Mardith's
wedding . . ."

That was all the strength left in him. His head fell to the side, and his chest stopped rising and falling.

I felt as dazed as if the flat of a blade had struck a ringing blow against my head. Mardith . . . about to be married? She was only a child! But even a child would have more sense than that, I told myself. I couldn't imagine Mardith, beautiful, innocent, spritelike Mardith, tied to some burly, sweating ground grubber. And that was the only kind of man to be found in the hills, other than thieves and out-laws.

The pain of Vorn's death, the death of an old friend, hadn't even registered yet. One undeniable thought sprang into my brain.

He had been killed because he was on his way to see me. I had already felt the coin pouch concealed beneath his furs. He hadn't been murdered by some street robbers.

And then his killers had come to find me. They were taking no chances, those three. Kill the messenger, then kill the one for whom the message was intended.

What was there about such a simple message—about being summoned to my sister's wedding, for the gods' sake—that had led to murder?

The answer to that question was somewhere in the hills, and I knew with a sudden sinking of my heart that I would be going back there, after all, and not as the Empress' bodyguard.

I closed Vorn's eyes, staring in death now, and stood up. "My vengeance for your murder has only begun," I promised him. I took another deep breath and didn't notice the stink of the city this time. "Are those three still inside?" I asked the tavern keeper.

He nodded, clearly puzzled by my question.

I went back into the tavern and cut their heads off, one by one. Wherever they were now, I hoped they felt it.

The hills never change.

The city was far behind me by the time the sun rose the next morning. Captain Galvor had not wanted to let me leave, but the Empress herself had overheard the concern in my voice and overruled the captain without even asking me for an explanation. Having a reputation for saving the Empress' life comes in handy sometimes. I had ridden all night and should have been tired, but somehow I was staying ahead of weariness. It was not far to my village now.

My village. No more. The place where I had grown up, perhaps, but no longer mine, through my own choice. I remembered the first time I had come to the edge of the hills at night and looked out across the flat land. Far, far away, I had seen the feeble glow of the city's lights, and I had known then that someday I would go there. Someday I would leave these bleak hills, with their promises only of hardship and death, behind.

But now I was returning, breaking my vow. Because an old man had been cruelly murdered, I told myself. That was the only reason.

Beyond the band of hills rose the mountains, a towering range that no one had ever crossed, to my knowledge. The mountains ran as far north and south as anyone had ever ventured. I had heard the young men boast, both in the hills and in the city, that they would someday cross the mountains and find out what was on the other side. Myself, I felt no burning need to know. There was world enough for me on this side.

I had seen the mountains. They were cold, unliving things. At least there was some vegetation in the hills, scrubby and thorny though it was. With hard work and luck, you could scratch out the bare necessities of life from the ground here. People aged quickly and died young in the hills.

Poor Mardith, doomed to such a life . . .

My horse crested a rise, and I reined in. Below me, in a small valley cut by the trickle of a tiny stream, lay the village. I caught my breath as I saw the little huts, unchanged in the last three years, shabbily constructed of the only building materials available out here, mud and brush. They clustered around the larger structure in the center of the village, a place I well remembered. The home of the village elder—my father—as well as the gathering place for any important happening.

Like a wedding.

A certain strangeness about the village struck me then. I saw no people going about their business, not even any of the mongrel dogs that infested the place. Bumping my horse with my heels, I sent her down the gentle slope into the valley. Despite my antipathy toward this place, I was frowning in curiosity.

It looked deserted . . . almost dead.

The sound of the horse's hoofbeats as I galloped up to the center of the village changed things. Heads popped out of doors, and I saw momentary terror etched on the faces that peered at me. Then relief flooded them. Voices were raised in cries of greeting, and people began to appear from the huts.

I pulled my mount to a stop in front of the entrance to the central hut. As I patiently sat the saddle, the curtain over the entrance was pushed back, and I saw the stern face of my father peering out at me.

"So you came," he said quietly. "I told Vorn you would not, but I had to send for you anyway." He looked past me. "Where is Vorn?"

"Dead in the city," I answered. "I gave instructions for his ashes to be sent back here." My voice was cold and flat.

My father paled, but that was the only indication of his shock at the news of his old friend's death. "The city is an evil place," he said simply. "I suppose thieves killed him for the coins he carried, or for his furs."

"No. He was killed because you sent him to find me."

I saw the stunned surprise in his eyes at this revelation, and I was glad. When you send a man walking blindly into death, you have to shoulder that responsibility.

"I didn't know . . . I didn't think things would go that far."

I swung out of the saddle and dropped to the ground. "Then you were wrong. Tell me why you summoned me."

Before he could answer, a smaller form crowded past him in the doorway. Mardith darted out of the hut and threw herself into my arms. "Ralna!" she cried. "You came! You really came!"

Awkwardly, I stroked her long blonde hair and hugged her to me. The years had changed her; she was no longer a child. She was instead a young woman, more beautiful than ever. Much too beautiful for these surroundings, like a bright flower amid gray, lifeless stones. She buried her face against my shoulder and held me tightly.

Little sister, sweet little sister . . . What in the name of all the devils and all the gods is going on here?

"What's this I hear about you getting married?" I asked, a smile on my face.

I expected the bubbling, love-blinded answer of a child caught up in her emotions. Instead, Mardith shivered, and a sob wracked her. "You've got to stop him!" she whispered raggedly. "You can't let him do it, Ralna!"

I patted her on the back and looked over her head at my father. His face was hard and composed once more. "Welcome, daughter," he said stiffly, formally. "Come into the hut."

Mardith's tears dampened my tunic. "It'll be all right, little one," I told her. "You don't have to do anything you don't want to do."

My father turned on his heel as I spoke. He stalked into the hut. With one arm around Mardith, I followed him, pulling the curtain closed behind me. The three of us went into the hut's main chamber. A small fire burned in the center of the room, the smoke curling up to the ceiling and out through the little hole there.

I had seen and heard enough outside to know what was going on. "You're forcing her to marry someone she doesn't want to, aren't you?" I accused.

My father shook his head. "I wish it were that simple, daughter. I'm not forcing her to do anything. Grond is."

"And who the devil is Grond?" I felt Mardith shudder as I spoke the name.

My father took a long breath before answering. "Grond is a man . . . I think. And he wants to marry Mardith."

"What does that mean? You *think* he's a man."

"He's a demon!" Mardith burst out. "A wizard! You've got to kill him, Ralna!"

I nodded slowly as I began to understand. "A wizard, is he? And what makes you think he's a wizard?" I had never met a wizard myself, though I had heard all the stories about them, and I wasn't sure if I believed in them or not.

"He's able to do things, things that—" My father broke off and paused for a moment. "Let me start at the beginning," he finally went on. "Grond . . . well, *appeared* is the only way I can describe it, several months ago. He wanted food and water, and he said he was a traveler who had lost his way through the mountains. He said . . . he said he came from the other side of the mountains." Awe was plainly evident in my father's voice.

"Quite possible," I said calmly. "We've never seen the other side of the mountains. There could be people there. Normal people like us. Or does this Grond have three heads and a tail?"

Anger flared briefly in my father's eyes. "You were always full of mockery, Ralna, but know you this: there are some things beyond even your understanding."

"That there are," I replied. "Such as why Mardith stays here and doesn't leave."

"I don't want to leave," she said softly. "I like it in the hills, Ralna. I know you don't, but I do. But I don't want to marry Grond!"

I tightened my arm about her shoulders in reassurance, then looked back at my father. "You said Grond can do things. What sort of things?"

"Naturally, when he came here, we offered him food, water, and shelter. We are a hospitable people, after all." There was a touch of pride in my father's voice, but it disappeared rapidly as he went on. "Grond wasn't satisfied with what we offered, though. He wanted more. He wanted all the supplies we had laid in. When we tried to stop him . . . he summoned a—a demon."

"What sort of demon?" I couldn't keep the disbelief out of my voice.

"An earth-demon," Mardith answered breathlessly. "A shape like a man came up out of the ground and attacked the village. It killed three of the men, and Grond took all of our food."

"Most of our food," my father corrected. "He left us barely enough for subsistence. But that was only because he wants us to work for him, to supply him with what he needs. And now he has decided that he . . . needs Mardith."

"Even a wizard needs a woman, he says." Mardith's voice quivered.

"Well, he can't have this one," I declared. "You sent Vorn for me because you thought I could slay this Grond, am I right?"

My father spread his hands. "You know that we're simple, peace-loving folk, Ralna. Only someone like you—"

"An aberration," I put in sharply. "A freak."

"Your words, daughter, not mine. We hoped that you could . . . deal with this situation."

"And if I can't?"

He shrugged. "Then Mardith shall have to marry Grond." She gave a little cry at his words, but he went on, "We have no other choice. I will not allow our village to be destroyed."

As far as I was concerned, there was little in this village worth saving, but Mardith . . . that was different. I couldn't ride back to the city and leave her to face the lecherous caresses of some slimy would-be wizard.

Besides, I wanted to meet this Grond. I was willing to wager that even a wizard couldn't stand up to cold steel.

"Where can I find Grond?" I asked.

My father didn't want Mardith to show me the way, but she insisted. "Ralna is willing to risk her life for me . . . for all of us in the village. I . . . I want to help her if I can."

She had swung awkwardly into the saddle, her long robes making such a maneuver difficult, and I could tell by the look on her face that the big, gentle plow horse frightened her. My horse was used to my weight alone and might well balk at carrying two people.

We rode out of the village and headed west, deeper into the hills. "Grond has raised a mighty fortress," Mardith told me. "It is a fine palace, worthy of a powerful wizard."

"Or so Grond says," I guessed. "You have no need to fear this man, Mardith," I went on. "He'll bleed, like any other man, when he feels the bite of my blade."

"Have you . . . killed many men, Ralna?"

"I am bodyguard to the Empress, child, a duty from which I am now sorely missed, I'd vow. 'Tis my job to bring death to any who would molest her."

She looked away then, would not meet my eyes. "I do not believe I could kill. Not even Grond."

"That's why I'm here."

We rode in silence for a few minutes. When Mardith finally spoke again, it was of mundane things. She told me of her day-to-day life in the village, and I could tell by the sound of her voice that she had no qualms about remaining there for the rest of her days. The dull routine she described in such cheerful tones would have driven me mad in less than a month, especially since I had been exposed to the fine cutting edge of life in the city.

As we emerged from a cleft between two ridges, she suddenly fell silent and pointed upward. "There," she breathed. "The fortress of Grond."

My eyes followed her gesture and found our destination. Perched on a higher hill so that it surveyed a commanding field of fire, Grond's fortress loomed over us. Fortress, or wizard's palace, or whatever you want to call it, to me it was only a large stone hut made of blocks quarried somewhere in the mountains. Sturdy and functional, but hardly the imposing, ornate edifice I had been led to expect. Still, to anyone accustomed to the simple dwellings in the village, it had to appear magnificent.

"I see the path," I told Mardith. "You can return to the village now."

"I . . . I can take you farther." But her voice shook as she spoke, and I knew she was terrified by the mere sight of the place.

"No need. The trail is easy and well-marked. I can find my way." I spoke the truth. The path rose gently up the slope and led directly to the door of the fortress.

"Well . . . if you're sure . . ."

I spurred my horse ahead and then turned to look over my shoulder at her. "When next I see you," I promised, "the mighty wizard Grond will be nothing but an empty, lifeless husk."

Bold words. I said them in a loud voice, and suddenly a cold formless thing moved along my spine. I stiffened involuntarily, then hoped that Mardith hadn't seen my reaction.

Ralna, you spend too much time making dramatic pronouncements, I told myself. I wheeled the horse, kicked it into a gallop, and raced up the path toward the fortress of Grond.

I didn't look back.

When I drew up in front of the massive iron door, I slipped my sword from its sheath and used the hilt to pound on the panel. "Grond!" I called as the blows echoed ringingly throughout the structure. "Come out and meet your fate, wizard!"

A small man, balding and bearded and clad in long, som-

ber robes, sauntered out of the door and peered up at me
with watery blue eyes. He smiled. "You must be Ralna,"
he said in a mild voice. "I've heard a lot about you."

He was within head-lopping range. "Prepare to die, wizard!" I drew back my sword. I had to strike quickly, before
he had a chance to work any of his arcane magicks.

I wasn't fast enough. He raised a hand and extended it
toward me, palm out. I had launched my sword in a mighty
slash, but suddenly it was as if the blade was mired in thick
mud. The blow reached its target, but so slowly that Grond
had ample time to duck beneath it.

He stepped back a pace and lifted both hands. I felt
something gripping me, something like a giant fist, tangible
but utterly invisible. Many times had I felt the grasp of a
physical enemy. To be held by . . . *nothingness* . . . was
both frustrating—and unnerving.

"Now just hold it," Grond said quietly. "There's no need
for all this barbarian posturing."

His odd, over-mountain phrasing grated harshly on my
ears. I found that my voice was unaffected by his spell.
"Monster!" I hissed at him. "Release me from your unholy
power, and you'll see how much posturing I do!"

He shook a finger at me and scowled. I expected to be
struck dead, but nothing happened. "I don't understand
you people," he said, his voice full of exasperation and
annoyance. "You don't seem to realize that you're dealing
with powers far beyond your comprehension here. All I
want is the respect and homage accorded to any wizard."

"Lizard is a better word for you," I grated. "How dare
you demand that my sister marry you."

He shrugged. "What can I say? I like her; she's the love-
liest woman around here, and I deserve the best, after all.
And as the wife of a wizard, she'd have a lot easier life
than if she stayed in that village. What a depressing place
that is."

I couldn't argue with his last statement. I just wished that
his power would wane, if only for a instant. That would
be all the time I needed to separate his head from his
scrawny shoulders.

He seemed to want to talk, to bring me around to his
way of thinking. Stalling for time and seeking to satisfy my

own curiosity, I asked, "Do you really come from the other side of the mountains?"

"Of course I do. Do you think I lied to the people in the village?"

"Are all the people in your land wizards?"

"No, just a lucky few like myself." His eyes rolled toward the heavens. "And across the mountains, people know how to treat a wizard. They meet his every need, instead of sending for some cold-blooded warrior to kill him. And in turn, the wizards take care of their people." He glanced around disdainfully at the hills. "You won't find places like this across the mountains. There, there is water in abundance, and the soil is fertile. Everywhere you look, there are fine crops."

"And you could do this . . . here?" Even under the paralyzing power of his spell, I felt my breath coming quicker with excitement.

"Certainly I could. It's simple. All you need is a few weather-controlling spells." His face and voice hardened. "But I won't. Not for a bunch of petty troublemakers." He spat on the hard ground. "Didn't want to give me their food, don't want to give me that girl Mardith . . . Why, they even sent for you! If I hadn't been listening in to their plans. . . !" His voice went up in a mockery of the villagers. *"Ralna can kill him, let's send for Ralna. Ralna will slay the evil wizard.* From the way they were talking, I expected somebody ten feet tall."

"Think you not that I am any less deadly because I'm a woman," I told him. "I can wield a blade the equal of any man."

"I know, I know. Otherwise you wouldn't even be here."

"Then you admit that you hired those three men to kill Vorn and then to dispatch me?"

He shook his head. "A wizard does not *hire* his lackeys. There were three outlaws passing through the vicinity. I merely made use of them."

So they hadn't come to the city of their own volition, hadn't killed Vorn and tried to kill me because they were being paid for the task. For an instant, I felt slightly guilty about cutting off their heads, but the feeling passed quickly. There were more important things to worry about.

"And now you intend to kill me? What will you do,

wizard, summon another earth-demon like you did in the village?"

"What earth-demon? I called up a whirlwind and some of those stupid villagers swallowed too much sand and choked. You'd think they'd have enough sense to keep their mouths shut."

Anger boiled up in me at his callous words. "You think you're above good and evil just because you're a wizard!" I snapped at him. "You're not, though. You are a vile and treacherous toad! Release me and I'll squash the life out of you!"

"Sorry. Can't do it. No, I'm afraid you have to die, Ralna. Even if you promised to go away and leave me alone, I wouldn't believe you. Oh, I know you warriors have your code and all, but you'd kill me if you got the chance, no matter what you said."

I drew a deep breath. With the force of the spell on me, it took a moment. Then I said, "If I must die at your hand, Grond, then have the good grace to grant me one boon before you kill me."

He considered for long seconds, then finally nodded. "Why not? What can I do for you, Ralna?"

Slowly, ever so slowly, I swept my free hand about me to indicate the sere hills surrounding us. "Make this a paradise, such as you claim can be found on the other side of the mountains."

He lifted an eyebrow. "That's all you want? I told you how simple that is."

"Then do it, wizard. Do it now. And then kill me, if that is your wish."

Again his shoulders lifted in a shrug. "Of course. Not a bad idea, now that I think about it. Your villagers might be a little easier to handle if they didn't have to scratch so hard to eke out an existence."

"And perhaps Mardith would be more kindly disposed toward you?" I gently prodded. I had always been more comfortable using my sword arm than my wits, but even in these desperate circumstances, I was beginning to enjoy manipulating this overconfident little piece of scum.

He stepped out away from the door of the fortress, past my magic-frozen steed, and spread his arms wide. The sleeves of his robe fell away from his arms. Gradually, I was able to turn my head until I could watch him.

His fingers moved in intricate patterns that defied any logic, and words fairly flew from his mouth. Strange words they were, unlike any I had ever heard. They sounded somehow *inhuman,* as if a man's tongue should not have been able to utter them.

And as Grond formed his sigils and mouthed his incantations, things changed.

The composition of the soil beneath our feet seemed to shift and shimmer as it became darker, richer, more fertile. Clouds gathered in the skies, and I heard the rumble of far off thunder. The sun went away and hid, and gloom settled over the hills. I felt a drop of rain, so rare in this dry place, splatter against my cheek.

Bushes that were scrawny, dust colored, barely clinging to life, became full and lush and green before my amazed eyes.

Grond was shouting at the top of his lungs now, and I knew by the prickling of my muscles that my wager was about to fall true. As the wizard became more and more enwrapped in the spells he cast, his control over me began to slip. Powerful though he might be he could not spread his energies over two such major tasks at once.

Mastering the climate was one thing; controlling the will of a warrior born was another thing entirely.

Grond shrieked out his arcane litany, and I was suddenly free. I whipped my sword around as I twisted in the saddle. Awkward though the position was, there was more than enough power behind the blow.

He sensed it coming and darted around just in time for the blade to take him in the throat. The impact shivered up my arm as his head popped up into the air, a look of pure surprise etched on his face, and then it fell to the ground with a thud. The lifeless body followed a second later.

And the rain, just beginning to fall, stopped. The sun slid from behind the clouds and beat hotly against my face.

Not all wagers pay off. And sometimes you only win part of what you desire.

Grond was dead, the threat of his dominance over the village erased forever. But his spells had evaporated with his life, and now the hope for change in the hills would never come about.

The hills have always been a hard place, I thought. *Why should they change now?*

The sudden drum of hoofbeats behind me made me jerk around and raise my sword. But it was only Mardith, riding toward me on the plow horse, face lit with happiness. She hauled back on the reins, leaped from the saddle, ran past Grond's body, and embraced my leg.

"He's dead!" she exulted. "You killed Grond, Ralna!"

I smiled down at her. "Did you ever doubt that I would, little one? No sister of mine will ever be forced to marry a wizard against her will. I think I told you to go back to the village, however."

She looked crestfallen. "I wanted to. I was afraid. But I had to see what happened. I had to see if . . . if . . . Oh, Ralna, I *never* doubted that you could kill him!"

Laughter welled up and burst from me. "Nor did I, Mardith, nor did I. Come. Let's go back to the village and tell everyone that they don't have to worry about appeasing Grond anymore."

She remounted her horse and we turned away from the fortress of the wizard, leaving his corpse for the carrion birds. Dust rose in little puffs with each step our horses took, and already it was as if the effects of Grond's magicks had been only my imagination. The hills looked as they always had.

But I hadn't dreamed it all. Mardith proved that by saying, "He was a mighty wizard indeed, wasn't he, Ralna? I was hidden behind a boulder, and I saw what he did."

"He . . . had some power," I said slowly. "But 'twould probably be a good idea not to tell anyone about what you saw today. I fear they wouldn't care for the fact that their village could have been a paradise and that chance is now dead."

Mardith nodded in understanding. "I'll tell them that you overcame the wizard's power and slew him. That much is true."

"Aye, that it is."

"I suppose . . . I suppose you'll go back to the city now."

"Back to the service of the Empress," I agreed. "These hills are not my home, Mardith. They never will be."

"I'll miss you." Her voice was soft and barely audible.

"And I you."

We rode on through the hills in companionable silence. I was glad that I had been able to help, glad that I had saved Mardith from an unholy destiny. And for this moment, even the hills, the hated hills of my youth, didn't look quite so bad.

We were almost back to the village when I noticed that Mardith was moving the fingers of her free hand in a strange manner and muttering under her breath. I tried to make some sense of her gestures, tried to decipher her whispered words, but they were all a mystery to me. She seemed to be concentrating quite hard, as if she was trying to remember something she had seen and heard and reconstruct it.

A shadow crossed my face. From somewhere, a tiny cloud had moved in front of the sun.

Mardith had been watching all the while, she said. She had seen Grond invoking his powers.

There is no natural law, I suppose, that says only one side of the mountains can have wizards. And if a girl from the hills can become personal bodyguard to the Empress, what's to stop another from reaching out and touching the unknown. . . ?

I smiled. Even a battle-hardened warrior can enjoy the soft kiss of a raindrop on her face.

HANNEGAN'S HEALTH
by Nick O'Donohoe

I

I start by saying, "Once upon a time," but it was probably more than once. There have been many princesses, and almost certainly more than one was spoiled.

Hannegan wasn't to blame for being spoiled—at least when she was a child: her parents were first busy, then dead. After that, because even the chambermaids felt sorry for her, she was flattered and given nice gifts. The Vizier, who was her guardian, had to spend most of the time running the country. When she was older, large numbers of people were paid to tell her she was beautiful and important. By the time she was sixteen, there was a high turnover in the people who told her she was beautiful and important.

Slowly, she changed. At first people said her face was pale, then that it was wan, then pinched. People still told her she was beautiful, but it was clear they no longer believed it. After a while, neither did she. Her hair (washed and scented whenever she asked, restyled almost constantly) went from full to thin to wispy. Her arms and legs were thin and weak, and she was tired nearly all the time.

One night, cold again in spite of the third blanket which she had taken away from the chambermaid, Hannegan strode down to the maid's in-palace chambers to take another. The chambermaid, she reasoned, was a healthy woman in her thirties who would do fine with less.

But she hesitated before charging in, and a good thing. With her ear to the door, inside she heard the Marshal of the Guard saying, "You should have told me. I'd have brought a blanket."

The chambermaid said, "I didn't know. She just came in and took my last one."

"How cold can she be?"

"Cold all the time now, I think." And she added something that, cold as Hannegan was, made her shiver harder. "Perhaps she'll waste away and die."

After that, she took care to listen at as many of the hundred doors and stairwells in the palace as she could. Over and over she heard, "Perhaps she'll waste away and die."

It frightened her that so many people said it, and frightened her still more that they sounded so hopeful.

It was clear to Hannegan that the only one who could help her was Weyrd. That was awkward.

Hannegan had shouted at Weyrd a week ago, during a tutorial session. Weyrd had quit her post, but had refused to move out of the palace, retreating to her apartments in the topmost room of the round tower once used as a lookout. Weyrd had quit before and had been tolerated, which was another way of saying that neither Hannegan's parents nor the Vizier nor the Marshal of the Guard had felt comfortable evicting her.

Sitting in the throne room, Hannegan sent for Weyrd. Weyrd didn't come.

Hannegan commanded that Weyrd come to the throne room. Weyrd still didn't come.

Hannegan declared that if Weyrd did not come, her possessions, her favor, and her very name would be forfeit.

After the last declaration had been delivered, the Marshal of the Guard returned without Weyrd, his eyes pleading silently to be given no more orders.

Shortly thereafter, Hannegan trudged by the stairs in the round tower, growing testier as she went. "It's inconsiderate to live so far up. And me so ill, trying to see her. From now on, I'll force her to live on the first floor."

The door threshold was actually the top step of the stairs. Hannegan, panting, flung it open and said, "You must—"

The stone step suddenly tilted out from under her, and Hannegan rolled down a circular ramp to ground level.

When she stood up, the stairs had steps as before. Hannegan, furious, took the first third of them two at a time.

At the top, she shouted, gasping as she pushed on the

door, "That's no way for a servant to—" She found herself rolling down again.

This time, she walked up. Her calves hurt, and she was beginning to wheeze.

At the top she prepared to give the door a nasty kick open, looked nervously at the steps behind her, and knocked instead.

A brisk voice inside said, "Much better. You may come in."

Hannegan swung the door open and stared. The room was circular and took up the width of the tower. Across from her was an unimpressive but remarkably lifelike tapestry of a manticore stalking a basilisk. Hannegan looked away from it; when she looked back, the manticore had caught the basilisk. She watched the tapestry carefully, but nothing moved.

She heard a liquid, whistling song. In a windowsill was a flowerpot; the plant had pursed its petals and was whistling enticingly to the birds in the tower rafters. A swallow darted down curiously; the flower opened wide and snatched at it futilely, then went back to whistling.

On the wall to Hannegan's left was a map of her kingdom, showing the castle, Prendarynn surrounding it, and all the rivers and roads. The water in the rivers and the traffic on the roads moved. The map also showed passing clouds and, though it was hard to explain how, the speed and direction of the wind.

To Hannegan's left stood a washstand near a plain wood-frame bed, a writing table, and a chair. Beyond them was an upright armoire for clothes; its doors were ajar, showing simple homespun robes, skirts, and one truly astonishing dress which changed color as she watched.

The writing table held a small bookshelf large enough for five or six books, it appeared to hold three. Hannegan squinted at it; the first book was labeled "Volume 1," the last "Volume 56." By peering intently, she could see volumes 2 through 56, one at a time between them.

In a chair at the table, her back to Hannegan, sat a slender, tall woman with long silver hair braided tightly and wound on her head. She said without looking up, "Thank you for knocking. Stare as long as you wish."

Hannegan, remembering herself, folded her arms. "Why

should I knock before entering anyone's quarters? This is my castle, every room in it is really mine."

"Ah, but there's one thing in it that isn't yours."

"What's that?"

"Good manners."

Hannegan glanced back at the tapestry. Two basilisks were hiding behind the manticore.

Weyrd turned around, her sharp silver eyes staring into Hannegan's blue ones. Weyrd smiled tightly. "For example, I should thank you for waiting while I finished writing. Thank you for waiting."

Instead of saying, "You're welcome," Hannegan blurted, "What are you writing?"

"Private things." Weyrd added, "I keep my feelings private."

Hannegan muttered, "I do, too."

Weyrd set down her pen. "Yes, you do. I, however, do it because I wish to. Tell me, right now, your feelings."

Hannegan stared out the east window, above the empty and hungry plant. "I'm lonely all the time."

"That's because no one sees you unless you order them to."

"Why not?"

"Because you've become unpleasant."

Hannegan said with a quaver in her voice, "You're unpleasant and people come to you."

"Very few—and I have a skill, remember. All you have is a crown."

"And I could put them all in the dungeon," Hannegan said querulously. "And they couldn't do anything about it." She finished incongruously, 'Why are they all so nervous around me?"

"Because you look very ill. Because they're afraid you'll die."

"Does that make them sad?" That seemed tremendously important.

"Not particularly."

Hannegan said, half to herself, "It makes *me* sad."

Hannegan stood. "Then you should become healthy."

"It's why I came here." Hannegan bit back an order. "Can you make me healthy? Can you do something?" She found herself in tears. "I'm so tired of being like I am."

Weyrd stood, her hand automatically grasping the Long Wand at her desk. She leaned on it. "Then I can help you."

Hannegan's hopeful look faded as Weyrd corrected herself, "Rather, I can tell you how to help yourself." She passed Hannegan the paper from the writing table. "Follow these directions. You must leave the palace and perform three deeds."

Hannegan perked up. At least there were only three.

"First," Weyrd tapped her pen on the page for emphasis, "you must go to a sinister place and kill a pitiless, vicious, brutal ogre at the bottom of a well."

"If it's at the bottom of a well, why bother?"

"Why do you think? Because it doesn't stay there. I'm telling you where you'll find it."

"Next, you must find an unexpected treasure in an unexpected place."

Hannegan said almost reasonably, "Once I look for it, I expect it."

Weyrd smiled crookedly. "Then be careful not to look for it. Finally—" she paused, possibly for effect, "you must seek a crystal bottle called the Elixir of Life, and in finding it you will save a life."

Hannegan said immediately. "My life. Do I drink it immediately?"

Weyrd shook her head. "You must return it here unopened." She sat back. "Undertake this quest, accepting its terms, and your health shall be restored." She waited for a nod from Hannegan. When it didn't come, she said, "Go now. Go east, on horseback. Take only a few clothes and your father's sword." Weyrd added, as though it was inconsequential, "And go alone."

"I'm too sick."

"Then you'll stay sick."

"Please." Hannegan said, her fingers clasped over each other, "can't I at least take my dog?" She had never cared much for him, but just now leaving alone seemed terrifying.

Weyrd raised an eyebrow. "See how good travel is for you? I can't remember the last time you said 'please.'" She added, "and no, you can't."

II

Hannegan packed alone and left without saying good-bye. She took a small duffel of clothes, and she took her father's sword, a relic of battles before she was born.

At her order, her stable hand brought forward Timan, a horse whom she owned exclusively but had barely ridden.

The stable hand looked up earnestly, tears in his eyes. Hannegan was immensely flattered; he was common and out of the question, but still, he was good-looking.

Timan paced docilely forward, responding well to the reins. Hannegan was relieved, then annoyed as she realized that someone else had spent a great deal of time breaking the stallion in. Clearly, the stable hand's tears at her departure had been for the horse.

During the first few days it rained intermittently, not enough to seek shelter. Each morning Hannegan woke stiff and chilled; each evening she went to bed cramped and annoyed. She snarled at the horse, who whickered back unoffended. Her first campfires were smoky and threw little heat.

After a few days she surprised herself with how intently she made fires. She was less stiff and cramped. She still disliked Timan, but had achieved a working relationship with him.

After a week, Hannegan rode into a strange valley, cut by a stream with alternating pools and falls. The pines were dark and ominous. On the hillside opposite her, at the end of a switchback lane off the road she had taken, was the silhouette of a huge, featureless, forbidding building.

As she approached it, Hannegan felt a fierce, angry joy in the fight to come, even though she had never fought a battle, and was clumsy with a sword. The week's travel had left its mark on her; she longed to attack someone. It never occurred to her that she might lose.

At the turnoff to the building she met a man with more fingers than teeth, more smile than sense. There seemed to be as much dirt on him as there was on the path he walked. Calling him a rustic would be charitable.

Hannegan pointed up the hill, using her sword for effect. "Who lives up that way?"

He looked surprised. "Why, Glundal of the Horrifying Secret."

She nodded and turned that way without thanking him. As she moved up the hill toward the house, the dark pines closed in to either side of her.

The house itself was unwelcoming from a distance; it had

huge, gaping eaves, doors and windows many times the right size, and the strange swaybacked roof slope which Weyrd had called gambrel—which certainly sounded strange and malevolent.

Hannegan was quite frightened by the house, if for no reason than that it wasn't a castle. "Travel," Weyrd had rightly if cynically told her, "is broadening; either you quit traveling, or you're afraid all the time, or you get used to things." Hannegan closed her eyes, concentrating, and resolved to get used to the strange house.

When she opened her eyes, she noticed things she hadn't before. For instance, it was hard to conceive of sinister window boxes full of flowers, and a sinister, carefully carved and whimsically painted wooden chicken and line of chicks on the lawn is nearly impossible.

The slate roof was dark and moss-stained, and sinister smoke curled from the chimney.

Hannegan paused, frowning as she sniffed the air. The sinister smoke smelled like cookies.

She pulled the sword from its sheath and flexed her muscles. She felt extremely confident about defeating an ogre who made cookies.

An enormous woman strode out, a huge, three-armed woman in a stone-gray dress fully the size of an army field tent. She had stone-gray hair and a stone-gray face and hands, and over her gray dress she wore a stone-gray apron. She walked from flagstone to flagstone, the thump of her steps breaking the morning stillness. Hannegan tensed.

The gigantic woman flapped her apron. Sparrows and finches flew in from all directions, grabbing at the crumbs almost before they hit the ground. A few landed on her third arm; she didn't shake them off.

Hannegan watched, disturbed. It's one thing to plan on killing someone, and quite another to murder someone who has just been feeding birds. She muttered to herself, "If only she'd do something brutal, something wicked."

A squirrel dashed in, startling the birds. The monstrous woman scowled, snapping the end of her apron in a threatening manner.

That was enough for Hannegan. She strode forward, trying to look as though she knew how to use her sword. In a sense, she did: swing it to hurt someone, look satisfied when it did, keep swinging till your enemy begged for mercy.

It surprised her quite a bit when the enemy begged for mercy before the first blow. Hannegan shouted, "Glundal!"

The large woman nodded cheerfully and stepped forward, hesitating only when she saw the sword.

Hannegan raised her sword with difficulty. "Come no closer," she said loudly.

Glundal stopped in place, cocking her head to one side curiously.

Hannegan added as loudly, "Surrender or die."

Glundal's hands, all three of them, shot up immediately.

More smoke issued from the chimney. Glundal, turning to look at it, edged anxiously toward the kitchen.

"No!" Hannegan snapped. "Stay where you are."

Glundal bowed her head, but couldn't keep from looking anxiously back toward her kitchen. In a few minutes, flames appeared in the windows below the now-billowing smoke. She turned back to Hannegan, arms spread in mute appeal.

Hannegan shook her head coldly. "Don't beg. I've defeated you, and now I'm going to kill you."

The giant woman stood sniffling, staring at the ruins of her kitchen.

"Don't snivel like that." Hannegan stamped her foot. "I have to. You're a terrible ogre."

The giant woman stopped crying and stared silently and unhappily at her with huge eyes. Hannegan had the nagging feeling that something wasn't right. "Aren't you supposed to be at the bottom of the well?"

Glundal looked blankly and miserably at her.

"Well, I suppose you can't stay in there all the time." But why did Glundal have a house, if she lived in the well? Hannegan waved her sword. "Stay here." Glundal looked anxiously toward the fire in her home. "Move, and I'll kill you."

The giant woman bowed her head and nodded. Hannegan dashed to the well and, looking over her shoulder to see if Glundal were following, peered down.

There was indeed a terrible ogre at the bottom of the well: vicious, unsmiling, remorseless, self-absorbed and brutal. Hannegan scuffed a pebble off the well's edge, and turned away, sickened, as the ripples erased it.

She went back to where Glundal was standing. By now the wooden portions of the house were in full flame, burning down to the soot-covered stone walls and slate roof. Not much of the stone house had burned; just the floor, the roof, and all the shelves, curios, and mementos.

Glundal watched bleakly.

Hannegan stood beside the giant woman and looked at the mess. Finally she sighed. "I'm sorry."

The woman closed her eyes and nodded.

She opened her eyes, startled, as Hannegan finished. "And I'll help rebuild."

Three weeks later, Hannegan packed up to ride away. The house behind her had new shelves, a new pantry, freshly washed and painted walls, and a newly sanded and finished floor. Hannegan had blisters, scrapes on her knees, and several new skills. At the last moment, the giant woman ran from the house, slung an absolutely huge bag of shortbread over the right rear saddle-knob, and heaved Hannegan completely off the ground to plant a kiss on her, using her third arm to hug Hannegan even more tightly.

Hannegan said, embarrassed, "I'll miss you too, Glundal. And those delicious cookies."

Glundal smiled broadly and handed her a sheaf of papers with recipes in, predictably, broad handwriting.

"Thank you so much." Hannegan said, astonished. She scanned the shortbread recipe and suddenly discovered Glundal of the Horrifying Secret's horrifying secret. "Mouse lard?"

Glundal nodded vigorously and put a finger to her lips. Hannegan, who had just eaten a cookie, felt faintly ill. "I won't tell a soul." She swallowed. "I promise."

Reluctantly, Glundal set Hannegan back on the horse, unwilling to let go. Hannegan said hastily, "Just one moment," leaped off and dashed to the well, looked down cautiously to confirm that the ogre was indeed dead, and ran back to the horse, standing on tiptoe on the saddle to kiss Glundal good-bye again.

On the way back to the road, she met the man with more fingers than teeth. He put his cap on his hand and asked, "Is Glundal all right?"

"Of course she is," Hannegan said, nettled and a little ashamed.

He smiled broadly then. "I thought you'd done for her. You looked a right nasty bitch."

Hannegan, red-faced, gave him the rest of the short-bread.

III

After a few days on the road east, she was discouraged. She had ridden long, watching the landscape carefully and speaking to passersby, but there was no sign, sight, or word of a treasure.

At midday on the fourth day she found herself passing a low stone wall with a gateway through it. Behind it lay a small pond, ringed with willows and, at one side, a sand dune higher than herself, relic of some ancient lake shore. Timan bobbed his head vigorously several times and turned toward the lake.

Hannegan was so anxious to get on with her quest that she nearly ignored him. However, she had grown fond of Timan in their days together, and hated to think of his going thirsty. She tugged on the reins, turning him toward the pond and clucking once softly.

She slid off as Timan drank deep, and looked around her. This looked like an inviting place to rest.

Thee was a post, upright and perfect for hitching, beside the sand dune; she led Timan to it. Before tying the reins on she paused, staring.

A teaspoon hung from a wire on the post, and below it a sign: HIDDEN IN ME IS THE WAY TO GREAT TREASURE—BUT ONLY FOR THOSE WHO LOOK CLOSELY.

Hannegan stared at it for some time. "An unexpected treasure," she said softly. She took the teaspoon off its hook.

For an entire day she moved sand with a teaspoon. At day's end, she slumped tiredly by the fire, looking at how little she had sifted, and how much sand remained.

She spent the next day weaving a sieve of willow branches and carving a shovel. In the last few minutes of daylight, she shoveled and sifted more sand than she had checked the day before.

On the fourth day, except for mounting the sieve on a movable tripod, she shoveled all day. Her muscles ached, but not so much as they would have before rebuilding Glundal's home. She shoveled the next day, and the next.

Timan, grazing and enjoying his rest, watched her solemnly. At first she resented him, but she realized that since she had sat on his back at rest while he worked, it was only fair that he rest while she worked. After a while she found herself talking to him; he listened indifferently, his ears twitching when his name was mentioned.

"The thing is, Timan," she puffed once, "not to give up." He bobbed his head up and down as though he understood. Hannegan paused and patted his nose, glad of his company.

At sunset on the sixth day, she found a small brass key. She polished it until the writing on the stem was visible: PUT ME IN A HOLE—

"Obvious," she said.

She turned the key over and polished the other side. HIDDEN WHERE YOU CAN MAKE NO HOLE.

She pocketed the key, thinking. Where can you make no hole? "Stone. No, because drills and chisels can make holes. Glass—no, you can make holes in glass, too. You can even make holes in iron—"

Timan, bending down to drink, nudged her and she stumbled, planting her hand in the mud to brace herself She pulled it out and smiled at it; a month ago she would have looked at it in disgust. Then she glanced at the mud where her hand had sunk.

The four finger holes and thumb hole were filling with water. Shortly they had disappeared.

Hannegan tied her skirt up and waded into the pond with a stick. After probing here and there haphazardly, she grinned at herself and waded back out. She pounded a row of stakes on each of the north and south sides of the pond, then a row each on the east and west. She unraveled threads from one of her dresses and strung them from shore to shore until the pond was laid out in a grid.

She stepped back out of the pond, shivering. In the middle it was up to her neck. She hoped that, over the next few days, the sun would warm the water.

It didn't. The pond was spring-fed. Hannegan moved through the pond for short periods of time, going out on shore to dry herself and try to warm up. She was amazed that, precarious as her health was, she didn't fall prey to a cold.

On the fourth night it rained: a steady downpour that Hannegan could barely see through even during the lightning.

Timan crouched under his blanket-canopy as Hannegan ran back and forth frantically, pounding in sagging stakes, tightening thread, ducking every time the lightning was too close and watching anxiously as the water rose.

In the morning her bare feet were filthy, her hair hung straight down like wet string, and she shivered constantly.

But the threads had held and she could finish searching the pond.

The pond water had risen to within a hands' breadth of the string, and Hannegan could no longer touch bottom in the center.

For the next four days, Hannegan swam, dove, rested and swam. From time to time she slogged to shore and rested her legs.

At night she built a fire, trying to warm herself and feel truly dry. Once, holding herself in the night, she remembered taking away the chambermaid's blanket for her own use.

At midday—she had lost count of which day it was—she struck something solid. An hour's diving, dragging, rising, and gasping brought the chest to shallow water. She made a rope of the reins and bridle, tying one end to Timan and pulling the chest free easily.

She had the patience to rinse the dirt and sand out of the lock before inserting the key. Finally she turned it carefully, listening as the long-frozen mechanism of the lock moved grindingly with the key.

For two weeks her life had been dominated by black mud; before that, two weeks of brown sand. Hannegan blinked at the range of colors in front of her: topaz, emerald, ruby, amethyst, lapis lazuli—and the gleam of gold, and the only black in sight the tarnish on the silver. Once, Hannegan would have quailed at the thought of polishing all that silver. Now it seemed the simplest of tasks.

She broke camp immediately and loaded the chest onto Timan, along with the pack. They began moving east again, in no hurry.

An old man, leaning on the stone wall by the road, watched her. He said solemnly. "So you found it."

Hannegan nodded. "How long have you known about it?"

"All my life." He saw her expression and added quickly, "Oh, I'm not jealous. I saw how you worked: sifted, waded, swam—"

Hannegan nodded uncomfortably, remembering that she had been naked when she swam.

"Seems like most of a month you worked down there. I've been here seventy-seven years, man and boy, knew that treasure was there, and never went after that chest the way you did." He shook his head deliberately, his beard lagging behind it. "Amazing, the patience you showed."

"I was afraid I'd quit," Hannegan admitted. "I nearly did, a few times."

"But you didn't, did you?" He waggled his head in neither a yes nor a no. "And now you have the reward, and I say you've earned it. Working day and night, sun and rain . . . patience like that isn't in everyone, mark me on that. That's a treasure, that is."

Hannegan, startled, said, "You're right."

IV

Both she and Timan seemed to sense the end of their quest. Their pace quickened; half the time, Hannegan was letting the reins lie slack in her hand as Timan galloped east over close-cropped grass, over rocky hills, through cuts in the cliffs near the Eastern Sea.

From time to time, as they rested, they would speak to strangers. Hannegan would ask them about the Elixir of Life. Some knew nothing; some knew legends. A few knew stories of guards for the Elixir, but the stories varied wildly. The closer they came to the sea, the fewer people they met, and the more nervous the strangers were.

She slung her sword where she could reach it, but tucked inside her bedroll; she found that it bothered strangers less there. She had no idea how she was making them so nervous.

*   *   *

One morning, the cry of gulls was constant overhead. The clouds rolled in constantly from the east, on a wind so strong it tore them to shreds as they moved. Timan was restless, and Hannegan could smell brine on the wind.

They rode uphill through a gap in the cliffs. On the way into a high, bowl-shaped valley, they were passed by a man who sprinted downhill desperately, blood streaming from a cut on his cheek.

She reined in Timan and called to him, "What is it?"

He said without breaking stride, "Homunculi." Shortly, he vanished behind her.

Hannegan looked thoughtfully after him. She was vague on what homunculi were, thinking them something like babies. Still, she pulled her sword free of the blanket, laying it across her saddle before continuing.

Hannegan rode forward until she could see the final line of cliffs, spray sometimes crashing over the black rock and soaking the moss and lichen with bitter salt. The rocks, cut with vertical lines and columns as far as she could see either way, were broken directly in front of her by a carved niche—

She caught her breath. The niche had a small sparkling bottle on a pillar intertwined with carved ribbons and snakes, a caduceus.

But in front of the pillar were a desperately fighting man, his fleeing horse, and, ignoring the horse but surrounding the man, a sea of creatures with spears.

They had the heads, torsos, and limbs of humans, if one ignored proportion. Their bodies, less than a third her own height, were broad-shouldered and muscular. They walked upright, legs spraddled, marching steadily and jerkily as though not yet sure on their feet.

The clop of Timan's hooves reached them, and they turned toward her. They had smooth, slick hair and bland, politely horrible faces, as though they had wandered onto the wrong road and weren't really planning to kill anyone here at all.

Hannegan slid off, sword in front of her. "Timan, go back down the path."

Timan shook his head, pawing threateningly at the turf. Hannegan threw a clod at him. "Go away. Now." He retreated unwillingly. Hannegan advanced on the homunculi, who were moving toward her.

From time to time they threw a spear, jerkily and in a low, hard arc with a great deal of force behind it. Now that they had seen Hannegan, several of them turned and threw at her.

She swung the sword. To her surprise, it moved smoothly and easily; her time spent digging and swimming had strengthened her considerably. She connected with the first grappling spear and knocked it out of the owner's hand.

Immediately, more than a dozen spears, held forward like lances, faced her. She parried quickly, but did not fall back. She was within sight of the Elixir of Life.

The homunculi, smiling indifferently, bore down on her, the largest ones first. Some threw their spears; others jabbed forward with them.

She killed one in a quick beheading. The ones behind him stared down curiously, but did not stop advancing.

She stabbed one in the chest. He fell quickly, and the others stepped over him.

Her third stroke, a desperate slash, cut one of them. His reaction startled her as much as the wound had him; the homunculus stared at his slashed biceps in disbelief, then at her sword. He clutched his arm, making a high keening sound, and fled. Several others, suddenly frightened, fled behind him.

Hannegan circled around until her back was against the upper wall. She sidled determinedly toward the niche with the crystal and toward the young man who was backed into a pocket of rock just beyond it. He fought on, his shield before him, but he watched her carefully.

One of the thrown spears went wild, knocking into the stand for the crystal. She saw the bottle wobble, then teeter, then fall with a heartbreaking slowness, just fast enough that she could barely reach it in time.

At the same time, the homunculi pressed toward the young man, and a spear smacked across his sword blade. He dropped his own sword.

Hannegan barely hesitated. She dashed past the niche, ignoring the crash as crystal struck stone and shattered. She swung the sword like a club, leaving instant, dark bruises on the homunculi.

The shrieking grew to full-fledged panic; only a third of the fleeing homunculi had bruises on them.

Hannegan ran to the young man's side. He was collapsed against the rock face, his shield sagging to the dirt before him. "Are you all right?"

He pulled his hair back from his forehead, breathing raggedly. Finally he said shakily to her, "It's not their fault. I don't think they're very bright; they don't mind death, but they're terrified of things that hurt."

She looked down at the back at the crystal shards. There was a dark splotch of dirt where the Elixir of Life had soaked in. She watched it until the first frenzy of growth, forget-me-nots, rue, and golden-dream, exploded into bloom, then turned away.

The young man had tousled black hair that looked as though it had been well-cut once; he stood very straight even when relaxed, and he looked at Hannegan in polite confusion. "Are you a hero?"

Hannegan nearly laughed at him. Then she looked at the fleeing squat forms, and she looked at the sword in her hand. "Just for now."

She added curiously, "Are you a hand— Are you a prince?" It was obvious he was handsome.

He glanced at his clothes. "Well, yes, I am. Prince Lowe." He bowed, and brushed dust off his trousers. "Not dressed for it, but well, the road, you know." He said wistfully, "Lotho the Fair—have you ever met him? He dresses better than anyone you've ever met; ermine, silk, satin, dragonscale cuff buttons—"

"Do you want to dress like that?"

"Well, no." He was very embarrassed now. "My father rather favored that style, and I suppose that's why I'm out here." He smiled at her clothes. "You don't seem to favor that style yourself."

She laughed. "I know. By the way, I'm Princess Hannegan." She felt awkward, using her title; it had been over a month. "Why are you here, instead of at home?" She looked at the flowers and the small oak sapling above the broken crystal bottle and hoped, suddenly and fervently, that he wasn't ill.

Lowe gestured vaguely at the niche. "I saw something

glittering up here. I'd hoped there might be a treasure; my kingdom could use it."

"You sound like my Vizier."

"A vizier?" He brightened. "Wonderful fellows. Hard to do without one. Had to lay ours off, though." He shook his head. "He wanted to stay for room and light board, running the kingdom, but that wouldn't be right, would it?" He sighed, looking suddenly tired. "My father was a good man, but he raised rather too many taxes, and the people loved him, but now they're—well, poor." He added, a touch defensively, "And they wanted to forgive his debts when he died, but that's just, well, I'm not letting that happen."

He shrugged into his backpack. "Thanks again for saving me. I'd best keep going. Somewhere there's bound to be a treasure."

Hannegan said, "Take mine."

"Beg pardon?"

"She pointed to the chest. "Take mine."

At first he didn't believe her. Then, when she whistled for Timan, he said he couldn't, but he clearly wanted to terribly. In the end he carried it over to his horse, who had also returned to the scene of battle and seemed delighted to find him whole. At his insistence, Hannegan picked out a few items she thought were nice—earrings and necklaces and a potentially magic ring—and left him the rest.

Before leaving he bowed to her. "If there's every any service I can give you—anything I can do—"

She shook her head. "I don't think I'll be needing anything, but thank you."

"Well." He bowed gain and fled happily, leaving Hannegan staring at the mass of blooms and the small oak tree growing from the niche in the rocks. Embedded in the fork of the new young tree were shards of broken crystal.

V

A ride home is always long, and longer still when you know you've failed in the one thing you needed more than anything.

On the outskirts of Prendarynn she passed a low stone

cottage. In the front yard, weeding a small patch of daisies, was her chambermaid.

Hannegan noted with amusement that there was a Guards' uniform drying on the wash line. The older woman stared at Hannegan, not recognizing her.

Finally Hannegan slid off the horse. "Hello. Your garden is nice."

The woman nodded politely, peering uncertainly at Hannegan.

"I didn't know you gardened."

The chambermaid—Claire, Hannegan thought, but realized guiltily that she wasn't sure—said, "Majesty?"

She nodded. "Yes. I'm back. Could I please have a drink of water?"

The woman dashed inside and came back with a glass. "Thank you," Hannegan said, and drained it in a single gulp. She noticed the older woman's stare and smoothed her tattered dress down self-consciously.

"Majesty?"

"Yes?" Hannegan was barely used to talking to people anymore.

She said firmly, "That dress is terrible." She ran inside the house and came back waving a blue homespun dress. "Here. I wore this to your mother's Coronation ball; it wouldn't look good on me now anyway." She gestured. "Come put it on."

Hannegan emerged, wearing it. "It's very nice." She had never noticed that she and Claire were the same size. "Thank you very much—Claire?"

The chambermaid was astonished. "Yes, Claire. You're welcome."

She fumbled in her duffel and reached into the paper-wrapped packet. "Why don't you take these earrings? I think it's a fair trade for the dress."

She turned them over and over, wondering. The stones were amethyst, and the setting gold filigree. "But these are worth much more than my old dress."

Hannegan said, "But you don't need the earrings as badly as I need the dress. I'll be at the palace. Could you come back, when you can?"

"Of course," Claire said dazedly. She clasped her hands

over Hannegan's and said impulsively, "It's good to see you come back to health."

Hannegan thought fully of her failure, and only said "Thank you" and rode on.

But the next person who recognized her said it was good to see her healthy. And the next. And so on, and some added that Hannegan looked beautiful, and some that she looked more fit than half her own sentries, and one even said she looked better than her mother the Queen had, so long ago.

She rode through the castle gate, but circled 'round to the stables first. She took the blanket off Timan, rubbed him down, fed him, and, impulsively, kissed his nose before leaving. The stable hand glared at her jealously.

Hannegan returned to the front door of the palace, where a crowd had gathered. The great door opened before she had a chance to knock. Trumpeters, assembled hastily, blew a fanfare.

When the Vizier saw her he knelt. "I was afraid you wouldn't come back." Hannegan had always thought his cheeks ridiculous and wrinkled, like a winter-dried apple; now the wrinkles were like tiny canals, salt tears breaking into tiny streams inside them. Hannegan had always thought he hated her.

She helped him up, kissing his cheek and offering him support. She wondered when someone she had thought of as stronger than her had become so infirm. There was a rustle of approval behind her, and she saw that a crowd had followed her to the palace.

"Thank you for waiting for me," she said uncertainly. "I'm truly sorry to have been gone so long—"

The crowd erupted into cheers.

As soon as possible, she climbed to Weyrd's tower and knocked firmly. A raspy but still-sharp voice said, "Manners *and* confidence. Oh, I like that."

Hannegan embraced Weyrd, noticing for the first time how bony Weyrd had become. "I've missed you."

"Odd." Weyrd gave her a dry peck back. "You never missed me when you were here."

Hannegan said simply and unguardedly, "Well, it's hard to miss someone you dislike." Weyrd laughed so hard she choked, and Hannegan poured her some water from the pitcher with the phoenix perched on it.

Hannegan told the story of her adventures and finished, "I don't understand it at all."

Weyrd sat back in her chair as though exhausted by Hannegan's imperception. "You did everything I said, didn't you? You killed the ogre in the well. You found a treasure in an unexpected place. Finally, you saved a life."

After a moment, Hannegan nodded. "But it didn't happen the way I planned."

"So stop planning."

"But I thought the Elixir would make me well, and instead people have done nothing since I came back but tell me how healthy I am."

"And aren't you?"

Hannegan said finally, reluctantly, "Yes. Better than I ever expected to be."

"Of course you are. I told you go to on a quest for the Elixir, and you'd be restored to health. Aren't you?"

"But I didn't drink the Elixir."

"I know." She seemed distracted and intent at the same time, waiting for Hannegan to say something she hadn't yet.

"And everyone says I'm beautiful and healthy."

She waved an arm. "Oh, that. All you needed was some exercise."

Hannegan, stunned, struggled for something to say. "Well, I guess it was worth it, then." She brightened. "And I did save Lowe's life."

Weyrd gripped her arm. "You saved his life? You're sure?"

Hannegan nodded. "Of course I'm sure. So are you; you said I'd save a life. It's like all the other tests you named; I thought I'd do one thing, and it turned out to be another. I'd thought, by finding the Elixir, that I'd save my own life."

After a moment Weyrd nodded. "I never thought that. But the Elixir?" she said with curious intensity.

Hannegan shook her head. "I ran past it when the homunculi knocked it over. It broke while I was saving Lowe."

A light died in Weyrd's eyes. She nodded abruptly. "Well, you can't save everything."

Three weeks later, Weyrd died. Before then, Hannegan tended her night and day.

In the mornings she carried meals, hot wash water, toast and tea to Weyrd's tower room. She said once as she set the tray down, "The steps go downstairs both ways now."

Weyrd lay back tiredly. "It was the least I could do."

Hannegan brushed Weyrd's hair, put an extra pillow behind her, and sat with her and helped her eat. In the tapestry, the manticore and several of the basilisks crouched side by side, watching her sadly.

Once she said to Weyrd, "You could have told me I was going for you."

Weyrd admitted, "At the time, I thought that was my joke on you."

"If I'd known you needed the Elixir, I'd have—"

"Let that young man die?" She closed her eyes. "Good thing you didn't know, then."

She fell asleep again. Hannegan tiptoed downstairs.

Hannegan spoke at her funeral, but courteously allowed the Vizier to speak last. It wasn't until now that she realized, to her astonishment, that Weyrd and the Vizier had been lovers. Nothing about her life had been as she expected.

After the funeral, she was host to a large banquet. She worked very hard at making everyone welcome, and at responding politely, but by the end she was staring at the sea of well-mannered faces and thinking of the homunculi.

Scarcely had the last mourner left when she heard a knock at the door. She glanced around helplessly for the guards, but they were in an a honor cordon around Weyrd's grave. She glanced at the Vizier; he was asleep from exhaustion. She answered it herself—

And stared at Prince Lowe. "Glad I caught you home." He smiled at her, then gestured at all the black bunting. "I'm awfully sorry about all this, whatever it is."

"Thank you." She realized that she was smiling back. "What are you here for?"

He held up a small leather bag which jingled as it swayed. "Well, I paid my father's debts, and there's still some left over from the treasure you gave me. I thought of sending it by courier, but I wanted to come thank you myself, and I really—" He coughed. "I really wanted to—"

Hannegan put a hand over his. "I really want to, too."

SEVEN GRAINS
by Kevin T. Stein

Mikalean pressed her fingers against the worn, obsidian handle of the kill ringer, cutting a shallow, perceptible notch.

"You'll soon need another barrel."

Mikalean sniffed once loudly. She held the ringer absently as she checked the new notch. Each notch was cut perfectly, as the life of the enemy was also perfectly cut. One bullet, one life.

"I'll be dead before then," she finally answered, dropping the ringer into its velvet pouch, held by leather drawstrings at her belt. She continued her scrutiny of the barrel. Forward from the cylinder, the plain steel barrel was lined with the lives of the enemy, notches, shallow cuts from when she first became Sheriff, to now. There was only about an inch left, and the cuts were only a hair's breadth apart.

Mikalean spun the pistol cast in steel hardened with her own blood, three times forward, twice back, as was the ritual, dropping the Gun into its leather holster. The powder she used for her bullets left an acrid smell in the air; the mix was making her nose run, and her pale eyes sting. This was a new problem she was having; it was a strangeness, a question that hung in the air without answer.

Frowning, she said, "I'll be dead by then, and you'll be the new Sheriff."

"Only if I'm ready."

"You'll be ready," Mikalean said. Her throat was dry, her voice hoarse. She would have to check the mix on her powder. Impurities must have crept in. Unlikely, but possible.

Reminded of the training and rituals that had made her Sheriff, Mikalean sighed heavily, tired, always ready. When she had been Deputy, her Sheriff had said the road to Justice was long. A simple tract, but ineffably true, she had understood for quite some time.

Mikalean's eyes narrowed at nothing, crow's feet where her skin had aged with the hard sun, and she jerked her head to the side, her single braid of dusty hair falling behind her. In all the ages of the land, each town had its Sheriff, and a Deputy ready to step forward. Always. It was ordained and ensured. It made no sense for her Deputy to think she might not be ready. Something not in the question but the reason for the question simply *being* nagged Mikalean, till she let it finally go.

Her deputy was young and strong, just over sixteen. Already she had the trappings, chaps, vest, simple shirt, tall boots, gold Deputy's Star. The Star, the talisman, would protect her until she was ready to become Sheriff, keep her from incidental harm. Her holster was empty. She had yet to give her blood to the Gun. And she did not know the secret of making powder for bullets. She did not know the seven grains.

With silver thread, her Deputy had embellished her holster and gloves with her family's heraldry, roses and stars. There was something about this that made Mikalean angry. It was her divine right as Sheriff to order her Deputy to remove the heraldic symbols, though she said nothing since she could give no reason for her feeling. Her own trappings were plain and efficient. The way they had been for every Sheriff for long, long, ages.

Mikalean saw that her Deputy knew of the disapproval, and was visibly uncomfortable. After a moment, her Deputy said, "There *have* been Sheriffs who displayed their crests."

"Name me one," Mikalean said evenly.

"Sheriff Gabrial, of the Age of Wheels . . ."

Sheriff Gabrial, the first Sheriff, was acceptable, but he was a myth. No trace of his Gun had ever been found.

"There's another."

Mikalean raised her head slightly, regarding her Deputy with little more than curiosity. No Deputy would make a claim unless ready to have it validated. Mikalean waited in silence for the answer.

"Sheriff Parcival," her Deputy finally said.

Mikalean did not need to check her remembrance of the

ranks of Sheriffs. She knew each by name and by Gun. There was no Sheriff Parcival.

"Of what Age?" she asked. She did not doubt her Deputy. This was a strangeness like her reaction to the powder, the words hanging still in the air.

"The Age of Ascension. And his Deputy wore heraldry, as well."

Mikalean frowned and peered up into the sky. Three carrion birds circled overhead in the hot, still air. The acrid smell of her powder cloyed at her leather. She sniffed again, her teeth gritty against her tongue. She was sweating from standing so long, standing and talking instead of completing the ritual of Victory.

Sheriff Parcival.

"They found his Gun in the Hall," her Deputy said.

"When?"

Her Deputy shifted, boots flattening the grass, obviously more uncomfortable now. The silver heraldry caught some of the sun, for a moment flares and brilliance threading the air. "There's another alcove in the Hall," she answered, her head bowed slightly. "Hundreds of Guns and Histories."

Hundreds. Guns and Histories, firearms and documents. New Sheriffs, new lessons. And changes. Her Deputy's heraldry, the stinging smell of powder, new Histories, new Guns. All these were different. Mikalean sighed again, loudly as before. It was her duty, her *charge,* to ensure that her town was protected from its enemies. To ensure that life did *not* change. As Sheriff, to ensure that life stayed the *same.*

"Retrieve the weapon of the Vanquished," Mikalean said without tone. She narrowed her thoughts on the ritual.

"Yes, Sheriff," her Deputy answered, bending to pick up the enemy's Gun in a gloved, protected hand. The man was an Outlaw, his Gun and powder inferior to those of the Sheriffs; but the Outlaws had numbers.

Her Deputy carefully dropped the Gun into a velvet bag, tying it closed with a length of hemp. She took out her firebox and spun the flintwheel, sending up sparks, igniting the wick. The bag was sealed with a drop of red wax, finished off with Mikalean's sigil, straight lines and crossbars and strength.

The birds continued their spiral, one calling out harshly to the others. Mikalean pulled the shovel from its place on

her horse, which had waited patiently since they had arrived a few minutes before. It would be discourteous to the
memory of the enemy to let him wait longer in the sun.

Mikalean strained her shoulders and sank the edge of
the shovel into the earth. She worked quickly, preparing
the enemy's grave. His Gun would be buried with him,
where his Gunspirit could cause no harm to the innocent
and the Protected. Her nose ran and she cursed, stopping
a moment to clean herself with a rag from her back pocket.

"Kaleigh," Mikalean said, replacing the rag, "help me
move the Outlaw's body."

Grabbing the enemy by the arms and legs, Mikalean and
her Deputy placed the dead man in his grave. Mikalean
dropped the velvet bag with the man's Gun in afterward,
handing the shovel to her Deputy.

Mikalean watched as the ground was filled. She could
not keep her thoughts narrowed on the ritual. New Guns,
new Histories. Changes were not part of her life. She let
herself wonder what her Deputy would face if things
changed beyond the Lessons. But only wonder briefly.

When she had been Deputy, Mikalean remembered her
Sheriff saying that a grave's first spade of dirt was the most
difficult to turn. Of all the Lessons her Sheriff had taught,
that was the one simply no longer true; no spade weighed
more than another when the enemy was killed to serve
the Protected.

This Lesson was the only one that had changed. It was
not something Mikalean thought of often. She could not
help but be reminded of her confusion when she realized
the Lesson was wrong, incorrect. She watched in silence as
her Deputy continued to bury the enemy, shaking her head
slowly, her eyes regaining their focus on the stark present,
letting the memory fade.

Mikalean could have done a number of things when she
returned to the town. Horses needed tending, the roof of
her home leaked, though the rains had been thankfully
minimal. She needed more powder. She would have to
make time to reap the harvests from the farmlands to make
powder for her bullets.

The door to the Hall was huge, steel hardened with the
blood of the first Sheriffs, they who had found the secret

of the powder and the forging of the Gun. There was nothing of note, nothing that changed, to notice. The same comforting darkness, the same smell of metal and age, and isolation. And protection. Mikalean drew her Gun slowly from the holster. She felt the Gunspirits protecting the door retreat; she was no threat, no enemy against the Protected. Only she and the town's Governors knew how to gain entrance to the Hall. They knew the combination. She had the Gun.

Mikalean pressed the tip of the barrel into the keyhole above the handled wheel set in the center of the door. She slowly pressed it forward, the many notches catching the rim of the keyhole, each groove ticking as it slid past. The cylinder pressed against the door, Mikalean turned the Gun to the right.

Inside, the door's cylinders locked into place, smoothly against the age of the metal and the minimal wear. The same sounds Mikalean knew for decades echoed briefly as the door swung back, taking the Gun with it in the keyhole. There were no weapons beyond those of the remembered in the Hall.

Mikalean had never paced in measure the length of the Hall. She could not see the end. The recessed lights which eternally lit the Guns and Histories sparkled dimly in the distance. Mikalean was tall, but she did not bow her head when she stepped onto the black marble floor.

Ten Guns held on pegs lined each side of the wall, the spirits of the Sheriffs at rest with their weapons. The respective Histories lay on shelves beneath the Guns. Mikalean passed by the Gun of her Sheriff, as notched as the rest, almost as her own. She had learned a great deal from that man when she was Deputy. Shoot straight. That was his greatest lesson, the one by which she lived in all things.

The walk was long.

The Hall sloped downward, and the echo of Mikalean's dusty boots died quickly among the shelved paper, smoothly plastered walls, wooden buttresses. She passed a number of recently discovered alcoves in the Hall. The Hall had, by her current Governors, been considered only one corridor, one path through the Ages. But they had found branches hidden, had found mystery where before there was only fact, assurance.

Mikalean had read through the few Histories found in these alcoves. All had been Sheriffs and remarkable. None had given reason for their being hidden. She had left them to their secrets; she had to train her Deputy, and protect, always ready.

With the discovery of the new alcove, the Governors had allowed others to enter the Hall, not unheard of but unusual. In past Ages, some Governors had been too infirm to walk the Hall, their retainers helping them when the town's problems called for Histories to be read, lessons applied. Retainers now sought for new alcoves. They had found a new Age called the Age of Ascension. An Age where Sheriff and Deputy wore their heraldry on their trappings.

Mikalean's Sheriff's Star, pinned to her vest, flashed gold in her eyes as she walked past a light. Stars were newly forged at the beginning of each new Age, denoting the passing of worldly pains and sufferings. New Stars, both Sheriff's and Deputy's, were forged from the old. Mikalean's Star had a bullet scar where a Gunspirit had nearly taken her life.

Mikalean found the new alcove. As her eyes cleared from the Star's reflected light, she noted that the buttresses were hinged perfectly to disguise their mechanism. The Guns and Histories on the false wall became part of the new hallway, all lit by the same eternal lights, leading to the edge of her vision.

She stepped forward into the new Age.

"Who are you?" The barrel of a Gun pressed hard into Mikalean's back.

There could be no one in the Hall. It was not possible; the Gunspirits would stop anyone, and nobody would consider such foolishness, not even the Outlaws. Mikalean tried to hear more of the enemy's sound, his breathing, his feet shuffling. The less Mikalean gave of herself, the less she *was,* the more she would find out about this man.

"The less I am, the more I become?"

The man's voice was smooth and even, tinged with anger. And he knew a Sheriff's Lesson. The question he made of the litany made it sour.

"Turn, Sheriff." The pressure of the Gun was withdrawn

a fraction. Mikalean turned slowly on her heel, clenching her hands to beat the intruder to death.

A Gunspirit. A man shimmering red in heat and fire, holding a cold, steel Gun. Impossible. No enemy Gunspirit could enter the Hall—

"Stop thinking of the impossible, Sheriff. I'm here to warn you." Each word was heat and metal.

Mikalean narrowed her eyes. She knew incantations, and she wore the Star. It would protect her against any harm but bullets.

The spirit touched the tip of his barrel to the Star. The Star grew hot and Mikalean's eyes widened in pain and curiosity.

"What are you?" she demanded, stepping back from the shimmering Gun. She could feel her lips pull back, sneering. Her flesh was blistered where the Star touched her vest.

"So angry," the Gunspirit said, venomous. "So many things changing around you. Cling, Sheriff."

Through the heat-shimmer, Mikalean made out the heraldry of the Gunspirit. It was nothing she recognized. She could see nothing of the face.

She needed time to form the Banishing. She bluffed. "Parcival."

The Gunspirit nodded slightly. "The enchantment on your Star . . . that is part of my doing. And the Banishing on your lips."

"How can you—"

The Gunspirit stepped forward a fraction and leveled its Gun to Mikalean's eyes. She forced herself not to step backward. "Somebody is going to end the struggle between the towns. And the Outlaws," the Gunspirit said. "And then your world is going to end."

Mikalean spat the incantation and the Gunspirit faded, stepped back. It raised its Gun again to her eyes, controlling the center, the line of battle. She did not know how the Gunspirit had come to enter the Hall, nor why its Gun had not been consecrated.

Why it did not fire.

Mikalean could have banished the Gunspirit with a single bullet blessed by her Gun and her words. Instead, she cut her palm on the edge of her Star and threw the blood into the Gunspirit's fiery eyes. It staggered back again and faded

to almost nothing. It leveled the Gun to her eyes a third
time. She could feel the Gunspirit's force of will against
the incantation.

"Your world is going to end, Mikalean. Someone will
end it. Don't find out who."

A final word from Mikalean, taught her by her Sheriff,
handed down through the Ages, and the Gunspirit was gone.

"This is the fourth grain," Mikalean said to her Deputy,
who knelt dutifully in the dirt next to the tall stalks of
wheat. The grains sifted across the scar Mikalean had made
tearing her flesh for the Banishing's blood. "With it, you
make bread for the innocent."

"Or Justice for the Protected."

Mikalean nodded, handing her Deputy a finished bullet,
one for each grain she learned; she now had four. Her
Deputy studied well. Such perseverance and dedication
would serve her in the difficult times. There were always
difficult times. Mikalean remembered when she had been
hard-pressed by Outlaws in a box canyon, remembered bullets tearing her body—

"What are you thinking about?" her Deputy interrupted.

Mikalean realized that she had wandered into her memory's far territory, riding silent, distracted from her present.
The crow's feet deepened, eyes narrowing at nothing, narrowing at herself. This was the second time this day that
she had ranged into silence, and precisely the seventh time
since she banished the Gunspirit Parcival.

"I've learned that the hardest time for the spirit were
often the trials of the body."

Her Deputy's silence revealed her question.

"Your body, your spirit, and your soul," Mikalean said,
pointing to her Deputy's stomach, heart, and hand. "They're
all related. They all affect the other. Except the soul," she
added, clutching her fist in the air, "is, above all others, the
one that cannot be hurt, the one that cannot be corrupted."

"The one from which a Sheriff draws strength," her Deputy said with a slight nod.

Mikalean pressed her thin lips together and nodded in
return. There was dust on her lips, and it made her mouth
dry. The dust on her clothes made her skin feel dirty and
aged. She had been trying to draw strength from her soul

for the past seven nights, but the words of the Gunspirit harassed her.

The words bound her with their truth; she had no doubt they *were* true. She could see it in the many changes around her, changes she did not want to recognize, could hardly bring herself to see. Someone was going to end the struggle between the towns and the Outlaws, and the world was going to end.

She had to find this person, put a stop to these events. She should have realized something like this long ago. It seemed . . . inevitable.

Staring into her hand, at the fourth grain that would make gunpowder, Mikalean rode through her memory. The Gunspirit's words trailed her as she rode after them. She could not escape.

"Who is the greatest Sheriff?" Mikalean asked.

Her Deputy opened her mouth to speak, but slowly closed it.

"I—I am the greatest Sheriff, aren't I?"

A number of answers passed over her Deputy's face, but Mikalean could see they all avoided the question. Such questions were never asked, not by Mikalean to her Sheriff, and not by Deputies to their Sheriffs throughout History.

"Greatest," her Deputy began, slowly, piecing together the words, openly ashamed that the question should have been asked, "is not important."

Mikalean narrowed her eyes, the Gunspirit's words clear. She shook her head slightly, enough to berate. Her Deputy pulled back a fraction. Mikalean knew the answer to the question. In these times, it was important for her to know.

Mikalean rode, reaching the home of Sheriff Constantine half an hour before the sun set behind the range of tall hills in the distance. Her horse was tired; the ride was the better part of a day across rocky country. Her Deputy had followed dutifully, and silent, the entire time, no more than a few hundred feet behind at most.

A Sheriff coming to see another was a grave event. Mikalean had seen questions in her Deputy's eyes when they left town, but had said nothing. As Sheriff, she answered questions as she chose. She did not feel a need to share what the Gunspirit prophesied; she did not feel anyone but herself could understand. Or stop what must happen.

The home was much like Mikalean's. A single room in the front that was a kitchen and reading space, and a bedroom in the back. The wood-shingled roof sloped down over the porch. Mikalean lashed her horse to one of the supports, standing and glancing inside the curtained windows. There were no lights; it was too early for the Sheriff to be home. Her Deputy sat still and alert, no other sounds except for the horses' snorting, shuffling.

Her Deputy continued to ask questions within her silence. Mikalean ignored them; she controlled her breathing, narrowed her thoughts on nothing. She had checked the play of her Gun before leaving. She preferred a firm pull on the trigger and tightened the mechanism's spring a quarter turn. She took enough ammunition for a long, hard trip.

As she anticipated, Mikalean did not wait long for Sheriff Constantine to arrive, his town nestled against the hills, its gaslights against the darkness flickering in the distance. She could hear his approach, feel the earth shake beneath her boots, long before she could see him as a shadow killing the town lights behind him. He and his Deputy rode their black horses hard.

Her Deputy began to unmount, but without turning, Mikalean gestured for her to stop. According to the Laws of Engagement, she was safe as long as she stayed on her horse. Mikalean heard her Deputy shift uncomfortably in the saddle, wanting to be part of this event. But there was no need for help in the fight; only in burying the body.

"What are you doing here, Mikalean?" Constantine thundered, riding up, his body blocking out the sky. His features were shadowed. Mikalean noted that the man was not weary from the journey, and though she did not take her eyes from him, she heard his Deputy breathing hard from exertion. The Deputy's gold Star caught the failing light of the sun.

Mikalean stood back from the Sheriff and his horse, drawing her duster open, tying it behind her back with the drawstrings. Her Gun was ready in the holster.

Constantine dismounted, throwing the horse's reins around a porch-rail, turning away from Mikalean. She knew Constantine was thinking about his next words; he always used words as a means of distraction, of creating doubt and fear. He was a big man, on the draw fast as a cat. Mikalean had no fear and no doubt.

The Gunspirit's words had seen to that.

"You're entering dangerous territory, Sheriff," the man finally said. He did not turn from the hitch, taking his time with the reins as if to ensure the horse would not wander off. "Very dangerous, as you no doubt know."

"I know," Mikalean answered, quiet and even. She moved farther away, stepping backward; the Rules of Engagement said nothing about when the duel must start. The dirt under her nails made her fingers feel tight, the dust on her hands reminded her of how her throat was dry from the ride. She concentrated only on the Gun and the duel, and the actions of this man.

Finally, Constantine turned toward her. Mikalean saw no move for his Gun, could feel no anticipation in the air of his being ready to draw. His features were still shadows, and he appeared as darkness with a great voice.

He let out a breath.

Mikalean drew and fired once, the bullet shearing Constantine's Star, spinning him, his Gun thrown clear of his hand, landing in the dirt. The echo of the shot still had not faded when the Sheriff finally hit the ground.

The acrid smell of gunpowder again made Mikalean's nose itch and run, reminding her further of the changes, the terrible changes that only she could stop. She spun the Gun three times forward, twice back, dropped into the holster.

"Aren't you going to mark it?" her Deputy asked.

Mikalean shook her head. "I will not mark my Gun with the death of a Sheriff. Not on *this* mission."

To Constantine's Deputy, Mikalean said, "Your Star."

The man on the horse said nothing. He was much smaller than Constantine. His features were obscured and dark. After a moment, he found his voice, steady, confused.

"What?"

"Your Star," Mikalean returned, holding out her hand.

"Give her your Star!" her Deputy commanded.

Constantine's Deputy fumbled with his shirt a moment before finally removing the Star. He threw it to Mikalean's feet.

Mikalean gestured for her Deputy to dismount. "Let us bury Sheriff Constantine in the Ritual of the Vanquished."

Mikalean removed the spade from her horse, and began digging the earth in front of the house. The echo of the gunshot was gone, but the scent of the powder remained. Mikalean ignored it as best she could, shoveling dirt to make the grave.

"I'll . . ." Constantine's Deputy began. "I'll tell my Governors to relinquish their lands to yours."

Mikalean ignored the young man. She continued to dig, her back growing stiff and her hands blistering on the palms near the fingers. Her Deputy dropped Sheriff Constantine's Gun into a velvet bag, and sealed it with a drop of wax and Mikalean's sigil. When the grave was finished, Mikalean buried the Sheriff, his Gun, and his Deputy's star with him. Her thoughts were partially empty, on the Gunspirit's words, to the question of greatness she had posed on her Deputy.

When she and her Deputy left, the smell of gunpowder still lingered.

"This is the fifth grain," Mikalean said. The poppy lay in her hand, wilting, dust from her palm dulling its yellow petals. "Medicine for the innocent."

"To heal the Protected," her Deputy replied. Mikalean gave her Deputy another bullet.

Her Deputy's answer had come after a moment's delay. Mikalean narrowed her eyes in scrutiny, but her Deputy revealed no reason for the pause.

Outlaw country was rough, untamed by large towns and plows. Outlaw Guns were rough metal, wooden grips, and their gunpowder was torn from the land, mixed minerals and powders, things dead, rather than the seven grains.

Mikalean's bandolier was heavy, each of the fifty leather loops had a new bullet. She had brought three extra cylinders; she did not want to rely solely on her reloading speed. She and her Deputy had been riding through this country for a week, and every day Mikalean changed cylinders to ensure her Gun's action was smooth.

Mikalean had pointed out to her Deputy the times when they were watched from the hills by Outlaw scouts. Mikalean guessed that news of Sheriff Constantine's death, at her hands, had reached the Outlaws. She had no doubt that they could not find a reason for the duel, nor why she would now by journeying into their territory. She was cautious. An Enemy confused is an Enemy most dangerous, the Lessons said.

The area they rode through was lined on either side by low hills and scrub brush. Their horses' slow walk was the loudest sound. Mikalean thought she heard a stream on the other side of the hills to her left.

Mikalean kept herself relaxed, her thoughts filled only with the Gunspirit's words. She glanced at the horizon; they had two hours of sun.

Her Deputy rode fifteen feet ahead of her, and to the right, her horse throwing up little clouds of dust. There was no wind, and the dust settled slowly. Her heraldry was dulled with dirt.

"Keep your shoulders relaxed," Mikalean said clearly.

Her Deputy straightened her back and did as commanded. Her body now moved with the horse's motion, instead of against it. Mikalean was satisfied. The Outlaw town was a few miles away, and she wanted her Deputy to be ready.

Mikalean stilled her breathing, listened as two men watched anxiously from behind the hill-line. Where there were two, there were more; Outlaws had to travel far to the towns, and they always traveled in force, at least five riding out. Mikalean guessed there were seven; her reputation warranted that.

"We'll camp there," she said, as loudly as before, pointing to the hill-line to their feet. Her Deputy wheeled her horse around and faced Mikalean with a blank expression. However, the question in her eyes made Mikalean nod slightly; her Deputy was wise for being so untested. They were making camp for a reason other than convenience.

Mikalean reined her horse and slid out of the saddle. Her legs were a little stiff from the ride, and her knees cracked. She removed her canteen, took her hat off, and poured water on her face to remove the dust. Some of the water trickled through her lips; she brought no liquor, but would have liked to clear her throat with something strong.

Throwing her pack on the ground, Mikalean bent and

untied her bedroll, opening it to its full length. The roll
had a familiar smell, and a bullet hole near one end where
her head had lain. Her Deputy unrolled her spread as well,
peering at the surrounding hilltops.

Mikalean's eyes flicked once toward the hills, and her
Deputy followed her gaze. The two men were gone.

"They're watching for us now," Mikalean said softly.
"They'll be back tomorrow."

"Why wait?" her Deputy asked.

"Experience," Mikalean answered.

In the darkness and still, the hammer of an Outlaw Gun
clicked loudly.

"We've got your Deputy, Sheriff."

Five men surrounded Mikalean's campsite. They all carried Guns, but two had Long-guns, barrels twice the length
of a Sheriff's Gun, twice the gunpowder in a bullet. Mikalean's Deputy rose cautiously to a sitting position; her Deputy's Star was pinned to her vest. The Outlaw who spoke
grabbed her arm and pulled her to her feet, holding his
Gun to her head. He hid his body behind her to shield
himself from Mikalean.

The horses snorted loudly from where they stood, the
stream on the other side of the hill-line the only other
sound. The men waited patiently, Guns ready, though after
a moment, the others also drew back their hammers.

Mikalean stepped out of the darkness from the scrub.
Her Gun lit the night and dropped the men with Long-guns
first, the most dangerous, her bullets tearing huge holes in
their bodies, killing two more before the first fell. Her Gun
pointed at the Outlaw holding her Deputy.

"If—"

Mikalean's gun dropped him as well, bullet between the
eyes, before he could level his threat. The shot echoed
quickly and died.

"We wouldn't have killed you, Mikalean."

Mikalean turned slowly. Two men stood behind her.
Their Guns were not drawn.

"I have no reason to believe that, McKay."

"No reason . . ." the man she addressed answered
thoughtfully. He toed the hole in Mikalean's bedroll and

smiled. After a moment, he added, "You would have at one time."

"That was before you went Outlaw," Mikalean replied. Her Gun was leveled at his throat.

McKay held out his hands. "I am the same man."

"You're not."

Mikalean stepped back, next to her Deputy. "Are you hurt?" she asked.

"No."

The simple answer said that her Deputy had more questions, could not find the answers on her own. As Sheriff, Mikalean had only spoke of the Lessons, never her personal life. Mikalean's Sheriff had said that the greater the Lessons were in your life, the more your life became the Lessons; Mikalean wanted only to train her Deputy in the Lessons and let the rest of life be learned on its own time. Her Deputy knew this was not the time to have her answers.

"What are you here for, Sheriff?" McKay asked, crossing his arms over his chest. Mikalean knew McKay was ready for the draw; his Gun's grip stuck out of the front of his pants. And he was good.

Mikalean said nothing. She slid from her Deputy's side.

"We've heard about Sheriff Constantine," McKay continued. "What's going on?"

Mikalean replaced her Gun in its holster. She circled farther away from her Deputy.

McKay's mouth pulled down slightly; his arms dropped to his sides. "Why are you here, Sheriff?"

Mikalean planted her feet in the ground. McKay's man finally stepped away, the expression on his face filled with confusion, alarm.

"Mikalean?"

McKay drew and fired as Mikalean's Gun fired its last bullet. The shot tore through McKay's throat and his spine snapped loudly as his body jerked; his bullet raked Mikalean's right hand where she held the Gun and scored her left shoulder as she turned her body.

Mikalean stood and bled, her teeth clenched against the pain, though her face showed little. McKay's man stood, his hand near his Gun, ready to defend himself against his friend and leader's killer. Mikalean reholstered her Gun. The man would try nothing.

Mikalean stood and bled, staring down at McKay. Things she remembered of the man were lost in the far territory of her thoughts, pushed away long ago when he had left for the Outlaws. There was nothing to feel, standing over his body, nothing to think about; only the words of the Gunspirit, and that she was closer to stopping the one who would end her world.

The smell of her gunpowder filled the still air.

"This is the sixth grain." The cotton seeds filled Mikalean's palm. "Warmth for the innocent."

"To clothe the Protected."

Mikalean gave her Deputy another bullet.

"The one who could end our world could only be an Outlaw or a Sheriff," Mikalean said.

The ten Governors and their retainers were yelling, loudly to each other, respectfully at Mikalean. They did not address her statement. They cared mostly for the issues of their offices; they were confused about her actions, about the prophecy, what it meant to them. Mikalean said nothing, her Deputy sitting silent, learning what these men and women were like when confronted.

"You have left the town unprotected now for over two months!" the Governor bellowed, angry enough to make his round face turn red.

Mikalean sat another ten minutes as the Governors agreed with one another that she had been gone that long. She shrugged off their outrage as pointless. The retainers were more tolerant, and Mikalean saw they shared glances with each other that spoke of their boredom and frustration.

"Have you found any new alcoves hidden in the Hall?" Mikalean asked one of the retainers, her steady voice cutting through the volume of raised voices.

The retainer shook his head, not daring to let his attention stray too far for fear of being reprimanded. Mikalean sighed; her absence had distanced her further from the town. More than her usual distance.

"You have tribute from the other towns," Mikalean said finally, standing, worn. The Governors fell quiet, their attention drawn to her. "The innocent prosper with these new lands. You have more now to govern, both in holdings and the Protected. The Outlaws have no leaders, and no direction. They are broken.''

The Governors said nothing. Heralds from the other towns, towns that now had no Sheriff, had arrived every day since she was gone, as had Outlaw messengers. Mikalean looked to each of the governors, stared into their eyes, could see their thoughts on their faces. They were frightened by her words, secretly by the words of the Gunspirit.

"I'm leaving again, for the last time," she said, straightening her leather vest, putting on her worn riding gloves. Her Star shone brightly in the lamplight. "My Deputy will stay with you to research Parcival's History."

Mikalean turned, purposefully catching her Deputy's gaze; Mikalean had made the decision to ride out alone on this final journey some time ago. This last man, this last Sheriff, had to be the one spoken of in the prophecy. Always ready, to serve the innocent and the Protected, she had to face him alone. Maybe her Deputy could find out more of Parcival and his Gunspirit's words; maybe she could find why his gun had not been consecrated.

Questions still unanswered reached out between them in the silence. The questions of her Deputy were the only ones that mattered, her Deputy still learning to be Sheriff, but Mikalean would answer the questions when the last Enemy was buried, when the threat to the world was ended. She narrowed her eyes, her expression saying to be patient.

Her Deputy's face revealed nothing.

In the last town, Mikalean faced the last Sheriff.

He stood no more than an arm's length away, having walked from his office to where Mikalean stood in the deserted main street in the dusk. His Gun was at his side. Like her, his trappings were plain.

The two faced each other. Mikalean could feel her soul in her hand, the spirit in her heart, guiding her body, making her ready. This was the one, the one prophesied.

The other sighed once, loudly.

Mikalean drew and fired. The heat from her bullet melted his Star and sent droplets of metal into the air, hissing, cooling, white hot turning yellow, orange, growing dark . . .

When Mikalean buried his body and placed his Gun in a velvet bag, sealed with her sigil, she saw that his cylinder was empty.

Mikalean rode into her town, shoulders relaxed, a light wind blowing through the empty streets, kicking up dust. She arrived a short time before the sun would set, when most of the Protected were already in their homes having supper or slipping into bed.

Her horse walked slowly down the street. Mikalean's thoughts were focused on the distance in her memory, the Lessons, each one in order, by rote, trailing after. The cloying smell of gunpowder filled the air around her, clutched at her clothes and saddle, but it no longer bothered her.

"Mikalean."

Mikalean blinked her pale eyes, coming out of her lethargy. She reined her horse to a stop, then turned in the saddle. Her Deputy addressed her from the street, trappings clean; but the heraldry was gone, torn from her clothes, from her holster.

The holster with the Gun.

Mikalean had not forged the Gun for her Deputy, with her Deputy's blood.

Her Deputy drew the Gun from its holster.

"Parcival's," Mikalean said. It could only be that Gun; she, herself, had Banished its Gunspirit, leaving it unprotected, accessible. She knew it must be loaded with the bullets her Deputy gained from learning the seven grains.

"What have you done, Mikalean?"

"I have saved the innocent. Saved the Protected. It is my divine charge."

Her Deputy shook her head. "The words of the Gunspirit were that one will end the struggle between the towns and between the Outlaws."

"And then our world would end."

"No, Sheriff, then *your* world would end," her Deputy interjected. "Your world. Not ours."

The Lessons continued to trail after Mikalean's thoughts. The side of her mouth jerked into a pained half-smile, her eyes narrowed, crow's feet deepening. She was beginning to understand.

"You've destroyed yourself," her Deputy said, Gun still

leveled. There were tears forming in her eyes, but her voice was steady, steady as Mikalean remembered her own addressing McKay, Constantine, the last Sheriff. "We all had questions, I had questions about your actions, and now that it's over, you can't answer the greatest question."

Mikalean remained in silence, thinking nothing.

"Who will destroy your world? It is you!"

The half-smile broke Mikalean's face again. Someone will end your world. Don't find out who, the Gunspirit had said. Don't find out who.

Her world was over. The towns were united into a great state, the Outlaws were broken and scattered.

"You are the greatest Sheriff," her Deputy said. Her voice finally broke. Tears flowed into the dust. But the Gun was steady. "Everything you've taught me, everything I've learned of the Lessons and Sheriffs and Histories is less than nothing now. We've no need of them. Or you."

Mikalean, the last Sheriff, stared at her Deputy. Her thoughts lost their narrow focus, her eyes taking in the town she had protected, measured in deaths along the length of her Gun's barrel. For the first time, she wished she knew just a little of life.

But she did not.

"Kaleigh," Mikalean began. She paused. she felt a pressure on her spirit, pushing her body away. She had to leave. Leave now. "Do you want to know the secret of the seventh grain?"

A cry broke out between her Deputy's lips, but it was bitten back. She shook her head.

Mikalean nodded. She turned her horse around, back out of town.

She said nothing as she left, her only company the Lessons and Histories, and the knowledge of what she had wrought. Her world was destroyed, she knew, but she could almost see how it would be better.

Almost.

As she rode past, Mikalean dropped her Sheriff's Star at Kaleigh's feet. And with it, her last, unspent bullet.

"Consecrate my Gun when you kill me," she said, staring into the open. "Use all six."

Kaleigh nodded but did not pause, loading the Gun and taking aim.

LOVE, TROUBLE, AND TIME
by Linda Mannheim

Amanda didn't phone first. She just came by. Drove all the way up here from the city, motioned for me to walk outside into the woods. We're up the trail, everything getting dim. Amanda, in her city clothes, has trouble walking. She tells me, "Lucia's going east."

I, wondering if I've misunderstood, if there's some code I don't understand, ask, "What?"

She says, "Lucia's out and heading east. She's going to see her grandmother. She wants you to meet her there."

Twigs snap beneath our feet, and small animals scurry. The brush scratching against the forest floor makes a sound inside my body.

"You mean she's been sprung?" I ask.

"No," Amanda answers.

"Aw, shit," I say.

"You know Lucia," Amanda answers.

"Shit," I answer back.

"You know how she's been about this thing with her grandmother."

I put my forehead against a tree and shut my eyes. I like the way the bark feels against my forehead. If I pushed harder, I could hurt myself.

"How come you know about this?" I asked Amanda, opening my eyes, twisting my head toward her so she looks as if she's standing sideways.

"Lucia called me."

"How come she didn't call me?"

"Too obvious," says Amanda. "They'd expect her to call you."

"I'm glad they do," I tell Amanda, realizing even as I say it that I'm sounding childish and bitter. "I never know when she'll call."

"She called me at the Y," Amanda says. "It was pretty good. Had me paged there while I was swimming. She knows I'm there every day at noon since the car accident."

Amanda puts her hand against my back, then reaches up and starts to give me a shoulder rub through my flannel shirt. "I'm her oldest friend," Amanda tells me. "You keep looking for signs that she doesn't care about you. I don't know why you're always looking so hard. She wants to see you. I've known you and I've known Lucia for a long time. I don't think I ever would have tried to fix you two up. It never would have occurred to me. Maybe this thing is some kind of turning point for you. Maybe you can sort out the things you can't sort out while you're apart."

I should be worried about her. I should be thinking about her. But I'm always worried about her. I'm always thinking about her.

How is she getting east? Is she hitchhiking? Did she make it to friends who have money? Where will the feds be looking for her?

The flight to New York seems unreal, the airport an entry gate to a world very far away from where I am living now, and, sitting next to all the businessmen on the San Francisco to JFK flight, fear pounds through me, as if they will recognize in a glance the look of a woman going to see a lover who's escaped from prison.

I shouldn't be feeling this lonely. I'll be seeing Lucia within hours if everything goes right. I shouldn't be walking the halls of JFK with a lump in my throat, half expecting someone to meet me when I know no one will, but every time I see the welcome anyone else is getting, the lump pushes up further. I find myself barely able to get words out at the information desk. "What's the best way into the city?" I ask.

"Depends where you're going," the woman behind the desk answers.

"Wa—" I start to say. Then, a wave of paranoia hits me. I know it's ridiculous, but I tell her, "Fourth Street," instead of saying Washington Square Park.

Skateboarders and jugglers and more people than I've seen in one place in a long time move around me as I stand

underneath the arch with all the other people waiting to
meet someone. Every woman who looks even a little bit
like Lucia becomes her before my eyes. I see someone
older than her, smaller than her, bigger, but with her hair,
who moves a little bit the way she moves, who has the
same jacket she wore when she went in, two years ago. Has
she changed since the last time I saw her, the last time I
sat across the table from her wanting to touch so badly, our
fingertips inches from one another? We had two chances to
hold one another, when I first came in and when I left.
Everything between that was static, staring at one another,
trying to do with our eyes what we could not do with our
hands.

I glance at my watch, shift, turn, shift, wonder which
direction she'll come from. To the south is NYU, where
the Triangle Shirtwaist Factory used to be, before it burned
to the ground and the women inside, mostly Jewish and
Italian immigrants, were trapped. All the doors were
locked. The factory owners did not want the workers leaving without permission. This was part of Lucia's thesis when
she was still in grad school. She would have come out to
California right after she got her degree in Labor History,
come to visit her friends, met me, destroyed the nuclear
missile system at the air base, in that order. "I wanted to
do something that would look good in the alumni newslet-
ter," she joked once.

Then, a voice behind me; "Helen."

I turn. A man, late twenties, with a few days' beard and
mussed up hair. His pale eyes are all that's clear in a face
that seems nearly abstract. He wears a torn, stained
fishermen's sweater, brown corduroys that are baggy and
tied on with a piece of rope. I stare at him. I'm so uncomfortable, it takes me a minute to realize he doesn't know
what to do. He waves his hand behind him, as if in slow
motion. He starts to say something, then stops. "The truck's
there," he motions.

I stare at him.

"I—I'm sorry. I'm going to take you to Lucia."

"You are?" I blurt out.

"She's . . . I'll take you there in the truck."

I look past him, to a beat up pick-up with Jersey plates.
"Who are you?" I ask.

"I'm . . ." He stares into space for a minute, his eyes becoming even more unfocused. "Doug," he says. "You can call me Doug."

I look at the truck again, at him.

"I'll take you there," he tells me uneasily.

Something in my gut says it will be all right. I know that, if I'm wrong, it will all be wrong, but something in my gut says to go. So I follow him to the truck, climb in, see the floor littered with sketchpads and empty food containers, cassette boxes. On my seat, there's a walkman jerry-rigged to the dashboard, and coffee can stereo speakers I know will roll around the truck when we take off. "Just," he says, throwing my bag into the back of the truck, "toss whatever you don't need onto the floor."

I put the walkman on my lap.

"Here," he says, "I'll take that."

The cab reeks of pot, bringing up a surge of bad memories and fear. He is too familiar, exuding gentleness that can give way at any moment. He reminds me of the past. He drives uptown, across the bridge and into New Jersey, playing Grateful Dead tapes the whole way. I feel tears well in my eyes. I know I can count on getting what I don't expect, but, somehow, this is beyond what I did not expect. I want Lucia. I want our last night together before she hitchhiked onto the air base, the rain washing the streets on the hill near Amanda's bookstore.

Be loving and kind, they told me. And I was.

Don't mind Helen. She seems so sad all the time. We wish we could get her to smile more.

I was too big to be pretty, too goddamned big, but I could make my horse jump higher than anyone else's.

The problem with Helen is, even when she's smiling, she looks like she's about to cry.

Through the green, patchy hills reminding me of then, of where I grew up.

"I always heard that South Jersey was nice."

He asks, "Huh?"

"South Jersey," I say. "Whenever I complained about how ugly New Jersey was— People always tell me that South Jersey is nice."

"Oh, yeah," he says. "Well, nicer than Fort Lee and stuff."

"How far are we going?" I ask.

"Not much farther," he says. "We're only gonna be about an hour from the city."

He pulls out a plastic bag with some pot and a carved soapstone pipe in it. "Here," he says. "Want some?"

I tell him no thanks.

"Well, would you mind filling the bowl for me then?"

I take the baggy from him, pull off some of a pungent bushy bud. How strange to have my hands in pot again, to be smelling this smell.

I hand the pipe back to him.

He tells me thanks, lights it, and takes a draw.

It occurs to me that I have no idea of what to say to him, no idea of what it is or isn't okay to ask. The truck looks as if it might be classic, but since it's fallen apart and been put back together with duct tape, it is merely old. "What year is this?" I ask, brushing my hand against the dashboard.

"1990," he says.

"I meant the truck."

"Oh, the truck. It's pretty old."

By the time we arrive at the house, I feel like my stomach has been put through a pencil sharpener. This is the scene where you hear strange rumbling noises coming from the boiler room, and you go to open the door. Either you find a puppy and microphone inside, or the entire room blows up and you're left standing with doorknob in your hand.

Doug enters the house first, motions for me to follow. First I see a skinny, brown-haired woman I don't recognize. Then, behind her, is Lucia. Very quickly, we grab each other's hands, then pull each other close to one another, and then, I am drenching myself in the taste, smell, and feel of her. I bend to put my face into her curls, and I feel her hair brush my eyelids. We discover, once again, that although Lucia is tiny to my awkwardness, our bodies fit perfectly.

"Hey," I hear a voice say, "when you two come up for air, the key is right over here."

Lucia looks up at the brown-haired woman. "Oh," says Lucia. "Sorry, Helen, this is my friend Sylvia. We went to high school together."

"Lucia drops in from time to time," says Sylvia, looking decidedly harassed and much older than Lucia. "Don't bother getting the phone. The answering machine is on, but do call me at Doug's if you need anything, and I'll leave my car here for you."

Doug stands in the hall, shifting-nervously. Sylvia's to the door before he is, calling out, " 'Bye girls!"

"Thanks, Sylvia," Lucia calls back. "Oh, and Doug, thanks for helping out with everything."

For a minute it's as if we're saying good night after a dinner party.

The door shuts behind them.

Lucia looks up into my eyes. "Hi," she whispers.

"Hi," I whisper back.

"Glad you could make it."

"Wouldn't miss it for the world."

Unbuttoning her shirt and the sound that fabric makes when you listen closely to it. She's wearing Sylvia's clothes, so the shirt is too tight, and the blue jeans cut into her belly, but the cuffs are rolled up so many times, she has to unroll them before she takes them off. I have followed her up to the loft, up the narrow, frightening stairs to the unmade mattress on the floor in the low-windowed slope-ceilinged room, and in that room, I forgave, for a few hours, everything ugly that ever happened in the world. And when I stopped forgiving, it was dark out. We were in a slapped-together house on the end of a long dirt road in part of the country I did not know as well as Lucia. I planted small, quick kisses on her chest, on her belly. "Lucia," I asked her, "what are you doing getting in touch with old friends from high school?"

"Sylvia?" asks Lucia, pulling me up to lie beside her. "I've seen her since high school. She's trustworthy. And besides, no one's gonna look for me here."

"You really thought this through," I say to her, "didn't you?"

"You know I did," she says. "Contrary to popular belief, I do these things after thinking them through for a long time."

Could have fooled me, I think. But instead, I ask her, "Have you seen your grandmother yet?"

"Not yet," says Lucia. "I was waiting for you to get here."

"For what?" I ask her.

"I want you to meet her."

I stare at her. "How will you introduce me?"

"As my lover," Lucia says.

"You will?" I ask, the words almost charging out in a cough.

"Helen," she says, "all my life, my grandmother was the one who pushed me to do what I want and study Yiddish and get a degree in something everyone else said was silly. And she would tell me about the village she was from in Poland, and she used to say that she wanted to study, but her father and her brothers and her husband were always yelling at her to take care of them. She said to me, Lucia, when you get married, I want to see you married to someone who will love you and care for you and help you do what you want. So I want her to meet you, Helen. I want her to meet you."

I stare at Lucia's face, wide-eyed, expectant, innocent as an adolescent's face when she first discovers love. All this time, when I have been alone and I have dreamed of holding her, talking to her, tasting her, I did not dream of a moment like this. I dreamed of her elusive, up before dawn as she was before, not open like this, not waiting, with me not knowing what to say.

'What?" Lucia asks me. "What?"

Even when I think I will begin to speak, I cannot get the words out. Instead, without notice again, the tears start to come. I feel them roll down my face, but I feel none of the emotions connected to them, only scared.

"What's wrong?" Lucia asks me, her face drawn into bewilderment and concern. "Did I say something?"

I nod.

"What?"

"I'm not sure," I tell her. Then, groping, "She didn't want you to marry someone who loves you. She wanted you to marry a man. Lucia, it's not a matter of telling her that you're with me. You haven't even told her you're a dyke."

Lucia takes my hand. Her voice quavers, so I know this sadness is contagious. "I just didn't know how. I planned to. Really I did. It was my mother. She kept asking me not to tell. She said my grandmother couldn't handle it. But I know that was wrong now. I can't let my grandmother die without knowing who I am."

We both stop crying then.

I look into her eyes.

"They're gonna nail you right there in the hospital, aren't they?"

"Maybe," says Lucia. "Maybe not. They're not all that efficient."

"Lucia, you kept trying to get them to let you see your grandmother, and now you're out. They don't have to be very efficient to figure this out."

"It doesn't matter," she says, looking down. "They're not gonna go after everyone who breaks out."

"You're not everyone," I tell her.

"Well, I'm not exactly famous," she counters.

"Luc, you are famous. You were in *People* magazine. You've been on prime time TV, and Amanda says that you're a hero in Europe."

"Yeah," says Lucia, "well, that was a long time ago. I haven't given an interview to anyone in about two years."

"Luc," I tell her. "*Commentary* ran an article on you last week."

"They did?" asks Lucia. "What did they say?"

"They said you were trying to be a female version of Abbie Hoffman and you've got a nose like a brussel sprout."

Lucia starts laughing. "They did? God, what was it for?"

"A special issue on how the left is dead."

"I don't suppose they said Abbie Hoffman was just trying to be a male version of Emma Goldman. Oh, well, never mind. It's nice of them to remember me."

She lies down on the bed and pulls me to her, so we feel each other's nearness, but are too close to see one another. "I'm gonna end up back in there," she says. "Even if they don't nail me in the hospital tomorrow, I know I'll end up back inside."

"How come?" I ask, tears welling up again.

"Because I'm not ready to live underground," she says.

"Why not?"

"I can't do it," she says. "I have to make up the rules for this."

"What about me?" I ask.

"You're beautiful and wonderful and I think of you all the time."

She kisses the top of my head.

"I mean what rules do I get to make up?"

"Whichever ones you want," she tells me.

"I don't think I get up to make any of them."

"You do," says Lucia. "But that doesn't mean you'll get me to follow them."

The playful giggle she lets out then annoys me. I pull back so we can see each other's faces. "Being lovers with someone who's in prison is suspiciously like being lovers with someone who smokes pot and drinks all day."

"What does that mean?" she asks.

"It means just what I said," I tell her, and sit up.

She puts her hand on my back.

"It means that probably I don't really want to be in a relationship, or else I would be with someone who can be in a relationship."

"I'd be with you if I could," Lucia says.

"I know," I tell her. "That's what I mean. You can't."

When we get to the hospital the next morning, Lucia's mother Dora is standing in the hall talking to a nurse. Dora is short, like Lucia, and a bit heavier. Her face is worn out from years of riding the subway to work and back, going to meetings where her voice rises raspy above all others. She looks like someone determined to not be taken by whatever it is that comes around corners in the city. Lucia and I stand down the hall from Dora and wait until she sees us. Then, with a look of astonishment on her face, Dora excuses herself from the nurse and walks toward us. She covers Lucia with hugs and kisses, weeping silently, and Lucia hugs her back. "Don't cry, Mom."

"Where have you been?" Dora asks, smacking Lucia's arm playfully. "The FBI's been bothering me and your father for a week now."

"It took me a while to get here," Lucia says.

Dora spots me, gives me a quick hug and a kiss on the cheek. "How are you, Helen?"

"Fine," I tell her.

"How's Bubbe?" Lucia asks her mother.

"She's not so good," Dora tells her. "She's had another

stroke and can't talk anymore. I think she knows who I am, but she can't talk to me."

"Did you try speaking Yiddish to her?"

Dora raises her eyebrows. "I didn't think of that." Also, Dora can't speak Yiddish.

"I was just thinking," Lucia says, "sometimes she remembers things that happened to her a long time ago, but she can't remember the recent stuff. She always knew Yiddish better than she knew English. Maybe if I tried . . ."

"Maybe . . ." Dora says.

We walk into the darkened room together, the room smelling of ruined things, things that are leaving, things that want to end the pain. Lucia's grandmother's face is wizened and bewildered at first. She is nearly hairless, and, like a baby, has trouble lifting her head. She says, across the room, "Lucia. Meiner Lucia."

Lucia goes to her and leans to give her a hug. It is very difficult, since Lucia's grandmother cannot get up at all. Then Lucia sits at the edge of her grandmother's bed and begins to talk to her in Yiddish. Dora and I stand at a distance, as if watching a movie. At first, Lucia and her grandmother speak pleasantly, saying, I imagine, kind things to one another and smiling into one another's faces. Then, I notice Lucia's grandmother's tone change to one which is reproachful, and weary too. I hear the word tsores a lot. Over and over: tsores, tsores, tsores. Lucia begins to look like a child trying to explain away the giant stain on the tablecloth. Lucia's grandmother looks at her as if she doesn't understand what she's saying. She starts to plead with her. Then Lucia says something accusing and her grandmother is silent for a while. Then she says something softly, but I can see that it hits Lucia right in the face. Lucia stars pleading now. I imagine she's trying to get back the common place where she and her grandmother once stood, telling her grandmother, *you taught me this, you told me to be myself,* because Lucia's grandmother's face softens for a minute, and she nods, and Lucia waves her hand towards me and I hear my name. I hear the word leib and then lezbianke. And then Lucia's grandmother begins to scream, her words spat like bullets. She sends a stream of Yiddish cusses at Lucia so powerful Lucia backs off, and I hear Lucia trying to scream back at her grandmother, but she can't shout her down.

An orderly comes, and Lucia grabs my arm and says to me, "Let's go." We run from the hospital as if we're being chased, as if we have just heisted something from the hospital and now we must make our escape. We run all the way down the street to where Sylvia's Toyota is parked, and Lucia stands by the driver's side saying, "Give me the keys. I want to drive." I throw her the keys over the hood of the car, and she peels out of that parking place, drives just a little too fast for the city streets. Soon, we're out of the city, back in New Jersey, and I can feel Lucia's relief. She won't slow down, though. The road is a ribbon that unfurls before her. She's staring at the road in absolute silence. I put my hand on her arm, rock hard. "Lucia, I'm sorry. I'm so sorry."

Lucia is unyielding. She glances at me sideways. "I wanna get something to eat. Do you wanna get something to eat?"

"Where?" I ask.

"We can find a diner."

"I think that's dangerous," I tell her.

"My picture's up in every post office, not every diner," Lucia tells me.

"We can get some picnic things," I tell her. "Go to a deli and then find a spot by a river and stop for a while."

"If I can't eat in a diner, it was hardly worthwhile to escape from prison," Lucia says, smiling. "See if there's some sunglasses in the glove compartment."

I look. There's a pair of black plastic sunglasses inside, covered with dust. I wipe them off and hand them to Lucia, who puts them on and asks, "How do I look?"

"Like someone who's trying to hide."

"Ah, good," she says. "I just knew that these glasses were me."

She takes the next exit off the turnpike.

"I think if we go down here, maybe we can find a small town or something."

"I heard South Jersey's pretty nice," I tell her.

"Yeah," says Lucia. "Isn't that funny? People always say South Jersey is nice."

We find a spot on the edge of a lake. The grass is wispy and spring damp, mud showing through the bare spots. We're eating sandwiches I picked up. "How did you get out?" I ask Lucia.

"I walked out," she says.

"You walked out?"

"There're times when the security isn't so tight, like when they have movies. You can walk out then, but they figure out during the count right afterward that you're gone. That's when they catch you. Everyone there gets nabbed when they start hitchhiking away. But I did things differently."

She smiles and takes a bit of potato salad.

"I don't get it," I tell her. "What did you do?"

"I didn't start hitchhiking until I was about fifty miles away. Until three days later."

I stare at her.

"I walked," she tells me. "I walked off the road, through the woods sometimes. One time, I had to walk through a train tunnel. I kept seeing a pink light on the tracks and I thought it was getting bigger, but then it looked like it wasn't. And I thought maybe I was wrong, but I couldn't go back on the road. I knew I wouldn't make it if I did."

I go to her, put my arms around her from behind. She eases back against my body, takes my hands in hers, and shuts her eyes. "I'm the first person to get away from there since 1972."

"What do you want?" I ask her.

"Credit," she says with a smile.

"What else do you want?"

She turns to me. "What do you mean?"

I shrug.

'I want a lot of things I'm not going to get," she says.

"But what do you want?"

Now she faces me and takes my hands. "Helen, if I went underground, would you come with me?" She laughs then. "I feel like I'm proposing."

Her eyes search mine. I can't say anything for a minute. Finally I manage to tell her, "I can't come with you."

She looks down, lets go of my hands.

"I thought you didn't want to go under," I tell her.

"That was before," she says quickly.

I ask, "Do you want to go back to the hospital?"

"Why are you doing this?" she asks.

"Doing what?" I answer.

"I ask you if you want to go underground with me, and you change the subject and ask if I want to go back to the hospital."

"Do you realize that's the first time you ever asked what I thought before you went and did something?"

"Yeah, well I guess I'm just a fuck up all the way round."

"Damnit, Lucia."

"What?" she snaps. "Don't you get it? It's the biggest joke in the world. If I'd been good, I would have gotten sprung in about six months. Instead, I break out, get disowned by my grandmother, and get into a fight with my girlfriend."

"Am I your girlfriend?" I ask Lucia.

Lucia rolls her eyes. "I can't deal with this right now."

"Well, pardon me for not giving you your dream escape, but you can never deal with it. First it was the trial, then being in prison, and now it's your grandmother. I know this isn't gonna be the way we want it to be. I just want to resolve enough of it so I'll be sure of what I've gotten into."

"Well, this is it," says Lucia. "You've got me hopping in and out of your life when you least expect it. I haven't got a fucking idea of what's gonna happen, and the only way you're gonna resolve it right now is if you break up with me."

"Don't make me break up with you," I say.

She takes my hand. Then we are holding one another, lying in the grass, looking at the sky, what's left of the early spring sun washing over us.

"I don't know what I'm facing when I go back," she whispers.

"We could go to Canada," I tell her. "Just keep driving all night. We'd be in Montreal by dawn. Before that."

Lucia shakes her head, smiling, tells me, "We can't do that."

I kiss her. "We could get a house up there," I tell her, "and have a garden, and raise Canadian geese."

"We don't have any money to do that." She pushes my hair from my eyes. "I have to go back to the hospital."

I stare at her.

"I think they're gonna nab me if I do."

I shut my eyes.

"Will you come with me?" she asks.

"I don't understand what you're doing."

"I'm going to make peace with my grandmother before she dies," Lucia says.

"Why?" I ask.

"Because I want to," Lucia says. "And she probably does, too."

"What did she say to you in there?"

"That I'm trouble," says Lucia. "That I used to be such a good girl, but now all I do is go around causing trouble. And she said that it was hurting my mother to have me be in prison. And she said—"

Lucia stops. Tears well up in her eyes.

"She said that she misses me and she wished I hadn't done this. I tried to remind her about when her friends went to jail in Poland, but she said that was different, and that she had a man who took care of her then, and she wanted to know why I wasn't married. So I said to her, 'This is my friend Helen. I'm a lesbian.' That was when she started screaming."

"You can't make her, Lucia. You can't make her accept you."

"She loves me," Lucia insists. "She'll listen to me."

Before we turn down the hallway to Lucia's grandmother's room, Lucia grips my arm, pulls me around the corner, and gives me a deep long kiss. "I think I can get in and see her," Lucia tells me, "but in case anything goes wrong, I love you and I didn't mean to mess things up this way."

I take her hand and we walk together toward the room. Lucia opens the door, and Dora turns around. Then Dora puts her fingers on her lips and comes towards us. She and Lucia grasp each other's arms, holding each other and keeping a distance, each making sure the other will not step closer. They stare into each other's eyes. Finally, Lucia breaks the silence. "Is Bubbe asleep?" she asks.

Dora shakes her head "Why did you have to tell her?" Dora asks.

Lucia squeezes her eyes shut.

"They're going to find you if you keep coming back," Dora says.

"Ma, please."

"I don't understand why you have to do things the way you do them," Dora says. "It's as if you like getting caught."

"I just want to say good-bye to her," Lucia says.

Dora lets go and turns toward the room. Before she can open the door, Lucia grabs Dora's arm and says, "By myself."

Dora stares at Lucia a moment longer, nods, and turns away. Lucia goes inside and I watch the door slowly swing shut. I turn to Dora, who looks very small and alone perched in the center of orange vinyl couch. I go to her. For a moment, Dora is silent, and she shifts as if to draw herself away from me. I consider that I might have made the wrong choice, that I should have stayed away, let Dora be alone, but it's too late now to get up and leave. Finally, Dora mutters under her breath something I don't quite catch. "Sorry?" I whisper.

"I said, I don't understand my daughter."

I don't know what to say.

"Do you?" Dora asks.

"Sometimes," I whisper.

I can't get my voice any louder than that.

"The FBI spends a lot of time at our house now," Dora says. "Do you know what I told one young man yesterday? I told him, 'You should be ashamed of yourself, bothering people like this.' He told me it was the best job he could get. Isn't that a hoot? Best job, my foot. I had a family to raise, but Lucia's father and I did it the honorable way, not tapping people's phones and following them around all day. That man could become a school teacher or a social worker like Lucia's father."

"Oh," I say, wishing words would come back to me.

"All the time," she says, "they came and they came and they came. Especially during the sixties, when Lucia was a little girl. They came asking about our friends. And Lucia would answer the door, and this little girl would tell them that she didn't have to answer anything. And the FBI agents would sometimes laugh, not knowing what to say. You'd think she would have learned, seeing all the things she saw when her father and I had to deal with that, but she doesn't. She drops out of school and goes and does this."

"Maybe what she learned was to be brave," I say.

"Maybe what she learned was to be stupid," says Dora. "If she'd stayed in school, she would have had her Ph.D. by now. My mother—from me she never took anything, but Lucia can do no wrong."

I glance away at the door to Lucia's grandmother's room.

"Let me ask you something," Dora says.

I turn to her.

"Helen, do you love my daughter?"

I feel the tears well again, say to Dora, "Pardon?"

"I asked you if you love my daughter."

Tears start to slide down my face. "Yes," I say hoarsely. "I do. Very much."

"Then how could you let her do something like this?"

"Pardon?"

"You heard me."

"Lucia pretty much does what she wants," I tell Dora.

I can see Dora trembling to keep back whatever is about to burst out. She's never been this nasty before.

"Lucia's poppa thought it was strange when she brought home her first girlfriend. Me, I wasn't surprised. I always knew Lucia had it in her, that she wasn't like other girls. It doesn't bother me at all. Really it doesn't. But I see the two of you together, and I wonder how you can stand being apart so much."

The tears keep falling steadily, silently. I brush them away and shift my feet.

"It's no life for you, Helen. I see. You cry so much."

"I always cried," I tell Dora. "Even before I met Lucia."

I glance up at a nurse who walks past and my legs start to shake violently. I think I must have my legs bent so I'm setting off some catalytic nerve, but when I shift positions, my legs don't stop shaking.

I hoard time, hungry for it as if I can consume now what will be taken later. I tick seconds on my finger, recount what could have happened if it had all been just a little bit different. If we had come there minutes earlier, and Lucia had said what she had to say, would everything have ended at the right moment? Would her grandmother have understood even a little, her dark eyes glaring, but opening over time?

They came in, rushing, their rubber-soled shoes and gray suits making them seem like caricatures of themselves, cartoon characters with special powers; they stop time, bolt open the door, pull out pistols and yell, "Freeze!"

RIGHTS OF MEMORY
by Gary A. Braunbeck

"To know that what is impenetrable to us really exists, manifesting itself as the highest wisdom and the most radiant beauty which our dull faculties can comprehend only in their most primitive forms—this knowledge, this feeling, is at the heart of true religiousness."
—Albert Einstein

"I have some rights of memory in this kingdom . . ."
—Shakespeare, *Hamlet:* V, 2

Sarah Hempel glimpsed her reflection in the protective glass of a vending machine in the nursing home's tiny lounge, looked into her bloodshot eyes, and thought: *The question is, can she do it?*

The prospect of deliberately ending another human being's life seemed less ominous when she thought of herself in third person.

She remembered something her aunt had once said before the woman's mental faculties took their final downward spiral: *What's wrong with giving the world a little Magic-Sight, even if it thinks it doesn't want it?*

Sarah rubbed her eyes—Christ, she was tired!—then wandered over to the lounge's only window and looked out.

An ornate, four-wheeled circus cage sat in the center of the courtyard. Inside the cage, lying on its side, was a huge stone sculpture of a woman's head. Shimmering gossamer webs blanketed the sculpture, holding it down like a weighted net; it tried rolling to one side, then the other, but the webs remained strong. Finally, defeated, the sculpture opened its eyes and pursed its lips; the darkness trembled with trills and arpeggios and flutings, echoes of a winter's midnight wind whispering *soon* on this late-August night.

What is it, Aunt Clarice? thought Sarah. *Some instance from your childhood turned into something only you can interpret? Is it meant to be some kind of message for me, or is it something more—the way you've felt your entire life, held captive by others' perception of you, their disapproval and scorn?*

Though part of her wished it otherwise, Sarah knew the cage and head were real; if she needed proof, she had only to look across the courtyard at other units where a few sleepless residents were leaning out opened windows: some stared at the head with childlike wonder while others, their faces masks of ethereal bliss, moved their hands back and forth in time with the music as if conducting a symphony of their own composing.

She turned away, got another cup of coffee, fired up yet another cigarette, and asked herself yet again if she had the nerve to do what had to be done.

Biting her lower lip, she watched the hushed activities in the corridor, glad to immerse herself in the sight of the Unmanifest in the midst of things mundane.

Nurses with dark circles under their eyes, their shoes softly squeaking against the polished tile, moved briskly along toward some pressing task, hastened not so much by urgency as the need to keep themselves awake; a middle-aged orderly who looked as if there were 2,341 other things he'd rather be doing at this moment whisked by with a snack cart full of chocolate chip cookies and tea—"Some goodies for us late-night folks," he said to Sarah on his way past; one of the restless ambulatory patients, his tattered robe hanging open, shuffled toward the front desk, a small globule of saliva creeping from the crusty corners of his mouth, bursting, then streaming down his chin; and, non-plussed by it all, the head nurse sat behind her desk, making notations on various charts.

One-forty-five AM on the Alzheimer's Unit and all was well.

As well as could be expected, anyway.

Sarah sat down, sipped the coffee, winced as it hit her stomach, covered the top of the Styrofoam cup with her hand, and cursed herself for not having gotten the hot chocolate instead.

For all of her years as Assistant Director of Adult Protective Services she'd counseled hundreds of families of Alzheimer's victims against giving in to the impulse to end their loved one's suffering; that thought, if not silenced *the second* it entered your mind, blossomed all to quickly into outright obsession, and now here *she* was about to do the unthinkable.

It was one thing to confront these feelings in others; it was something quite different when you yourself were grappling with them. Intellectually, she knew what she was going through was simply a stage in a process, one that she'd seen countless family members experience (always advising them to create some kind of emotional distance, erect some temporary psychological barrier, and *hot-damn* wasn't that sound, professional advice?); emotionally, though, now that it was she in the midst of this, her heart thought her intellect was full of shit.

No one had wanted to deal with Aunt Clarice when she started going downhill—Mom and Dad had never particularly cared for her (*"She's too much of an oddball, always has been."*), Sarah's brothers and sisters saw Clarice as more an object of amusement than an actual human being (*"People think she's funny—an old broad like that who never married, a Wicca member, New-Age weirdo, and arteest. Something freaky got into the gene pool when she was born, that's for sure!"*), and her coworkers at APS had given Sarah no small amount of grief when she'd decided to apply for legal guardianship herself. (*"It's not a good idea, Sarah; you're too close to the woman, and you* know *what happens when personal feelings start to override professional duty."*) Yet none of their protestations had swayed her; she knew things about Clarice she could never hope to make the rest of them understand.

That knowledge hung around her neck like chains instead of pearls.

(*"There are three Aspects to becoming an Earth-Witch and Joining with the Goddess and Her Magic,"* Clarice told her when she was younger. *"The first Aspect is Recognition—to* know *that something is* Magic, *that it fulfills the purpose of affecting the manifest through the Unmanifest; the second Aspect is, simply, Belief—to believe that the Magic is out there, even during those times you can't—or won't—See it; and the third Aspect—perhaps the hardest one*

*of all—is Embracing: because when you Embrace Magic,
when you allow it to wholly enter your heart and spirit, you
will be forever Gifted with full Sight; and from that moment
on, hon, no Magic will remain hidden to your eyes and
senses. You'll be living in two very different worlds at the
same time."*

"I'm not sure I understand, Aunt Clarice."

*Clarice had laughed her wonderful sandpaper laugh and
put her arm around Sarah's shoulder. "Imagine that you're
in a movie theater, okay? Only somebody screws up, and
instead of just* one *movie being projected onto the screen,
there're* two *up there at the same time, one superimposed
over the other. But the thing is, you can't have someone go
up to the projectionist's booth and tell them to turn the other
movie off so you can see just one. You have to watch both.
All the time."*

"Is it hard?"

Clarice's eyes misted over. "Yeah, hon, it is, because this
*world doesn't want to See the other one, which is really
sad—because if it did, then the two might start to become
One, which is the way the Goddess wants it to be. So much
pain would be eased, then; no loneliness, no sickness, no
more tears."*

"No more death?"

*Clarice shook her head. "Oh, no, hon—people and things,
they'd still die—everything has to die when its time comes—
but their lives would be so much fuller until then.*

*"You've already reached Recognition, Sarah, and Belief.
You're already capable of some Sight. I hope that, when the
time comes, you'll be strong enough to reach Embracing,
because I'm going to leave all my Magic for you, hon. An
Earth-Witch has to pass on her magic when she dies, or else
it'll die with her."*

*Sarah had begun to cry. "I don't ever want you to die,
Aunt Clarice."*

*"Oh, hon. Like it's high up on my list of 'Things I Most
Want To Do.' Ha!")*

Sarah was jolted from the memory when an old, dry,
eggshell voice scattered out from a room somewhere down
the hall: ". . . abeewan . . . abeewan . . ." then became
louder, alarm on the edge of full-blown panic: "Baby . . .
I want my baby! *I want my baby! I WANT MY BABY!*"

A nurse whisked toward the woman's cries with a muscular orderly in tow. The orderly was clutching a baby doll (missing both of its hands) under one of his massive arms. A few more cries, these less panicky, and soon the eggshell woman was cooing a brittle, misremembered lullaby in a voice full of dust and regret and emeralds.

Sarah crushed out the cigarette and pulled her hand away from the top of the cup. The coffee had turned into hot chocolate—complete with a few of those mini-marshmallows she'd loved as a child.

"Nothing up my sleeve," she whispered.

There's Magic for you, Aunt Clarice; I can turn coffee into hot chocolate but I can't make you better—hell, you told me yourself early on that I'm not supposed to try to make you better. "It's getting near my time," you said. Then you started humming that old Byrds' song, "Turn, Turn, Turn" and laughed.

What good is Magic, then? I know what this world is like, Clarice, and in my hands Magic would only be a way to put a Band-Aid on a shotgun wound.

She closed her eyes and lowered her head.

Sarah Hempel did not want to embrace magic the way she had wanted to embrace it as a girl of twelve; as far as she was concerned now, that was the last refuge of the hysteric: A final, frantic attempt to explain Chaos—or at least give the *appearance* of having explained Chaos. Not for her; not for someone who grappled with the all-too-grim realities of the day-to-day world, who felt morally compelled to abide with Chaos all the way until the last and dreadful hour, plugging along until she had either answered all the questions at hand, unraveling the tangles in life's unseen cat's cradles, or else succumbed to the snarl altogether. She was an always cautious, sometimes emotional woman, not a romantic one, who prided herself on being clear-headed, especially during a crisis; but that particular clarity now lay shattered like so many shards of imploded glass. She'd swapped pragmatism and determinism for magic and fantasy—or, rather, had found that they were being swapped on her behalf.

She sipped the hot chocolate and thought again of how Clarice used to have her come over for the weekends when Sarah was a child, how the two of them would make hot chocolate and watch the marshmallows melt while Clarice told her all about Earth-Magic and healing rituals and the Goddess' Gift of Sight that could lift the Veils of Perception. Sarah hadn't understood exactly what it was her aunt was talking about then, but she'd loved listening to her; Clarice seemed to be of another world, another time, like something out of a neverending fairy tale.

Only now it was Sarah who was being forced to write the final scene.

This last of it had begun some seven-and-a-half hours before when the head nurse from the Alzheimer's unit called. Sarah had had a particularly bad day at work, having nearly gotten herself slapped with a Contempt of Court charge when she vehemently argued with the judge against granting guardianship of an elderly Alzheimer's patient to the patient's son—who was not only misrepresenting how he spent the poor woman's Social Security money, but was (Sarah strongly suspected) physically abusing the woman. Sarah had just about had her fill of bureaucratic bullshit and its glibly justified dismissal of APS' suspicions. Maybe it was time to get the hell out while some part of her soul remained her.

The call was the last thing she'd needed.

"Ms. Hempel? This is Emily, from the Cedar Hill Healthcare Center. I'm sorry to bother you, but it's your aunt."

"Is everything all right?"

"Yes and no. I need your verbal authorization to strap her into her bed. She's nearly fallen out twice now and we're concerned that she—"

"I understand."

She not only gave them permission to strap Clarice into her bed at night but when she was in her wheelchair, as well.

Sarah hung up the phone, went into the bathroom, washed her face, then stared at the weary, wary eyes reflected in the mirror.

Well, let's take stock of what you've done to her so far, shall we? she thought. You've made her a No-Code—meaning that they are to take no extreme medical measures to prolong her life, just as she wanted . . . not that that makes it any easier; you've let them put her in diapers because she messes herself so much; you haven't seen her in almost thirty days, knowing full well no one else visits her; and now you've said it's okay to tie her up like some prize hog on its way to the slaughterhouse—or a witch on her way to execution. Even today, with all the world's learned about the true nature of magic and witchcraft, you're allowing her to be treated like some cauldron-happy hag from the prologue of *Macbeth*.

What else could she do? The last time she'd visited, Clarice barely recognized her, only sat in her wheelchair staring at the television. Occasionally she'd look up and say something cryptic—"Lord of death and the Summerland" or, "I am the heart of the Four"—then take hold of Sarah's hand with more reflex than intentional affection. After a while her grip would loosen and her hand would drop to her side and she'd sigh and close her eyes as one of the nurses spoon-fed her oatmeal and spoke in the same condescending singsong voice most people use with children—

—*Okay, she was bad before you put her in the nursing home, sure, no question about that. She was becoming a danger to herself, leaving the stove on or a ritual candle burning too close to open tubes of oil paint, hurting herself and ignoring the wounds until they became infected, not bathing or changing her clothes, performing Gaian-Praise rituals nude in the back yard in full view of the neighbors . . . pretty bad, yes—*

—*but she'd still been* driven, *argue that. She'd still been able to mutter complete sentences and carry on brief conversations, enjoy a TV movie, laugh at jokes, savor the taste of wine, and RECOGNIZE YOU! She was impatient because she was growing old and there was still so much to hear, taste, see, know, understand, imagine, and do—and not nearly enough time to experience all of it. She'd still been able to look at her sculptures and paintings and sketches and talk about how she wanted to improve them, still wanted to teach you about the ways of the Goddess, instruct you in Healing Practices and how to train your Gift of Sight—*

—*she still seemed to want to live.*

Then came the nursing home and a downward slide so sudden and all-encompassing she might as well have been stoned to death and burned at the stake.

Face up to it, damn you. Once you put her in there, she gave up, *surrendered, became so weak and pathetic and . . . sad. She* had *to've seen it as your refusing to Embrace the Magic of the Goddess, of rejecting everything dear to her that she wanted to pass on to you, the only member of her family who didn't mock her, hold her in contempt, or feel embarrassed by her practices and beliefs. Maybe she would have accidentally killed herself if you hadn't put her in there, but she would have died at least goddamn happy, believing in her magic ways and your faith in her, feeling that she had some worth and integrity and was still a viable, worthwhile, preciously* unique *person and not some sputtering, somnambulistic sideshow attraction with no shred of the power, wit, grace, and radiance that marked her at her best.*

Sarah began to cry—a luxury she rarely allowed herself these days.

I'm sorry I put you in that place, Clarice, but I'm thirty-five years old and I don't have anyone special, my family doesn't know what to make of me, and I'm wondering if my life will mean anything—working at APS, fighting day after day against a system intent on creating enough red tape to blind itself to its responsibility to the elderly, then not wanting to hear about what happens when it fails . . . watching you die is more than I can handle right now, so I draw walls tighter around me, do what little I can at work, pay the bills, clean the apartment, and ignore the Emerging Sight that keeps me awake at night and forever separate from the world I want so much to be a part of. If I crack it will all come spilling out, ugly and incoherent. I'm lonely, Clarice, and I can't get myself to embrace the magic you say is out there— I can recognize *the power of the Goddess, I can even* believe *in it in the same way I believe in cruelty and loneliness and duplicity and pain, but even though I'm Gifted, I'll always be one of the Unmanifest because I feel banal, pointless, and ineffectual. I go through the motions, watching movies, listening to music, and reading books because there has to be something in my life to pass for purpose. You had that once, didn't you, before I signed the papers and put you away? I don't want you to die, but sometimes I wish you would. Most of you is dead already, and that one last part that's hanging on by its fingernails can't be too far behind. And when it goes, when that last part finally says "fuck it"*

*and gives up the ghost, when that pale, clammy shell that
was once you rattles out its last, slow, muck-filled breath,
they'll all shake their heads and whisper, "Isn't it a pity?"
and never, ever know that I'm the one who condemned you
to death. I might as well have strangled you in your sleep.*

The phone in her apartment rang again, wrenching her
back to the present.

"Hello?"

"Ms. Hempel? Emily. I'm sorry to bother you again so
soon, but . . . well, something's happened."

Sarah felt the tissue connecting her muscles turn into
bone. *Please say that she's all right. Please say that she died
a few minutes ago. Please say she's fine. Please—*

"I don't understand how, Ms. Hempel, but your aunt
is missing."

"She's *what?*"

"We do a bed-check every thirty minutes. The first time
I called you was just before we made the rounds. I don't
know how this happened—Clarice has been incapable of
independent mobility for a long while now—but sometime
in the last half-hour she got out of her bed and wandered
off the unit."

"Have you checked the rest of the buildings?"

"Yes, and she's not been seen anywhere. I've got staff
members out checking the grounds, and the immediate resi-
dential areas. I've called the police and given them a de-
scription, but . . . oh, Lord, Ms. Hempel, I'm so sorry.
Nothing like this has ever happened on my watch before."

"It's all right, Emily, it's not your fault. I'll be there in
about twenty minutes."

She hung up the phone, terrified, the echo of Aunt Clarice's voice resounding in her mind: *You'll know when the
time comes for you to perform the Earth-Witch Requiem
and the Awakening of Magic Awareness ritual, honey, because what's left of me'll take itself a little spirit-stroll. Don't
you worry none about my body—hah! Silly old thing—
'cause I'll hide it someplace for a while, until I'm done with
what I need to do before you can perform the rituals.*

Though every rational instinct told her not to do it, she
nonetheless went into the back of the bedroom closet and
removed the black airline carry-on bag Clarice had given
to her. *Everything you'll need for the two ceremonies is in*

here, Sarah. Don't worry if you forget any of the words or anything—not that I think that'll happen; Lord, hon, I'll bet you could probably do them in your sleep we've gone over them so many times . . . I'm rambling, aren't I? Sorry. Anyway, everything's all written down for you. Just do like the instructions say and everything will be like it's supposed to be.

Sarah had promised Clarice that, when the time came, she'd perform both the Requiem (to honor her aunt and compel Clarice's transmigration from flesh into the bosom of the Goddess) and the Awareness Ritual (wherein Sarah herself would Embrace the power Clarice left behind for her, in essence taking her aunt's place).

Knowing that she would perform only the Requiem, she drove away from her apartment building three minutes later.

She was taking a shortcut to the nursing home—driving along a winding, poorly lighted stretch of Cherry Valley Road—when she saw the statues . . . or what she at first *thought* were statues.

They appeared in her headlight beams so suddenly she almost didn't have time to stop.

They weren't statues at all, she saw, but costume head-pieces worn by a large group of revelers as they crossed the road. Some turned to wave in apology, others in recognition, and a few, oddly, in invitation.

The giant papier-mache heads many of them wore were reminiscent of the stone monoliths on Easter Island—but where those ancient heads were solemn, inspiring awe, wonder, and even fear, those worn by the revelers were quirky and whimsical, inviting laughter and good cheer with their comically elongated noses and jaws and stiff, pointed horse's ears. Some carried banners that flapped in the wind, others had large bottles of wine cradled in bamboo baskets, a few held leather harnesses with sleigh bells above their heads, jingling and jangling as they twirled by, and one carried a well-used bodhran, using its thumbs to strike the surface of the goatskin drum.

Sarah stared at them, wondering where in hell they'd come from and what they were doing. It was too soon for any Halloween parties, and the local Wiccans wouldn't be conducting their Autumnal Equinox celebration for a few more weeks.

Maybe someone just decided to have a costume party for no good damn reason, she thought. People did that. It was called Having Fun.

Despite her anxiety and impatience to get to the nursing home, she couldn't help but watch the merrymakers, noting how elaborate and meticulously-detailed were their costumes; not just in the shape and design of the headpieces (she wondered how some of the revelers maintained their balance, so big were the adornments), but in the craftsmanship of the robes, gowns, and togas, as well.

Then one of the giant-headed figures blinked its eyes, parting its lips in a smile. Sarah realized that they weren't costume headpieces at all; these beings were real, corporeal, flesh and blood . . . and utterly fantastic.

A man with the head of a black hawk wearing a feathered headdress, a turtle with a small antlers, a raven-headed woman in a golden flowing gown, a lion peering out from behind the visor in a suit of armor, a wolf in multicolored bandoleers, a mouse with angel's wings, a steer-skull being wearing the uniform of a Spanish Conquistador, a glass owl, a crystalline buffalo, a jade spider; dressed in deerskin shirts and breechclouts and leggings, with medicine pouches and beaded necklaces, holding flutes and horn-pipes and ceremonial chimes, their music and soft singing became the unbound wings of time, holding the Earth's spirit in the spell of a lullaby.

The antlered turtle—who, from all appearances, was a child—came over to the car, its right hand making a small but insistent circular motion: *Roll down your window.*

"Hello," it said in the voice of a little girl.

"What are you?"

"The first moment your aunt ever dreamed about falling in love," replied the turtle-child. "She wants you to know that it's time, if you've got the courage."

Sarah shook her head. "It's not that simple."

"Why not?"

"Because I can't allow myself to embrace it the way she wants me to."

The turtle-child nodded its head. "She thought this might happen. That's why she let us out tonight. She knows there's a chance you won't take her powers—that you won't take *us*—into your heart, so she gave us the closest thing to our true physical forms and is allowing us to wander the world tonight, to see things as she saw them, to hear, taste, feel, and experience this side. It might be our only chance."

Sarah almost smiled. "And how do you like it, so far?"

"I think it's pretty neat, most of it. I could do without the dirt and chemicals and anger, the pain and violence, stuff like that, but . . . wow, *the stars and moonlight!* The smell of damp leaves. Paintings, a baby's laughter, churches, space shuttles—Charlie Parker records! There's . . . *so much* to enjoy."

"And just as much to hate."

"If you accepted the Power of the Goddess, you'd have the ability to change things. When the real world gets too horrible, then the real world has to be altered; you would have it in you to do this."

"Oh, for chrissakes! There's too much pain, there're too many—"

The turtle-child—who told Sarah its name was Then-Again—reached out and took hold of her hand. "The problem with being able to believe in magic, Sarah, is that people think too much in terms of the *big* miracle, the Earth-shaking miracle, when the whole secret is what's born and kept alive in the heart: a true love, a right hope, a good will. No adversity can stop you if *that* is the magic you first Embrace."

"I can't even embrace that much," whispered Sarah, ashamed. "Not after all I've seen over the years."

"That doesn't make any sense. You've already reached Recognition—"

"—and Belief, yeah, yeah, blah-blah-blah; don't you think I *know* this already? But I can't . . . I can't be part of two movies at the same time, you know what I mean?"

"No," said ThenAgain sadly. "No, I don't know what you mean at all."

Sarah stared at ThenAgain, her eyes tearing—but she did not allow herself to cry. "I can't Embrace it because . . . b–because I don't see how I can use it the way it *should* be used. It scares me, that Power. Christ! I have authority and power in my position now, and *I can't change a damned thing!* I feel like a fail—oh, damn! . . . no; I won't whine about it. Listen; the idea of Embracing Magic and *still* not being able to make a difference is more than I can deal with, because if I fail with Magic on my side, then there's . . . there's no point to my life.

"To fail within the boundaries of the Unmanifest world is one thing; to fail with Magic would . . . would render me *purposeless*. Can you understand that?"

"Clarice thought the same thing, early on."

"But I'm not her."

ThenAgain sighed. "You would have been a worthy Earth-Witch. You would have given the Goddess even more presence on this side.

"Just remember, Sarah; you can still change your mind, you can still Embrace. But when Clarice dies, when she Moves Toward the bosom of the Goddess, we'll go with her."

". . . I know . . ."

"Good-bye, Sarah," whispered ThenAgain. "I hope someday that sadness will be lifted from your eyes and your heart."

Then she turned around and ran back to the others.

"Wait!" cried Sarah, but the group was now only a dark, oddly-shaped silhouette moving in the twilight shadows.

When Sarah finally arrived at the nursing home, Clarice was back in her bed ("I *swear* I don't know where she got to or when she came back," said a perplexed but infinitely relieved Emily), securely strapped in place and looking not only peaceful in her last hours but strangely content.

"You here to fix my television?"

Startled, Sarah looked up to see the ambulatory patient from earlier standing in the doorway clutching part of his tattered robe. The man's chin shimmered with spit. The deep, discolored lines that had burrowed into his features were all too clear, souvenirs from a life that had been too long and too hard, filled with too many disappointments and heartbreaks, a life now measured not in weeks or days or hours but minutes—possibly even seconds—because that was all his damaged, dying brain could retain.

"Don't gawk at me like that," said the man. "I asked you a question. You here to fix my television?"

"Uh . . . no, no I'm not."

The old man sneered. "Well, ain't that a pisser? I been on them to get someone out here for weeks. Can't watch my programs if the damned TV don't work!'' He shambled over to the window and looked out, his eyes widening. "Well, lookee here, why don't you?"

Sarah turned around in her chair to face the courtyard. The stone head was still whistling and some patients were still pointing at it, pretending to conduct private symphonies . . . then creatures that had been hiding in the darkness came slowly forward and began dancing around the cage.

One was a lithe female figure with the head of a black horse, its ears erect, its neck arched, vapor jetting from its nostrils; another was tall and skeletal, with fingers so long their tips brushed against the ground: it hunkered down and snaked its fingers around the bars of the cage, as if absorbing the sound through vibrations. Some hopped like frogs, some rolled, some scuttled on rootlike filaments that were covered in flowers whose centers were the faces of blind children. All of them sang and danced.

"Kinda pretty," said the old man.

"My aunt made them. Some from clay, some she painted, some were only sketches."

The old man turned back toward Sarah. "I can't watch my programs anymore. What'm I supposed to do?"

"I'm sure they'll get someone out here real soon."

The old man stuck out his chin and defiantly adjusted his robe, tying its frayed belt with palsied hands. "They told you to say that, didn't they?"

"Who?"

"Don't you try it. Don't you be sneakin' into my room and trying to take away my television, you hear me? I'm not the one who told on Katie Lynn. I oughtn't to be punished for that. I mean, sure, everybody saw how bad the cut on her face was, that it needed stitches and all, but I saw her fall off her bike, all right? *I saw her.* Her daddy didn't beat her like she said. She just said that so all the kids'd feel sorry for her. Everyone picked on her, y'know? She smelled kinda ripe and always wore them old dirty clothes. Shameful, it was." A tear slipped out of his eye and ran down his cheek, dangled at the corner of his mouth, then tumbled onto his chin. "I loved her, though, really, I did. Once you got past feelin' sorry for her, she was kinda sweet. Do anything for you, she would. A sweet girl. Terrible thing, don't you think? Her daddy touching her like he did, then beating her up all the time so she'd not tell and making her say that she fell off her bike. I saw him pound on her." He made a fist and swung it down toward an invisible target near his hip. "Just hammered on her like she weren't supposed to feel a thing. Poor girl. She made me promise I'd tell folks I saw her fall off her bike. Poor girl. She was sweet. Do anything for you. I felt sorry for her. Them dirty clothes all the time. She used to help me on my paper route and tell me stories that she made up—and they was clever ones, to boot. Dragons going shopping at the bakery, elephants dancing the ballet. I got to know her on account of them stories, and she was pretty when you got to know her. She gave me my first kiss. Her lips tasted like fresh strawberries. And her in them dirty clothes. I loved her. She's dead now, sixty years. He pushed her down the stairs and she—" his voice cracked on the next word, "—*smashed* her head against the radiator and then she went away. She was only ten. I miss her something terrible. I wish I'd've married her, that she'd've lived that long. I'd've treated her tender, y'know? But I never told her I loved her. Don't think anyone ever did. Someone should've loved her and told her so. Now I can only see her on the TV, and it's all broke." He clamped his mouth closed, his rheumy eyes releasing a few more tears. His body swayed a little to the left, then he shuddered, snapping himself from his wistful reverie. "You here to fix my television? I got it right here. Just a little portable thing." He held up his hand, fingers and thumb curved into a crescent as if grasping a handle.

Sarah felt something in her chest wither and for a moment stood outside the tableau, staring into this too-bright room at a pair of sad, lonely people; an old man in a draughty hall, a younger woman seeking absolution for the sin she was about to commit. The storms continue to come. The nights only grow darker. What use was there, then, for tenderness? Swaddled in this darkness, a word of mercy within a word of despair, unable to speak either one, proffering deeds to oblivion and love to the prosperity of the grave: This old man; this frightened woman; this harsh light; this skirling sorrow like lingering smoke.

"Let me take a look at it," whispered Sarah.

The old man meandered over. "You be careful. This's

the only one I've got and I can't afford to replace it. Probably can't afford your prices, either, but we'll work something out.''

Sarah stared at the empty spot on the table where the TV was sitting. "This one'll be on the house."

"Best get to it, then," said the old man, looking on his wrist at a watch that wasn't there. "Almost time for my programs."

Sarah gave him a half-smile, nodded once, then reached into her purse for a metal nail-file which she used as a screwdriver to repair the loose antenna in the back of the set.

"Nice television," she said, squinting at the complicated detail work as she removed the back panel and replaced one of the electronic chips.

The old man watched, glistening-eyed and anxious.

A twist here, a tightening there, then replace the back panel; Sarah gave the antenna a jiggle to make sure it was securely in place, then turned the set around and asked the old man to try it now.

"Hey, you do good work," he said, his smile still haunted by the ghost of the handsome devil he must have been in his younger days. He picked up the small television—now as corporeal as both himself and Sarah—and turned it on. "Picture's clear as a bell. Thanks."

"My pleasure, sir. My very great pleasure."

The old man shuffled toward the door. "She ought to be on pretty soon. I miss her, y'know? Poor little thing. Do anything for you. Kids shouldn't've picked on her so much. That's all she ever knew, people picking on her. . . ." He rounded the corner and was gone. The empty space in the doorway ached with his absence.

It occurred to Sarah that she hadn't asked the old man what his name was, or what Katie Lynn's last name had been. Too bad; she wouldn've liked to have known.

Only then did she allow the enormity of what she'd just done to hit her.

Jesus.

She'd done it. The coffee/hot chocolate incident, that had been one thing, but *this*—it was like Aunt Clarice had said, she had only to visualize it in order to make it so.

What's been in me for all these years, Sarah, is in you, as well. You've never really felt quite at home with folks, have

*you? Even family. They don't want to believe in these things,
so that's what they've taught you—not to believe. But you
still* feel *it in there sometimes, don't you? Late at night when
you're just about to fall asleep, you get this sense something
in you's only now coming awake, only now being set free.
That's the power of the Goddess in you, honey, trying to
give you the life you* should've *been allowed to have, the
power you* should've *been allowed to embrace and use. But
this world—ah, hell, honey, this world, it doesn't* want *to
understand, let alone believe. Too much concrete beneath
folks' feet, it makes them look at it for too long until they
think that's all there is. You have to accept that your powers
are real, that* the magic *is real.*

"No," said Sarah through clenched teeth; "It's still just
a Band-Aid on a gunshot wound. Nothing more." She drew
in a ragged breath and looked down.

Were a murderer's hands supposed to shake like this?

She paced around the lounge, lit a fresh cigarette—*that
makes almost two packs since this morning, you idiot—
doesn't that tell you something about the shape you're in?*
For the umpteenth time she reexamined the pattern.

She'd seen it many times during her years with APS:
They closed all other doors on the unit when someone died.
No doctors were on call between eleven PM and eight AM,
barring a medical emergency—which death in this place did
not qualify as. After the doors were closed, the head nurse
went into the room, noted the time of death, then called
the doctor's answering service and left the information. If
the next of kin was present at the time of death, they were
allowed to remain in the room and wait for the funeral
home to come and pick up the body.

The *funeral home.*

Which meant no doctors.

Which meant no autopsy.

Which meant there would be no way for them to know.

She crushed out her cigarette and went back to the
window.

A flock of coelacanths and paddlefish swam around the
cage as if their long-ago vanished prehistoric ocean still
existed in the spot.

She clenched her teeth, steadied her hands, spun around,
and walked to her aunt's room.

There was Clarice in her bed, her aged, emaciated hands
lying against the soft cotton blanket like the desiccated
shells of dead starfish along an abandoned shore.

Sarah inhaled deeply as she stepped into the room and
began closing the door. Emily wouldn't think twice about
the door being closed while Sarah was in here, she knew
how much Sarah loved her aunt, how precious these last
few hours were; shutting the door had been Emily's suggestion in the first place.

As the door thumped softly closed, a last gust of air from
the corridor slipped in, carrying smells of antiseptics and
detergents, of aged ladies' perfumes and musky bath salts
accented by the aroma of dying flowers, the scents blending
in a pathetic effort to disguise the underlying stench of old
urine, feces, and vomit which seemed as permanent a part
of the building as the mortar between the bricks.

Sarah moved toward the bed.

Her hands increased their trembling.

Jesus! Get a grip!

They were alone in the room. The other bed was empty,
its occupant having died three nights ago.

Sarah felt a thin bead of perspiration slide down her
cheek.

She stared at the pillows under Clarice's head.

She listened to her aunt's breathing; slow, painful: Death
pausing to savor the moment and admire the agonizing poetry of its handiwork.

Sarah crossed to the chair where she'd placed the carry-
on bag earlier and began removing the items she'd need
for the ritual; a makeshift altar (two large books of magic
spells and a section of wood, plus a silk cover); white and
black taper candles; a white votive candle in a white con-
tainer; a vial of water, a vial of salt, and small dishes to
hold them; incense and burner; a small bell; a hand-sized
black stone; some rosemary (for remembrance); a small
spool of red yarn; a square of paper; a red-inked pen.

She set up the altar facing North, placing a vase of flowers near the back; the white taper candle (for the Goddess)
went on the left, the black taper candle (for the Horned
God) went on the right. She arranged the other items according to Clarice's instructions, purified the water, blessed
the salt, and mixed the salt into the water.

She set flame to the wick of the white candle—

—a remembered moment: Clarice saying a prayer for Sarah's dying kitten when Sarah was seven, then saying, "It's not the kitty's time, hon, so don't you worry none," and sure enough, two days later, the kitten made a full recovery and Sarah was so happy because it meant that there was wonder, and magic—

"Oh, Great Mother Goddess, who gives birth to all that is . . ." Then she set flame to the black candle, whispering, "Oh, Great Horned God, Lord of Death and the Summerland, I ask that both you of you be with me tonight and bless this ritual." She lit the incense, stood, parted her arms, turned in a complete circle, and chanted: "Oh, Mighty Ones of the four Quarters—Air and Fire and Water and Earth—I ask that you attend and empower and bless this rite.

"Hear me as I say that Clarice Hempel, a friend and sister in the Craft, is passing beyond the veil."

(*And what about Tommy Butler? Remember how you wanted him to ask you to the ninth grade dance but figured he didn't like you because any time you tried talking to him he made up some excuse to leave, but then Aunt Clarice performed some kind of ritual and he did ask you to the dance? You got so mad at Clarice because you thought she made him do something he didn't want to do, but then she'd said, "Oh, no I didn't; that's the worst misuse of Magic there is; I only gave him a little push to act on what was already in his heart, so you can stop looking at me that way now."*)

She rang the small bell three times, hoping none of the staff would get curious and come to investigate the sound. "Tonight I remember her and honor her spirit as I bid her farewell." Next, she laid the red spiral of thread in the center of the altar and said: "She travels soon on the Great Spiral of Death and Rebirth. Infinite and eternal is the cord which binds us to the Mother Goddess."

(*. . . the whole secret is what's born and kept alive in the heart: a true love, a right hope, a good will . . .*)

"Night leads to dawn, winter to spring; endless is the Spirit's journey and ever the Circle shall turn." She lit the votive candle and placed it in the middle of the red spiral. "Dearest Clarice, whom I love so deeply, may your spirit be rekindled in new flesh; may you arise in peace. I bid you farewell on your journey through the shadows. May you find rest and peace in Summerland."

The rest of the ritual she performed exactly as she'd been taught, and only started to cry again as she reached the last, sprinkling rosemary and the purified salt-water in a circle around Clarice's bed. "B–blessed is the Great Mother, who gives life to the universe. From Her we all proceed and unto Her must we all return. She is the Ground of Being that dwells within us, giving us Her Power, allowing us Sight, changeless, boundless, and eternal, and Her love is poured out upon the Earth.

"Blessed be."

A rattling, wheezing, painful sound crawled from Clarice's lungs.

Sarah, standing next to the bed, put her hand on her aunt's head and whispered, "*Atlas Shrugged,* huh?"

"*Right,*" echoed the memory of Clarice's voice. "*What if it were possible to simply* will *the world to stop spinning on its axis?*"

"*The planet would go hurtling into the sun, and we'd all be ash in a millisecond,*" Sarah had replied.

"*But not if you didn't* want *it to happen—work with me here, will you, hon?*"

"*So, what do you do while the world goes on, unnoticing of the wonder you've performed? Answer: You perform another. You pull a* Fountainhead, *do a Howard Rourke, and build the most astonishing building, a fantastic piece of architecture the likes of which haven't been seen since the Tower of Babel, then you tear it down and build an even better one—only in this case, since the rest of the world— the Unmanifest—can't consciously register what you're up to, you recreate the world, making it this fabulous, mind-blowing work of art and—oh my, look at me, will you? I'm shaking, I'm so excited. Better pay attention, hon, this is 'A' material here.*

"*Think of it—ha! You could recreate the world a million times over, and no one but you would know it.*"

"*Until you decreed otherwise?*"

"*Bingo. And by then it would be too late for anyone to stop you—but why should they want to? When the real world gets too horrible, then the real world must be altered—*"

one kind thought, one good will, one heart at a time. That's *one of the Goddess' most profound lessons: Purify one heart, lift the sadness from one set of eyes, and* nothing *is impossible for you.*"

Sarah wiped the tears from her eyes, then reached underneath Clarice's head and gently slipped out one of the pillows.

Realizing the curtains were still partially opened, she put the pillow down near the altar and went to pull the curtain all the way closed.

She froze, one hand clutching the curtain's edge, and saw that the bacchanal around the cage had stopped; all of the creatures were looking upward.

Sarah unlatched the window, opened it, leaned out, and craned her neck for a better look.

Up in the night sky the moon had become a shimmering silver rose, its petals formed by the wings of the hundreds—maybe thousands—of angels perched around it, looking down like spectators into an arena.

They were watching a pterosaur twice the size of an airplane pump its mammoth wings and fly in wide, graceful circles.

It was not alone.

A WWII German pursuit plane with twin machine guns mounted on its wings—a latter version of the 1916 model designed by Anthony Herman Gerard Fokker (Clarice's favorite kind of plane)—was engaged in an intense but playful dogfight with the flying reptile. The plane turned in tight, precise maneuvers as the pterosaur tried attacking it from below. The machine guns strafed without mercy or sound, a silent-film prop spitting out bursts of sparking light, firing off round after round.

The creatures seemed to be smiling at this harmless little entertainment.

Sarah quickly shut the window, yanked closed the curtain, and grabbed up the pillow.

Clarice pulled in another strained breath, and though there was no sound this time Sarah thought she could hear a scream, silent and gnarled and endless: *Help me.*

She marched over to the bed and whispered, "If you can hear me, Aunt Clarice, if there's some part of you that can still comprehend what's said to you, please forgive me. I don't have your faith, or your strength, or your joy for living. I love you, and I will remember you and miss you every moment of every day for the rest of my life, but I . . . I *can't* Embrace the Magic. I'm too much a part of this world now, and it *scares* me to let that go.

"I can't perform the second ritual, I'm sorry."

She gripped the pillow in both hands and held it an inch or so above her aunt's face and moved to press it down. *That's it, all you have to do is cover her face, she's weak and can't fight back, so just do it already why don't you, press against her nose and mouth and bear down with all you've got, make it stop, make it go away, whisper* Forgive me *and hope it doesn't take long, grip it hard at both ends, just like you're doing, yes, just like this, use both hands and press down, down, down, down, go on, GO ON, GO ON DO IT FOR CHRISSAKES IT'S ALMOST THERE NOT FAR TO GO EVERYTHING HAS TO STOP, IT HAS TO, YOU KNOW IT, YOU KNOW—*

—and then she remembered something else; something that had almost nothing to do with magic, or the Goddess, or Sight and Power; something very simple, something she'd thought she'd forgotten about:

Ten years ago. New Year's Eve. She had decided to skip the party she'd been invited to and spend it with Aunt Clarice because Clarice hadn't been feeling well lately— not only from a cold she couldn't seem to shake but because she'd been feeling ". . . a little lonely these days." They had made a pizza, said a prayer to the Goddess in thanks for the New Year, then planted themselves on the couch to watch Clarice's favorite movie, *Pride of the Yankees,* starring Gary Cooper. Sarah had never seen it before and was surprised at how well-made it was, how intelligent and compelling, and when it came down to the famous final scene, the one where the Coop stands in the middle of a packed stadium and delivers the famous *Today-I-consider-myself-the-luckiest-man-on-the-face-of-the-Earth* speech, then turns around and walks out as the crowd cheers, disappearing into the darkness of a hallway next to the dugout just as an unseen umpire shouts, *"Play ball!"*—at that moment she'd turned to see her aunt in tears—and not those wimpy little raindrop tears, no; these tears were the big, fat crocodile kind, and Sarah had laughed and said, "Well, you old sneak! Look at you. All these years claiming you haven't got a sentimental bone in your body!"

Clarice had blown her nose and wiped her eyes and said, "Oh, stuff you, honey: That's a helluva scene, rakes me over the coals every dang time. Ha! Y'know what?—*Everybody* ought to be given a chance to go out like that, one grand, glorious, untainted moment where they get the chance to say what they hope their life has meant, and what it will mean to those folks they're leaving behind. You die twice when people forget you were here, and everybody ought to be given a chance at the end to make damn sure that folks will remember them. *That's* how I want to go out, like the Coop there; I want to leave the world with something that it'll never, ever forget . . . even if it's just a kind thought. Is that . . . is that too much to ask?" Clarice was still crying, but now it was obviously because of something more than the movie.

"No, it isn't," said Sarah, scooting closer to her aunt and embracing her. Clarice put her head against Sarah's shoulder and wept a little more.

"Ah, Sarah," she said (so mournfully), "I know what everyone thinks of me, that they'll be glad in a way when I'm gone, but sometimes I . . . I wish I could get just one of them to understand what I'm all about. That I want to mean something to them, that I want my life to mean something after I'm gone. God, hon, usually it's not this bad but I realized tonight that I'm sixty-two years old and I've never been in love or had any real close friends because of . . . of being a witch and all, and I just got to feeling so lonely . . ."

"I'm here, Aunt Clarice. And I love you. Your life means something to me."

"Thanks, hon. You always were kind to me. You never made fun of my beliefs." She pulled back, took Sarah's face into her hands, and looked straight into her niece's eyes. "Promise me that when I die, if I don't get a chance to do a number like the Coop did in the movie, that you'll do it for me. Is that asking too much?"

"No," said Sarah. "Not at all. If you can't tell people, then I'll do it for you. I'll remember it all for you."

Standing over her aunt now, Sarah realized she couldn't do it, and so pulled the pillow away and leaned down and listened for Clarice's breathing.

There it was; strained, ugly, and painful, but she was still alive.

She pulled back the curtains and opened the window.

The creatures had moved the cage closer; the stone head sat less than a yard away from Sarah—its face now revealed to be her own—and as she stared into its eyes, she thought about magic, in all of its forms, and what it should mean to the world. The lessons of magic taught that every human being should understand the necessity of using art, language, music, and faith to carry the Now into the Yet To Come so as to give human memory in all its frailty some form of permanence. If you were lucky and Chaos had its back turned at the moment, you might find someone to whom you could pass on your beliefs so they might use it to keep art, music, language, faith—all of it—from slipping through humanity's psychic filters. A good will, a kind thought, passed from keeper to keeper. "Remember this for me when I'm gone." Moment to memory to scroll, page, canvas, stone; permanence; history; ritual: Magic.

Do a number like the Coop did . . .

She stared at the webs weighing down the head.

"You're the Goddess, aren't you?" she asked. "Or, at least, the *aspect* of the Goddess my aunt wanted me to Embrace?"

The stone head blinked its eyes; once, very slowly: *Yes.*

"I put those webs there, didn't I? My fear and cynicism?" *Yes.*

She looked once more at her aunt.

Begin with one heart, that's what you said, wasn't it, Clarice? "Can't change a thing until you change what's in your own heart, hon, and you can't do that until you open yourself up to the possibilities."

"Atlas Shrugged?"

"Ha! You're catching on, hon, you're catching on."

Sarah took a deep breath and felt something in the center of her chest expand, ever so slightly—a space between heartbeats just large enough for a breath to pass through—and realized that she was being selfish, so selfish; Clarice had not learned how to use her Magic overnight, so why would she expect Sarah to do so?

Begin with one heart.

A true love; a right hope; a good will.

Could there be any more worthy an embodiment of those things than the woman to whom she'd just good-bye?

Could there be any better way to honor the memory of her life than to—

—no, of course not.

And look at it this way, she thought: *At least you'll have tried. You owe her that much.*

"You owe yourself *that much."*

"Have mercy upon me, O Goddess," she chanted, beginning the Awakening of Magical Awareness Ritual. "Blot out my transgressions and wash me thoroughly of my iniquities, cleanse me from my sins of unbelief."

She parted her arms and slowly turned in a circle. "Create in me a clean heart, and renew the Spirit within me. Give to me the Sight, and the Power of Your Love and Healing. From my heart of being I cast off the chains of the Unmanifest, I extend this circle of power, of Awareness and Gifting. Let no evil or discordant influence enter my heart to blind me to Your Goodness and Strength and all Your Magicks."

She faced south, standing with her feet together, arms still spread so as to make a cross with her body. In her mind Sarah envisioned a column of holy flame rising from the center of the Earth, passing through her aunt and accepting Clarice's Power, then moving across the room and entering her own Center, making her One with Infinity.

"Before me," she whispered, "is Michael, Lord of Flame, Lion of the South; behind me is Raphael, Lord of Air, Angel of the North; on my right is Gabriel, Lord of Water, the Eagle of the West; on my left is Uriel, Lord of Earth, the Bull of the East: The Four surround me." Her voice was Bliss; her inflections Redemption.

She raised her hands above her head.

"Fire above."

She lowered them to her waist.

"Water below."

She brought her hands together over her heart.

"I am the heart of the Four; I am the center of the universe."

She opened her eyes and stared directly at her aunt.

"I love you, Clarice, and I will remember all you taught to me, all you gave to me. You offer me Empowerment . . .

"And I happily accept your gift. Happily, I Embrace the Magic."

Around the cage, as the webs fell away from the stone head, ballerinas pirouetted on the backs of marble manticores, starlight and meteor dust flowing from their fingertips; dwarves with leopards' heads tumbled over one another, becoming the base equations of infinite mathematical theorems; selachian angels, their luminous wings like the pectoral fins of stingrays, arose from the bosoms of tigers; scores of young lovers emerged from glass chrysalides, brining forth their past and future generations in an unending pageant—

—and all of them sang of magic, and faith, and Acceptance.

"Come to me," whispered Sarah, feeling like herself for the first time in her life; unbound, untainted, empowered.

Free.

Afterward, when Aunt Clarice had passed on quietly, Sarah was on her way out when she caught sight of an old woman—such beauty in her aged face—wandering toward one of the rooms near the end of the hall.

Her clothes, though old and somewhat tattered around the edges, were at least no longer dirty.

She looked like a sweet little thing.

Do anything for you, she would.

The woman found the room she was looking for, knocked lightly on the half-opened door, then entered.

"Oh, my," said an old man's voice. "Oh, Katie Lynn, you—*oh, my!*"

Sarah smiled to herself, catching the echo of her aunt's voice somewhere in the back of her mind.

So it begins?

One good will. One kind thought. One small miracle in the human heart.

She winked at the horse-headed dancer only she could see, straightened her blouse, and walked confidently down the corridor to introduce herself to the TV man and his long-lost love.

This time she'd make sure to ask their names.

"So it begins," said Sarah.

It was a song of rejoicing.

In loving memory of Pat Sims and Nancy Paynter

SHADOW
by Felicia Dale

Shadow ran through the crowded, sunny streets without a pause to find her way. Her tough brown feet made no sound on the hot stones as she slipped effortlessly through knots of slower-moving pedestrians as neatly as her namesake.

She took to the alleys to avoid the crush of the central market and was soon at her destination. She paused, panting, her heart thumping in her breast. The sign that hung on the iron bracket over the door showed a green serpent devouring a white star. This was the house of the wizard Irilzar, and Shadow was to carry a message for him; so her master had ordered.

After a short but intense internal struggle with her dread of what might lie on the other side of the door, Shadow raised her fist to knock, but before she could touch it, the door opened. A short, wizened red imp of the common type stood before her, glaring at her from milky, pupilless eyes that burned sun-white under the beetling, red, hairless brows, glared and then grinned and popped a ridiculous bow.

Then it bowed again and held the door wide open, inviting her into the dark maw of the hallway.

"I'm the m—messenger," Shadow stammered, taken aback. Usually she was handed a scroll or pouch, given directions and sent on her way. The imp bowed and grinned obsequiously but with a hint of worry beginning to cloud its wrinkled, ruby face. It glanced over its shoulder as if it was afraid of what might happen if she hesitated too long. Reluctantly, Shadow stepped over the threshold.

The hall was cool and dim after the hot, brilliant streets. The floor was cold and very smooth under her callused soles, and she wiggled her toes with the novelty of the luxurious surface. The imp shut the door and scurried away.

Shadow hurried to follow, staring at the curly tail that decorated the posterior of her guide. There was a silvery ribbon tied in a bow around its tail, just before the barb at the end. Shadow found her eyes so drawn to the twinkly, bobbing ribbon that she did not see anything of her surroundings until the imp stopped, threw open another door, and then vanished in a silent puff of ruby smoke.

"Enter." The voice came from the room beyond the door and Shadow obeyed.

The wizard was a small man, plainly dressed, plump about the middle with thinning gray hair. There was a certain tension around his eyes that Shadow later came to realize was the sure mark of any dealer in magic. He stood at the end of the room and except for a small stone table beside him and an open window behind him there was no other thing in it. The wizard looked at her so long and hard that her skin began to prickle.

"Come closer," he said.

Coming forward, Shadow saw that the table was not empty as she had thought. There was a tiny scroll and an anklet of soft leather cord braided and knotted with beads and bells resting on it.

"Your message and a small reward for service," he said and he held up the anklet for her to see. One of the beads winked bright red, and a soft jingle came from the brass bells. Shadow felt her hand reach out for it, but the wizard was at her side and he knelt and tied the trifle around her ankle. He gave the knot a tug as if to secure it and then stepped back.

The tug was like the tap of a hammer on a bell. There was no sound to this ringing, but Shadow was so filled with the vibrations that she fell to the floor. She felt her body writhing uncontrollably, bruising itself against the stones. The wizard loomed over her. He seemed to have gotten very tall, so tall that he nearly touched the ceiling with his head. Shadow screamed in terror, and her voice was not her own, but a piercing whistle. The wizard bent over her. Shadow struck at him but he deftly evaded her blows and pulled a black hood snugly over her head.

The sudden darkness shocked her into stillness. The hood was like a sponge, absorbing her fear and rage, compelling her to hold still. Swiftly the wizard pinioned her arms to

her sides and hefted her easily up under his arm, holding her
ankles together with the other hand.

There was movement—the wizard was carrying her
somewhere.

Shadow's body ached and trembled, her heart was
pounding so hard she could feel it shaking her breast. She
panted open mouthed, glad the hood did not cover her
mouth or nose. Her arms were strangely bent, pressed
against her sides by the wizard's strong grasp and in his
other hand her feet clenched and clawed the air.

There was the jolting of stairs, several flights of these,
and then fresh desert air came to Shadow's nose. A door
was unlatched (she could hear the scrape of metal) and
passed through, and then the hot sun pressed down on
them in a familiar, silken wave and pierced the hood by a
tiny hole, making a golden star in Shadow's right eye. The
wizard fussed at the leather thong on her ankle and then
with a quick movement tugged the hood off her head.

The sudden brilliant light made Shadow blink and pant
angrily, ready to shriek again. She could feel the cry welling
up, rising on a hot tide of rage. The wizard stood her on
his wrist and steadied her with a hand under her breast.
She put out her arms to catch her balance, disdaining his
touch. There was the metallic blue sky above and the white
city throwing back the glare of the sun below.

Shadow's anger faltered a moment as she gazed around
her, surprised by the clarity of her vision. Perhaps it was
only the bright sunlight after the darkness of the hood, but
it seemed she had never seen so clearly or with such detail
before—why, she could focus on the tiniest feature and see
it perfectly though it might be inches or thousands of feet
away. She looked to the horizon, and there were mountains, distant and blue, yet plain to her were trees, rocks,
the shining line of a river, animals grazing on the lower
slopes. Shadow swallowed and clenched her feet on the
wizard's wrist.

With a smooth swing, the wizard threw her over the
edge.

Shadow shrieked with the fear of falling and then again
when she didn't fall but flew. Looking to each side she saw
wings instead of arms and she began to realize what had
happened. Awkwardly, her new body carried her in a circle

around the wizard's tower. He still stood on the balcony
from where he had launched her. He pointed north and
east. Her understanding was completed. She was still a messenger, she was just now in bird shape.

That explains the flying, she thought, in a strangely lucid
moment between the dizziness of height and giddiness of
slipping and sliding on the air.

The wizard's pointing hand must have been a magical
gesture, for it made the direction she was to take indelible
in her mind. There was a sense of distance as well, but this
was less defined. A gust of wind rose under her wings and
her new shape seemed to bring its own wisdom with it, for
she sculled away as if she had always known how to fly. In
just a few moments the wizard, the city, and all she had
ever known, was behind her.

As amazed as Shadow was at being transformed into a
bird she was completely disconcerted by being forced to
leave the city. She had imagined many fantastic fates for
herself, but going outside the city had never occurred to
her. And now, in a few strokes of her new wings, it was
passed over and left behind and all there was below her
was the narrow band of cultivated fields on either side of
the winding river that twisted through the region. Then
there was scrub land dotted with sheep and goats and other,
smaller creatures that made her mouth water. There was a
swelling of reddish hills that had a current of hot air rising
from them. This lifted Shadow far into the sky, pressing
under her body like a great hand and driving her onward
out over the high desert.

The city was left in a moment, but the desert was not to
be so readily passed. As far as she could see in every direction was dun-colored sand shaped into smooth formations
by the constant wind. The blue mountains she had seen
from the wizard's tower were no longer visible and even
the white hump of the city swiftly vanished in the haze of
heat that hung over the land. The sky was an implacable,
unnamable color, the sun a glaring white fire that beat on
her back and dazzled her eyes. She saw little that lived with
her sharp vision, only the occasional lizard standing on tiptoe to cool itself on a high spot, or a distant dot that moved
in the air as did she, but as the sun rose high toward noon

even these creatures hid themselves and waited for cooler hours. Her own shadow cast on the sand was the only other thing that moved in the world.

Soon she was bored with just flying northeast, and she tried to experiment with her new form, but she found that she was magically prevented from turning or stopping. All she could do was fly on in the direction the wizard had indicated. Shadow found this very irritating and at last lost her temper completely. She fought the magic that constrained her, squawking and contorting with effort, but it was useless. She could not even close her wings to fall but must at least glide onward. As soon as she came near to stalling, her body simply resumed working to keep her in the air. Shadow loved her work and took it very seriously. She cursed the wizard furiously, angry that he had not understood that he could have trusted her, even as a bird, to deliver her message. But she was never angry for very long, and as that emotion eased, she felt a wave of homesickness. If a bird could have wept, Shadow would have sprinkled the sand with tears.

After a while she was forced to admit to herself that the wizard had been wise in using magic to enforce the delivering of his message. Her desire to return was terrible, and she could see that she might not have been strong enough to resist it. She would have failed to complete her task. This stung her pride, and she chided herself for being so weak. She was not a good messenger if mere homesickness made her want to turn tail like a baby. She must be brave and do her work well—no one would keep a slave who did not do her duty. Shadow tried to think of her unexpected adventure in a more positive light. After all, it was not every day that such things happened, and there might be some unknown benefit at the heart of it that she could not yet perceive.

Gradually her sadness abated and she became more lighthearted. She flew on with a will, dreaming about the future and wondering what lay ahead of her.

The sun reached its zenith and began its long descent. The magic that forced her on also seemed to provide her with the energy that water and food would have brought her so that she did not suffer thirst or hunger nor did her wings tire. The hum of her feathers pressing the hot wind behind her, the featureless waste passing below her and the lack of mental effort needed to continue on her way lulled her into a trance. The morning's events seemed as distant as some odd dream and gradually Shadow slipped deeper and deeper into a comfortable forgetfulness. She had always been a bird flying over the desert, there was no other reality, all else was a fading illusion. She had never been a girl, she had never run on two feet, she had never had a name. . . .

Deep inside her mind was a protest at this.

I do so have a name, came the thought, but then she couldn't remember what it might have been, nor could she remember just what a name was. Something hot welled up in her breast, and she was suddenly alert and trembling with fear.

"Shadow! I am Shadow!" she said out loud, or tried to. She wished she could laugh at the sound of her bird throat and mouth trying to make human sounds but what rose in her was a sob of terror. Her bird's body was complete in itself, having all the knowledge it needed to be a successful hawk and only her memory of herself as a girl was what kept her human inside it. She wondered if she could be returned to human form if she forgot what being human was like. Interesting as it was to be in bird-form and exciting as it was to fly, she found she had no desire to spend the rest of her life as a hawk.

Determined to remain more attentive, she looked around and was surprised to see that the day had passed and night was falling. The sun was not quite gone but the land was already dim, a mottled blur beneath her, and the wind had ceased to blow. Swift as a dart in the air Shadow went, but faster still was the coming of night.

A turquoise light stained the sky, following the sun to the horizon where it sank in white glory. She could only see this by turning her head and looking below her wing, which she often did, for ahead of her was a darkness that loomed, growing fast as the sun fled downward to the world's rim. One moment the sun hung whole and brilliant just above the horizon, then in three blinks it was gone with only a dying glow to show where it still traveled on.

For a moment despair filled her, as if the sun had truly

died, eaten by the World Snake as in the old myths, and was not just passing over in its endless path inside the Crystal Sphere. She had traveled with the sun all day and despite its pitiless glare she missed it all the same. Swallowing the lump in her throat, she turned to face the darkness ahead of her—and there were the stars to comfort her, so brilliant and numerous they flooded the night with a haze of silver.

The gentle, cooling glow soothed the anxious girl-hawk so that she might have slipped back into the trance that had almost engulfed her before, but this time she held on to her name like a tether and repeated it to herself every now and then. She didn't say it out loud, for she couldn't bear to hear herself trying to say words again, but she tried to think of it every time her mind started to wander. After a while it came fairly easily. She was so successful that she actually fell into another trance, her name becoming part of the swift beating of her wings and the rushing of the endless wind.

She was still flying, it was still night, and the stars still poured out their milky brilliance, but something had changed and caught her attention. She yawned, shivering all over with a delightful stretch. Despite the sameness of everything around her she felt a kind of anticipation rising in her breast. She remembered the vague sense of distance when the wizard had pointed her on her way. Was she almost at her destination? She tried to look ahead, but the light the stars made was too fine and ethereal to show her anything helpful. Still . . . was that something other than desert ahead? She glided, trying guess what it might be.

There was a darker spot on the dark desert floor, long and narrow, one end rounder and broader than the other. Perhaps it was a ravine or a patch of brush. She shrugged and flew on, watching as she drew nearer mainly because it was the only thing besides the stars to look at.

The sudden scent of water filled her nostrils, and she blinked in surprise. In that moment she realized she had reached her goal.

There was no time to slow down, no time for fear, just a sense of something very large and very close, then the shadow on the desert rose up and dealt her a crushing blow. Pain rose like hot air off the sand and carried her into darkness.

There was no desert, no sky, no wind, no day, no night. She was not even aware of her own existence but for a sense of a voice saying her name, over and over again. There was no time, but it seemed that after a while Shadow realized that, though she had no mouth, it was her own voice speaking. She had no eyes, but it seemed that she opened something that let her see.

She could see two directions, inward and outward.

Outward was a grayness that was neither space nor light but an endless realm of possibility. Inward was a darkness that was not the absence of light but the presence of a single possibility. Neither direction pulled her; she was balanced between the two in a perfect stillness. She felt that her name was the thing that created the stillness that held her and if she stopped speaking the balance would change.

She heard her voice say her name countless times while she contemplated the two directions and the balance between them. Then she ceased speaking.

Instead of silence another voice was there, this one calling plaintively with the last of dying hope in it. She realized it had been calling to her all along, but her own voice had obscured it so that she could only hear it now that she was quiet. Who was it? She knew no one who would call her with such despair, such hope, such wistful love. Something like a laugh filled her.

Balance was lost, and she fell outward, expanding until grayness filled her consciousness and the dark presence within her was forgotten.

Her eyes were open for a while before she realized she was looking through them at a room. Candlelight reflected off white stone walls and lost itself in the low vaults of the ceiling. A fire was burning in a hearth, casting a rosy warmth. The smell of wood smoke reached her nose, and then other smells came also, not all of them pleasant. Sweat, an earthy dampness that had a faint bitterness underlying it, the sweetness of drying grass.

There was a boy lying on the floor near the fire, and this was so interesting that Shadow stared at him for a long time. She could just see part of his face and his bare feet. He had very pale skin, lighter than any she had ever seen. He was wrapped in a ragged blanket that could have given little protection from the cold of the stone floor. Shadow then noticed her own bed. She was lying on a pallet of grass and burlap on a wooden shelf that hung from the wall by two chains and hinges. A blanket covered her, but otherwise she was naked. Even the neck chain that marked her as her master's property was gone. She didn't remember losing it. Perhaps it had slipped off when the wizard had turned her into the bird-shape. Shadow looked again at the sleeping stranger, wondering what had happened to her.

She remembered being changed into a bird and flying over the desert all the day and into the night, then there was a sort of dreamlike memory of pain and a strange voice calling her name. Now, she was human again, but that was all she could say for sure.

The stranger by the fire opened his eyes and looked right into hers.

Hello, he said. *You came back.* His voice was not in her ears, but inside her head. It was a very odd feeling, almost ticklish, but Shadow smiled because he seemed so glad to see her awake.

Not just awake, but alive, too, he said. *How do you feel?*

She found she could not answer out loud or with her mind, but she could smile again.

Good. Sleep more and you will be better yet.

She could not disobey him. Her eyes closed and she drifted off.

Shadow woke later to the sound of wood being laid on the hearth. The boy was very thin, and his bony hands trembled as he worked. The fire had gone to coals and ashes and took some coaxing to restore, but at last he sat back and basked in the fresh flames before he turned to look at Shadow.

How do you feel now? he asked, coming closer and kneeling next to the pallet. Now she could look at him easily, and she examined him with interest.

His face was fine-boned, marked with hunger and some other trouble but patient in expression. His eyes were a dark hazel-green, a color she had never seen before, heavily

fringed with lashes and dark-circled. His hair was dark and
dull, not black, not brown, a thick tangle that he had tied
back with a piece of string.

"How do you do that? Talk in my head," she croaked
out loud.

The boy shrugged and looked away.

It's just how I am.

Shadow looked at him until he turned his gaze back on her.

"You're the one who was calling me," she said and this
time her voice was not so rough. "What happened to me?
Where was I? Who are you? Where am I now?"

The boy couldn't help smiling at her flood of questions.

*You were spelled to fly in the window of the wizard's
chamber, but you came faster than expected and the window
was closed. You hit the shutter. He found you outside on
the ground and brought you in. The wizard turned you back
into your proper shape—otherwise you might have died,
though you nearly did die anyway. Now you are his slave,
as I am.*

"Is he a kind master?" Shadow asked, worried by the
boy's worn face.

He is a wizard, the boy said as if this explained all, and
turned away again. *I brought you water. Can you sit up?*

Shadow found that she could, though she was weak and
uncoordinated and not particularly thirsty. The boy held
out a small, dented metal cup which looked light, but she
found she was not quite strong enough to hold it herself,
so he held it for her and let her guide it. Water, cool and
metallic, filled her mouth. A flood of feeling rushed from
her mouth and spread outward through her whole body so
that goose bumps rose on her skin and a great shiver shook
her. Then she was aware of a terrible thirst that the mouth-
ful of water only made more consuming, and she clutched
at the cup with a sudden desperation and drank until it
was empty.

"More," she said and shivered again, but the boy put the
cup aside.

Put this on, he said and he guided her arms through
sleeves and buttoned the front of the garment for her when
her fingers were not able to. It was a long tunic of old
material, once fine, now frayed and colorless with use and
washing. The boy snugged the blanket around her legs.

Then he filled the cup again from a wooden bucket near the fire and let her drink again.

This time the water blunted her thirst, and she sighed with relief. Then she could no longer sit up but had to lie back. Though her body demanded rest, her mind was not so much exhausted as excited and questions bubbled up in her faster than she could speak them.

"You didn't tell me your name," she said, "Or where I am. I can guess I'm in a cellar of some kind, but that's all. What happened to my clothes? And where is my collar? My master is the only one who has the key, but then maybe the wizard undid it. I don't suppose it would be hard for him, what with magic and all, though I must say I'm not impressed that he misjudged my arrival and left his window shut. He can't be too powerful a wizard if he can't look forward that far."

He was distracted, the boy said. *You lost your clothes and your collar when his colleague turned you into a bird. And we are in a cellar. I think they used to keep wine here back when it was a real waterkeep and not a wizard's home.*

"Will the wizard keep me here, or am I to be sent back?" was Shadow's next question. It had not escaped her that the boy had still not told her his name. Perhaps it was one that he hated. Owners usually picked their slaves' names and sometimes it was not a kind one, so Shadow did not press him for it. She would learn it soon enough.

The wizard is getting very old. When he stole me, he thought I would make a good host for him, but I have certain powers that would disappear along with my self if he took my body against my will.

"What do you mean? I don't understand."

I am a healer. That is why I am here and you are alive. The wizard took me prisoner a few years ago and forced me to keep him well past the time he should have died. His body is wearing out. Not even wizards can live forever, and he has lived in this body a very long time. He needs a new, young body to house his mind so that he can continue living. He wanted to take mine, but he would lose my magic since I won't give him my body willingly. He has a terrible fear of dying, and that's why you were sent. He asked his colleague in your city to send him a good host, and here you are.

"Me!"

Yes, you. He was furious when he changed you to your real shape and found you were a girl.

"What a shame," Shadow said wryly. "Has he gotten over his shock or died of it, I hope?"

For the first time the boy's face lightened.

No, though I never heard him curse so creatively before. He is planning a revenge of some kind at the moment, but I doubt it will work. The wizard in the city would hardly dare making him angry if he could not defend himself. Though he is clever and ruthless . . . The boy's thoughts trailed off.

"Is there no way to escape?" Shadow asked, looking around the room as if there might be an answer written on the bare, cold walls or hidden in the shadows overhead like a roosting bat.

I've tried, the boy said, and Shadow felt his discouragement as if it were her own. *He is a powerful man, and my own magic is not so much. If only my parents could find me, I know they could defeat him. I'm sure they've looked for me, but he keeps me hidden inside the keep. He has spelled the stones of this place so that no one can see in or out. I don't even know where I am.*

"Well, I flew northeast for a day and most of the night. I don't know how fast I was going, but that's something, anyway. Do you know what kind of hawk the wizard changed me into or how fast such a bird can fly? It felt very fast, but maybe it was a magical flight and not a real hawk's speed. How complicating magic must be."

Yes, it is, agreed the boy, but something in the mental voice that Shadow heard was lighter and more hopeful than before. They looked at each other and smiled. Then, the boy hesitated but forced himself to speak, turning his face away as if he were going to say something shameful. *You are a slave, aren't you? I thought so. If we get out of this, I promise I'll ransom you. My parents are wealthy and would do anything for someone who helped me.*

Shadow was struck speechless. Being ransomed was an idle dream of every slave she had ever known, but she had never heard of it actually happening. She could only look at the boy and wonder who and what he was that he should feel bold enough to make such a promise when there

seemed no chance of their escaping this strange prison. He
had seemed purely defeated, yet now a subtle change had
come over him as if new determination was growing in
him. Perhaps having someone more helpless than himself
in danger with him, and partly because of him, pushed him
to a new effort, but neither he nor Shadow thought of this
at the time.

Then a listening look came over him and he got up from
the floor.

I have to—he began to say, and then he vanished.

Shadow slept for a while, once the shock of her friend's
sudden disappearance wore off. The fire dying, a piece of
wood breaking in two, woke her some time later. She lay
quietly for a while, her body still weary from the flight and
her encounter with death. She thought about this for a
while and the boy's saving her and then of what he had
told her about the wizard. After a while something tickled
in her brain rather like the boy's inner voice did. An idea
came to her, shyly, rather like a very young child who has
something precious to show a grownup and is not sure if it
will be well received.

What if the wizard took her body instead of the boy's?
Could he somehow hide her self so that she would not get
lost or die but be ready to take back her body if he and
his parents could somehow defeat the wizard?

Excitement filled her, and she had to get up. Her body
did not hurt, though parts of it felt numb. Her face, arms,
and shoulders were particularly unfeeling, but she found
she could sit up and even walk, slowly, to the fire and the
water bucket. After a rest she looked around and found
the other kind of bucket well off in a corner. She made use
of it and then came back to the fire. It was in need of
wood. There was not much to draw from, and what there
was looked like pieces of old furniture rather than wood
for burning. One stick was definitely a chair leg and another
flat piece had faded gilding on it. The flames ate eagerly at
the offering and she watched for a while to make sure it
would not die. It would be a cold room without a fire.

The fire was a fairly good companion while the boy was
gone, but she soon found herself missing him and worrying
about what was happening with him and when he might

come back. Shadow got up and searched the whole room trying to find a door, but all was white stone blocks tightly fitted together and there didn't appear to be any way in or out other than the way the boy had left earlier.

The search exhausted her. She stumbled back to the pallet and fell under the cover and into sleep as fast as she ever had. She slept a long time or a short time, she never knew which, but she woke to the boy shaking her shoulder and saying,

Wake up. He wants both of us right now but I think I have a plan. Will you help me? It might not work.

"I have an idea, too," Shadow said, but she was confused by drowsiness and could not say her plan before the boy said his.

I will give you my healing powers and then the wizard will take over my body. I will not leave my body but hide inside where he will not be able to reach me. He will not be pleased, but he will have you to keep him well, and if we ever get outside this place, I will be able to send a message to my parents. I know they will come to us right away. Will you do this? I know it might not be easy, but I think we can do it.

"But can't he hurt you if you are both in the same body? If he can change bodies, why can't you? If the two of you can be in the same body, why don't you come to me instead? Then you would be safe from him and even more likely to get a message out. I'm really good at finding my way in strange places, and I bet I could get out of here, once out of this room, anyway."

The boy stared at her, barely breathing as he thought this idea over. Giving up his magic and his body terrified him and he had been even more frightened of how he would have had to compress himself to fool the wizard into thinking that his "host" was uninhabited.

I don't know if it will work, or even how to do it but . . . you are willing to do this? How can you trust me?

"You saved my life and offered to ransom me. How can I not trust you? I've never done anything magical in my life, so it will be up to you to decide and choose what's right, but anything's better than losing everything. We can't beat him if we're not both alive to do it."

There was a moment of silence. The two children looked

at each other. They were strangers to each other and yet each knew then that the other was the friend they had always looked for in others and never encountered until this time.

He's calling us, the boy said then, and the room dissolved around them.

It was a strange feeling to be transported by the wizard. Shadow could feel the boy's hand in hers, a point of warmth in the cold moment between the two rooms, and she clung to it desperately. The boy felt her panic and squeezed her hand tight for an instant as the new room appeared around them, then he let go.

The wizard stood directly in front of them. He was a short man, not much bigger than the boy, but as ground down by age as a man can be and remain alive. All she could see of his body was his head and his hands; the rest of him was covered with a long robe of purple-and-green phoenix-cloth. The fabric cast its own light about the room, dyeing the white stones with its radiance. His mottled skin was without wrinkles, stretched tight over the angles of his cheekbones and the dome of his skull. A plain ring of dark metal circled one bony forefinger. It did not reflect the robe's colors but seemed unaffected by light. The wizard's eyes were of a similar quality, dark-pupiled and red-rimmed with no touch of light to them at all. Shadow felt his gaze fall on her and she trembled in terror.

"You are afraid of me," the wizard said in a dry, thin voice. Shadow saw he was pleased.

"Of course, master, how could I not be?" Her teeth rattled together so that she could hardly speak. Suddenly her legs buckled and she fell to her knees. She had thought she was afraid of her master or of the city guards or of the wizard who had turned her into a bird but this was different. This wizard might be human in shape, but he had long ago abandoned any of the frailties that would stand between him and the getting of anything he desired. Nothing human looked from his eyes, not even a snake had as cold or as calculating a glance and Shadow quailed before him.

"Now this is the way a slave should behave," the wizard said, turning his attention to his other prisoner. "You have never acted as I thought you should but always resisted me and tried to cause trouble. I am sure that this girl, puny and stupid as she is, will make a far better servant than you ever have, will you not?" and the wizard pinned Shadow with his lightless eyes.

"I always do my best, master," she gasped, feeling a strange, clammy pressure all around her that seemed to emanate from the old man's eyes.

"Good. Then it will not be necessary to punish you often. What have your masters called you before you became mine?" he asked, twining his fingers together slowly.

"I have always been called Shadow, master," she replied, unable to do anything other than suffer under the growing pressure that was beginning to limit her breath, though the wizard left her enough to speak with.

What are you doing to her? the boy demanded. *You will have everything you want from us, why are you hurting her?*

"He is master," Shadow gasped and would have writhed, but the pressure squeezed her too tightly for movement.

"Yes, I am master," the wizard said slowly, looking at her with a pleased, though somewhat puzzled expression on his bony, dry face. The pressure eased a minute amount and Shadow managed to draw a breath. "It is not for you to question, boy. Now you will yield up your magic to her and your body to me or I will continue crushing her until not even your powers will be able to heal her."

Yes.

"Good. As soon as you give her your magic, I will relent and she will be unhurt."

Shadow could no longer breathe. She began to faint, darkness filling her vision. She felt the touch of the boy's mind on hers, as if he were going to speak to her, but this time there were no words. Something sweet and cool poured into her from the touch and suddenly she was no longer fainting but perfectly conscious and well. The pressure was still there, but it did not trouble her. It could still kill her, but that seemed unimportant. She felt the boy's magic filling her as water fills a cup. There was just enough room for it. She felt it brimming in her, a beautiful living thing without thought or consciousness, drawing awareness from her own perceptions which its being within her augmented. *How wonderful,* she thought, surprised. Dimly she noticed voices. The wizard and the boy were speaking;

"Is it done?"

Yes.

The pressure eased somewhat but not completely. Shadow was able to take a deep breath and open her eyes. The wizard and the boy paid no attention to her, they were completely involved in each other. The wizard was smiling, a ghastly expression that threatened to tear the fragile skin covering his skull. Shadow could feel the tension in the man's skin and she felt the boy's magic in her reach out automatically to ease the discomfort he was feeling.

"Very good," the wizard almost cooed, surprised that the girl should be able to use the transplanted magic so quickly. "But waste no time on this old body. Come, boy, give yourself up."

Shadow was ignored again and she watched without being watched, unable to turn away from the bizarre scene before her. The old wizard's teeth were bared in a rigid grin, his whole face frozen with effort as he gathered himself to leave his dying body. The boy stood in front of him, white-faced, his head thrown back as if he tried to look over his conqueror toward something better. Then he closed his eyes, and once more Shadow felt his mental touch.

Again something entered her mind, something large and complex that wound itself up in a frightened, trembling coil and settled to one side like a dog chastised and sent to a corner.

There was a rustling sound. The old man's body collapsed in a heap, the phoenix-cloth shimmering more beautifully than ever with the movement. Then the cloth rose from the discarded body and Shadow watched as it draped itself cozily around the boy's shoulders. The rags vanished and the boy's pale skin gleamed with the light from the cloth. No light came from the now darkened eyes and she quailed under the cold gaze of the wizard.

"Where is the boy's spirit? It is not here or in my old body. I did not mean for him to escape so readily." The wizard looked at Shadow very hard, and she squealed because the eyes gazed right into her head with a knifelike pain. She could not hide anything from him, then, but the frightened thing that was the boy's spirit buried itself under her memories of him and so escaped detection.

"How silly of you to love something so easily," the wiz-

ard said, withdrawing his gaze. "You have gained nothing
from it and he can no longer help you in your puny plans
to escape me. You are mine now. Forget everything else.
Nothing is important to you now except for me and my
continuing health. This body is tired and weakened by lack
of care. Heal it."

Shadow did not know how to obey, but the magic within
her reached out on its own and did what the wizard commanded. It was dreadful to see the wizard looking out of
her friend's eyes and somehow even worse to see the dark
circles lighten and the starved look leave the still-pale face.
Shadow could feel the magic working in him, restoring all
to rights. Hunger left the sunken belly, the hands stopped
trembling, even the tangled hair softened and seemed to
weigh less heavily on the boy's head. *No, it's not him, this
is the wizard now,* she corrected herself, sickened by what
she saw. The healing completed, the wizard gestured lightly
with his now plump, young hands and sent her back to
the cellar.

The water was drunk, the wood burned to ashes, the
candle a hardened puddle of melted wax. Shadow did not
know how long she sat in the dark, hungry, thirsty, and
alone. She felt the magic keeping her alive, and she tried
not to be too frightened, but she could not help crying now
and then. She had never been alone before, not for any
length of time. Always there had been crowds of people,
brilliant sunlight or moon-washed nights, lamps, torches,
candles. . . . The remembered voices seemed to reverberate
in her head, and Shadow thought she might see fires and
candles and stars, too, if she wanted. But it wouldn't be
magic, it would be madness. She looked inside her head
with the magic the boy had given her to see if she could
find him, but he might as well have disappeared along with
the rest of the world.

Without warning, she felt the pallet under her vanish to
be replaced with the stone floor of the wizard's chamber.
The light was dim, but still it blinded her after the long
darkness.

"Heal me," was all the wizard said, holding out a
bloody hand.

Shadow did as he commanded; the magic stopped the bleeding and closed the wound.

"Please, master, I need water—" Shadow began, but already the light was gone and she was back in the cellar. Tears ran from her eyes, and she sobbed uncontrollably. This was terrible, worse than any fate she had ever envisioned. To be left alone in the dark, starving and dying of thirst, but never to actually die was a terror she could not face. At first she could only weep, but after a while she felt anger rising in her and she sat up in the dark and wiped away her tears.

There must be a way out of here, she thought. *At least, no one builds a cellar without a door to get things in and out.* She had looked before and didn't see an opening, but what if the wizard had just hidden it really well?

Shadow sat in the dark and thought about the room she was in. She remembered it clearly enough, and she set to work picturing it well in her mind as it had been, with the fire burning and the boy sitting near her.

The magic stirred softly inside her, as if the thought of its former home could rouse it. Shadow turned her attention to the magic inside her. It really was alive, an entity complete in itself, but in no way she had ever experienced life before. She tried talking to it, both out loud and inside her head, but it did not reply or appear to take notice, though it remained alert. She felt it soothe an itch on her shin almost before the itch became noticeable and even more wonderful, drawing moisture out of the air to keep her from dying of thirst.

It wants to heal, she thought. *What is there in the room that needs healing besides me?*

The magic responded, surging out of her and casting about the room. In the dark, Shadow's eyes were useless, but she found she could see if she watched through the magic. She did not understand what she was doing exactly, but it was as if the magic was showing her the room through its own method of comprehension, reporting back what it found to her brain. It was sight without eyes, touch without nerves, not merely of the surface of things but deep within as well.

The stones that made the room no longer appeared as flat, dressed surfaces. The magic revealed to her the three dimensions that comprised the stones, and then showed her the inside of them, particle by particle. There was no sense of scale, one part was not larger than another, but all was interconnected—not just within the stone's own fabric but with the air as well, the mortar in the joints, the cold ashes on the hearth. Shadow turned the magic on herself and found that she was made the same way, smaller bits of stuff organized into larger bits that became blood or bone or thought or breath.

Looking outward again, this time she saw readily enough where the door had been. The wizard had forced bits of air and stone and mortar to look as if they were part of the wall, not archway and air leading into a hallway. It was plain where he had worked and Shadow almost sneered at the clumsy job he had done. *I would do better than that,* she thought, *if I knew how.* She left the pallet and walked directly to the opening and stood before it. She knew if there had been light, she would have seen solid stone before her, but in the dark she saw perfectly well that there was nothing to stop her from walking right through. Should she go now or wait?

Wait.

It was only one word, spoken more softly than a whisper, but Shadow recognized the boy's voice instantly. It did not come from outside her as it had before but from within. She yelled with delight and hugged herself as if she could somehow hug the boy by proxy. The magic retreated in a flash and left her sightless again in the dark, but now she didn't mind nearly so much. She wasn't alone! The boy was still alive; he was hiding inside her as he had planned. There was still a chance he could send the message he had spoken of before, and if he was right, if his parents could rescue him. Then she was sure to be free also. But why hadn't he wanted her to take the doorway and find the way out?

She was so deep in thought, eyes tightly closed against the darkness, that she did not notice the wizard had called her from the cellar. Only a sudden graying of the world beyond her eyelids alerted her to the shift.

"Heal me!" demanded the wizard and instantly the magic leaped to do what it must.

Shadow's eyes streamed tears, stinging from the light.

Still she could see that the wizard was dreadfully injured.
His face was red with blood and the phoenix-cloth robe
was dim and torn. It would heal itself and gradually regain
its brilliance without the help of the Shadow's borrowed
magic, but the wizard's stolen body was in dire need of aid.
It took only a moment, though, and then he was as well
as before.

This time he did not send his slave away immediately.

"What do you do in your cellar?" the wizard asked, regarding Shadow with expressionless eyes.

"Nothing," Shadow said. Her throat hurt with the unaccustomed task of speaking aloud.

"We will be leaving this place soon," the wizard said,
and sent her back to the cellar.

Shadow did not dare leave by the doorway she had discovered for fear the wizard would not find her where he
expected her. She did not want to lose this chance of even
a brief escape, but she was also afraid that she might not
be able to get outside the walls before the wizard caught
her. He would surely be angry and might even suspect that
she had a motive besides escape for wanting to get outside.
He might guess that the boy was hidden inside her and find
some way to harm him.

So she waited, sometimes sleeping, sometimes dreaming,
most often exploring the magic the boy had left with her.
She learned a great deal about the nature of the bits that
things were made of. There did not appear to be a great
deal of difference between the living bits that made up her
own body and the bits that made up everything else around
her. She inspected the work the wizard had done hiding
the doorway and contemplated how the work could be
done better. She wanted to try rearranging the deception
but she did not. Several times she started, but each time
something held her back. It was not the magic that was
reluctant, it seemed perfectly willing to consider this a matter of healing, but she wondered whether the wizard would
notice if she changed anything. She might be safer if he
kept thinking she was helpless.

So Shadow passed her time in the dark.

The next time the wizard called her up out of the cellar

she could watch what happened to her body and the world around it. Fascinated, she forgot her fear of the wizard and only dumbly obeyed his order to wait, reluctantly ceasing her investigation of the world through this new way of knowing and turning to her own senses.

Shadow cringed under the assault of light, dim as it was. She had been so long living inside her head that it was hard to turn her attention outside. She was weak from lack of movement and from starvation and thirst. She looked around the room, but it was bare of anything except the stones that made it. There were two windows but these were barren; any view outside obscured with a thick, gray mist. She heard voices outside the room speaking in a strange, hoarse tongue, the wizard's voice ordering in the same accents, then his footsteps as he returned.

"We are leaving this place. You will follow me and do what I say. You will not move or speak except to obey me. Come." The wizard turned and led the way out of the room without a glance to see if she complied. Shadow followed, legs trembling with the novelty of walking.

The wizard led her through the door and a long hallway, down several flights of stairs and another long hallway. Here and there were windows out of which nothing could be seen but the same mist as in the first room. There was no one else about, no owners of the hoarse voices, but her skin prickled at every step as if eyes were pressing on her from every side. By the time they reached the end of the second hallway, Shadow was exhausted and only the healing magic kept her from falling down. The wizard paused, and she saw that he was opening a door.

A molten flood of golden light poured in the doorway. Shadow nearly wept at the beauty of it, wondering what lamp or magic could cast such a perfect light. As she stepped through the door, she realized it was the mid-morning sun. She blinked and blinked, stunned by the brilliance and shivering under the velvet blow of it on her skin. The scent of grass flowers was overwhelming, sweet and strong as the sunlight, mixed with the coolness of water nearby. As her eyes grew used to the light, she was able to look around and see where she had been kept prisoner.

It was a waterkeep, an ancient round structure built next to an oasis. It was not meant to defend the water so much as make a place for wanderers to take shelter. As she looked at it, Shadow realized that it was not large enough for all the stairways and hallways she had been led along by the wizard. *Magic,* she thought, more curious now than afraid.

As she gazed around her, a movement in the sky caught her eyes, causing her to look up. It was only that common watchman of every desert, a vulture, black-fingered wings spread motionless on the constant wind. After the long confinement it seemed a miracle of elegance and beauty, as indeed it was despite its indelicate behavior with corpses. Surprised by her feelings for a creature that usually she ignored except to ward off with crossed fingers as a sign of bad luck, Shadow extended her healing magic to inspect it more closely. The moment she made contact something inside her darted up to it along the path the magic made, like a flash of light runs along polished wire. Then a blow like a fist knocked her down.

"What are you doing?" the wizard exclaimed, furious. He stood some distance away, a thick roll of material under one arm. "You are not to use that power on anyone or anything but me, unless I command it. Understand? Now come here."

Shadow nodded, picking herself up off the ground and wiping dirt from her mouth. She did not dare look up again at the vulture or to try and contact it with her magic. She was sure that the boy's spirit had left her and was now flying overhead in the black bird. If she caused the wizard to notice the bird too closely or if he guessed what she was thinking he might destroy, the creature, or worse, so she came at his call as quickly as she could.

The wizard took the roll of cloth, spread it out on the sandy soil, and stood on it, gesturing for her to do the same. When she stood beside him, he took a long look at her. He frowned, murmuring to himself,

"No, this will not do." He considered and then reached out with one hand and touched Shadow on the forehead. A chilling breeze fluttered all around her. He smiled. "Much better," he said, pleased with himself. Then he clapped his hands.

The rug beneath them stiffened and lifted off the ground, spilling Shadow to her hands and knees. The wizard stood, proudly indifferent as the rug carried them swiftly away from the oasis.

Shadow gripped the dusty, dark material with both hands and tried to keep her head. The wizard's blow still dizzied her and so did the rapid movement through the air. She looked behind her and thought she saw the vulture soaring far behind, but she might have been mistaken.

It seemed only a few minutes of flight, but when the rug descended to the ground, Shadow was stricken to see where they had come. She was back where her life had begun, just outside the walls of the white city. The main gate was only a few hundred yards away, yet none of the many people using the roadway had noticed their arrival.

The wizard stepped off the rug and made Shadow do the same. The rug rolled itself up, and he tucked it under his arm. He turned to Shadow.

"We are back where you were born, my dear, and doubtless you will see many old friends and acquaintances. Make no attempt to talk with them however, for I have taken away your voice and given you another appearance. Anyone who looks at you will not see a girl-child but a common blue imp. Be sure that I will punish you severely if you try to escape me. I made many enjoyable experiments on my former slave whose body I now inhabit, and I would not mind repeating and refining my efforts."

Shadow tried to speak but found that she couldn't, just as the wizard had said. She could only stand before him and bow her head, hoping he wouldn't choose to demonstrate his threats right away.

"Now follow me. I have work to do."

The wizard led the way to the road and thence into the city. No one appeared to notice them, yet the way was always open before them. The guards standing to either side of the gate did not even blink as they went by.

The wizard took a house in the best part of the city, right in the shadow of the royal palace. He changed his appearance so as to seem a handsome man of middle age and set himself up as a great doctor, calling himself Ylinilzar. Soon he had a devoted clientele among the rich and idle of the higher classes who were delighted to have such a capable healer to shower with petty problems and rich

rewards. Shadow, of course, did the real work, but she soon
found that she was not put forward but must stand to one
side and do her healing without thanks or any other notice.
The only times the wizard spoke to her was to command
her here or there, and for that she was profoundly grateful.

The word of this new doctor soon reached the royal family and caught the attention of the oldest daughter of the
king. She had recently spent too much time in the sun and,
fearing that her complexion was ruined, she called the great
doctor to see what could be done. Shadow's borrowed
magic soothed the windburn that roughened the princess'
cheek, and Ylinilzar was a great hero. Soon after that the
King had indigestion, which the magic also cured, and the
wizard's good fortune was assured, but he was happiest of
all when his brother wizard, Irilzar (he who had changed
Shadow from girl to bird), was forced to call on him to
have a demon-inflicted bite healed.

This was the hardest healing the magic had been called
upon to do. The wound was not deep, but the demon's
poisonous saliva lingered in the tooth marks. When the
magic entered the bite to heal it, the poison, being magical
in nature, attacked it as it had the wizard's flesh. As Irilzar's
painful wound was healed, he saw the false doctor's attendant imp stagger as if in pain, and he guessed that it was
not the doctor who did the healing but the slave. He did
not give away his discovery, but merely thanked the doctor
and paid him his fee, which in this case was a book of rare
construction containing ancient spells that Shadow's master
had long coveted.

Returning home, Irilzar gazed into a scrying bowl and
took a long hard look at the blue imp that went with the
new doctor wherever he went. He soon pierced the simple
magic that disguised the slave. Looking on the girl as she
followed her master into the royal palace, Irilzar found that
he desired to have the slave and her magic for himself. He
knew that Ylinilzar would never give up this wonderful
resource and that the magic was the kind that would be
nullified if he tried to take it by force, so he must come up
with a way of obtaining his desire by guile. All he really
had to do was steal the slave and hide her while he convinced her to give up her magic voluntarily. That should

be easy enough, he thought, and began to study how he might achieve his aim.

Ylinilzar rose quickly in the royal family's esteem and soon became a regular attendant in the daily gathering of the court. He amassed great wealth as he attended to the ills of anyone who could pay his high fees. The royal physicians could only step out of his way and fume with fury behind polite facades as he took over their former importance and eclipsed them with the ease with which he allayed every ill, small or large. During the King's waking hours, he made himself completely available, professing his love and loyalty to that personage and his family. In his free time he continued to study his art, aided now by the wealth at his disposal, purchasing what he could not obtain by his services as a doctor.

Shadow was always with him, except for the times that he desired privacy but he noticed his slave less and less, except in moments of boredom. She dreaded his attention as he was inclined to experiment on her to attempt to obtain the healing power for himself but she thought of the boy and his promise and managed to refuse Ylinilzar his desire, trusting in the magic to heal the wounds he inflicted on her and trying to not be afraid of the pain.

The boy . . .

In her rare moments alone Shadow always thought of him. The memory of his kindness and of the warmth of his hand in hers gave her comfort. She still believed that he would rescue her if he could, but she was beginning to give up the hope that he had been able to communicate with his parents as he had said he could. Or had he gotten lost in the vulture shape as she had nearly become lost in the hawk's form? She had not had the chance to warn him about this peril, and she tried to believe that he was wise enough to see the danger for himself and not succumb to it. Yet as time passed and there was no sign of him or any message, she began to fear the worst.

Being in the white city was strange, for though it had been her only home, she had never been out of the common streets where her messenger work had taken her. Here, she walked in the most luxurious surroundings possible, ignored by the most powerful men and most beautiful women of the city. At first she was lonely, being a naturally friendly and gregarious girl and wished she could have even one friend among the servants and other slaves, but she found that they were supremely contemptuous of a mere imp, and a common blue one at that. The few other imps about turned up their noses at her because they knew from her scent that she was only a somewhat clumsily disguised human. Out of fearful respect of her master they did not tell the secret, so Shadow was left severely alone.

Being ignored proved to be an excellent way to observe those around her. She was amazed and disgusted by how her fellow humans behaved when they thought no one of importance was watching them. Ylinilzar noticed this by accident, and he thought to make use of her as a spy as well as for healing. He gave her back her voice for a while in the evenings and made her repeat to him everything she saw and heard during the day, pressing here to linger about certain personages to obtain information that might prove useful to him later.

Shadow hated this and resisted doing it, even when Ylinilzar threatened her and made her life even more miserable than before. He gave up on this tactic once he realized that with his new wealth he could bribe or hire willing informants and insure their silence with the same methods he practiced on his slave. More than once Shadow was made to heal some stupid servant or petty noble who thought he or she could threaten Ylinilzar with tale-telling and found that the wizard took immediate steps to punish such silliness.

It was after one such night's work that Shadow was allowed to retire to the closet that the wizard had given her as a sleeping place. Ylinilzar had been particularly cruel to a young serving maid. Though the magic had healed her body perfectly, Shadow was haunted by the girl's terror and by the wizard's deep enjoyment of his hobby. Ylinilzar had erased the maid's memory of her torture, but Shadow could not forget.

Shadow laid herself down on the blankets she had foraged for herself in a forgotten storage chest and closed her eyes. She felt unspeakably weary in body and mind alike. Even her heart was sore, like a terrible bruise in her chest.

She wished she could cry, wondering if it would help her, but she had no energy for tears.

The magic stirred softly, easing her bodily fatigue and though it could not soothe her other pains, she felt comforted just knowing it was inside her. It was like a big soft orange cat curled up in her lap. The bed was hard and the space was small, but it was her own and she took comfort from that as well. She knew it would probably be taken away from her at some point, but at least it existed now and she could hide herself away, away from people and especially away from Ylinilzar.

How Shadow hated and feared him! These two emotions filled her constantly now, wrestling with each other in an agony of incessant agitation. She wished she could destroy him, she wished for any kind of escape, almost to the point of hoping for death. She did not know how much longer she could wait for rescue and she had been unable to think of any way to escape the wizard.

When the wizard had tried to make a spy of her, she had tried to just walk out of the palace. After a certain point she found that her footsteps were no longer taking her where she wanted to go but in a circle so that she would end up back where she started. She tried to walk out again, but each time the same thing happened. When she returned to Ylinilzar, he gazed at her with a bored sneer and did not even punish her as if it were not worth the effort. She had not had another real idea about escaping since then.

Shadow sighed a deep sigh, glad to be resting. At any time Ylinilzar might call for her, but at least she had this moment to herself. It might not be right away, for he was lost in the study of a newly obtained book. Usually, if he started reading, she might have as much as several hours of rest.

Weariness gradually pressed her down into the blankets. The floor no longer seemed hard, her body felt as though it might actually fall through the floor to the next room below . . . no, she was not heavy but light, so light she was floating above the blankets no longer touching anything. The relief was so great she fell asleep.

Shadow was awake for a long time before she knew it. She lay perfectly still even when she did know because the dream she was having was so pleasant. She was dreaming

of being in a soft, warm bed, with white sunlight shining
somewhere in the room, not too bright but just cheerfully
so. There was a pleasant scent of desert in the room, not
the jangling perfumed reek of the city but a subtle breath
of sand, dry soil, fragrant grasses, and water somewhere
nearby. She was also dreaming that she had slept for hours
and hours and that in that time she had been carried a long
distance and hidden safely away where Ylinilzar could not
ever find her. She dreamed her imp facade was gone, that
she looked like herself again and could even speak if she
wanted to.

It was so lovely and so realistic that Shadow fell back
asleep again.

The next time she woke, she was still in the same dream,
but this time someone was calling her name. It was so like
the last time she had been called awake by a voice and her
name that she bolted upright in the bed, eyes popping open
expecting to see the boy beside her, himself again.

Instead, an old man, vaguely familiar but not immediately
recognized, sat beside the bed.

"Hello, my dear," he said. "Awake at last?"

Shadow only nodded, heart pounding in her chest, looking about her with wide eyes to see where she was.

"Do you remember me?" the old man was saying, peering into her face with a friendly persistence. "I'm afraid I
didn't treat you too kindly last time we met. I am the wizard who sent you off to Ylinilzar in the shape of a bird.
My name is Irilzar."

Shadow could only stare at him wondering what in the
world had happened. Was it as she had dreamed? Was she
safe from Ylinilzar or had she just fallen into a new danger?

"I mean you no harm," Irilzar continued. He reached
beside him and Shadow followed his gaze to a small table
which stood near her bed where a pitcher of water and cup
waited to be drunk from. "Are you thirsty?" He poured
her a cup of the water and held it for her to take. She
made no move toward it, but looked around the room
again instead.

It was not a large room, but it was airy and full of fresh
light from two windows. She could see blue sky outside and
the tips of a leafy bush that waved in the breeze. A door
into another room, also full of light, stood open across from

the bed. Shadow felt under the covers and found that she was dressed in some sort of garment, though not what she had been wearing since the boy had woken her so long ago. Eyeing the wizard suspiciously, Shadow got out of the bed on the side away from him and stood for a moment, just to see what he would do.

Irilzar did nothing, merely watched her in a patient fashion as if he knew what she was about and was not surprised nor concerned.

Shadow walked out the door and into the next room. Here was a sitting area with soft chairs and cushions strewn about, not rich but comfortable. There were two doors here besides the one she had used to leave the bedroom. One door led into another room and the other led directly outside. It was not even closed but wide open so that she could walk right out without stopping for even a moment.

Desert stretched in hilly sameness all around her. It was like a paradise after the city and the cellar. The healing magic inside her moved softly and then settled again to stillness. The sun shone down out of a pure blue sky, hot and bright but not punishingly so. Bushes with long, dusty green foliage dotted the hillsides and waved their branch ends in the gentle wind. A few small birds were flying about here and there, making their living in the wilderness. Shadow turned all around, taking in the whole scene, wondering where she was and why and how. Behind her was the house she had exited. It was a simple construction made of mud bricks with a slanted pole and tile roof, rectangular in shape like any average person's home in the city just transported to this wild placed.

Irilzar came out the door carrying a tray on which were several plates with various things to eat and the cup of water.

"How long has it been since you have had food?" asked the wizard. "Come, I know you have every reason not to trust me, but I carried you away from Ylinilzar because I am sorry for what I did. I should never have taken you away from your rightful owner and subjected you to such a terrible fate as you found. Please accept my apologies and let me prove to you how sincere I am."

Shadow listened to him though she could not believe him, not yet. However, she was very intrigued by the food.

She had managed to snatch a few things to eat here and there in the city, but she had not had a full stomach since her change into bird-form, nor enough to drink as well.

"Go away," she said. Her voice grated unpleasantly in her throat, and she coughed.

"All right." Irilzar set down the tray of food on the ground. "You are safe here from most danger, but please don't wander too far from the house. There is a well around the other side if you get thirsty. I'll come back in a while." And the wizard clapped his hands and vanished.

Shadow stood for a long time just waiting to see what would happen. After a while, when only the sun and the wind moved about her and the small birds, she walked over to the tray, kneeled beside it, and looked at the food.

There were dried fruits and green vegetable stalks of some kind. There was bread, a clay pot of something dark and sweet-looking to spread on it, and a blunt knife to spread it with. It all smelled fresh and good, so as a test she sipped carefully at the water to see what would happen. Nothing happened, so she thought she would try the bread next.

The first bite tasted of nothing, as if her tongue had forgotten how to work after so long a time of not eating. Then saliva rushed into her mouth and she devoured the bread in three more bites, not even waiting to put on any of the stuff in the pot. This she ate with the fingers of one hand while the other reached greedily for the dried fruit and the vegetables. In just a few moments the whole tray was empty. She ended her feast by finishing the cup of water and getting up in search of more.

Shadow walked around the outside of the house and found the water that Irilzar had spoken of, not so much a well as an upwelling of water in a stony crack in the desert hillside. Water pooled, reflecting stones, green grass, and blue sky in the crystal surface before it trickled away to seep into the dry soil. Shadow dipped her cup and drank deeply, the sun filling her eyes as the water slipped coolly into her mouth.

Am I free? she thought. *There is only one way to find out.* She drank once more from the pool of water and then set the cup down on a stone and walked away from the pool, away from the house up the hill and over the crest, leaving it all behind her.

It was hours later when Ylinilzar called her and received no reply. He went to find her and found only the old blankets that made her bed. Shadow was gone.

Ylinilzar was so surprised that he stood looking at the empty blankets for several minutes before he could react. She could not be gone. There was no way for her to go more than a certain distance from him; he had made sure of that first thing. He tested the spell as a weaver tests the tension of the threads of the loom and found everything intact just as he had made it. No . . . there was a tiny portion that was not quite as it had been. Someone had been here and stolen away his property and carefully remade the spell so that it appeared that nothing had broken it, but he knew his own work and recognized that of another.

Irilzar.

Fury made him hot all over and he stalked away from the empty closet. How could this happen? What he had hoped for most of all had finally occurred, and he needed the healing magic, right now, right away. How could Irilzar have stolen it away just now when he needed it most? Oh, he would suffer for his actions! Ylinilzar paced around the room in agitation, stopping once to gaze out the window that looked over the desert.

There, slightly beyond the cultivated lands, a beautiful palace had appeared with the sunrise, growing with the light as if it were a great flower opening to the sun. Ylinilzar felt a shudder of fear and delight as he looked at the beautiful construction. Only the most powerful of wizards or enchanters could make a place of such size and intricacy appear overnight. It had caused quite an uproar this morning. Everyone tried to catch a glimpse of the magical palace. Even now there was a great crowd of gawkers on the outermost wall.

Soldiers had been sent out to see what this might mean and were greeted by men all clad in golden metal so that even their faces were hidden behind flat, featureless visors. They were not hostile. Instead they carried a message scroll

addressed to Ylinilzar. One of the golden men returned
with the soldiers to deliver the message and even now
waited silently in the next room for Ylinilzar to go back
with him to the magical palace.

The wizard gripped the scroll so hard that the fine parchment was crushed. Taking over the powers of the white city
was just a diversion to him while he waited for word of his
healing abilities to spread through the world. He had
turned down thousands of petitions for healing, taking only
those that would certainly advance him either in wealth or
power or in notoriety in hopes of attracting the attention
of such workers of magic that are so beyond humanity that
they live on other planes. From these superior beings he
might gain immense knowledge, that though common to
them would be as swords are compared to stones in this
reality.

The message asked for his help in healing a person in
the magical palace and promised great reward if he was
successful. Ylinilzar could not ignore this summons. He
must go, but what should he do? His own powers lay more
in the areas of destruction rather than the opposite. Well,
he must go. Perhaps he would think of something.

Ylinilzar allowed the golden-clad man to lead him out of
the building. Once outside, the golden man clasped him by
one hand, and with a pop they vanished from the city and
reappeared at the high-arched, delicate doorway of the
magical palace. Again the golden man led him, this time
through the doorway and into a spacious, open courtyard
where servants, human in appearance, were waiting for him.

Never had he seen such beautiful men and women. They
were all perfectly alike, dark-haired, dark-eyed and pale-
skinned, slim and quiet in movement, dressed in soft robes
of silky, brilliantly colored material. They were like living
jewels created just to adorn the magical palace. They did
not speak but guided him with gestures and by the lightest
of touches through a long, high-arched hallway more gor-
geously made than the finest rooms in the white city.

Ylinilzar felt his heart pounding with excitement and a
certain amount of fright, though he ignored this as best he
could, telling himself that it was only the lack of his slave
that caused his fear, not the proximity of beings so obviously greater than any he had dealt with before. His pride

and the intoxication of his surroundings made him strut a
little, thinking that he cut a fine figure with his phoenix-
cloth robe and the illusion that covered the boy's features
with the appearance of an older, distinguished man's form.

The servants showed Ylinilzar through another set of
doors, these tall and narrow, blood-red in color and bound
with gold and verdigris metal. Here was a great room, a
huge, echoing chamber that was far larger than any Ylinilzar had ever seen before. The floor was of tile, indigo and
glossy as water, the walls were of dull, cream-colored stone
and rose high overhead before a series of windows pierced
them just below the arched roof. The sun drifted in but did
not disturb the twilit room, merely picking out the golden
traceries that decorated the arching ceiling. Delicate columns supported the structure, like the fine bones of a
giant fish.

Ylinilzar might have stood staring about him for far
longer but a whisper came to him. No, not a whisper, but
a clear and masculine voice in his head.

Come, the voice commanded. *Come and stand before me.*

Then did Ylinilzar notice that at the far end of the long
room was a dais and a pair of thrones. In one throne was
a figure, the other was empty. Beside the thrones, also on
the dais was a bier on which rested a second figure.

Ylinilzar tried to stride forward in his surest manner, but
instead he stumbled the first few steps, taken aback by the mental voice. His breath came quicker than before, and he wondered if he had perhaps made a mistake in seeking the
attention of otherworldly beings.

It was a very long walk from the doors to the dais, and
the wizard had plenty of time to collect himself and recover
most of his usual composure. Yet, when he reached the
thrones and met the eyes of the man who sat there, once
again all his calm evaporated.

The man was the very twin of the body that Ylinilzar
wore, only quite a bit older. Gray streaked the heavy hair
and a deep frown marked the pale brow. His eyes were
golden green and flashed even in the soft dusk that filled
the room here where the sun did not reach. His clothing
was dark and severe in cut with no jewels or embroidery
or other decoration denoting rank, yet Ylinilzar knew he

was in the presence of a king far higher in station than the one in the white city.

You have not brought your healing magic with you, though you inhabit the body that once carried it. Where is it now? asked the man with a certain quality of impatience that carried more threat than a hundred words might have in another's mouth.

Ylinilzar stammered, dismayed to find his illusion so easily pierced and the truth so brutally spoken. He had become used to the long discourses of endless variation and little or no meaning in the palace of the white city and he was completely taken aback by this bluntness. The king stared at him and Ylinilzar felt a coldness in the pit of his belly.

You have lost the magic; you do not know how except that you suspect one of your fellow wizards to have stolen it. You thought to trade it for great secrets, you hoped for immortality. You may have your immortality, if you want it but only if you heal my wife of her illness and give up this body you have stolen.

"But—but I will dissipate without it, I will die! How can I achieve immortality if I am dead?" Ylinilzar exclaimed.

I will give you a new body, one which is indestructible and undying. You will have no need to eat or sleep. An hour of sunlight every few days will be enough to keep you alive for as long as you can bear it.

The wizard was again confounded. His heart's desire was being offered to him and all he need do was find the stolen girl and make her heal this man's wife to take on unending, imperishable life.

"H–how do I know you will do what you say?" Ylinilzar asked, pressed by his suspicious nature for some guarantee. Then he quailed before the anger that shot from the man's eyes like lightning from a cloud.

I never lie, said the man, and the mental voice was taut with loathing. *Do not attempt to return before you have recovered the healing magic. Now go!*

Ylinilzar felt a heavy pressure on his shoulders, turning him and propelling him down the long room. He tried to keep his feet under him, but his sandals slipped on the slick floor. The pressure did not let him fall but kept him upright, rushing him toward the red doors much faster than

he could have run on his own. He saw the doors come
closer and closer until he thought that he would be crushed
against them, but they opened before him and closed with
a clap behind him. Then the pressure ceased and the wizard
ran on his own, panting and gasping with terror out of that
beautiful place.

Ylinilzar ran nearly all the way back to the city before
he was forced to stop by shortness of breath. As a lesser
man would adjust a hat after running from an angry dog
so did the wizard seek to adjust the illusion that made
lesser humans perceive an older man rather than the boy's
body he inhabited, but to his consternation he found that
the illusion was intact. He made his way back to his rooms
in the palace, thinking hard all the way.

Shadow woke in the same bed she had found herself in
the last time she had come out of sleep. It was the same
bed in the same room though there was no sign of the
wizard Irilzar. Sun poured in the windows and the wind
played with the leaves of the bushes just as it had the time
before. She lay in the bed thinking of the hard ground she
had fallen asleep on, miles, she thought, from this house
and this bed.

Irilzar is no different from Ylinilzar, she thought, becoming aware of a strange numbness growing in her breast. She
was just as much a prisoner here as she was in the palace
or the cellar. Soon Irilzar would return and attempt to gain
the healing magic from her, probably starting with kindness
and then turning to cruelty when he found she would not
trust him, would not give up this terrible gift.

For a moment she thought of the boy and wished she
had never survived the crash that had nearly killed her. It
seemed so very long ago now. Then the boy's face came
more clearly in her mind, the hollow cheeks, the trembling
hands, the hope that had flamed up in the hazel eyes just
before Ylinilzar had called them up before him.

Well, I won't give up on him just yet, she thought, swallowing her disappointment at being back where she had
started the day before. She forced herself to climb out of
the soft bed, her body aching still with the unaccustomed
exercise even though the healing magic had done its best

to take the soreness from her muscles and the blisters from her feet.

I'm soft! I who used to run all day long and never mind a step. That's something I can change, anyway.

Shadow left the bedroom and the house, preferring the outdoors to the false comforts inside. There was another tray of food in the middle room but she left it with only a brief glance of regret. The magic would keep her alive and she could drink water from the pool. She was determined now not to accept a single thing from another wizard ever again.

All day Shadow spent roaming the desert hills. She did not bother trying to escape the house that Irilzar had made for her, but she did not keep it in sight, either. She returned once to drink deeply from the pool. She gazed long and hard at her reflection, but somehow she could not recognize herself in the face that looked back at her from the bright surface. Returning to the hills, she found a high place to sit, shaded by a slightly larger bush among the many bushes. Here she remained until the sun began to go down into the west, the red-and-gold rays warming her face.

The beams felt good, softening a coldness that had numbed her all day. She cried and felt better for it, even smiling at a bird that flew by and startled in midair at a slight movement she made.

A thought struck her, and she reached out for the first time that day with the magic that rested inside her. The magic cast about for something to heal and found the bird, not far away. Shadow looked at the creature through the un-eyes of the magic. It, too, was made of the same bits that made everything else, the air, the clouds, even the sun. . . . The magic soothed the bite of a louse which the bird had been unable to reach, and the silent gratitude it felt at this relief made Shadow want to cry again.

The magic was so enormous in its capacity for good, and up to this point she had been forced to use it only for the furthering of greed and power. Well, she was not under anyone's thumb right now. What was there to be healed here?

The magic stretched itself with a bound, like a creature used to vast spaces let out of a too-small cage. It spread itself all around in every direction and a wave of wellness followed it that affected every one of the tiny bits of stuff that made the world. Shadow felt the spell that bound her to this part of the desert dissipate and vanish, felt the house shiver and disappear back to the white city where it belonged, felt thousands, millions of living creatures healed of myriad ills, small and large, felt those creatures shake themselves and go on with their lives, one worry the less. The magic went to the ends of its limits, doing all it could, and then when it was done, it returned to her, none the worse for its work, pausing only to ease a cramping muscle in one of Shadow's legs before it settled in its accustomed spot inside her.

Shadow opened her eyes and found that the sun was rising behind her. The healing had taken all the night and just now was finished. She felt rested as though she had slept in that soft bed, but better for the freedom she knew had been given her during the night. She yawned and got up to stretch. When she looked around, she found that she was no longer alone.

Irilzar and Ylinilzar faced each other in a flat spot not far away. They turned at her movement.

"Give me the magic," they said in almost perfect unison, and then glared at each other and at her with equal fury.

"It's mine, I found it first," Ylinilzar said through clenched teeth.

"You don't have it yet," Irilzar retorted, sneering. He looked then at Shadow, trying to smile in a winning way, though his voice was strained. "Haven't I been kinder to you than this old thief? I really was sorry to send you to him, you looked like such a likely girl. I thought you might make a good apprentice and I wanted to keep you for myself, but . . . well, I made a mistake. You do forgive me, don't you? Give me the magic, and I will protect you from this posturing idiot. If you don't, I can't guarantee that you won't get hurt. I would never do anything to you, but this one has no conscience, and I'm not sure I can keep you from harm without the magic on my side."

Shadow laughed, a single explosive syllable that erased the attempted smile from the wizard's face.

"I told you she would never believe you," Ylinilzar jeered. "Defend yourself, if you can!"

The first clash stripped Ylinilzar of his illusory appearance and threw Shadow off her feet and against the ground so hard she was stunned. As soon as she could, she got to her feet and ran away, putting some distance between her and the wizards. Then she turned to watch, frightened but unable to look away.

The two wizards merely stood facing each other, their spells nullifying each other as fast as each was cast, each one striving to trick the other into a false step. They did not move except to mutter words of power or to wave their hands in magical gestures. All around them lightning flickered and thunder clapped, the air shimmered with disturbances, first blue, then green, then a sickly yellow. Clouds formed overhead and wind gusted hot and cold from all directions, raising dust and ripping leaves from the bushes that bent humbly beneath the disturbance.

Shadow covered her eyes with her hands to protect them from flying debris, but she continued watching the two wizards through her fingers. After the first shock of seeing them, she found she was not afraid of them anymore. She watched their display with a strange detachment, thinking rather unkind thoughts about their ostentation. The healing magic moved inside her, alerted by the attempts at injury, but she quieted it and did not let it reach out as it might have done unrestrained.

An ominous calm descended on the two wizards. The lightning gradually ceased, the wind fell to nothing, there were no gestures, no words of power spoken. They still faced each other, tense with effort, eyes unseeing as they strove to destroy each other. Suddenly Ylinilzar smiled, a ghastly bare-toothed grin, and Irilzar gave a terrible cry of pain.

A flicker of something like lightning danced all around Irilzar's body and with a brilliant, sickening flash ate him from the inside out. There was a last peal of thunder and Irilzar was gone.

Ylinilzar staggered, but he held himself from falling with a great effort. The face that he turned to Shadow still grinned but it was a spasm, not an expression of joy.

"Heal me," the wizard croaked.

Heal this one, too.

Beside her stood another man, so like the boy that Ylinilzar had stolen that she had to blink and look from one to the other, seeing so many resemblances that she quickly guessed this must be the father that the boy had spoken of. The man looked at her as well, his hazel eyes catching hers and holding her gaze so that she could not look away. With that look he read her every secret, knew her every thought, everything that had happened to her from her birth to this moment.

My son chose well whom he trusted with his gift. One more healing now and then we will see what comes next, he said.

Shadow thought he spoke grudgingly, as if he had not expected to find any worth in her, and she felt irritation at this idea and at being so completely examined without so much as an introduction. *Wizards,* she thought, annoyed, *They are all the same,* but she followed his gesture willingly to turn the healing magic on whatever or whomever he desired.

The man stepped to one side and there on a pallet of rich materials lay a woman. She was delicate of feature, pale-skinned and dark-haired like the man, but there was a gentleness in her face that the man lacked, or repressed. Her eyes were shut though she was not asleep. She was more deeply unconscious than sleep. Shadow felt her heart go out to this strange woman even as the magic leaped to its work, even as she knew that the magic could not heal all that was wrong with her.

The magic returned to her at last, yet though the woman breathed more easily and deeply and a fine color rose in her cheeks, still she did not wake or stir.

Ylinilzar chose this moment to come forward, striking Shadow a blow with his fist, knocking her down.

"Come on, heal her, use the magic and make her well," he shouted and would have kicked her, but the man stopped him with a glance.

The magic has done what it can. She will not wake yet, and that is only through my own fault. I was hoping for too much too easily. The man sighed. *I will be true to my word. Do you still desire immortality and an undying body?*

"Yes!"

Will you give up this body as you promised before?

"As soon as you give me my reward," Ylinilzar said, attempting to smile ingratiatingly.

Shadow could hardly bear to look at him, his face was so ugly. Turning away, she caught sight of the man and her heart was filled with pity for him. She had barely known the boy, and it hurt her to see his body, his beautiful face charged with such an evil spirit. What must it be for him, his father, to see the same thing?

Here is the body I promised you, the man said. He gestured slightly and yet another figure appeared on the hillside.

It was a man but apparently made all of gold, expertly molded into the perfect likeness of a human. Its eyes were closed and it did not move, merely stood where it had been called forth like a statue.

Ylinilzar stood nearly as still as the golden figure, completely taken aback.

"This is what I am to inhabit?" he asked after a moment, evidently not quite sure what to think.

Yes, the man replied. *I promised you immortality, undying life. This is the best way to achieve it so far as I know. No weapon can pierce it, no illness can attack it. It is completely indestructible except perhaps in the furnace of the sun. Even that may not destroy it, I do not know.*

Ylinilzar regarded the golden construction for a long time. He did not appear eager to try it on, much as he might look at a coat that, though beautiful and useful, was not exactly of the fashion or size he was looking for.

Then, without warning, the boy's body crumpled lifelessly to the ground. The golden man opened its eyes, and Ylinilzar looked out from them for the first time.

"Wonderful . . . wonderful . . ." the wizard murmured, and the golden lips moved into a shape like a smile.

The dark-haired man smiled also and reached up to put his hand on the golden one's shoulder. As he touched the construction, there was a click and the golden man froze in mid-smile and did not move again.

Quick, please do not let my son's body die, the man begged, turning to Shadow, but the magic was already in the abandoned body doing its work to keep breath and blood moving.

"Where is your son? Is he not with you?" asked Shadow, as the man went to the body and gently straightened the tangled limbs and smoothed the heavy hair back from the blank face.

No more than is his mother. The man sat back on his heels, regarding the two silent figures, ignoring the third and golden one which seemed to have lost any interest for him. *My son came to us, but at first we did not recognize him. We did not expect him to return to us at all and certainly never in the shape of a vulture. It was my wife who first realized why the bird had sought us out and she tried to communicate with him but—*

"But he was lost in the bird shape and she became lost with him," Shadow said.

How did you—the man began, then stopped. A faint color rose in the pale cheeks as if he might be blushing. Shadow stared at him, surprised at her lack of fear.

"Have you forgotten reading me? You know more about me than I do. I spent time as a hawk before I met your son. I was nearly lost in that shape before I discovered the danger. Your son saved my life, twice in one effort, for my body was badly hurt and my spirit had gone very far toward death. he healed my body and called me back to life."

Yes, of course. the mental voice held a strange tone to it. Shadow thought he sounded almost embarrassed. *Can you—would you do the same for him?*

"I will try," Shadow said. "Where is he now?"

The man pointed up into the sky. High above the desert were three black birds soaring.

He is one of those three.

Shadow started to turn the attention of the magic from the boy's body toward the three birds but immediately she felt its breath slow and the heart begin to fail. She let the magic go back and steady the abandoned body while she tried to think of what to do. She watched through the healing magic as it spread itself out happily in its old home, but it nosed about restlessly as if seeking the missing spirit.

I never learned his name, Shadow thought.

We named him after the custom of your people. We named him Islinisildir, came the answer. *Though his mother called him Slini when he was a baby.*

Shadow repeated the unfamiliar syllables a few times while she seated herself on the ground near the boy's body. She closed her eyes the better to use the magic for sight.

Where is Islinisildir? she thought to and through the healing magic. The magic coursed through the boy's body, hunting for the missing spirit. *No, not here, somewhere else,* she thought, *but you can't completely leave his body to look for him, you must keep some of yourself here to keep him alive while we find him. Is that possible?*

The magic responded as quickly as she thought the problem out for it. She felt it spread out again but in a new way, changing from a warm, wide presence into a narrow, hot band like a beam of light. It made a bond between her body and the boy's, then, directed by her thought, into the sky to the soaring birds.

Shadow and the magic worked together, touching first one then another of the three birds. In each bird mind she said the boy's name and in the third one she thought she heard a faint echo, a resonance that had not occurred with the other two. She let herself and the magic go deep within the bird, past the bird's awareness of wind and sky and the endless hunt for food. She began to call the boy's name, over and over, setting it up as a beacon in the darkness that was behind the bird's conscious mind, beyond the subconscious and into the depths that reached back and out and in all at the same time.

The magic had taught her already that every part of the world around her, both seen and unseen, was made up of the same kind of bits of stuff and here she found a similar consistency. The bird had not the intelligence or awareness of a human nature, it had its own variation on these things, and yet behind that was the same well, the same source from which came all intelligence, all awareness. It was only in the creature it was expressed through that the differences came to be.

Shadow and the magic pressed deeper and deeper into the darkness, still calling the boy's name. She might have been impatient, for there was no response yet beyond the slight resonance that told her she was doing the right thing, but she had begun to remember her own experience of being lost. She remembered that the boy had called to her for what seemed like a very long time before she ever noticed his voice, so she did not despair, merely continued calling. Time ceased to have a linear meaning for her. It was something outside of this place, this experience. Shadow called and called into the darkness, teasing the resonance over and over. Was it growing stronger?

It seemed another voice was calling to Islinisildir. It was very faint but as Shadow noticed it, it also noticed her. They both paused in surprise.

Who calls my son? came the question, and if a mental voice could be rough from overuse, this one was nearly worn away.

A friend who wants to help, Shadow replied, hope rising in her. *Who are you?*

His mother, came the reply. *I have been calling a long time but he will not return to me, he is too far lost to come back. I have only been able to keep him from leaving altogether. Perhaps together we can bring him back.* But the distant voice was gloomy and hopeless.

Well, we'll never entice him back this way, Shadow thought to herself, but Islinisildir's mother heard her.

What do you mean?

Shadow paused for a moment before she answered.

He and I were both in danger when he left his body to the wizard and set off in the vulture to find you and his father. The wizard was very cruel to him. Perhaps he does not know that it is safe to return. I was a bird for a while also and it would have been very tempting to remain as one. It is a simple and straightforward life: no wizards to torment you, no magic at all to deal with, just the hunt for food, and mates, and the joy of flying. Perhaps we need to remind him of the good things he is missing by trying to leave us. I only knew him for a few hours, so you must think of all the things that he loved or enjoyed or desired to do in the future. Send this to him while I keep calling his name. Maybe that will bring him back.

Tentatively, Islinisildir's mother complied.

Shadow saw all that she sent, though much of it was incomprehensible to her. There were visions of silver ships without sails, a black sky filled with unblinking, many-colored stars, crowds of people essentially identical in appearance to Islinisildir and his parents . . . But there was other information that she understood all too well. Shadow thought he might be driven completely away, so sad were the thoughts and memories that the woman called up.

Islinisildir's mother brought up all her memories of her

son being born, the joy that the infant brought to the lovers, the delight in his swift intelligence and gentle nature. But, as the boy grew and learned to question as all children do, trouble began. The son and the father began to disagree on the answers to the questions Islinisildir raised. At first the son deferred to the father, but when he continued to question things that the father thought should not be questioned, he began to be more forceful in his insistence that his own view was the correct one and that he thought Islinisildir's persistence was unpleasant and unnecessary.

Then began the struggle in earnest between father and son. The mother was left out except to be appealed to by one or both for support, which she did her best to provide. This was a difficult thing to do, for she loved both of them and did not want to anger the one by agreeing with the other. So she was left to give no opinion at all, and this only made them both angry with her because she would not take sides.

There came a last argument. It ended with the father striking his son across the face. This was a common thing in Shadow's world, but in this society a blow like this was nearly unheard of. Islinisildir did not retaliate; he simply left, and where he went after that his mother did not know.

This is awful, Shadow thought, dismayed. *He will never return to us if this is what we use to call him. I'm surprised he's still anywhere to be found. What is it that is keeping him?*

Desperate, she cast her own thoughts back to when he had rescued her from the very fate she was trying to save him from. She remembered how surprised she had been that anyone would know her name, and how that alone was nearly enough to bring her back. Of course, she had not known the fate that awaited her—if she had, she might not have returned. No, she decided, she would have come back anyway. The love and concern in the boy's voice had been what really lured her back. No one had ever spoken to her like that, and remembering it made a warmth spread out in her own voice that still called the boy's name. She wanted to hear it again, wanted the boy to speak to her as he had before.

Islinisildir, she called, putting all her heart and mind into the name, thinking of his face as she had first seen it bending over her in that dreary cellar, the clear hazel eyes shining so happily at his success.

The slight resonance that responded to the call grew stronger and Shadow rejoiced and redoubled her efforts.

Islinisildir's mother listened hard to Shadow's voice, striving to understand the change in tone. It took her only an instant to comprehend, and then she cast aside all the thoughts of past anger and sorrow. Instead her voice carried the image of Islinisildir the baby who drew his parents into a new understanding of love and responsibility. Weariness faded, and she called with fresh hope, her voice clear and sweet in the darkness, chiming in with Shadow's.

Again Shadow felt the response grow, but she also felt his hesitation. She remembered how comforting the darkness was, how she had wanted to fall into it and let everything go. She tried to think of something else that would tip the balance in their favor, but before she could worry over it too much, another presence joined them.

Humble and a little shy, fearing he might be sent away, Islinisildir's father joined them. His voice added a new dimension to the call, his vision of Islinisildir in the future, a proud and independent man, free to disagree, loved and respected for himself as he was and not as others wanted him to be.

The three voices blended, the three visions merged into one and each perfectly balanced the others so that together they made a joyous song of calling into which Islinisildir rushed as if he could hold himself back no longer.

There was a wrenching as if the world had turned upside down and inside out, and Shadow found herself back in her body. She was lying on her back, sand and dead leaves in her hair, cold and stiff from the hard ground, Overhead, the sky was just turning the darker blue of twilight, sprinkled with a few early stars. She heard someone else stirring not far away, and turning on her side, she saw Islinisildir just opening his eyes. He looked up at the sky as she had and he smiled. He just had time to turn his head to look at her before his parents scrambled to his side and gathered him up in their arms.

Shadow lay back again and left them to their reunion. She was surprised to find tears coming from her eyes, and she wiped them away with one hand. When she had the strength, she sat up and found that the family was just separating enough to turn their attention on her.

Thank you, the mother said. *I never would have known what to do without you.*

We both would have been lost without you, Islinisildir said.

And I, as well, his father added. *I could not lose both my son and my wife without wanting to follow them.*

"Well, I never would have known what to do if you hadn't rescued me," Shadow said. "And I would not be here without your magic—which I want to give back to you right away. I never wanted it to begin with, and I don't want it now!"

That was all it took. The magic made a leap and was gone, leaving a numbness behind where it had rested inside her.

Shadow tried not to cry, concentrating on the expression of joy and completion that came over Islinisildir's face, trying to be glad that he was whole again. Then the magic reached gently back inside her, easing the numbness so that it woke into a kind of pain. Slowly the pain faded until she felt only a glow like the warmth she had felt when Islinisildir had taken her hand so long ago in the cellar. This time when the magic left her, she did not mind so much. She knew she would miss it, but relief was already welling up in her, too. Then Islinisildir spoke, and for a while Shadow forgot all about magic.

I made you a promise, Islinisildir reminded her. *What is the ransom for a girl-slave of your age in the place you come from?*

A slave! exclaimed Islinisildir's mother

Ransom? asked Islinisildir's father. They looked at each other fondly, for they had spoken at the same moment.

Islinisildir explained in a rush of thought that took only an instant, giving his parents the whole story of the time he had spent with Shadow in the cellar and what he had promised her. Shadow saw only a glance pass between them for the thoughts were too fast for her to understand. Another look went between father and mother. For a long moment her heart nearly stopped beating, for the man seemed to hesitate. Islinisildir's eyes darkened, his mouth beginning to set itself in a stubborn line, but the woman spoke before her husband.

No matter what the cost, it cannot be more than we owe you for the return of our only child, she said. Shadow had the odd impression that she did not refer to a monetary cost but some other, more subtle payment.

Her husband nodded with a look of relief as if he had been stopped from making an old mistake.

How do we do this thing for you? And where will you go once you are free? What is to keep you safe while you grow up? You are only a child, after all. Have you no mother or father or other relative to take you in?

Oh, can't she come with us? asked Islinisildir, but both parents shook their heads as one.

You know the laws, Islinisildir, said his father, but his voice was gentle. *You broke them by coming here and falling into trouble and drawing others in after you. We will do this ransoming but more than that would be wrong.*

"I can take care of myself," Shadow said, firmly. She did not want to be the cause of any trouble. "Once I'm free, I need fear no one. I will soon find a place as a messenger again or some other thing that needs doing."

Well, then let us do this thing. I want to return with my family to where we belong, Islinisildir's father said.

Father, Islinisildir said, as they got up from the ground and dusted each other off. *What is that doing here?* He pointed at the golden man standing nearby, silent and still in the gathering dusk.

Nothing, his father said. *We'll return for it later.*

Hands, said Islinisildir's mother softly, and they reached out for each other, Islinisildir taking Shadow's hand in his. Shadow was glad of the contact for the thought of seeing her master again made her heart beat uncertainly. What if he would not free her? What if—

In a blink the desert was left behind, and they stood in the heart of the city outside the very door of her old master's dwelling. There was music and the sound of laughter. Anberious was entertaining. Islinisildir's father drummed his fist on the door and after a moment it was flung open.

"Go away, too late for business," Anberious drawled and then interrupted himself saying in surprise, "Why, Shadow,

dear, where have you been? I had just about given you up
for rat-meat."

"Hello, master. How much do I cost, master?" Shadow
asked. "I mean, to ransom," she added, thinking, *has he
always been so short and dull-seeming?* She looked at her
old master while he answered, trying to remember what he
looked like, comparing the memory with what she saw now.
It was then that she wondered just how long she had
been gone.

"Ransom? Er, let's see," Anberious dithered in greater
surprise than ever. Shadow's eyes were uncomfortably
piercing and he wished she wouldn't stare at him so. "Your
cost would be, um, at the market, on a good day, if you
had a bath, about fifteen trets, perhaps eighteen with a new
tunic and a little luck, so your ransom . . . I would think it
would be about double that—"

"Oh, master, I would never cost so much!" Shadow
laughed at him when his face fell, laughing as much at his
expression as at her own relief that Anberious had not
simply refused to consider freeing her. "I think I cost you
all of five trets four years ago and so double would be ten
at the most. Isn't that closer to the truth?"

"Well, yes, but you've grown so, especially since I saw
you last. Where have you been all this time? You did complete your assignment, didn't you?" Anberious would have
gone on, but he was stopped by an impatient motion of
Islinisildir's hand. Abruptly, the old man noticed the people
around his door. His mouth gaped open, and he stared
at them so that Shadow was torn between laughter and
embarrassment at his stupid, fishlike expression.

Islinisildir's father held out his hand. There was a single
piece of gold in his palm, not the triangular pierced coins
of the white city but a simple lump as big as a green fig.
Anberious's eyes popped open at that, and when he began
to gabble something about not being able to make change,
Islinisildir's father merely dropped it at his feet and turned
and led them away.

Anberious picked up the lump of gold and stared after
them, musing over what had just occurred. That man—so
imperious and disdainful. He must be a king or a great
wizard. Such strange coloring as well. Then he thought of
Shadow and how she had looked at him, and he shuddered.

She had made him so nervous with those sharp eyes of hers raking him from top to bottom that he had forgotten to take off her collar. Come to think of it, she hadn't been wearing it anymore. How had she slipped it? Perhaps the wizard had taken it off of her for some reason.

Anberious hefted the gold in his hand, thinking he was glad she was gone. She would have been more trouble than she was worth with those sharp eyes of hers and anyway, he could buy any number of youngsters to take her place with this ridiculous quantity of gold. He turned to go back into the house. There was a burst of laughter as he paused on the lintel and a voice called for him to come and enjoy the joke. Anberious hesitated, looking back down the lane, but there was no one there.

"That was much too much gold," Shadow said.

They were outside the city again. The desert was sweet and dark all around them, stars shining overhead and a young moon just rising.

No matter. I could not stand to hear another word from that stupid man. Islinisildir's father seemed disgusted.

Are you free now? asked Islinisildir. He was still holding her hand and once again Shadow found herself clinging to it as desperately as she had in the cellar. She shrugged at his question, not daring to speak. She knew they were about to leave, and there was a lump in her throat bigger than the piece of gold they had paid for her.

Come, Islinisildir's father said, and might have insisted, but his wife took him gently by the arm and led him to one side.

Good luck, Islinisildir said. *I'll miss you.*

"I'll miss you, too, though I hardly know you," Shadow said. "Will I ever see you again?"

Not if my father has anything to say about it, Islinisildir replied. He squeezed her hand tightly and then let it go. *But then, that never stopped me from doing what I wanted to do before. That's how I met you, after all.*

There was a short silence between them. Islinisildir's face was only a pale blur in the starry night, his eyes glinting a little as he looked at her.

I have to go.

"Good-bye, then. Don't get into too much trouble," Shadow managed to say.

No, not without you around to rescue me, he said. Then he turned and walked to where his parents waited. They took hands, and without another word or look they vanished from her sight as if they had never been.

Shadow stood alone for a long time without really being aware of anything around her. After a while she wiped the tears from her face and started to walk back toward the city. Her feet felt very heavy, and it was hard to keep going. The road was quiet at this time of night, only a few travelers making their way along the dusty track. Shadow went unnoticed, slipping along the verge out of long habit. She was not thinking very clearly but one thought went round and round in her head. What to do next?

She had spoken boldly in front of Islinisildir and his parents but the reality of her situation was not as bright as she had suggested. While it was true she might be able to find work, it was more likely that she would be picked up for what the city guardsmen called loitering and turned over to be put in the general pool of unclaimed vagrants. She would be put to work, but it would be the same as being a slave without the protection of a master who had made a monetary investment in her, and the chances of escaping again would be slim at best. If she was very lucky she might get a position as messenger, but more likely she would be sweeping streets or washing pots in someone's kitchen. She could return to Anberious and ask him to take her on as a free agent but the thought of that made her annoyed. She did not want to work for him again, free or not.

The gates of the city were not far ahead. Torchlight spilled out into the night and there was a distant sound of men laughing, then raucous shouts.

Shadow stopped.

Worse things could happen to an unfriended girl than being picked up by the city guards and made to wash pots. Night was not the best time to be wandering around the city. Perhaps she should just head back out into the desert and find a safe spot to sleep in. Yes, that sounded like a better idea than going into the city now. Perhaps tomorrow

she could explore around the farms near the river and find
work there. She was just turning to carry out her plan when
the harsh call of trumpets came from inside the city,
guardsmen calling for reinforcements.

There were shouts of alarm, the sharp clatter of metal-
shod horse's hooves on stone, and suddenly out of the gate
came a small company of riders galloping full speed out of
the city. Two or three had drawn swords, one had a sling
and was shooting stones back over his horse's rump, aiming
high to frighten, not kill. Shadow jumped farther away from
the roadway, keeping a wary eye on the company as they
went by.

The riders were laughing, already putting away their
weapons, slowing their mounts to a canter as if completely
sure of their ability to protect themselves from mere city
guardsmen.

They were past in an instant and lost in the milky, moon-
lit dark but Shadow jumped up and ran after them as fast
as she could, following the patter of hooves and the sweet
sound of women laughing into the night.

THREE CHOICES:
THE STORY OF LOZEN
by Jane Lindskold

Everything written on these pages is true, except for what is not, of course, for that is the way of legends. This is the tale of three choices and what those choices meant not only to a woman but to the Apache people, for these choices shaped their history.

The girl was born to the Mimbres Apaches, a tribe whose nomadic life carried them both through the mountains and into the land of Old and New Mexico. Although these lands had food and hunting, the Apaches regularly preyed on the Mexicans, stealing horses, crops, and slaves. Tribal lore held that the Mexicans had been created by the Mountain God, both to raise the crops that the Apaches could not and to provide sport for the warriors.

One of the infant child's first memories was the warriors' faces striped with bands of red or white clay across the eyes and nose. She wept in terror the first time she saw the paint transform her father's handsome face in preparation for a raid. Her shrill cries were immediately silenced by her mother who swung the cradleboard in front of her and offered the baby her breast.

"Hush, daughter, hush," Mother crooned. "You must never cry aloud. There are enemies everywhere—not only the Mexicans, but the white men."

"And the bears and the snakes," piped up Big Brother, eager to be part of the conversation.

"Never say those names," Mother said sternly. "If you say their names, they may believe you are inviting them to visit, and then what would you do?"

"I would fight them!" Big Brother answered, sighting down the barrel of an imaginary rifle.

"Perhaps," Mother chuckled softly. "Perhaps."

As the girl grew older, caution was her first and most important lesson, but she learned other things as well. There was the seasonal pattern of foods to pick, dry, cook, and prepare for storage. There were the different camps the Mimbres moved between, each place becoming so special to her that she could not have borne to leave one place if it were not for anticipation of the next.

Once she could walk, the girl helped her mother care for the younger children, both her own brothers and sisters and the children of kinfolk whose mothers had died and whose fathers must be free to go on raids and to fight for the Indéh, the People, on raids and in war.

Sometimes her adopted sisters and brothers had neither mother nor father. The little girl was careful not to show her pity for them, but she was very conscious of her own wealth of family. Not only did she have both mother and father, but Big Brother remained her close friend, even while they were inducted into the mysteries they would need to know when they joined the adult men and women.

Big Brother never mocked her as clumsy or big-footed as many boys did girls. He praised her for her stealth, helped her learn to shoot a bow, and to handle a knife. When their father was part of a raid that captured a wealth of horses, she and Big Brother were each given a horse of their own. Together they rode, exploring the mountains of their current camp, bringing back treats for their mother.

Because she and Big Brother were so inseparable, the girl came to be called Little Sister, a name she wore with pride, dreading slightly the day when she would need to put it off and take on a name that could never mean as much to her.

Aside from her games with her brother, Little Sister's favorite thing of all was to listen to the stories her mother and grandmother and aunts recited in the evening. They told how Yusen, the Life Giver, had drawn the world up from the waters of a vast lake. She learned how White-Painted-Woman had cleverly saved her son, Child-of-the-Water, from the Owl Giant.

Other stories told how Child-of-the-Water had grown to be a great warrior who killed the evil creatures of the world—even the Owl Giant. After such stories, Little Sister would fall asleep and dream. In her dreams she was Child-of-the-Water, but the monsters she slew were not bulls, bears, and prairie dogs. Instead they were Mexicans and Anglos.

When she told her dreams to her mother and grandmother, they nodded solemnly.

"These dreams are not to be ignored," Mother said. "Remember, Child-of-the-Water is a warrior, but he is also the one who shaped the first people from the mud. Today men are the warriors and women make new people."

Grandmother nodded. "This is true, but it is also true that women of the Indéh know how to be warriors when the need arises. Sometimes a faithful wife will accompany her man into battle. She paints a yellow stripe across her eyes and fights alongside him. Other times, when the warriors are away, the women and the old men defend the camp. Perhaps your dreams are telling you that someday you will be called upon to defend your people."

Little Sister listened carefully, glad that they did not laugh at her. Big Brother also did not laugh.

"If you may be called to be a warrior," he said seriously, "then I should show you what the old men are teaching me."

"And I will teach you women's lore," Little Sister promised. "That way you will know the best plants for food and healing so that you will never be in need when on a raid."

Years unrolled through their cycles. Grandmother died. The father of Big Brother and Little Sister was killed on a raid. Their mother mourned, never permitting their names to be spoken again lest the ghosts be drawn from the spirit world and the family die of ghost sickness.

In time, another warrior offered for Mother. He was an older man, a friend of their father. Mother had taken in one of his children when his wife died in childbirth. Now he took her and her children under his protection.

When the time came for Little Sister to celebrate her Puberty Feast, the da-i-dá, Step-father was as generous as if she had been his birth-daughter. Mother made her a skirt and blouse of fine deerskin, embroidered with sacred patterns in tiny bird bones. With the help of her sisters and daughters, Mother prepared enough food for a four-day feast.

Little Sister worked with her aunt, her mother's elder sister, who was her sponsor and teacher in the ritual. There were many things to remember. She must not touch water. She must share blessings with the people when White-Painted-Woman came to her. She must not stumble when she made the four ritual runs. When she had completed the runs, she must shake her buckskin mat to the four directions.

There were also dances to learn for the end of the ceremony when the Crown Dancers, who represent the Mountain Gods, would join the celebration. Sometimes, Little Sister wished that she could just run away from it all, go riding or gathering piñon nuts in the hills with Big Brother. She put these childish longings from her. Trying to deny her womanhood was as foolish as Coyote's desire to fly.

On the fourth day of the da-i-dá, her runs completed with flawless grace, her people confident that the Mountain Gods would smile upon her, Little Sister joined the Crown Dancers for the final celebration.

Alone of all those happily celebrating her womanhood, she felt disquiet for, although she had performed as she had been told, she had not felt White-Painted-Woman descend upon her. She had not felt herself become the mother goddess. Even as she went through the ritual dance steps, she wondered if she should tell her mother that the blessings she had given were empty.

"Why would you believe that?" said a voice from just behind her. It was female, sweet-toned but strong. "You were painted with yellow tule pollen by your sponsor; everyone you touched believes themselves blessed by White-Painted-Woman. Why do you doubt?"

Little Sister realized that she could no longer hear the drummers, no longer hear the footfalls of the Crown Dancers on the hard-packed earth. Not losing step with her silent partners, she turned her head. Behind her danced a beautiful Apache woman, clad identically to Little Sister in buckskin blouse and skirt. Only the white clay painted evenly across her features revealed her for who she was.

The mother goddess smiled. "Do not doubt the power of the blessings you gave, Little Sister. Sometimes the recipient, rather than the bestower, is the only one who can judge what is a blessing and what is not."

To Little Sister's right, a Crown Dancer broke step with
the others. As he turned toward Little Sister, she realized
that the one who faced her was not a Dancer, but Child-
of-the-Water, the son of White-Painted-Woman. His face
was painted with the wide, red stripe worn by the warriors.
He was bare-chested; his embroidered buckskin loincloth
touched his knees in the front, touched the ground in the
back.

"You already show the makings of a di-yin, a medicine
woman, Little Sister," the handsome warrior said. "On this
day of your da-i-dá, we have come to offer you a gift. If
you will devote yourself to the welfare of your people, for-
saking a family of your own to take the Apaches as your
children, then we will give you a power no di-yin has ever
possessed—the power to know where your enemies hide."

Little Sister danced, her feet keeping the steps, even as
her mind swirled. No family? No sons and daughters? No
husband?

Yet, if she could tell where enemies hid, how much safer
would her people be! The warriors would never need to
follow a wrong path, never need to risk ambush. Children
and women could camp without the fear that their enemies
would strike unexpectedly.

Yet . . . no children? No husband?

White-Painted-Woman danced in front of her, dancing
through the body of the Crown Dancer nearest to Little
Sister. Child-of-the-Water danced beside her. Little Sister
could see the sweat on his body, the scars from his battles
with the evil animals. He carried a rifle in one muscular
hand, a rifle that reminded her of her brother's newly ac-
quired weapon.

Little Sister felt her decision take shape within her. Bow-
ing low before the two Mountain Gods, Little Sister stated
her choice.

"I will take your gift, White-Painted-Woman," she said.
"I will protect my people as your son protected us at the
dawn of all days. I will show my people their enemies."

White-Painted-Woman smiled upon her; Child-of-the-
Water raised his rifle in salute.

"When you would know where your enemies hide,"
White-Painted-Woman instructed, "go a distance from the
war party. Lift your hands to the sky and pray to Yusen,

the Life Giver, for guidance. Then spread your hands with the palms outward and spin a slow circle. You will feel where your enemies are then."

"I understand," Little Sister said, "and thank you."

The sound of the drums within her ears, the thudding of feet upon the earth, the chanting of the crowd was her only answer.

Some days later, with the aid of Big Brother, Little Sister tested her new gift. Praying fervently to Yusen, she held out her hands. Almost immediately, her palms burned slightly.

"To the west," she said to her brother. "I do not think there are many."

Big Brother shrugged. "Good, we do not need many to prove that you have been divinely gifted. Let us scout. If there are indeed enemies, we will return and tell the warriors."

Her burning palms directed them west, then slightly north and west. Within an hour, they found a small encampment of Mexicans.

"I recognize those men," Big Brother said. "We took some horses from them. Perhaps they look to take them back."

The warriors they told of their find were somewhat unwilling to believe in Little Sister's power. Over the months that followed, however, they grew first to believe, then to trust in it.

The gift of White-Painted-Woman and Child-of-the-Water did have its limitations. First of all, it would not work within the tribe. It only worked slightly better on other Apache tribes, as if the Mountain God, wished to remind the Mimbres Apaches that the other Apaches were not enemies, even when there were differences of opinion and custom.

The power was almost useless on a raid, unless that raid was on proven enemies. Additionally, Little Sister must invoke the god's gift or it would not warn them, even if the enemy stood directly outside of their camp. However, when invoked and used against enemies, the gift was flawless. From the intensity of the burning sensation, Little Sister could tell not only the direction of the enemy band, but she could guess their proximity and numbers.

Around her family's fire, Little Sister would retell the tale of her spirit vision, of how she was approached by the Mountain Gods, and of the price they exacted for her gift. At first no one much minded the cost, but as Little Sister grew into a fine young woman with shining black hair and such high cheekbones that her face was almost diamond-shaped there were those young men who grumbled softly.

Because Little Sister did not wish any to think she could secretly be courted, most frequently she chose to ride with Big Brother's war party. At his side, she was both valued and her modesty was defended against reproach.

When Big Brother grew older, he courted a woman of the Chiricahua, also called the Warm Springs Apaches. When he married her, he became a member of the Tchi-hénè, the Red Paint People. The band's name was taken from the stripe of red clay that the men painted in a mask-like fashion across their eyes when they went into battle.

His new family called him Bi-duyé. Little Sister learned to call him by his new name, for a rising young warrior could not be called by his childhood name.

As his successes grew, Bi-duyé insisted that Little Sister have her place in the Tchi-hénè warrior's circle—that she be given the warrior's salute and be permitted to paint her face with red clay as well as with yellow.

He said to the assembled men, "Little Sister is as my right hand. Strong as a man, braver than most, cunning in strategy—Little Sister is a shield to her people."

Only a few warriors protested, for more and more frequently the war bands were coming to count not only on her magic, but also on her healing and fighting skills.

Thus it was that Little Sister was sitting with the warriors when the stranger called Gray Ghost was brought before the fires of the Chiricahua.

"We found him riding with a small band," said a proud young warrior, displaying his catch. "He does not speak our language, but this one—" here he indicated an elderly Mescalero Apache, "—is his interpreter. He says the man is Gray Ghost, a chief come from lands far east of here, looking for a new homeland for his tribe."

Little Sister thought that the stranger looked like a chief.

He was taller and leaner than was usual for her people, strong and handsome. Although most of his clothing was Apache in styling, the patterns on his jewelry were alien.

Showing no fear, Gray Ghost studied the Tchi-hénè warriors. His gaze lingered on Little Sister, and she felt her breathing quicken. She was glad that the darkness and the noise as the warriors shouted their questions at the interpreters gave her time to recover her composure. Still, she was certain that Bi-duyé noticed and was grateful that he did not comment.

At last the debate resolved to two sides—those who said Gray Ghost was an enemy spying for the Mexicans or Anglos and should be slain, and those who said that he was merely a stranger and, as a guest of the Apaches, should be treated as a guest until he proved himself unworthy of the privilege.

No one even suggested that Gray Ghost be taken as a slave. The Apache word for "slave" means, roughly, "they had to live with them." Not even the hottest of hot-headed warriors would believe that the powerful, handsome man who stood proudly before them as if indifferent to the fact that they were discussing his fate, could be made to live anywhere that he did not choose.

Little Sister signaled that she wanted to speak, and the warriors fell silent out of respect for this di-yin and warrior.

"We cannot speak to this stranger except through his interpreter and even an honest interpreter can be fooled by clever word," she said, her voice strong and clear. "Yusen, the Life Giver, can see into this stranger's heart and know if he is friend or enemy. Let me go a distance from our camp and pray to Yusen. If my palms burn, then he is an enemy and should be slain. If my palms remain cool, then let him be treated as a visitor and guest."

The gathered warriors agreed with the wisdom of this plan. Not sparing another glance at Gray Ghost, Little Sister strode from the camp. With a gesture, By-duyé gathered a few of his warriors and followed his sister to guard her as she prayed.

Alone, Little Sister raised her arms to the starry night sky. "Yusen, Life Giver, powerful one who drew the world up from the waters and began all, once again grant me the blessing of knowing enemies from allies, ones who would do harm from those who are merely unknown to us."

She prayed with all her heart, immersing herself in her humble plea. Then, closing her eyes and holding her palms outward, she began to spin. Her palms remained cool even after she had completed a full revolution.

"Yusen sends no sign that the stranger is an enemy," she said, holding out her palms so that Bi-duyé and his men could see them. "Unless they act otherwise, I believe the gods wish us to welcome the strangers as guests."

Bi-duyé and the others hastened back with the news. Little Sister followed more slowly. Although her palms remained cool, her heart burned as it never had before. A revelation as swift and certain as her vision during the da-i-dá told her that Gray Ghost was the man for her, that with him she could bear strong children, could build a family that would survive disaster to the end of time.

As she walked back to the warrior's circle, she felt her isolation as she never had before. Although the warriors saluted her as one of them, and the women respectfully asked for her advice, she belonged neither to one group nor to the other.

Bi-duyé loved her, but he had married several times, had sons and daughters to carry on his line, to welcome him when he returned from battle. She had nothing but an empty wickiup and the hesitant friendship of the Tchi-hénè, many of whom feared her as much as they loved or admired her.

Gray Ghost would end her solitude. Had she not served the Indéh long enough? How many had she saved by her use of the Mountain Gods' gift? Surely the coming of Gray Ghost, the power of love she felt for him, was a sign that her time alone was ended.

Returning to her seat in the warrior's circle, she listened as, through his interpreter, Gray Ghost told stories of his journeys. While he spoke, she noticed how frequently his gaze came to rest on her. However, through the night's storytelling, she never offered a question or acknowledged his regard.

Gray Ghost and his interpreter stayed with the Tchi-hénè for several days. Little Sister went on with her duties as if he was not there—neither avoiding him, nor seeking him out. Still, she noticed that he continued to watch her with admiration, that he frequently wandered near where she was working as if by accident.

When, at last, Gray Ghost left with his interpreter and a small war party, Little Sister watched him go, her heart burning with a love equaled only by her duty to her people. She had never spoken a word to Gray Ghost nor he to her, but she would never forget him. Nor would they ever meet again.

The years following Gray Ghost's departure were busy ones for Little Sister. Bi-duyé was rising in reputation as a war leader. The Mexicans had dubbed him "Victorio," perhaps as a salute to his prowess in battle. If that was the reason, they should have called Little Sister "Victoria" for she was one of the main reasons for his success.

Perhaps they did not realize how much the war leader owed to the lovely di-yin who rode into battle with him. However, they did notice her, dubbing her "Lozen." By this name she came to be known, not only by the Mexicans and Anglos, but also by many of the Apache and other Indian peoples as well. Certainly, continuing to call an increasingly legendary warrior and di-yin "Little Sister" seemed inappropriate.

To her family, Lozen remained Little Sister. Although she did not have children of her own, her brother had several. The eldest was a serious little girl who quite admired her warrior aunt. Sometimes Lozen would take the child with her when she gathered medicinal herbs or tended to the horses.

The horses needed much care. Lozen would clean and trim their hooves. Other times, to harden the hooves, she treated them with a paste made of deer liver, powdered ash, or limestone. Even greater protection could be gained by making coverings of rawhide for each hoof, but this took good hide and time. And, like many things, time was becoming more and more difficult to obtain as the Indéh fled their enemies.

Other times Lozen and her niece would string red beans and white seeds to make protective necklaces. Lozen would tell the little girl stories, the same stories she had heard as a girl from her mother and grandmother. Often, the little

girl would beg to hear the story of Lozen's da-i-dá and
Lozen would oblige.

These were good times, but there were not as many of
these as either Bi-duyé or Little Sister might have hoped.
Despite their best efforts, the Apaches were losing their
war with the Mexicans and the Anglos. Repeatedly, the
Tchi-hénè were forced to move from Warm Springs to
other, less hospitable areas. At some of these, like the San
Carlos Reservation, the conditions were barely survivable.

Forced into crowded quarters, side-by-side with other
tribes, many of whom did not share their customs, many of
the Indéh despaired. Some of the women used the corn
ration to brew tulapai, an alcoholic drink. Fights broke out
frequently, ironically confirming the low opinion Anglos
had of the Apaches.

Victorio, as he was more and more frequently called, since
his followers liked the promising omen in the name, was one
of those who did not take well to reservation life. His response was to shun drinking and brawling. Instead, he gathered a band around him consisting not only of the Warm
Springs Apaches but of Mescalero Apaches as well. He was
welcomed as an equal into conferences with Geronimo,
who he did not trust, for Victorio considered Geronimo
prodigal with the lives of the young warriors.

Through all of this, Lozen was at her brother's side.
Using the gift of the Mountain Gods, she advised him
which of the Anglos he could trust. Sadly, almost as soon
as they had established rapport, many of these Anglos were
removed from their posts by their own people because they
had "gone soft" on the Indians.

Other times, Lozen and Victorio fled the reservation to
go raiding. When conditions at San Carlos grew intolerable,
brother and sister led a band of their people, including
women and children, back to Warm Springs.

During part of the journey, Lozen carried her favorite
niece before her on her horse, cheering the child with stories of how Child of the Water had defeated his enemies.
Privately, Lozen wondered if she and Victorio could possibly win their battle. Always there were more Anglos, more
Mexicans. Always there were fewer and fewer Apaches.

Surprisingly, the Anglos left Victorio's followers alone
when they returned to Warm Springs. The Tchi-hénè built

wickups, planted crops, and settled in. Even though conditions were immeasurably better than they had been at San Carlos, the land would not support the small group without the supplies gained by raiding—nor, even if they could have, would Victorio have let his men forget that they were warriors first, that warriors take what they need from the weaker.

Victorio's band paid a high price for their raiding. One day they returned to the sound of weeping children and the smell of smoke. While they had been gone, soldiers had come and destroyed the camp. Lozen searched diligently until she found her favorite niece. The girl was alive and unwounded but in shock. She had seen her mother shot before her—all that had saved her had been the soldier's need to stop and re-load his rifle.

Carrying the still weeping girl, Lozen sought her brother. He was standing in the center of the ruined camp directing this man to gather the horses, that one to salvage supplies, another to bring the women and children together. His eyes were hard as he looked at the destruction.

"Little Sister, they have killed our mother," he said. "They have killed the mother of the child you hold. Why?"

"They are mad," she answered. "Only fools and cowards kill women and children. I think that they seek to frighten you so that you will stop raiding, so that you will return to the reservation."

"How can they frighten me further?" Bi-duyé said. "If I surrender, my remaining children will die of sickness in the reservation. The only way for us to survive is to claim our own land. I am finished with negotiating with the Anglos or with the Mexicans! If they want my land, they must kill me for it!"

Despite her desire to find a safe, hidden place for the child trembling in her arms, for all the children who remained, Lozen could only nod agreement. There were no quiet, hidden places left, certainly not for Victorio and his sister. The only answers were imprisonment or death, and Lozen had been Apache and warrior for too long to accept imprisonment.

Gently, she set her niece on the ground, shooing her over to join the rest of the children.

"We must begin to plan," she said. "The others can handle the salvage. You and I must decide where we will go after the funerals."

Now what the Anglos would call the Victorio War flared in earnest, but it was the Lozen War, too. Sometimes the entire band traveled with the war-party but increasingly, they left the women and children in the relative safety of a reservation while the warriors went out against the enemy.

Most of the booty from those raids was used to fuel their war. Whenever possible, Lozen would reserve some food or clothing to sneak in to their imprisoned people. These gifts were accompanied with a stern warning never to reveal from where they had come, even to the other Apaches.

Daily Lozen prayed to Yusen, and when she did her palms burned instantly. Sometimes the skin grew purple-red and inflamed as if screaming protest at the sheer numbers of those who opposed Victorio's band. Yet, though the cause was hopeless, scattered warriors continued to join Victorio. His reputation for fearlessness in battle was only part of the attraction. He alone of all the war-leaders could claim the continuing counsel of a di-yin whose favor in the eyes of the gods was obvious to any who cared to look.

Sometimes these new recruits would bring with them the ragged remnants of their families. In these cases, Victorio's counsel was harsh, but unvarying. Unless the women and children could support themselves in the mountains, then they must go to the reservations. When the Anglos gave the Apaches back their land, then the families could be reunited with their men.

Occasionally, a family would choose to stay in the mountains or flee into Old Mexico. However, most accepted Victorio's counsel. Whenever possible, the war-band escorted the women and children part of the way, trusting Lozen's gift to warn them if the soldiers were near.

During one such trip, a pregnant woman—a young mother expecting her first child—went into labor. Lozen rode to inform Victorio that the woman could no longer ride.

"What can I do?" Victorio said. "If I stop here, the soldiers will have time to find us. Only if we keep moving are we safe."

"I have a plan," Lozen said. "You go on with the warriors. I will stay with the woman until she has her baby.

Then I will escort the women and children to the reservation before rejoining you."

Victorio frowned. He could not protest that Lozen was incapable of doing just what she had outlined. She rode better than most of his men, was fleeter afoot. Only a handful were her equal with a rifle. Additionally, as a di-yin, she knew the mysteries of childbirth far better than any warrior.

"Can you find us again?"

"I know where you are heading," Lozen assured him, "and I am a good tracker."

"I know you are, Little Sister," Bi-duyé tried to smile. "Didn't I teach you how to track myself?"

"You did, Big Brother." She reached to embrace him. "Go carefully. There are enemies where you ride."

"There are enemies everywhere," Victorio said. "But that does not mean I will disregard your warning. I saw how dark your hands turned when you prayed to Yusen this morning."

Lozen swung onto her horse. "I will rejoin the woman now. There is an old woman with her, but she is too exhausted to serve as a midwife."

They did not say "good-bye," for there is no word in Apache for "good-bye." They simply parted to their duties.

The young mother did not give Lozen time to feel sad about her brother's departure. The woman's labor was long and difficult, in part because she was small and undernourished, in part because the baby insisted on coming into the world feet first.

For many hours, Lozen despaired that she would lose both mother and child. In the darkness around their camp, coyotes howled, attracted by the smell of blood and the scent of weak things. Lozen set the other refugees to watch the four directions with orders to toss stones into the night if the coyotes grew too bold.

At last the baby was born, a surprisingly strong boy who eagerly took his exhausted mother's nipple. Lozen rigged a carrying sling for him from a length of fabric she had saved as a gift for her niece. Then she insisted that the rest of the group sleep while she stood watch. Victorio had left them a horse. In a few hours, she would put the mother and baby on it. The old woman and the smallest of the children could ride Lozen's own horse. They would travel until the worst heat of the day forced them into hiding.

They covered the miles in this fashion for several days, resting during the hottest part of the day, moving after dark when both coolness and concealment were in their favor. Lozen trapped lizards and snakes for them to eat. The old woman was horrified and refused to touch the food.

"We do not have the luxury to be delicate, old mother," Lozen said with quiet firmness. "You need to eat this, both for the strength you will get from the meat and for the moisture."

"But tradition says it is forbidden to eat the meat of poisonous things, lest you become poisoned," the old woman protested. "We did not even eat turkeys because turkeys eat snakes."

"I would welcome a turkey," Lozen said, "but we are unlikely to find one here. Eat the meat and be quiet, or I will leave you here."

Such was the force of Lozen's personality that the old woman fell silent and obeyed.

They were several days' journey from their destination. When Lozen prayed to Yusen her palms began to burn. Taking one of the horses, she rode out to scout. When she returned, she was in good spirits.

"There is a small cattle camp a few miles away," she explained. "Tonight you will travel without me. I will steal a couple more horses and some supplies, then rejoin you in the early hours of the morning."

Predictably, the old woman began to protest, the small children to weep, but Lozen did not listen. Instead, she shook some powdered red clay from a pouch at her belt and spat to moisten it. Carefully, she drew the red stripe of the warrior across her face. Then she added a thin stripe of yellow beneath the red. When darkness fell, she checked to see that no enemies were in the direction her charges would go.

"All seems to be clear," she said. Taking the eldest of the children by the hand, she pointed to the sky. "See that bright star? Travel toward it and you will not become lost. That is a lesson my brother, Bi-duyé, taught me when I was smaller than you."

The boy nodded. "I will watch, both the star and for the coyotes. You will come back, won't you?"

"In the morning," she promised. "They put the horses in a corral at night, but free them into a pasture in the morning. I will take one when they first set them out, so that they will not miss it until the evening."

Lozen turned away.

"Aren't you taking one of our horses to ride?" the young mother asked.

"No," Lozen smiled. "I can run swiftly over such a short distance, and you will need the horses more than I do."

She slipped away, running almost soundlessly over the sandy ground. There was just enough moon for her to see, not enough to make it easy for her enemies to see her. If she had thought about it, she would have realized that she was happy. For too many days she had been burdened by her responsibilities to the ones she led and by her duty to her brother. Now, she was free.

Reaching the cattle camp, she scouted carefully. There were a few dogs, but she would try to stay upwind of them. In any case, the heavy scents of cattle and horses should cover her own. A supply shed stood temptingly just a short distance from the main house and the bunkhouse. She thought she could easily get in there once the Anglos were asleep.

When all the lights from the kerosene lamps dimmed and the fires were banked, Lozen slipped down into the cattle camp. The dogs did not notice her as she glided between the buildings. She startled an opossum on its own scavenging route. First, she studied the horses in the corral, noting the best choices for theft.

Then she went to the supply shed. It was latched with a heavy bar meant to keep animals, but not people, out. In this isolated area, theft was hardly a consideration. Lozen studied the latch, comparing it to those she had seen in other places. When she had it puzzled out, she rubbed both it and the hinges of the shed with some of her gun grease. They opened smoothly then.

One of the dogs on the porch of the main house stirred, but when the noise was not repeated, settled back into sleep. Lozen slipped inside the shed, leaving the door open to let in the moonlight. From what she could see, the camp must have recently been restocked. There were sacks of dried beans, rice, smoked hams, flour, jerky, salt, and canned fruit.

Methodically, she began removing what they could use most easily. Carrying it in small loads, she cached it in some rocks a few miles north of the cattle camp. She worked steadily for several hours, restraining herself from eating anything but some jerky. Although greed made her want to clear the entire shed, she took only what she thought she could load on a horse.

Next, she found some waterskins and filled them from a well behind the barn. The restless stirring of the cattle covered any noise she made.

Her task completed, she cut open one of the cans of fruit and made her dinner seated in the crotch of a cottonwood tree. Safe from anything on the ground, she dozed until morning. The noise of horses greeting the wrangler woke her.

Unmoving, she watched as he fed and watered his charges, then turned them out to pasture. A few were kept in the corral, presumably those who would be needed today. She was vaguely disappointed to see that her two first choices were among these, but accepted philosophically that even an Anglo could have an eye for a good horse.

When the wrangler had gone inside, Lozen dropped from her tree. Moving quickly but steadily, she approached a quiet old brown mare. It was not the most beautiful of the horses, but it was steady. Lozen roped and haltered it easily. Her second selection was an attractive brown-and-white paint. This horse was more lively, but was also accustomed to accepting anything a human on horseback did. She roped it and then led the two, stopping periodically to erase their trail with a cottonwood branch.

The entire process took only a few minutes. Once she was out of the valley that held the cattle camp, she urged the horses into a trot. She paused to collect the supplies she had cached the night before and to reward the horses with some salt. A few minutes' work with the branch eradicated the last of her trail.

Then she sped up. By the time the day had grown hot, she had rejoined her charges. They did not cheer or shout, for to do so would be to admit their fears she would not return, but she saw the worry lines melt from their faces.

"Two horses *and* all of this food!" the old woman said admiringly. "How many Anglos did you kill?"

"None," Lozen said. "I did not wish them to follow us. If I had killed one, the others would most certainly have pursued us. Now, if the Mountain Gods smile on us, the Anglos will think that the horses wandered of their own accord. They many not even notice the missing food."

"Were you afraid?" the little boy said. "When I am a man, I won't let anything stop me from killing Anglos and Mexicans. I won't be afraid."

"Sometimes fear is a good thing, Little One," Lozen said thoughtfully. "And sometimes killing only causes trouble. Perhaps taking only what one needs is the wiser course."

The old woman studied her, but did not say anything. Perhaps it was because her mouth was filled with canned peach, perhaps it was because of the sorrow she saw in Lozen's eyes.

Lozen took her charges within a half-day's walk of the reservation before leaving them. She gave them the quietest of the horses and all of the dried beans and rice.

"If you wish to thank Victorio and me," she said, "do not tell anyone of our involvement with this, do not boast before those who may tell the Anglos. And if you can, find Victorio's wives and children and share some of the food with them."

She wheeled her horse then and rode away. Enemies were near, and her dreams had been dark and haunted.

Now she set herself to the laborious task of both avoiding enemies and finding her brother. The gift of the Mountain Gods did not desert her, but she could find no trace of Victorio or his men. Finally, discouraged, she rode into a Mescalero Apache camp. There she learned that Victorio and most of his men had been slaughtered at a place called Tres Castillos.

From that day forward, Lozen never again spoke her brother's name, neither did she answer to the name "Little Sister," for she was no one's sister, daughter, or mother. What she remained was the Mountain Gods' means of warning their people that enemies were near.

She joined with Nana, who had taken over leading Victorio's band. For five years she served as a scout and emissary for Nana, Geronimo, and the other Apache leaders.

When finally they all surrendered, she surrendered with them.

"You live better off the land than anyone I have seen," whispered old Nana. "Go. Surely the Mountain Gods will protect you. I have even heard rumors that Bi-duyé left a vast treasure hidden in the mountains. Perhaps you can find it."

"There is no treasure." Lozen said. "You know that. I know that. The story of the treasure is a story to give hope to dreamers. I made my choice during my da-i-dá to be the Mountain Gods' servant to the Indéh. I made the choice again when I might have given up the gift for love. Now I make it a third time. If I can no longer be a warrior, I can still be a di-yin. I think our people will need a medicine woman in this place called Florida."

Old Nana chuckled dryly. "Surely, there will be no end to enemies, even though there is an end to our war."

"Surely so," said Lozen, "and our people will need warning against them. The Mountain Gods will not stop listening to our prayers just because we have been taken from the mountains."

The one photo of Lozen that has survived to this day was taken as she waited to get on the train that would take her to Florida. She is still beautiful. Her dark eyes hold both wisdom and sorrow.

And, remember, everything written on these pages is true, except for what is not, of course, for that is the way of legends. I leave figuring out which is which to you.